THE

TOURIST

Robert Dickinson

orbit

www.orbitbooks.net

ORBIT

First published in Great Britain in 2016 by Orbit

1 3 5 7 9 10 8 6 4 2

A CIP catalogue record for this book
is available from the British Library.

ISBN 978-0-356-50818-4

Typeset in Bembo by M Rules
Printed and bound in Great Britain by
Clays Ltd, St Ives plc

Papers used by Orbit are from well-managed forests
and other responsible sources.

Orbit
An imprint of
Little, Brown Book Group
Carmelite House
50 Victoria Embankment
London EC4Y 0DZ

An Hachette UK Company
www.hachette.co.uk

www.orbitbooks.net

THE
TOURIST

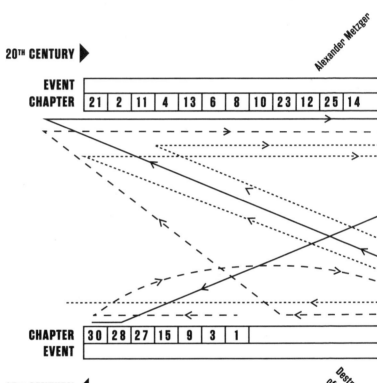

20TH CENTURY ▶

Alexander Metzger

EVENT
CHAPTER | 21 | 2 | 11 | 4 | 13 | 6 | 8 | 10 | 23 | 12 | 25 | 14 |

CHAPTER | 30 | 28 | 27 | 15 | 9 | 3 | 1 |
EVENT

25TH CENTURY ◀

Destruction of City Two East

TIMELINES:
Spens ————
Karia ·············
Riemann - - - - -

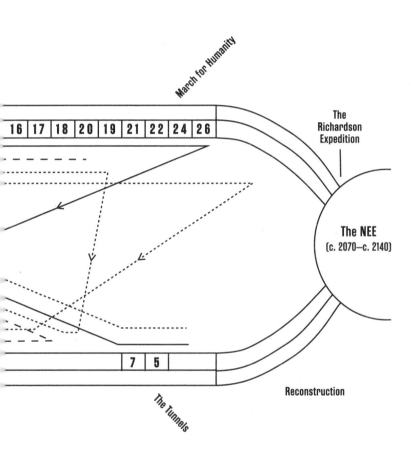

March for Humanity

| 16 | 17 | 18 | 20 | 19 | 21 | 22 | 24 | 26 |

The Richardson Expedition

The NEE
(c. 2070–c. 2140)

| 7 | 5 | |

Reconstruction

The Tunnels

NOTE: ALL TIMELINES SUBJECT TO CHANGE

'88

You're staring at the wall when it's announced. You spend most of your days staring at the wall. If anyone asked you'd say you were gathering your thoughts.

Visitor, says the voice.

Your thoughts scatter like cockroaches. You stand up so quickly you feel dizzy.

You don't have visitors.

Room Six, says the voice. The door of your cell slides open.

The corridor outside is white, brightly lit. There are no obvious doors in this corridor but you know they're there, flush with the walls. Twice a day, when you walk to Room Two to eat, you knock against the walls as you pass. You don't expect a reply but if there's another prisoner they might take heart from knowing they're not alone.

You don't have visitors. Isolation is part of the sentence. Your captors have a horror of solitude and believe you share it. The only living things you see are the doctors (for monthly examinations) and the doctors' guards, and, once a year, the Consideration Panel. The rest of the time there is only the

1

voice. It tells you when to wake up, when to eat – always in Room Two, a room hardly bigger than your cell, where the food is left on a tray chained to the table and the table is bolted to the floor. It allows you an hour to eat before it tells you to return to your room.

The voice hasn't changed in all your time here. You suspect it isn't human. Synthesised, a machine. It sounds like your own voice, or how you imagine your voice sounds.

The corridor leads to an enclosed courtyard with an opaque glass ceiling. You can't tell the colour of the sky, or if the diffused light is the sky. You stop for a moment and look up as you always do and wonder if what you can see is daylight.

The door to Room Six is already open.

Keep walking, says the voice.

Room Six is three times the size of your cell. The only furniture is a single metal-framed chair that faces three other chairs. All of them are bolted to the floor. This is where the Consideration Panel – a Safety, a Happiness, a Facilitator, different people each time – sit in judgement, with a guard standing by the door behind them. You've never seen that door open but know there must be another room beyond it with people watching. The meetings are the same every time: the Consideration Panel ask questions and you stare at them until they send you back to your room. This has happened seventeen times. Or eighteen: you seem to have lost count. Each time they expect you to talk about what they call your crimes. Saying nothing is a small victory.

Your visitor is sitting in the middle chair. He's wearing the formal greys you expect for a Facilitator but his posture is military. He's familiar. Your first thought is that you've noticed a family resemblance and he's the son of an earlier guard. He's barely out of his twenties. You've been here long enough for that to be possible.

Sit down, says the voice.

You sit.

Your visitor looks at you carefully. His hair, you notice, is cropped and patterned in a way that was popular before your sentence began. The style must have come round again. "Karia Stadt," he says. "I expect this is a surprise for you." It's small talk, meant to put you at your ease. It sounds rehearsed.

Normally you wouldn't talk at all, but there is something different about this man. "I don't get visitors. My people are dead." Your voice sounds dryer than you expect. You wanted it to sound like a reproach but it comes out like self-pity.

"You grew up in City Two East." He relaxes, but only slightly. "That's the reason I'm here."

City Two East is their name for your old home. It's their way: give everything a number, erase the past. Pretend they had nothing to do with the old world. Your city had a name. You resist the impulse to correct him. "You're military."

"No." He says it firmly, as if the suggestion is offensive. "I should introduce myself. My name is Riemann Aldis."

The name stirs a memory.

"I'm with Awareness." He follows his script. "I have been seconded to the Safety Executive in order to find one of their people and a high-status Happiness. The evidence suggests they're in the vicinity of your old home."

You don't believe him. "And?"

"You're the last person familiar with the terrain."

"Don't you have maps? Satellites?"

"Nothing reliable. Your people didn't make maps and nobody goes there now."

"Why should I help you?"

He blinks. "I'm giving you a chance to return to your home city."

"How is it home? Everybody I know is dead."

"The alternative is that you stay here until the end of your sentence. Twelve more years, isn't it? This is your chance to leave."

"Under what terms?"

"You'll be in my sole custody. If you agree to help it will count at your next Consideration Panel." He seems to realise this is a weak argument. "You can see your old home," he adds quickly. "Or you could stay here."

You realise why he's familiar. It's the way your memory works: you try to remember a name or a place and find a blank. Minutes later, when you're thinking about something else, the name or place comes back, making you forget your latest train of thought. Riemann's name is familiar because it's the name of the man you met back in the 21st. That Riemann had been an older man, talking about an event in his past. Standing on a street in the 21st, asking why you were there, hinting he already knew. The memory is vivid. You remember the name because you were told to remember it. You had a good memory then. You'd been told to remember everything he said. *One day, a long time from now, you meet me again.* You assumed it was a lie, a trick to make you talk.

You study the face opposite you. It's young, genuinely young, not reconstructed the way some of them are. You can tell by the eyes. Either it was a different man or the events you can remember are in this one's future.

There's a phrase they use: *travel is confusing.* You heard it all the time when you were pretending to be one of them. They say it as a joke. They say it and it stops the conversation. You can understand why: when you try to think of what his presence means your head starts to ache.

You decide to say nothing. If this is the man you once met it might be information you can use later. Or you might have misremembered. It's been a long time. Your visitor could have given you any name and you would have adjusted your memory to make it fit. "When would I leave?"

He gives a thin smile. "We made the application for a temporary release before you were sentenced. It was approved five years ago." The smile is familiar. "If you agree you will be out of here in the next two hours."

It has to be a trick. "How have you done this?"

"That's not your concern." He's pleased with himself. The other Riemann had been smug, keen to make it clear he knew something you didn't. "Do you accept my offer?"

"Is this true?" you say aloud, not to him. "If I agree, am I free to go?"

You can go, says the voice. *You are not free.*

Typical 21st

It should be simple. A coach ride from the resort to the attraction, the kind of uneventful trip I've accompanied before. According to the brochure the journey takes thirty-five minutes and we stay at the attraction for two hours. There's a novelty: the journey back will take longer because of an accident. It will be a minor accident, nobody hurt, the coach barely dented. Some of the clients are excited by the prospect. Some of them have booked the trip *because* of the accident. It's something new. There's a hint – but no more than a hint – of danger.

I count the clients – fourteen of them – onto the coach. On the way I give them the talk about the attraction, a typical early-21st shopping mall. It's the kind of thing they've seen in the old entertainments or heard about from kin who have already made the trip. "This may be the early 21st," I tell them, "but it's still an advanced and sophisticated civilisation." I give them the standard warnings about the food, the reminders about changing currency: "You may be offered a better deal, but there are strict protocols governing this. If you see something you absolutely have to buy, use the plastic cards provided. They are as good as currency. If you're not sure about anything, come and talk to me." I end with the joke about not offering to buy anybody's children. A few listen. The rest stare out of the window, shocked at how ugly and crowded everything is. Tri-Millennium Travel has a grand name but it's cheap and doesn't attract the most adventurous travellers. For many of them this is their first time outside the resort.

I'm bored of the early 21st. I've been doing this for a year and a half now, and I'm tired of the cramped houses, the noise, the crowds, the gathering pollution, the omnipresent advertising. I'm unmoved by their entertainments (they use pictures, even for grown-ups) and bored, mostly, with the company of the other reps. The only thing that keeps me going is the knowledge that in three weeks I'll be sent home for breach of protocol. (Four years after that I join a kin, and forty after that is an end date. I've seen my record.) I have a few more weeks of shepherding these cautious people from one heavily monitored location to another and living in the off-resort accommodation that's supposed to make me a better rep. There's a theory that you can't really understand an era until you've had an affair with one of its natives and unless one of them has a radical change of diet and hygiene that isn't going to happen. I'm definitely not going to join the extemps and pretend I belong here. I want to go home and find out which kin I join. And then I want to go to the early 19th, the era I actually studied.

I'm curious about the breach of protocol that gets me sent back. A fling with a client? I look up and down the transport. I can't imagine having a fling with any of these. Apart from a woman at the back who keeps her hood up and avoids eye contact, they're all at least my parents' generation.

We reach the coach park of the attraction on time. I count them off, a little ritual of reassurance, and tell them that if they need help I'll be in a particular coffee shop on the upper level. Tri-Millennium has an arrangement with this shop: they reserve a reps' table that gives a view of nearly the whole shopping area. We're allowed free coffee and one of their least disgusting pastries. They know that a quarter of the tourists will get bored after about an hour and join me. (I usually take a bite out of the pastry when they turn up: it gives them a thrill to see one of their own eating this era's notorious food.)

They have the usual wariness about getting off the coach and walking in the open air. I tell them they don't need suits, and point to all the native shoppers in their drab period costumes. *They're* not worried. Some of the older clients are sceptical. I can sympathise: you never really get used to the sky. They jog across the car park as if the atmosphere here will kill them (the Near Extinction Event isn't for another sixty years, but these people's grasp of history is shaky at best, and some of them grew up with stories of the Cloud). Once inside, I point them in the direction of our preferred stores (Tri-Millennium has deals with them; their staff are supposed to have had special training) and take the escalator to Coffee Monarch.

Li Tran is sitting at the reps' table, wearing earphones attached to a native mobile. I'm pleased it's her. Most of the other reps are second- or third-gen Happiness straight out of Further Ed. We're both a few years older and weren't always Happiness: after my parents died I'd been identified as having potential but, without any other Happiness in my kin, had to work the Tunnels to qualify for the education. It's not the usual rep progression. Most of the people who work the Tunnels end up in Safety; the ones who enjoy it get requisitioned by the Millies. I had the usual offer from Safety but turned it down in favour of more education.

Li's path was also different. She's from City Three North, a rough place, although she claims it's not as bad as its reputation ("We have power and clean water, you know. And schools with teachers. It's not like we're City Two East.") And she travelled before she became a rep, which is rare.

The other thing we have in common is that we're shorter than the average Happiness. Not by much – nobody would mistake us for natives – but just enough to make it clear (if only to us) that we don't quite belong.

Li nods at me and takes off her earphones. I can hear a snicker-snicker sound like shuffled cards. Native music. "Spens," she says without smiling. "Welcome to hell."

Li works for Heritage, a slightly more expensive operator. Her clients come to the same attractions as mine, but they're ironic about them. They'll wander around, pointing and laughing and quoting the guidebooks to each other with knowing little smiles.

I don't like Heritage clients. Li likes them even less.

I sit down. "Problem?"

"I knew today was going to be a bad day. I didn't realise how bad."

"What's happened? Or going to happen?"

"Nothing on the record. But the record doesn't include how annoying people can be. The Shin family." She looks down at the main shopping area. Our clients stand out in their shimmering jackets and dark visors. Also in the way they gather in doorways, blocking the flow of foot traffic, transfixed by the pictures of things for sale. (The early 21st loves pictures. It's like people have grown tired of reading.)

Our clients – Heritage or Tri-Millennium – are not impressive. The natives walk round them without any overt signs of resentment. Not that I expect any: they've had ten years to get used to us. "How about you?" Li asks. "Anything about to happen?"

I tell her about the accident. "Some of mine are looking forward to it."

"At least they won't have to go to a hospital. That's an adventure." Li spent a night in a hospital after being punched in the face at a musical event in the 1970s when she was here as part of a research team. The hospital was scarily primitive, but Li considered it part of the experience. Nineteen seventy-six was wild, she says. It's a period before we made our presence known, so everything had to be clandestine. Li had been chosen for the team because she was clever and short enough not to stand out. She'd had to dress like the natives and speak their language. Early 21st is tame by comparison, she says, but she liked the popular culture. She still goes to gigs, as she calls them, and, earlier this time around, had a two-month affair with a native which ended because he kept asking about lottery numbers and sports results and didn't believe her when she told him she didn't know. He couldn't understand how that information was lost, and she couldn't tell him about the NEE. If she had, she said, he'd either have refused to believe her or thought he could do something about it.

A lot of the natives think if they've been warned about an event they can stop it from happening. Li calls it the Terminator Fallacy, a reference to one of their entertainments. Li has an anthropologist's interest in their culture.

I don't share it. I prefer a different kind of music: Beethoven. His 22nd December 1808 concert is my favourite recording, and one day I mean to go. It won't be soon. Early-19th Vienna is difficult. It's a long stopover and there's a lot of prep: languages, medical, plus the usual hazards of being a freakish outsider in a war zone. "Anyway," Li says, "have you found out what your breach of protocol is yet? It can't be long now."

"Three weeks."

"It might not happen."

"It's on my record."

"If you can believe that."

Li isn't typical. She enjoyed the 1970s and she's one of the few who hasn't checked her record. She doesn't trust them: she claims we can't be sure they're from the 25th and for all we know the authorities made them up. And if they are real we *shouldn't* trust them. We've had long conversations.

Back home, when records from the 25th suddenly appeared a lot of people made a point of refusing to look. Eventually nearly everybody gave in. The records were, it turned out, scrappy: my employment history stopped with Tri-Millennium, then had the year I joined a kin – just the year, with a symbol next to it that was never explained – and an end date (2388). Other people had lists of occupations but no dates, or they had kinship history but nothing else. The fact some had no end dates led to speculation they would still be alive when the records were compiled. It's more likely the records were corrupted, deliberately or not, before they were released, either by the 25th or our own authorities. Too much detail might reduce our sense of agency.

Agency has been a concern since the early years of travel. It's still the subject of most entertainments. If you know your loved one is going to be killed in an accident do you try to stop them leaving for work? If you find out they're going to commit a crime do you try to talk them out of it? The entertainments always give the same answer: you can't change what's going to happen. You warn somebody about the accident; they take a different route, which results in the accident. You warn them not to commit the crime and it turns out you gave them the idea. The 25th is, if anything, even more cautious. They discourage travel – the last few attempts to get there were bounced back – and they never visit. Apart from these skimpy records nothing has come from them: no tech, no art, nothing. I'm not sure if this is from some high-minded moral objection or because they just enjoy being mysterious.

Li is pensive. "I'll be sorry to see you go."

"You can't be here for much longer."

"Five more months. Unless something happens."

"Haven't you checked?"

"I want it to be a surprise."

"Knowing doesn't take away the surprise," I say. "The records are always incomplete. I don't know why I get sent back. And all I know about this afternoon's accident is that it happens on the journey home and that nobody gets hurt."

"But isn't even that too much?"

"No. For some of them it's comforting." I nod down at our clients in their shimmering coats. Some of the braver ones have entered the shops.

"And you? Do you find it comforting?"

"I don't find it anything. The company record makes my job easier. My personal record – it doesn't tell me anything I couldn't have guessed."

"That's what's different about here." Li looks at the shoppers below. Our clients are outnumbered three or four to one by the natives. "The people here don't *think* they know what's going to happen. Or when."

"Does that make them better than us?"

13

"It makes them less fatalistic."

"I'm not fatalistic. Apart from a few details, I know just as little about my life as any of the people down there." I'm careful not to say *natives* in front of Li. She doesn't like the word.

She turns back to me. "A few details. You mean like thinking you know when you're going to die?"

"I know the year. It's only a date. And it doesn't give an age. Travel changes everything."

"I don't know how you live with it." She looks down at our clients again. "Why do you think they come here?"

"It's a shopping mall. They're a defining feature of the culture." Once it was temples and cathedrals, then railway stations. In this era it's shopping malls and airports. Tri-Millennium don't organise excursions to airports (the natives have security concerns); occasionally a few clients will make the trip by themselves just to watch the planes.

"But why the 21st? What do they expect to see here?"

There are lots of reasons. The main one is this period has a fixed link: spend a month here, go back and find a month has passed at home. Our clients are here for a holiday. They're not roughing it in the fourteenth century or trying to establish if King Arthur actually existed. The early 21st has short travel time, amenities and relative security. Our clients choose it because it doesn't need much medical preparation, they can understand some of the language and the natives are sophisticated enough not to burn them as witches or worship them as gods. "They're here to see something they can't see at home. They'll feel they've done something adventurous and be glad to get back."

"It doesn't seem much."

"Not everyone is like you, Li. The 21st is available, so they come here."

14

"But they could go anywhere. They could go to the 1920s."

"Have you seen the schedules?" I might not be a tech but, because I'm interested in the early 19th, I've studied them. "The 1920s are difficult. If you want to come back you have to sit it out until 1943. That's a bad time for any kind of travel."

"I'd send the Shins to the 1920s." Li watches a particular group as they block the door to a sportswear store. "There they are. Spoiling my day." There are five of them: two women and a man in their fifties, and two men in their twenties. They've surrounded one of the natives and are looking intently at something in his hands. "You know, I think they're about to buy some currency."

"Shouldn't you stop them?"

"I've given them the standard warnings. If they choose to get robbed that's their concern." Heritage travellers have higher status than Tri-Millennium clients. They're paid more and are occasionally confident enough to leave the resort unaccompanied or try to talk to a native. (Living History are the most reckless: they'll use public transport and eat in restaurants.) As we watch, the Shins stand aside to let the native walk away, then gather in a circle. Then they appear to argue. The younger ones start looking around, obviously trying to find the native who sold them whatever rubbish they've just bought. He's gone, of course. One of the women points up at us. "Here they come," Li sighs, as they make their way to the escalator. "Time for the Heritage smile."

The Shins march towards us in single file, one of the older women at the front, the younger men hanging behind. They knock empty chairs aside as they approach. They are unmistakably in a bad mood. Li stands up, beaming as if she hasn't noticed. "How are you enjoying your excursion?"

"We've been robbed," the woman at the front says. "Robbed," the other woman and man repeat from behind her, like a choral accompaniment.

Li looks concerned. "I'm sorry to hear that. Tell me what happened and I'll take you to the police."

At the mention of the police the Shins hesitate. But it isn't long before their sense of outrage bubbles over. "We don't think this is a matter for the police. We think this is a matter for Heritage. We think we should have been warned."

Li sounds less sympathetic. "I'm sorry that you think that. Can you tell me what happened?"

"We changed some currency," the man says. "We were robbed."

"Was this at an approved bureau?" There's steel in Li's voice now. "Because you *were* warned about the dangers of changing currency at unauthorised outlets."

"We should have been warned," the woman insists.

"You were warned." Li smiles again, this time coldly. "I told you on the way here that people who approach you offering to change currency are criminals and you should refuse."

"It was a good rate," the man says. "Very good," the second woman adds, implying the offer had been so good they'd have been fools not to take it.

"We gave him two Dors," the woman says. "And this is what he gave us." She slams what appears to be a small wad of £10 notes onto the table. Li does not touch them. "I think Heritage are responsible."

"So, let me make sure I've understood you. You were warned not to deal with touts who approach you. You were told they would almost certainly try to trick you. Yet you made a deal with one of them and were tricked. And now you think Heritage is responsible for you making that decision. Is that correct?"

"We should have been warned," the woman insists.

"You were warned. You chose to ignore the warning."

"No. *We* should have been warned."

Li pauses. Some of our clients really don't understand the logic of travel. "Do you mean I should have warned *you* personally that *you* were going to be tricked?"

"It must be on our itinerary."

Li pulls a paper from the small pile on her table. Heritage uses paperwork. It's a period touch, supposed to remind their clients that this isn't home. It's slightly anachronistic, given the 21st is beginning to abandon paperwork. They're moving their information onto servers, which is why so little of it survives the NEE. "No. Remember it would only be on your itinerary if you were to lodge a formal complaint."

"Well, we want to lodge a formal complaint."

Li tries to look serious. "I see. You want to make a formal complaint that, while engaged in an illegal activity, you were cheated out of two Dors. You understand that I will be obliged to refer this matter to the authorities here. That does mean the local police. I should warn you there are protocols governing what actions they can take against people from our era who take part in illegal activities." Hardly any clients have read the protocols. Most don't need to: they're too cautious to take any chances. The merest hint they might be held in one of this era's appalling prisons should be enough to stop the Shins making a fuss. "Even if there is no criminal charge, you understand there would be implications on your return? So," Li concludes brightly, "do you want to make a formal complaint?"

"We'll think about it," the first woman says. "We'll write

to Heritage when we get back," the man says. Disgruntled but beaten, they slouch away, not even picking up their small bundle of notes.

"They won't write," Li says once they're back on the escalators. "And they don't travel with Heritage again." She picks up the notes they've left behind and counts them. "Two Dors." She flicks through the notes. They are, for once, actual currencies, rather than strips of newspaper. "Forty pounds, a hundred Bulgarian lev and the rest is Turkish lira. They've been cheated, but it's not actually bad. I've had customers hand over twenty Dors and get less." She puts the notes into her satchel.

Time passes. I drink a coffee, slowly. It tastes as bad as it did the first time I came here, but I've grown used to that. Coffee is probably one of the few things I'll miss. That, and the park near my flat where I sometimes sit before going to the resort. There's a particular spot where there's just enough of an elevation to give a view across part of the city. There are no particular monuments, nothing I would bring any clients to see: just rows of different-sized houses exposed to the sky. On a winter morning I'll sit on the bench and listen to the bells ring out the call to prayer as the lights in the houses come on. It's one of my own rituals of reassurance, and helps put me in the right frame of mind for dealing with the clients. The ones who come here in winter can be the most difficult. They come because of the shorter days and rarely leave the resort, which means I spend longer in their company. On those mornings, with a long day ahead of me, I sit on the park bench and wonder about the lives of the people who live in those houses. There are children in them, perhaps, who will live to see the NEE. I don't know what form it takes here:

there might be something in the records at home, but because I didn't know where I'd be assigned I didn't check before I left. Perhaps there's the outline of a cellar somewhere, with some relic of everyday life in a locked box. That view from the park is something I'll miss. Perhaps, when I get home, I might try to find the place again. I have the co-ordinates. The hill is probably still there.

Fifteen minutes before the coach is due to leave the clients have all assembled in Coffee Monarch. Some of them have actually bought cups of coffee, which they sip experimentally. The rest watch as I cut a Danish pastry in half. I eat one of the halves, an act closer to a party trick than the absorption of nutrition. I offer the other half to them to try, but they're too cautious. This is usual. Children are sometimes tempted to try a mouthful, but even they have trouble dealing with food that is simultaneously tasteless and excessively sweet. When I announce it's time to go back to the coach everyone is relieved. Tri-Millennium's excursions are brief, at least compared to Heritage – Li's clients will be here for another half-hour and then they're taken to a cathedral. I compliment her on the way she handled the Shins, and she reminds me about a farewell party for another Heritage rep at Bar Five. It's the kind of event we'd both usually avoid. I tell her to send me a reminder. Even this slight delay makes my clients restless. Brief as the stop has been, they're still impatient for it to end. It's understandable. The shopping mall quickly gets dull, especially if you're uncertain about the etiquette of buying and there is nothing you really need. The clothes are odd: it's hard to get anything in our size, and they have never really been fashionable. There was a brief fad in the 30s (*our* 30s), but that was limited to one tiny clique in City One West and lasted about two months. So clothes are out, and

communication devices, hilarious computers – has
n novelty value but won't work when you get home.
only things our clients usually buy are books and disks
of entertainments. The natives are proud of their entertainments: they think cinema is their greatest contribution to culture. It's like a Stuart courtier telling you the masque is the art form of the future. The 20th's real contribution is radio drama, the forerunner of all our serious entertainments. Unfortunately, thanks to travel, it's become acceptable for grown-ups to watch the old movies and serials. It started with students, who used them as a way of prolonging their childhood, and then spread to older people, like our clients, who take them seriously. Watching them doesn't feel childish because they're historical artefacts and the language is different (not that you need the language to follow most of them: you only need to recognise a few simple visual conventions). Still, you can only buy so many disks, and after an hour all the clients usually want is to get back to the resort and tell the people who didn't come that they're pleased they did it but it was a bit disappointing and they wouldn't do it again. Today's clients are typical.

Plus some of them are looking forward to the accident.

I settle the bill for the clients who tried the coffee. Some of them stand next to me so they can hear me talk to the barista. They're often impressed when they hear me speak This English even if I'm not as fluent as Li. "You sounded like one of them," they'll say, though the language isn't difficult and it's not as far from Modern as they think. Later, on the coach, I'll explain how this era's language eventually became the language we speak today. I'll tell them how Agneta, the barista we met that afternoon, is from one of the countries that disappears in the NEE, which isn't strictly true – I don't know where she's from – but it's the kind of detail that gives them a thrill. They'll feel sorry for her because she treated them politely, wasn't alarmed at their attempts to speak what's probably her second language and is almost as pale-skinned as we are. How sad, they think, even though she'll probably die long before the NEE begins. Our clients don't always have the strongest grasp of history.

I lead them out of Coffee Monarch. There's the usual half-jog across the open space of the car park and then I count them back onto the coach, where, with only the driver to hear them, they become voluble, eager to share their experiences. And then one of them asks, "How much can you tell us about the accident?" He's about sixty, a thin, neat type who's probably worked in maintenance or low-level industry. There are no visible augs. He reminds me of my father. The older Tri-Millennium clients often remind me of my parents: hard-working, patchily educated, facing new experiences with bewildered decency. If my parents had lived they would have travelled with Tri-Millennium and congratulated themselves on their daring. This one has been quiet until now. I suspect he's an enthusiast for ancient tech and has only joined this trip because of the accident. I tell him all I know is what's on the itinerary: somewhere between the attraction and the resort we will collide with another vehicle. "You must know more than that," he insists, convinced I'm holding something back. Clients often think we're holding something back. Sometimes, of course, we are.

I tell him it's going to be what the report calls *a minor accident*, which means it won't involve the native police or the terrifying emergency services. The delay is for the driver of our coach to exchange insurance details with the driver of whatever other vehicle is involved in the accident. I expla

21

what an insurance company is. The client still looks sceptical. Of course, I say, if you wanted details of the crash you'd need to look in the insurance company records, and, in our time, most of those are lost, and, while in this time they still exist – but not yet, because the accident hasn't yet happened – there would be problems getting them. Private companies don't make their records publicly available. You'd probably have to fabricate an ID or pretend to be somebody else, which is theoretically possible if you can get the right approval, but unlikely: approval is usually only issued for serious historical or scientific research and the prep can take years. And in the case of *a minor accident* the only additional information you'd find would be the approximate time and location and an estimated repair cost – assuming there's even damage that needs repair. It would be a lot of work for information we don't really need, and, besides, isn't it better not to know these details? Doesn't it add a little thrill to an otherwise dull journey home?

He accepts all this, without quite believing me. I'm used to that. They think that because this is the past we should know everything. They're travelling in the open air, in a country of seventy million people, in a vehicle powered by the internal combustion of fossil fuels, and they still haven't grasped how different this century is, and how little we know about it. Most of the reps couldn't name the current Prime Minister or guess which party is in charge. Why would we need to? For most of our job a blurred outline of history is enough. If something we hadn't expected happens we can always consult the Arc when we get home. (The version of the Arc at the resort is heavily edited – agency again.) As we're driving through a street of small, old-fashioned shops (newspapers, flowers, takeaway food) a car suddenly pulls out in front of us. Our driver brakes, but there's still a noticeable jolt as we bump gently against it. A small cheer goes up, and the clients gather round the windows with the best view. Our driver gets out to talk to the driver of the car. It all seems amicable. I wonder how this delay is going to take fifteen minutes. Then the other driver's face hardens: he's noticed who's on the coach. It's an expression I've seen before. Natives often look at us and see the money they hope to make. This one starts rubbing the back of his neck and miming sudden pain.

Some of the clients ask if they can get off of the coach and look around the shops. It's an unexpected request from Tri-Millennium clients. Presumably they've been emboldened by the shopping mall. I give them the usual warnings and open the door: let them have their experience of the varieties of early-21st retail. A few of them get off. They stand in the street, looking at the shop windows. One, the man who asked about the accident, actually goes into a shop and emerges a few seconds later triumphantly holding a newspaper. Meanwhile, the driver who pulled out in front of us has stopped rubbing his neck and is now looking animated. I suspect he's trying to persuade the driver to back his claim, probably by offering a share of the damages. Our driver has seen this kind of thing before and doesn't budge. Eventually the other driver caves in and details are exchanged. Our driver signals to the clients, who are now gathered incredulously around a menu in the window of a takeaway. They jog back to the coach, exhilarated, the man waving his newspaper like a trophy. The driver looks up and down the street, climbs back in and we move on again. The rest of the journey is uneventful. We're soon out on the motorway and, a little while after that, we can see the dome of the Resort getting gradually nearer. Fifteen minutes later we have driven through the short glass-sided tunnel into the coach bay, our coach has pulled up in its allotted space (#24) and the clients disembark. I count them off for the last time as they file past thanking me for the interesting experience. I thank them for coming. It's only when the last of them has stepped off the coach that I realise there's a problem.

One of them is missing.

A good subordinate

The transfer happens quickly, as if, having decided you could leave, your keepers want you gone. You return to your cell. A bag has been placed in your bed. *Pack what you need*, the voice says. You do as instructed: a change of clothes, your pills. The bag already contains a bottle of water. Afterwards you sit on the bed, waiting. You're nervous. Your life has become a series of simple routines; you've grown used to thinking the same thoughts in the same order. Twice a day you shuffle to Room Two to eat and each time you tap on the wall and wonder if there are any other prisoners. You stop outside Room Six and look up at the ceiling and wonder if what you can see is daylight: the same thought each time. How will you cope with something different?

Room Six, says the voice.

Riemann is still sitting in the chair. He glances at your bag. "Is that everything?" The door behind him opens. "Follow me."

As you'd suspected, the door leads to an observation room with two rows of empty seats and large blank screens set in the wall. Beyond it is a corridor as white and bare as the one outside your cell. After a hundred metres it turns right. A door at the end of it opens as you approach. You go through to a high-ceilinged, windowless room with black panels set in the walls. Riemann walks quickly, as if being timed. The door on the other side of the room slides open. You recognise daylight. Your prison was on the surface after all; the diffused light outside Room Six was the sky. A transport vehicle is backed up against the door, open, revealing two bench seats facing each other.

You still haven't seen anybody except Riemann. You follow him in and sit on a facing bench, panting slightly, which he finds amusing. He bangs twice on the panel to his right. The vehicle doors close and you hear the low hum of its engine. It's the first time you've been in a vehicle since you were brought here. Not much seems to have changed. It's another cell, this time on wheels. Riemann seems to relax. You watch him, asking yourself: Is this the same man? You try to picture the one you met in the 21st, but the image is indistinct. And you can't ask the man sitting opposite because if he is the same man those meetings are still in his future.

Instead you ask, "What happens now?"

"They drive us to our first stop. It will take about four days to reach City Two East."

Once again you resist the impulse to correct him about the name. Four days. How long is it since you spent more than a few minutes with any other person? You look around. "It's just you."

His expression stays blank. He is so young.

"No guards." You spell it out. "I thought I was an important prisoner."

"Important, perhaps." There's a flicker of amusement. "But not dangerous."

"So it's just you."

"And the driver."

"Who do you work for?"

"I told you. Awareness, seconded to Safety."

You feel the old contempt for the names they use: Happiness keeps them quiet; Safety keeps them in place; Awareness spies on everybody else. "And you're taking me" – the word sticks in your throat – "home."

"That's right." He watches you carefully. "To help me find some people."

It sounds implausible. All this trouble to find missing people? It's more likely to be an execution. They've grown tired of keeping you alive so they tell you they're taking you home and then drive you to the nearest deserted spot. And this is the man they've chosen to do it: someone young, compliant. *Go there, carry that, shoot this person in the face.* "These people you're looking for, what are they doing there?"

"A translation error." He pauses, considering what he can tell you. "An accident caused by a power fluctuation. Apparently it put them on a trajectory towards the 25th. And you know what happens then."

You don't. You've never thought about the 25th. You will still be in prison by then, or dead.

"The 25th don't like travel," he says, like he's talking to a child. "If they see something coming they send it back. It must be easy when you have the details in advance. This one they sent back to City Two East. It should reach there in the next day or so."

"Why send them there?"

"They don't give reasons."

"That's all you know?" You would have told a better story: they were kidnapped or there was sabotage. There would be a

27

reason, an enemy and a moral. There would have been clarity. "What happens if you find them?"

"There'll be a medical transport waiting for us at the perimeter. When we find them I'll send the location and they'll collect us. Then I return with them."

It's a lot of resources for two people. "And if you don't find them?"

"I find them." He speaks as if the outcome is already known. "And when I do you return here and go back to your room."

And then it strikes you: the reason he's travelling with you in a sealed vehicle. The reason there was nobody else present as he led you out of the prison. That cropped and patterned hair isn't a style that's come round again. They're being careful about what he's allowed to see: in this case, nothing outside the vehicle. Riemann is just as much a prisoner as you. "They've sent you forward, haven't they?"

He stiffens, tilts his head back. Military. "That's not relevant."

"Why have they sent you? If they know where these people will be, why don't *they* find them? Why weren't they *waiting* for them?"

"They have their reasons."

"Because they don't want to go themselves," you say. "Because it's still dangerous."

"They have their reasons." He's not going to be drawn. A good subordinate, the best in his class, pleased to have been chosen for this. Compliant. They send him forward, they send him back. He follows orders and doesn't think unless he's told to. You feel, for a moment, almost sorry for him.

"This translation error, was it a charter?"

"A fixed link."

"I thought they were safe."

"This one wasn't. And how would you know? You people didn't travel."

"What have they told you about me?" You watch for his reaction. "I travelled. When I was your age. A fixed link." Offer a shared experience and they will start to think they can trust you.

He's sceptical. "Didn't you think it was impossible? Where did you go?"

"The 21st. Where else are there fixed links? You can launch a translation from inside a transport." You don't think he'll know this. "There's a procedure, a panel. You open it. There are switches. You have to throw them in the right sequence. Twelve switches," you tell him. "It's so simple a Happiness could do it. But you have to remember the sequence. If you get it wrong it doesn't work." Your right hand jabs at the air between you, faltering at the fourth switch. You start again, and stop at the same place. You let your hands fall. "I used to know it," you insist. "I had a good memory."

"They didn't tell me you were talkative," he says flatly. "It's going to be a long ride. You might as well tell me about your city."

Happiness Executive

"Are you sure?" Erquist is perplexed. He calls up records on the display panel on his desk. The screen is local tech, adapted: we don't make them at home. Our industries have other priorities. "Are you really sure?"

"I checked the list."

"Have you checked it more than once?"

"Three times." Her name is Adorna Mond. She was travelling alone. "Are you saying you didn't know this was going to happen?"

"Are you certain it *has* happened?"

We're in his office, behind Entertainment Area Two. Erquist's office is in the style of home: sparely furnished, softly lit, windowless. Erquist has been Resort Supervisor for two years and has never left the resort. He rarely leaves his office. Most clients will spend their month in the 21st without ever having seen him. Even for one of us, he's noticeably pale and soft, like a mushroom that's acquired human form and a talent for administration.

He stares at the display as if he expects the record to

change. "It's not on any report. Who do you think is missing?"

I give the client's name. "And she's not in the resort. I checked with Safety."

"Is it possible you've made a mistake?"

"No. She's missing. Isn't this the kind of thing we report?"

"Is it possible Safety have made a mistake?"

"They've checked twice."

"She hasn't found the blind spot?"

"No." Reps have been looking for resort blind spots ever since their existence was first theorised. Nobody has ever found one. "She isn't in the resort."

"How about the approach?"

It's the one place where the sensors might not find her: the approach to the travel zone, right at the heart of the resort, a winding corridor with nothing to see and an unsettling ambience where equipment frequently breaks down and the techs report hearing voices. Clients will have walked along two of them to get here; they're not usually eager to repeat the experience, and there's a Safety at the gate to discourage the ones who want to try. Besides, to get there she'd have to cross areas where the sensors *do* work. "She won't be in the approach."

Erquist is untroubled. "Are you sure she was on your excursion?"

"I counted her on. We must report this."

"Perhaps we do." Erquist looks up from the display. He's concerned, but only mildly. It's the management style. Erquist is pure third-generation Happiness Executive. He's probably incapable of anxiety. "But it's obviously not important enough for it to be sent back."

"And the accident was?"

"That's different. The accident could have upset our clients. They had to know in advance it wouldn't be serious. It's a matter of operational importance. One client wandering off – it's important to you, but it doesn't create an operational problem. If it's not in the forecast it must be because she turns up safely."

I feel a moment of hope. Perhaps Erquist is right. Perhaps she's made her own way back, her signature contaminated by an electronic product from the 21st picked up at the shopping mall.

Except Safety hasn't reported any clients returning alone. She can't be in the resort.

Erquist is still tapping at his desk. "Have you said anything about this to your section chief?"

"I came straight to you."

"Good." Erquist waves away the records and settles back into his chair. "We can keep him out of the cone for now. I don't see this is a problem. She's not on the records because we didn't report her missing. Which can only mean that you're going to find her quickly and we're going to decide the whole thing was a fuss about nothing. After all, assuming our client left the group, she did so through her own agency, didn't she?"

He's saying this to cheer me up. It's typical Happiness: a contented employee is a productive employee, anger and stress do not solve problems – basic stuff, the precepts they're taught from an early age. And it's possible our missing client is slightly more adventurous than the average and travelling with Tri Millennium because we're cheap. She might have followed her own itinerary and slipped away with a scholarly guide or ancient travel text.

Or she might just have been careless. She might have turned

a corner and become so engrossed in some picturesque aspect of the 21st that she failed to notice the coach pulling away. She might be there still, alone, not speaking the language, with night falling, in a street the guidebooks don't mention. She might be waiting for us – for *me* – to go back and collect her.

So the street is the first place I ought to look.

Erquist can see I'm concerned. "It'll be fine, Spens. If it wasn't we'd know about it. You'll find her. She can't have gone far. Or she's on her way here now, in a taxi." He says *taxi* tentatively. Erquist isn't quite sure about the terminology. He's never caught a taxi, or a train, or a bus. Despite his time here he's still unused to the idea of paying for travel through space. The local obsession with turning every aspect of life into a financial transaction is something he understands only on the most abstract level. Outside this resort, he'd be help-less. "Go back to the place where you think she got off the transport. Take one of the natives to drive you. You'll find her in no time." He hesitates. "No, wait. It's probably best if you don't take a native. We'll keep this quiet for now. You can work on your own, can't you? You know how to drive their" – he gropes for the word, gives up – "their things?"

"I have a licence."

"Good. I'll authorise the use of a thing." He makes hand gestures over his desk. "And don't look so glum. You'll find her in no time."

Despite his reassurances I remain glum. I don't like the way he keeps saying *in no time*. I know it's an archaic survival, but you'd think a Resort Supervisor in the travel business would be a little more sensitive to the nuances.

But he could be right: if there's no record of anything going wrong, it should mean nothing goes wrong. It's the logic of travel. The company could hardly keep quiet about losing a client. For a start, there would be questions from the kin.

People have travelled and not returned before, but they were either on official business or scholars like Brink and Nakamura, who knew the risks and travelled knowing they might not come back. Or they're extemps, supposedly *alienated* from their own era, who want to live in a *simpler, more natural society.* Extemps are supposed to need official approval before they leave, but there's always a few who think it's easier to pay for a trip with one of the companies and simply not come home. Usually they're unimportant enough to be allowed to stay. Perhaps our client is one of these. Perhaps her kin don't complain. Perhaps they're glad to see her leave.

Before I go to the vehicle pool I stop by the Safety Office again. I add our client's details and a signature tracker to my handheld and see what Tri-Millennium knows about her. Most extemps are humanities types: history, literature, music, religion, art. According to her travel application Adorna Mond was science, working with various environmental teams. I'm not a tech, but most of it looked like junior-level research: toxicity analysis, soil reclamation projects, worthy but dull, and nothing like the high-end physics required for travel. At twenty-six, she's younger than a typical Tri-Millennium client. I study her image. We catch all the clients' images as they arrive in the resort. It's a concession to the native authorities, so they can tell their own people they're taking every precaution. Adorna Mond is the hooded woman who sat at the back, staring out of the window and not asking questions. Her behaviour hadn't seemed significant at the time. I've seen it with younger travellers: they're with us because we're cheap and they don't mix with older people outside their kin.

While in the office I consider comparing our image with

CCTV from the accident site. I decide against. Erquist hadn't authorised it, and I wasn't sure if the street even had CCTV, or if it would be accessible. Besides, it's an inefficient system. You might as well post teams of near-sighted people with sketchbooks.

Finally I set the internals to bip me if she turns up while I'm out.

The vehicle pool is deserted. Occasionally we'll get a retired tech who's read about internal combustion engines and wants to see one for himself (we'll show them but we don't let them touch); more often, though, the clients will get away as quickly as they can. They don't like the smell, or are keen to share their impressions of the outside world with less adventurous friends. Our native drivers usually head straight home or go to the sleeping quarters/café we built for them just inside the dome wall. I suspect they find too much time with our clients makes them uncomfortable. I know that spending time with natives makes me nervous, even now. I've learned enough of their language to follow their news and watch their entertainments but I still miss too many nuances.

Beyond the coach parking bays are Tri-Millennium's stock of smaller vehicles. They've been customised with the usual recognition tags, so the one Erquist has authorised for me clicks and flashes its lights as I approach.

I get in and tell it where I want to go. The key is in the ignition. I plug the handheld into the control panel, start the engine, engage the security protocol and drive very slowly and carefully towards the exit. I have a licence to operate this vehicle (four doors, a Japanese brand that's become slang for somebody who works hard but has no character). Three checkpoints later I am on the open road, the handheld on a two-kilometre sweep in case our client is heading back in the other direction. I switch on the radio: the last user, probably a native, had been listening to the monopulse of ancient dance music. I click through talk shows until I find a Mozart piano concerto; not my first choice, but tolerable. It's a recent performance – recent, that is, in this era – made by someone who hasn't heard the composer's own recordings, so the speeds are all slightly wrong. I don't know if they haven't heard the originals (we only made them available here a few years ago) or if they're among the natives who think our recordings are faked. Some do, but then there are supposed to be twenty-seven per cent who don't believe in travel. They think we're actors in make-up and odd costumes talking a nonsense language as part of an international conspiracy, or aliens out to enslave humanity. Most of the sceptics come from the States, China or Russia, big countries that don't like the idea they're technologically backward, even if the people who have outstripped them are their own descendants. And then there's the DomeWatch crowd, who accept we're from their future but don't trust us for other reasons. The pianist and conductor in this performance probably aren't as crazy as them. They still cling to a way of playing that's been shown to be wrong.

It takes me longer to reach the accident site than it took our driver to make the opposite journey. In part that's because I drive more slowly and use the safety protocols. I don't, like the natives, trust to luck. I see the results of two accidents on the way there: natives standing beside their dented vehicles, probably asking themselves how it could have happened to them.

It's starting to get dark when I reach the site. I have to park a few streets away, outside a row of squat little houses where nobody seems to be at home. I unplug the handheld and slip it into my jacket pocket. The shops are still open, their lights making more of a contrast with the shabby street. The street lights aren't yet on and the rooms on the upper storeys are still dark. There's a scent of spiced food overlaying the usual sewage-and-petrol miasma and odd little gusts of wind throw sharp dust in my face. The client isn't here. She isn't waiting forlornly in a shop doorway and the handheld doesn't find her signature anywhere in the neighbourhood. I walk the length of the block, cross the road and walk back, glancing in each shop as I pass. She isn't in any of them, and I'd be surprised if she was. There's still no signal from my handheld. It sits in my pocket, inert. I might as well be carrying a pebble.

Well, I think, perhaps she's lost. She's had two hours, plenty of time to wander off on some unguided quest for help, and long enough to have caught a train or a taxi and be in a different part of town, or even a different town altogether. I begin to feel anxious. Erquist might say we don't report this because it's not important, but what if we don't report it because it is? What if it turns out we kept quiet because reporting it would be disastrous for our company? What if I go back empty-handed and Erquist invokes some Tri-Millennium protocol that means this can never be discussed?

She's had two hours to get somewhere else. Or be taken somewhere else.

Travellers have been kidnapped before, but not in this era or in this part of the world. This isn't the sixteenth century, or any of the numerous dark ages where people are frightened of strangers, and, this early in the 21st, England isn't as bad as it becomes during the NEE. Kidnapping shouldn't happen. There have been only five recorded instances since we announced our presence, none of them in this hemisphere.

Now we have an official presence we take kidnapping seriously. Our people are rescued within a matter of hours.

It could be done in minutes, but there are usually negotiations with local governments about using our own Safety Teams. What happens to the kidnappers is never disclosed. It's assumed they're killed on-site, although there's a rumour among the natives that anyone who survives the initial assault is sent to a more inhospitable era. The vagueness is one part of the deterrent – only the dimmest native criminals want to spend their last hours in the Permian. The main deterrent, the feature that keeps would-be kidnappers from trying their luck, is the obvious one that we're from the future. Our Safety Teams will know where to find them because, from our perspective, *we've already found them.* So why allow kidnappings in the first place? The rumour among the reps (and we love rumours as much as any native) is that the victims *wanted* to be kidnapped. They knew they were never in danger. They were Safety, dressed like tourists or diplomats. They could afford to wander without a bodyguard through a city known for its high kidnapping rate and trigger-happy cartels. When they were bundled into unmarked vehicles we suddenly had leverage with the native authorities: if you can't ensure the safety of our citizens then we'll have to. And the Safety Teams show up very soon afterwards with serious, serious firepower. The kidnappings always happened in recalcitrant states. They provided an excuse for a demonstration of our efficiency that usually speeded up any negotiations.

So she can't have been kidnapped. This is England in the early 21st, an advanced, sophisticated civilisation. Nobody should be that stupid. Our client should be fine.

Except I have a feeling something is wrong.

Subjective feelings are not, of course, reliable. They can be prompted by any one of the thousand bad smells in this city: the rotting food, the exhaust fumes, the updraught from decaying sewers, the stench of dead meat that arises whenever large numbers of natives gather. (Individually they have chemical overtones. Collectively they stink. You spend your first few days in any city convinced there's a large dead animal just around the corner.) And then there's the noise: the continuous throb of waiting engines, the pop music that pounds out like a musical analogue to a child's tantrum, and, below all that, the infrasonics. The combination can trigger a sense of unease. Spend too long in the early 21st and you learn to mistrust your instincts.

The handheld is telling me our client is not in this area. None of *us* are in this area: I can't get a single signature. But then this is a native quarter. There are no passing groups from Heritage, or extemps. Why would there be? There's nothing of architectural interest here, nothing of any historical significance has ever happened. The only reason to live here is because you were born here or can't afford to move somewhere else. I head back to the car. Now I'll have to look up transport routes and hand the case over to Safety. And then Erquist will send me home for breach of protocol.

I don't want to give up so easily. I go back to the little row of shops. Along with the newsagents, the takeaway and the one with flowers outside is a taxi office. It can't, I think, hurt to ask.

There are two men behind a glass screen. On this side there's a dark blue carpet and four orange plastic chairs which look as though they would warp if I sat on them. The walls are a dirty yellow. The man at the counter is reading a native newspaper which is mostly pictures. The other man sits behind him, watching a tiny, inaudible box with a screen. Despite my time here, I'm getting no better at guessing the ages of these people: the newspaper reader might be fifty, or a socially deprived twenty-five. The television watcher is probably younger, but only five or six years away from coronary failure. Neither looks up when I walk in. It's possible they think I'm here by mistake.

"Excuse me," I say in This English.

The older one looks up. His expression doesn't change. He doesn't say anything. I doubt he speaks Modern.

"I'm looking for somebody." I take out the handheld and project the face of our client onto the yellow wall. At home, we wouldn't use an image for identification. It's too easy to change your appearance: eye colour, a different nose, a new jawline. Signatures are a more reliable guide. But this is the early 21st. A picture will have to do. "Have you seen this woman?"

The man glances at the image, still expressionless. The native behind him doesn't take his eyes off the television, which shows three men sitting in a studio. From the picture of a trophy behind them they're talking about football, a native obsession (Tri-Millennium offers a trip to a local stadium). The older man looks back at his newspaper without answering.

I stay calm. I remind myself this is probably the first time he's spoken to one of us. "I was asking you," I say, "if you have seen this woman."

"No." He doesn't look up. "We haven't."

I have the impression he wouldn't help even if he could. "Thank you for your time," I say, partly because it is Happiness policy to be polite and partly because I suspect it will annoy him, I leave. It's dark now. The handheld still isn't reading anything. Stage two. Return to the car, perhaps even drive around for a while in case our client has decided to walk back to the resort and set off in the wrong direction. She's had two hours. Even moving slowly, on foot, she could be ten kilometres away. If I don't find her in the next hour it's back to the resort.

Street lights are starting to come on, along with a few house lights. Motor traffic is getting heavier as people drive home. There are more pedestrians. I'm conscious of their sidelong attention. This is a poor neighbourhood, after all. For all the talk of the economic benefits we bring it will always be poor, at least until the NEE drags everywhere else down to their level, and then lower again. I've been in neighbourhoods like this before, when Li tried to educate me about native culture. I saw their pubs and heard their musicians. I thought it would make me a better rep. You get used to the glances, the murmuring in corners, the sudden flash of someone taking a picture – taking pictures is as close as most people get, unless they're Domeheads. *They'll* talk to you. Some of them have even learned Modern. They have questions: Is it true that, Do you really. And listen wide-eyed to whatever you tell them. It's surprising, the things they believe about us: that we live for hundreds of years and can read each other's minds ... They want to be our friends. They dress like us and copy our hairstyles. They want to come back and live with us in our fabulous underground cities. They're a minority.

I doubt there are any in this neighbourhood.

"What are you doing here?" A man's voice, behind me. Modern.

My handheld hasn't registered any of us in the area. I turn, expecting a tragic misfit. And my first thought is that it *is* a native. He's dressed like one: black coat, businessman-style. Taller than usual, thin, with a lined face and white hair. Fifty-odd, I think, and he's spent a lot of time outdoors. He smiles: something amuses him. "Spens," he says, "I always wondered how you got involved."

I look more closely. Not a native. An extemp, then, who's been here so long he's lost his wariness about sunlight. But an extemp would have a signature, and the handheld in my pocket hasn't moved.

He looks down at my feet. "I suppose I should have guessed."

I don't say anything. We're supposed to have signatures. If we don't it's because we've gone to expensive trouble. It occurs to me that this man might be dangerous. There's no overt threat, but he has an unnerving way of standing very still. And why is he so interested in my shoes? I realise he's looking for Safety-issue footwear. He's assessing how dangerous I am.

And he knows my name.

My shoes are standard Happiness Casual. Yellow, harmless.

He smiles. "You don't recognise me, do you?"

"Should I?"

"It's Riemann. Cantor's brother."

I stare helplessly. Cantor was a friend from school. I lost touch with him when he went to Tech Ed and I went to the Tunnels. Riemann had been his little brother. The last time I'd seen either of them on my line had been six years earlier.

Riemann had been ten.

"Riemann?" Travel is confusing. "The last time I saw you—"

"It's been a while. For me, anyway."

"You've changed."

"And you're shorter than I remember." His smile becomes almost friendly. "And heavier. Have you had augs?"

"In the Tunnels."

"I remember when you left. I was sorry to see you go. You were one of Cantor's nicer friends."

"Thanks." My departure is, for him, a remote childhood memory. If I'm right about his age it would have been, for him, forty years ago. "When did you get here?"

"About fifteen years, give or take. You – is this your first trip?"

"You've settled?"

"Hardly." A wry grimace. "But, you know, you go where the work takes you."

Fifteen years in the early 21st. "What kind of work?"

He looks up and down the street. Natives walking home. Sidelong glances. Does Riemann look like a native to them? "You're probably wondering why I haven't got a signature."

"A little." It's either shielding, which is supposed to be impossible, or de-augmentation, which would require official approval or a lot of currency. Official approval isn't supposed to happen. "Are you able to tell me?"

"I can't. You can draw your own conclusions."

"But you've been here for fifteen years."

"As I said, you go where the work takes you." He becomes sombre. "And it wasn't always here. Most of the time I was in South and Central America. I can tell you that much. But how are you? I'm glad to see you. And what are you doing here?"

"Looking for a missing client."

"A client." This seems to amuse him. "I remember Cantor telling me you'd become a rep. Who are you with?"

"Tri-Millennium."

"The cheap one? And you've lost a client?"

"She got out of a coach near here and didn't get back on."

"And you're concerned about her?"

"She's my responsibility."

"Do you think she's in trouble?"

"That's what I'm trying to find out. Do you know anything about it?" It's dizzying. Her disappearance doesn't get reported, but here he is, being mysterious not far from where she disappeared. "I mean, is it a coincidence you're here?"

"No," he says. "Nothing is. You know that. You also know why I can't tell you anything."

I can guess. "Agency."

"Exactly. What I can tell you is you don't have to worry about your client. She isn't lost or frightened. She left of her own free will. You can tell your Resort Supervisor and Safety Chief that it's not worth worrying about. You don't need to mention me. But then you don't, do you?"

"No." Because if I say anything it will be part of a record he's already seen. "I suppose I don't."

Or perhaps I say something and that part of the report is removed from the Arc. Perhaps he knows I report it and is warning me anyway because that's the procedure: he has to warn me, even though he knows I'll ignore him. Perhaps I include his warning in the report and an official deletes the whole thing before he sees it.

Or he's just being polite. Good travellers don't reveal what they know about other travellers' lines.

It's dizzying.

He takes out a handheld. It's been modified to look like 21st tech. Or it is 21st tech. He sighs. "I have to go. It was nice seeing you again, Spens. I always liked you." He pockets the device and strides off. I'm frozen in place for a few seconds. A few years ago he was ten: now he's twice my age and knows about our client. Thirty years after she left for the 21st she's important enough for a man without a signature to be following her.

I tell myself it's not my concern. I go back to the car, plug in the handheld. No signatures in a five-kilometre radius. I boost the range: a couple the Arc identifies as known extemps, but nothing from our client, or Riemann. On the drive back I find a concert of last-century music (Bartók, Martinů) which calms me down a little. The music is seventy years old by the local calendar. The announcer talks about it as if it's modern. It takes my mind off the meeting, at least while I'm driving. Li bips me a reminder about Bar Five.

Kat

The world was simple. There was your home, Kat, and there were the Number Cities. Numbers, not names. Slaves instead of people. Slaves who were drugged and pampered and didn't even realise they were slaves.

Now there are only the Number Cities.

Kat, you tell Riemann, was two cities: the old one from before the Collapse and the new one alongside and underneath it. Your city remembered its past. It kept its ruins. It was beautiful. "Our cathedral was famous. World famous."

There is no harm in telling him this.

"Everybody thinks their home city is beautiful," he says. "Even City Three North."

You've heard their jokes: City Three North is supposed to be poor while One West is pompous and Two West is dull. Five South is ambitious.

"Beauty's all very well." He gives up waiting for you to laugh. "It would be more useful if you had maps."

"They would have helped an enemy."

"What enemy?"

"You."

"Do you think you're our great enemy?" He keeps lapsing into the present tense. "You aren't even a nuisance. Your city's a joke. We're more concerned about the weather."

"When you left, it hadn't happened, had it?"

He pauses. Calculating how much he can say. Of course you're both being watched. A prisoner and a man who's been sent forward – neither of you should be here. Everything you say is being listened to or recorded. "All I know is that I came here expecting negotiations. I thought my job was to be an escort. When I got here I was told there wouldn't be any negotiations because City Two East is dead." He lets the word *dead* hang in the air. When he speaks again he tries to sound neutral: "Instead of simply collecting people from a prearranged point I'd have to find them myself. And you were the only available guide. I didn't think I'd need one and that I could just track the signatures. But it turns out there's no network so I can't do that. I have an effective range of two hundred metres."

Signatures. You can't remember how many you've had. Three, four? "You rely too much on those machines."

"They're usually reliable. So, without maps, how did you find your way about?"

"We knew the city."

You tell him you were raised in a home two blocks south of Corn Street, behind Cathedral Square, and sent to a school four down from the Parliament Building.

"Simple enough," he says. "Where I grew up there was nothing older than sixty years."

It's the Number City way. They ask you questions so they can talk about themselves. You tell him there were rules about giving directions: if anyone asked you how to get somewhere you were supposed to refuse. If they had a good reason to go somewhere new they would have been given directions along with their orders.

"What if they were strangers? How were they supposed to know?"

"They weren't." If you saw anybody you didn't recognise you were supposed to avoid them and alert the authorities. If it was somebody you recognised and they were in the wrong place you did the same. "We were warned against spending too long in the old city."

"I've seen some of the old cities," he says, and looks surprised at his own words. "The Tunnels."

"The buildings were unsafe. There were criminal gangs. Thieves. Deserters. There are always selfish people. We were told to be careful."

That was the pattern of your life. You were told certain things were true and gradually discovered they weren't. The old city was not as dangerous as your teachers claimed. All the children, given a chance, explored or took shortcuts. The ruins had been made safe – or safer – by the labourers who'd lived in them when they built the new city. Anything that hadn't fallen down long ago was buttressed or shored up. Sometimes you'd find traces of recent occupation – the ashes of a fire, animal bones, shit. You rarely saw people, and then only at a distance, fleeing. They were scared of everybody, even children. If they were reported and caught they'd have to become citizens, which meant working in the waste farms and insect factories.

A memory comes back unbidden: the room where the girls lined up to hear the latest announcements. *Don't stop, don't take shortcuts, don't talk to strangers. Yesterday our scouts saved more people fleeing from the enemy.* How many mornings did you stand in that room? Lined up with the other girls, then sitting with them in classes, waiting for those moments between classroom, mess hall and dormitory when you could slip away to some alcove or cupboard and be alone.

"Were you a believer?" Riemann's voice drags you back. "The cathedral. Did you worship in it?"

"It was unsafe."

The room had thick pipes overhead which, at twelve, you could reach up and touch. It was always too cold or too hot and there was always a smell of damp and shit and at least one girl would be crying because she was new and didn't understand the language. After the messages and lessons there would be songs: stories from history, reminders of the need for discipline and others which you'd thought were nonsense until you learned they were from *before* when even the language was different. The teachers were determined to teach you the old songs. It is your culture, they would say. It cannot be lost. You remember the time one of the girls made a mistake and instead of shouting at her the teacher cried. It was the first time you'd seen an adult cry, or show any emotion other than anger or stern resolve.

"Why did you keep it?" His voice is gentle. "I didn't think you were religious."

He's still talking about the cathedral. "We weren't." There had been believers, different sects allowed to pray in private if they thought it helped. "We were taught to rely on ourselves."

"Because everybody else was against you?"

"Everybody *was* against us."

You can't remember any of the songs now, only fragments. The first line of one, a refrain from another. There was a song about a birch tree. You didn't even know what a birch tree was, but you sang the song with the other girls. You knew the words then. You could be the last person alive who once knew those songs and you've forgotten them all. What would the teacher say to that?

He's long dead. He wouldn't say anything.

The real danger in the old city, you tell him, was from other children, particularly the boys from the home under the courthouse – the older girls were full of stories about what happened to girls they caught. If you saw them you were supposed to stay hidden until they moved on. But even the boys weren't so terrible. They were more interested in getting away from the city, heading west, hoping to avoid patrols. The girls shared stories about tunnels, hidden rooms, boltholes where you could disappear; the boys told each other how to leave the city.

"Your whole city was mad." He shakes his head. "So you had a cathedral that was unsafe and you didn't worship there. Why didn't you demolish it and build something useful?"

"Because we weren't you. We remembered our past." You're pleased with your answer. You'd be more pleased if it hadn't occurred to you after a long and awkward silence.

He goes back to staring at the side panels. There are three small dents at eye level. He's probably wondering what caused them. Now that you've started thinking about your old city you can't stop. Your favourite hiding place was a room beyond a room on the second floor of an old school building: you liked it because there were two ways in, both hidden, and because it had been your discovery. It had been some kind of storeroom, and still contained a single shelf of rotting books. There was a crack in the wall through which you could watch people hurrying along the old street: other girls, teachers, workers. It was like being invisible. Whenever you could slip out of the home you'd come to this room and stand by that gap in the wall. You spent hours there. It was the solitude, the view of the street. Sometimes you'd take a book off the shelf and turn the damp, gritty pages in the dark, trying to imagine what they said. Other times you'd pretend to be a sniper, deciding who lived or died. The memory of the room is vivid, but when you try to remember the view the image that comes is a mistake, a street from the 21st with ancient vehicles and people in old costumes. You blink.

Riemann is watching you. You close your eyes and pretend to sleep.

Bar Five

Bar Five is in the city centre. It's a native place, in that it's owned and run by natives, but its customers are extemps and reps and the more adventurous clients. The name is supposed to remind us of home. It's bright and white, a vision of a streamlined future that's retro even by native standards. The staff speak Modern, or something like it, and, while they sell the usual local drinks, they've learned not to stock ones we can't metabolise. Natives occasionally come in, but they never stay for long. Even if they can afford the prices they don't like the atmosphere.

Sergei, the rep who was leaving, had booked the room at the back. By the time I arrived he was already asleep at the head of the table. Li jumped up when she saw me. "Spens, glad you could show. This is getting dead." Sergei wasn't the only one not entirely in the room. Kelson and Petra had their heads on the table, and a man I recognised from Living History was awake but staring at the plain white wall with more interest than it merited. There were a few others I didn't recognise: typical Happiness engaged in typical Happiness conversations about kin ramifications and where they studied, except at about half the usual speed. "It started early," Li says.

That's the problem with rep events: tonin. They get nostalgic for an old-fashioned T-break, inevitably somebody has a supply, and they don't moderate. That's why rep events are held in back rooms.

I haven't taken T since I was in the Tunnels, when it was part of the end-of-shift routine and recommended by the Tunnel Authorities. They wanted to keep their workers sane. Tonin won't make you forget but it distances the experience so you don't have flashbacks or bouts of unfocused aggression. If I take it now it just makes me think of rambling discussions about what you'd rather be doing with your life and a particular orange stain on the ceiling of my room. Li doesn't take it for different reasons. She'll drink alcohol or listen to music to change her mood but thinks chemical intervention this precisely targeted is cheating. She also hasn't had any elective augs. "Another typical rep farewell," she says. "Do you want to go somewhere else before Ivan turns up?"

Ivan is the other problem with rep events. Unlike most extemps, he actively seeks out the company of reps, if only because he thinks we'll provide him with tonin. Somebody will usually oblige. I disapprove: if he's an extemp he ought to stick with the native population's range of narcotics. Isn't that why he's here? Instead he pesters us. If there's a farewell party he'll sniff it out, even if he hasn't been invited.

Li says goodbye to the few reps who are still awake and we head for the door. "I've never liked this place," she tells me, which I knew already. "There's a bar not far from here that's not bad. And cheaper."

Cheaper. Li is concerned about money: she says it's because she's from City Three North, which rarely had any. Her wages are supposed to pay for her future travel. She doesn't want to spend them in Bar Five.

"Wherever you like." We're out in the main room. A few reps, a couple of clients looking around in wonder. It's still early evening.

Before we can reach the door Ivan steps in from the street. He's wearing native clothes, layers of drab, inert materials. He's rolled up his sleeves so that everybody can see his tattoos. They're the kind you still occasionally find on Tri-Millennium's older clients. Ivan's in his forties but belongs to that generation. He's been in the 21st ever since it became possible to live here openly, and still thinks he's a pioneer, full of advice and interesting stories. "Li." He sees us and grins. "Spens."

Li nods at the back room. "Sergei's in there."

Ivan stands in our way, arms folded across his chest so we can't miss his antique body art. "I'll be sorry to see him go." The snake tattoos writhe slowly around his thin arms to emphasise how sorry he is. "No, I'll chat to Sergei later. But it's you I wanted to talk to."

He's looking at me. This is unusual. I'm not a source of tonin. "Yeah?"

"What's this I hear about one of your clients wandering off?"

"I don't know, Ivan." I wonder how he's heard anything. It's only been a few hours. News travels quickly but so far I've only told Erquist. Unless a client on the trip noticed and talked to another rep . . . "What have you heard?"

"⊓ ⊓⊓⊓⊓⊓⊓⊓, ⊐⊔⊔⊔⊔⊔. ⊔⊔⊔⊔⊔ ⊔⊔⊔⊔⊔."

"I wouldn't worry about it." I don't like Ivan. He's simultaneously sleazy and boring – actively, aggressively boring. He can take a subject dear to your heart and turn it into ashes.

Plus I'm uncomfortable with somebody of my grandfather's generation scraping tonin from reps. It's undignified. "There's nothing to it."

"I've heard there's something." The snakes on his arms freeze. "I mean, you know who she is, don't you?"

"Of course we do."

"But you know *what* she is?"

For a moment I wonder if Ivan knows about Riemann. They've both been here for years. Somehow I don't think Riemann would stoop this low. Plus Riemann spent most of his time in South and Central America. I don't think Ivan has ever left this city. "We're not concerned."

"Aren't you?" Ivan looks pleased. His snakes resume their sinuous weaving. "So you don't think she's in any trouble? There isn't a Safety Team trying to find her?"

"Why would there be?"

"Just curious. It can be dangerous out in the anterior." The anterior: the slang that reminds you he's not a contemporary. "I thought you might be taking precautions. Li!" He unfolds his arms and hugs her. She shudders and twists free. Ivan is known for his hugs and hand clasps. They're part of his native affectation. "I'm sure Li knows all about the risks."

She says, "It's not so dangerous."

"So where are you going?" For a moment it looks as if he's about to invite himself along. "Looking for your client?"

"Just a pub." Li's step back was part of a move to circumvent him. "If you want to say goodbye to Sergei you'd better hurry up. They started early. It might not last."

This works. Tonin isn't addictive, yet Ivan has all the traits of a native addict. He grins and scuttles towards the back room, ready to give anybody still conscious a hearty greeting. He probably thinks he's a larger-than-life figure. Ivan Ho, the one who went native, the one you need to know to find out what's going on. It's pathetic.

Before the door can close behind him a woman runs out. She clutches Li's arm. "Take me with you," she pleads. "You can't leave me in there with him." She's one of the reps I haven't seen before. Tall, with the casual perfection and high gloss of a typical Happiness. I should be scornful, but when she smiles at me I smile back and notice she has piercing green eyes. The new fashion, just breaking as I left. Striking now, in a few years her illuminated stare will be as passé as Ivan's tattoos.

"This is Edda," Li says flatly. "She arrived last week."

"It's my first time out." Edda continues to smile. "Are you going to a native bar? Please let me come with you. I can't stand that man."

Li doesn't look entirely happy. She wanted to talk to me, not babysit this new arrival. We step out to the street. "I don't want to put you to any trouble," Edda says. "It's just I didn't come here to sit in a back room and pretend I'm home. And I've already met Ivan."

"I thought you said it was your first time out," I say.

"First time without clients." The illumination fades slightly. "I had an excursion yesterday. He followed me around for an hour."

"The place we're going is quiet," Li says, as if this might discourage her. She leads us down a side street. It's dark and lined with containers for unwanted food and other rubbish, the kind of street you walk through on your way somewhere else, the kind Tri-Millennium's clients would avoid unless they had a guide. "This is already more interesting," Edda says, touching my arm.

"Wait till you've been here a year," I say.

Two-thirds of the way along, Li stops and pushes a button

next to a wooden door. There's a sign next to the button, illegible in this light. I assume this must be one of Li's discoveries, a place where she takes only her hardiest clients.

The door opens. I expect to hear music, but there's nothing, or nothing I can distinguish from the ambient city noise.

"Logan," Li says.

The native at the door is short, round-faced, pale, bearded – a neglect beard rather than a style beard, though, for some of Li's friends, neglect *is* a style. "Li," he says. He seems disappointed there are only three of us.

"This is Spens," Li tells him, as he stands aside to let us in. "And Edda." He mumbles something as we pass. I don't think it's an actual word. When Edda smiles at him he looks pained and turns away.

The door leads to a corridor as dark as the street outside. I still can't hear anything that indicates we're heading to a place of entertainment. The man opens another door. Beyond it is a storeroom, more brightly lit but just as quiet, with a few cardboard boxes on dusty metal shelves: paper towels, bar snacks. The boxes look like they haven't been opened in years.

"It's a quiet night," the man says.

The next room is like a darker version of the back room at Bar Five. Low black sofas against the walls, glass-topped tables. It's brighter than the storeroom but not by much. There's another room beyond it, larger and brighter still, with some natives on stools by the greenish glow of a bar.

Logan looks at us nervously. "What are you drinking?"

I almost answer: Nothing, yet. Li recognises the idiom and orders beers. She pays in cash. I wonder if it's the same money she took from the Shins. Edda sits next to me on the sofa. Li says, "What do you think?"

I can see Logan and a native girl behind the bar where three customers have gathered. Two others sit at a table in the middle. The music – some kind of slow, angular jazz – is just loud enough to drown out whatever they're saying. "You're right. It's quiet."

"But at least Ivan never comes here." Li leans in. "So is it true what he said? Have you lost a client?"

Edda is immediately interested. "You've lost a client? Is that even possible?" Her eyes seem to light up. They're troubling. I knew people with layers like this in the Tunnels: first generation, functional, with a photosensitive switch for night vision. The catch was that the layers on each eye responded independently. We discovered that if you sneaked up behind somebody and covered one of their eyes it could trigger an immediate migraine, a joke which soon wore thin. I preferred to work with torches and helmet lamps.

"There are rumours about your clients," Li says.

"What sort of rumours?"

"The main one is about tone." Li glances at Edda, wary of talking about this in front of her. "If your client is missing it could be she's a courier."

"Carrying tonin?" This is something I hadn't considered. "What would be the point? It's all over the resorts already. And you saw Sergei."

"That's reps and clients. Small stuff. If she was carrying it would have been for extemps. They're a market."

"Really? Why don't they do what Ivan does and scrape it off a rep?"

"Not all of them are close enough to a resort." Li is patient. "And not all of them want anything to do with reps. They're extemps for a reason."

"But they still want tone," Edda adds. "There are some things they can't give up."

"And they can't make it here," Li says. "And there's no legal market outside the resorts. So they rely on our clients."

"Or *your* clients," Edda says. "Tri-Millennium is notorious."

"No." It's one of those moments when you realise you're not as observant as you thought. "Notorious?"

"Because you're the cheapest," Edda says, as if it's common knowledge. "Your clients can get a free holiday and still make money. Three-quarters of all the tone in Western Europe comes from your clients."

I wonder if Erquist knows this. I wonder how Edda knows this. I ask a stupid question. "Where does the other quarter come from?"

"Geneva." Li looks surprised I haven't heard. "But that's not the point."

This is less of a surprise. Geneva is the closest we have to sovereign territory in this era. We made a show of negotiating for islands, but we always knew we'd have Geneva and once we'd repurposed CERN nobody wanted to argue with us, even if they weren't sure what we'd done. If there are any charters to the early 21st they come through Geneva. Geneva enforces the protocols and decides how much information we're allowed to see.

It's reassuring to know they're not perfect.

"You said that was one of the rumours." I try to keep the bitterness out of my voice. "What are the others?"

"There's one that the locals have started taking the stuff," Edda says. "You know what the locals are like with drugs."

I know. The users will try anything and the authorities will ban it as soon as they find out. The perfect conditions for ensuring a product is expensive, adulterated and supplied by criminals. If the natives start taking tonin those criminals would soon be involved. They couldn't allow a drug that works properly to compete with their inferior product. I'm a little put out by the confident way Edda says it: she's only just got here.

Still, gang violence over a drug from the future might explain the involvement of someone like Riemann. Damage limitation, tidying up. Assuming he's on the side of virtue. South and Central America are where a lot of native drugs are produced.

"No," I say, with more force than I mean. I'm not sure what effect tonin would have on a native. Probably the same as on us: a few augs aside, brain chemistry can't have changed much in two hundred years. Certainly not as much as gut flora. "Surely we'd have heard about that. It would be more than a rumour."

Li sighs as if I'm a slow learner. "We don't *think* they use tone. But just because it doesn't get reported doesn't mean it didn't happen."

"Or they're taking it and calling it something else," Edda says. "El Niño. Or something completely different. Like float. Or wankdust."

I assume these are native culture references. Even Li looks impressed.

"So, are people saying our client made a deal with natives?"

"Maybe not a deal," Li says. "And maybe not your client. But they might have found out about tonin. Some extemp trying to impress his new friends. You know how that can happen."

"Right." It's exactly the kind of thing I can imagine Ivan doing. *Look at my tattoos. Try my wonder drug.* "So they might be interested in her. What are they going to do? Offer her a better price?"

"She could be in danger."

Which, again, might explain Riemann. Except he'd insisted

she *wasn't* in danger. "They won't try anything. They don't try anything," I say. "If they did they must know it would involve a Safety Team."

"These are drug dealers, Spens. Most of them are drug *users*. They're not the smartest people around."

"We don't think she's in trouble. Even if she is a courier, she could be staying with whichever extemp paid for her holiday."

"But you have to be careful with this. This could be serious."

"Possibly." I suspect I know better than Li. I've seen Riemann, who said it doesn't affect me. I'm just a rep. In a few weeks I go home. "Don't worry. I'll be careful." Saying it when I'm not in any danger makes me feel slightly fraudulent. "We really don't think she's in any trouble."

Li isn't appeased. "Because there's nothing on the record? You know you can't trust those. They'll say whatever Geneva wants us to think."

Logan collects our empty glasses. We don't talk about Geneva or records in front of natives. Logan might not look like a Domehead but there's a chance he knows some Modern. I change the subject to Ivan. Edda joins in and somehow the conversation moves to her asking Li about her earlier visit and about how someone with my background came to be a rep. It's all standard Happiness: they smile as if they're pleased to see you and ask questions as if they care about your answers. It's not an act (they *are* pleased to see you, they *do* care); it's more like a conditioned reflex. And you can't help responding. Li tells her hospital story and I tell her I used to work the Tunnels, which Edda claims to find fascinating ("I *thought* you had augs."). She's intrigued again when she finds out I don't live at a resort and, once the subject of kin is raised, I end up saying more than I intended about how my parents died (an industrial accident when I was twelve), a story I hadn't even told Li. (They had been working in a recovery team. I was staying in a hostel when I heard the news. There was a memorial service one morning; I was excused classes for the afternoon; the hostel became my home until I went to the Tunnels.) Edda listens sympathetically. It occurs to me she would make a good interrogator. Unusually for a Happiness she doesn't talk about herself. I can't tell if this is modesty or another level of training.

Two hours later Li and Edda have caught the bus back to their resort and I'm making my way to the Metro. I'm not paying as much attention to my surroundings as I should because I'm thinking about Edda. She isn't a typical Happiness. That she took an instant dislike to Ivan is a point in her favour; that she knew Tri-Millennium clients carried tonin for extemps is worrying. I've been here a year and a half and didn't know something she'd learned on her first week. What else have I missed? I'm so intent on this and the conversation I need to have with Erquist I don't notice the doorway ahead of me isn't the entrance to a nightclub and that the two native men standing in it aren't bouncers, even if they are bouncer mate-rial: big for natives, heavy-set, though the tallest is still a head shorter than me. The older and squarer of the two is wearing a dark suit, like an office worker. The taller, leaner one is in a shiny black jacket. If they're following the usual native dress codes the man in the suit is in charge. They step out from the doorway, blocking my path. I'm belatedly alert. There's a wall on one side, parked cars on another, these two ahead of me. Nobody behind. They're acting alone.

"You," the Suit says. "You're with Tri-Millennium, aren't you?"

It's This English, a Southern dialect I recognise from their entertainments, where it signifies either low status or criminal. It's the first time I've heard it addressed to me.

"Yes." I keep a distance. I'm not frightened by these people. They're big, but only by local standards, and Suit is out of shape. He wheezes when he talks and he's only said six words. Black Jacket is younger and probably has old-fashioned gym muscle. He shouldn't be a problem either. I worked in the Tunnels: I've had augs.

"One of your customers is missing," Suit says. He's wary, but getting more confident, rolling into his prepared speech. "We're tryna find her."

He must have followed me since Bar Five. Or somebody had let him know where to find me. I blame Ivan. Ivan's the sort who would make friends with these people.

Suit says, "We know about your signals." He pauses to see my response. I don't give one. "Every single one of you. A signal that can be tracked." He seems to think I'll be impressed that he knows this. He nods at me, waiting to see what I have to say.

"We don't call them *signals*," I say. "They're signatures."

"I don't care what you call them. We know she's not at the resort." Again, the nod. I'd thought it was for emphasis but it's beginning to look like a nervous tic, the consequence of some old cranial trauma. "I want to find her," he gasps. "That's why you're going to give us her signal."

It's a bizarre request. I wonder if he has the equipment to track a signature. I can imagine him trying with some early-21st tech. It's laughable. Unless someone like Ivan has traded him an old Safety handheld.

It's laughable but I don't laugh. I don't do anything.

"Did you hear me?" Suit's voice drops a minor fourth.

"Don't pretend you can't understand. You are going to give me her signal."

Laughable. "I can't release that information."

"I'm not asking you." That's when he comes forward in a rush. He probably thinks we're about the same weight and that his momentum will be enough to give him the advantage. That, and whatever brawling experience he's picked up over the years.

He's heavy, but I lifted heavier weights in the Tunnels. I grab his lapels, lift, turn and release. It's enough to throw him clear over the front of a parked 4x4. I hear him land in the road on the other side. Black Jacket's right hand moves towards his left armpit. My first thought is that he's reaching for a gun. They're supposed to be illegal in this state but the early 21st is patchy about enforcing its laws. He pulls out a long blade, the kind you'd use to hack through heavy vegetation. I stay out of reach. Black Jacket's expression doesn't change. I show him my handheld. "Stop, or I use this."

It's a gamble. He stops. He doesn't know it's not a weapon. It can produce a beam of focused light that's mainly useful for pointing at things, but unless I catch him directly in the eye he won't even notice a change in temperature.

He doesn't move. I suppose he's thinking this through. Could it hurt him? I'm from the future, after all.

I level it at his face. "I warn you. I will use this."

He lowers the blade and backs away, watchful. He still hasn't said anything. I wonder if he can. Perhaps he has a stammer, and that's what drove him to violent crime. I wave the handheld. "Go help your friend.

He glances at the road where Suit is still groaning, and carefully slides the blade back into its scabbard, or holster, or whatever. He zips up his jacket and lumbers off round the car.

I walk away quickly, the useless handheld still ready, until I've turned the corner. Then I start running. Riemann told me not to worry about my client. It doesn't look like I'm going to be able to take his advice.

Spad

You're fourteen when the Defence Committee chooses you. Fourteen is your official age. It's a guess. Your parents were refugees, displaced when the Number Cities started moving east. When the scouts from Kat found you sitting next to their bodies you were too young to tell them your age. They gave you a new name and decided you were five.

Later you overheard a nurse say malnutrition might have retarded your development. You didn't understand this: you were taller than most girls your age.

The woman from the Defence Committee is stern. People don't smile in Kat the careless way they do in the Number Cities. In Kat if people smiled it was a sign of trouble. *Karia Stadt*, she says. *We see you haven't made friends with the other girls.* You watch her from the other side of the desk. *This is not a bad thing. You could be the kind of person we need.*

You try to mirror her expression. You want her to look across the table and see someone as serious as herself. "For what?"

To help us fight, the woman said. *Don't you want to fight against the people who killed your parents?*

They talk about your parents as if you remember them. You ask, "Would I leave here?" You wanted to leave.

Not yet. Perhaps in a year. If you work hard at your classes.

"What do I have to do?"

The woman smiled. *Just do as your teachers tell you. And stay alive.*

Do as your teachers tell you. This is easy. You're a good pupil. Some of the other girls forget minutes after they're told and can't pay attention, but you remember everything: lists, dates, names, formulae. The only problem you have is when the teachers expect you to deduce other facts. *Think, girl.* It would be easier if they told you what to do. Gave you rules and lists and left you alone.

Two other girls were seen by the woman from Defence. They talked about it in the dormitory. *They want us for secret work*, they boasted. *They're going to send us to the cities with bombs.* They're overexcited. They mix up their history.

You watch them talk and say nothing. The other girls have learned not to ask you questions.

Sex work, the older girls jeer. *They'll take you to special rooms and make you fuck old men.*

The older girls always talk about sex. This guard, that teacher, everybody knows, don't let them catch you on your own. You carry a knife in your jacket. You've made a special pocket so it won't cut you by accident or fall out.

You listen to the other girls argue. You know the ones who boast won't be chosen.

All you have to do is stay alive. You start counting the days.

A year passes. Ing is stabbed in the kitchen; Mana is killed by a soldier who saw her in the yard and climbed the wire fence to reach her. Some of the girls insist they know the details of her injuries and why nobody heard her scream. Prudi is found hanging in the shower block. Zinza and Jenfer simply disappear. It's an average year.

You manage to stay alive.

Kat had four satellite towns: Mosk, Spad, Sver and one you can't remember. The loss of the name pains you. You had a good memory once: you can still remember the names of the girls who died or disappeared. Mosk, Spad, Sver. Why not this? You repeat them under your breath hoping the fourth name will come. They sent you to Spad. You remember the journey, a long drive in a sealed vehicle. And here you are again, travelling in another one. You have to remind yourself you're not going to Spad. Riemann is not an instructor.

That journey was at night. They didn't tell you why it had to be at night. You thought it was because they didn't want you to see any landmarks. You travelled with six girls you'd never seen before and couldn't sleep because you didn't trust them. It was the furthest you'd ever travelled.

You've walked further since. Back in the 21st you travelled across Europe.

Mosk, Spad, Sver. You won't tell Riemann about Spad. It was a military secret in his time. You wonder if the Number Cities ever found out about it. You can't ask.

You sat in silence until the battery on the truck failed. You had to walk the rest of the way, hurried along by your instructors, who were, you soon realised, terrified. They pointed in the direction they wanted you to go and slapped anyone who asked questions. You listened for noises – dogs, wolves, other people – but all you could hear was the wind. You didn't know what Spad looked like but you'd been told several thousand people lived there. You expected to see lights after the next hill or the next, but each time you reached the top of one there appeared to be nothing ahead. You wondered if your instructors had taken you there to see who could survive in the open. Or if they were spies who meant to kill you or sell you to the Number Cities. Just as the horizon started to grow brighter they signalled you to stop. You'd reached one of the entrances. In the dark it had looked like another hill.

You'll never forget that walk. Still tired and shivering, you were greeted by the woman who had recruited you. Her title was Assistant Director of the Defence Committee, External Division. You can't remember her name; you can't remember if you ever knew it. She was always addressed by her title: "Yes, Assistant Director. No, Assistant Director." You liked that: to be known by a title rather than a name. Everybody had a name: a title – a function – had to be *earned*.

You were privileged to have been chosen, she said. You will be part of the struggle against the Number Cities. "Are you ready to learn how to fight?" You have never been happier.

In Spad they told you the truth about travel.

Official official

I tell Erquist the next morning. I start with the possibility that our client was carrying tonin. He finds this mildly interesting. "If she's working for extemps it wouldn't be illegal." When I tell him about the attack he says, "I think they call it a *machete*." Finally I tell him about the earlier meeting with Riemann. I don't give his name or say how I knew him, only that he was one of us and didn't have a signature. This makes him sit up straight: "And there was no reading? Nothing at all?"

"Nothing. And he made a point of making sure I noticed."

"And he's been here how long?"

"Fifteen years. At least, that's what he said."

"South America usually means materials acquisition." Erquist thinks through the implications. "Except there wasn't a fixed point fifteen years ago. That means he must have come here on a charter. That probably means he's here on official business, reporting directly back to Geneva." I've never seen him so animated: a man like Riemann is the stuff of entertainments, the suave authority figure who arrives at the end to solve the problems and save the day – of course Erquist finds him intriguing. "Or possibly *they're* not supposed to know about him either," he says carefully, awed by the idea Geneva might not know something. "The signature – or the lack of it – means he's not official. Or not official official."

"And what about our client?"

"There is nothing in the records to indicate she becomes a problem."

"Do they mention me being attacked or a man without a signature?"

Erquist becomes, by his standards, firm. "Those are not necessarily serious problems. I admit the attack is a concern, but you were unharmed. That said, if the natives are aware of tonin that might be a cause for concern, especially if Tri-Millennium is the source. Is there anything on the Arc?"

"I checked." It didn't take long. The resort Arc's account of native drug culture is tailored to the needs of our clients: a list of popular synonyms (dope, coke, horse, molly, acid, skunk) with cautions about quality and asking for refunds. I'd been the first person to look at it in years. Tri-Millennium clients don't get involved with the local drugs. It's hard enough to persuade them to try the local food. "There was nothing."

"Don't you have a connection to their internet in your accommodation?" From the way he says *their internet* I can tell that, for him, it's as much a mystery as anything else outside the resort. "You might find something on that."

"I've already looked." Among the local tech at my flat I have a laptop. Their internet is like a lawless version of the Arc: there's a lot of information mixed in with misinformation and opinions and attempts to sell you products that may or may not exist. Its main use for me is to find out what people *think* is happening, or want to believe is happening. It's monitored by their governments, so you have to be careful. I'd confined my searches to corporate media and public health sites. All I'd found was complaints about the legal status of their own drugs and more lists of synonyms. None of their street drugs had effects that seemed to match tonin. If the natives had discovered it they were keeping quiet. "No traces yet. I also looked at DomeWatch." If anybody was going to accuse us of destroying their society with drugs it's that crowd. A search of their site showed their main drug complaint is we haven't yet given them a cure for cancer. Then I'd wasted ten minutes reading some speculation about what they called our plans to steal their drinking water. "As far as I can tell there's nothing out there."

I'd thought better of searching for *Riemann Aldis*. Their authorities might not be the only ones watching.

"Good work." Erquist clears his desk. "Well, after this business with the *machete*" – he seems to relish the word – "do you want me to organise a room for you in the resort?"

"I'll stay outside for now."

"Right. But if you feel you are in any danger ... What do you have this afternoon?"

"A walk across the moors. Then a pub lunch."

Erquist shudders. "That sounds grim." I know he's never walked across a moor. I doubt he's had a pub lunch, even though Restaurant Three in this very resort offers versions of 21st-century meals so you can prepare yourself for the real thing. "How many have booked?"

"Only five." Our younger clients. We're not scheduled to have any accidents and the pub has been given instructions about preparing the food. We should avoid allergic reactions this time. "I'm not expecting any difficulties."

"Good. I'll talk to Hayek. Don't look so concerned. I'll keep it unofficial."

"I'd rather not involve Safety."

"You've been attacked. They have to be informed. Protocol, you understand. Besides, it's likely they already know. They've probably been watching you since you borrowed the tracker. No, we need to keep Hayek inside the cone on this. And don't worry: he's more accommodating than he looks."

When we first announced our presence to the early 21st the natives had a lot of questions. Their scientists had thought travel was either impossible, or theoretically possible but impractical (requiring more energy than exists in the universe, etc.), or possible in only one direction (I forget which). And the people who weren't scientists assumed we could pick a date and go back or forward to whenever we pleased.

The reality is different. Yes, it does take a lot of energy (and of course we don't tell them how much or how we generate it), and, no, you can't just pick a date. There are constraints. There is a fixed link between here and 2345 (which happens to be the year I left). That's how the tourism business is able to function; that's how City One West has two grand pianos. But fixed links are expensive, and you can only have them in periods with a certain technical sophistication. There aren't any before the beginning of the 21st and none after the beginning of the NEE. If a traveller from 2345 wants to visit anything earlier they'll need to charter, which requires a lot more energy (and therefore official approval) and has a longer stopover. The further back you go, the longer it gets. If you want to see 1850 the nearest you can get is 1845 and then you have to wait until 1857 to get home (from a well-concealed site in Australia). Some of the 18th-century stopovers are even

74

longer: 1736 in, 1762 back (from Siberia). These are the trips that have to be planned carefully. There are no trained reps or Safety Teams. If Riemann came on a charter it means he has serious backers. To come here on a charter *without a signature* means they are *very* serious.

Our client might not be the only reason Riemann is here: she might be second to last on his top secret to-do list. The question is: *is she important to us?* Is she our problem? That is, is she *my* problem? Or do we just carry on as usual and leave it to the professionals?

I think about this on the walk (not far but enlivened by exciting rain). When I get back there's a message: the Chief Safety Officer wants to see me.

The lock on the outer office releases as I approach. Two Safeties are sitting at monitoring desks. They don't look up as I pass. The door to the inner office slides open.

Hayek Englebrot has a desk like Erquist. He has a more elaborate chair he's said never to leave. There's a display screen on the wall to his right, and nine smaller ones in a 3x3 block to his left. 21st tech, and not the latest, but good enough for a tourist resort if you have the right adaptations. His desk has a slight incline, so I can't see whatever he's looking at when I walk in. The other ten screens are blank.

Hayek is more than typical Safety: he's like the platonic ideal of a Safety Officer. Heavy, augmented. His eye tech is definitely not cosmetic. I used to know people like him when I worked in the Tunnels, but only *like* him, with bone-and-muscle augs and retinal enhancements. Compared to him they were still in the larval stage. Hayek is the mature adult, connected, modified and contemptuous of the merely human. He's been here ten years and has never left the resort. This isn't, as with Erquist, through choice. Hayek isn't allowed to leave, except under very specific and very unlikely circumstances. The natives aren't supposed to know that people like him exist.

"About our girl," he says. "It's interesting." Girl. He refers to unmodified adults as girls and boys, as if he considers them children.

"You mean you haven't found her?"

"I didn't say that." He gives me his Safety Officer stare, the one where he calculates to the microsecond how long it would take to kill me. Thanks to the Tunnels I've had combat training and standard bone-and-muscle augs. As far as Hayek's concerned they might as well be hair extensions and a manicure. "We can use their communications networks to confirm a signature," he says. "The problem is without a tracker they're not very good for *finding* them." He explains why: a combination of a tech mismatch and network charges. I understand about two-thirds of it. He summarises: "To find somebody I would have to know where to look. I tried the usual tourist destinations in this city and found no trace. I had to ask the question: where might an adventurous tourist go? And I found her." Hayek approximates a smile. "She's in London."

It makes sense. London has a lot of extemps. They like the romantic thrill of living somewhere that doesn't survive the NEE. If she's selling tonin that's where she'll find a buyer. "Why are you telling me this?"

"Because you lost her." He looks at me with what might be amusement. "And because I don't want to involve a Safety Team when it's possible there's an innocent explanation. Geneva are sensitive about interventions. Also, if our girl is dealing with the locals we might need to speak to them as well. My people are good at what they do, but they can be unsubtle, and they're not recruited for their languages. You can talk to the locals, and, from what Erquist tells me, your former training hasn't been entirely wasted. You are the ideal person for this." He pauses: new information has arrived. "She's still our client. It would be irresponsible not to take an interest." This is presumably the defence he'll offer if it turns out he wasn't supposed to get involved. He gestures at the large screen which shows a high-angle shot of hundreds of natives in an enclosed, high-ceilinged space, most of them standing still and looking in the same direction. My first thought is that it's some kind of temple. Then I notice the shops. "Victoria station," Hayek says. "The concourse. Is that our client?"

A woman, obviously one of us, is walking through the native crowd. She doesn't look lost or frightened. She seems to be alone. "It could be."

"It is. Once I knew she was in London I started looking for her face. Geneva allows us access to some of their cameras . . . " He explains how he narrowed the search: one of those explanations that contains just enough tech detail to demonstrate his mastery. "Now watch."

He finds a camera at a lower angle. It's a view from behind; our client stands out, a head taller than anybody else. She's heading straight for one of the platforms. She passes through the ticket barrier. It's rare for a Tri-Millennium client to use public transport. They don't like the attention and the seats are too small. Our client moves with a lot of assurance for somebody who's only been outside a day. Hayek switches to a view from the platform itself. It's from a higher angle and she doesn't look up, but her face matches the hooded woman's from the coach. Hayek is triumphant. "Is that our girl?"

"It's her."

"So where is she going?" Hayek searches timetables: the next train from that platform is heading for the south coast. One of the stops is an airport.

She could be planning to leave the country.

"Interesting," is all Hayek says.

We watch her board a train. Then, before Hayek can find another camera, I notice something familiar. Limping through the ticket barrier is a squat native in a suit followed by a taller man in a black jacket.

Hayek has noticed my interest. "Do you know them?"

"They're the ones who attacked me. They asked about signatures."

Hayek appraises them. "And they can still walk?" The implication is he wouldn't have made that mistake. "As for the signatures, they must have heard it from an extemp." He turns to me. "So now what?"

"What do you mean?"

"What should we do?" He fixes me with a look. "Does she need help or has she arranged to meet these people? Do we intervene, or sit back and watch?"

I hesitate, which amuses him. He wants me to know he'd have no doubts: he's probably been augmented for decisive action. He's surprised when I stand up. "You've found her," I say. There was a Tunnel principle: if somebody doesn't come back from a patrol you look for them. I might have become a junior part of the Happiness Executive but I still have the reflex, even if it means I'll spend the rest of the day following a single client. "You keep watching her. If she gets off at the airport, find out what plane she's likely to catch. If you can authorise a flight I should be able to reach her destination first."

"Not bad, Tunnel Boy," Hayek says. "It's the beginning of a plan. What will you do when you find her?"

It occurs to me that I've chosen the very thing he wanted me to choose. "I'll think of something."

He turns back to the screen. Suit and Black Jacket have moved out of the picture. Before Hayek can change the view I notice something odd about the image, a blur, like a thumbprint on the lens. Except this is a smudge that moves. Hayek notices it too. He stares at it, rapt. I can almost hear his augs at work, applying new resolutions and filters. "Interference," he finally says. "Everything comes through Geneva. There must be degradation."

"Keep me informed." I'm already at the door, which, this time, doesn't open at my approach. It won't open until Hayek tells it to.

"Have no doubt about that." The door opens. "I'll be watching."

I go back down to the car pool. My plan is to head south and east to the old USAF base in Essex we lease under the pretence we need an air ambulance service. Provided our client isn't going to the other side of the world Hayek should be able to get me a place on a plane. It won't necessarily be faster than anything she catches, but there will be less bureaucracy when I land. I should be able to catch up.

Conventional cars, conventional aircraft. Some of the natives used to think that because we travel we must also be able to teleport. There were experiments in the early days, when High Energy Generation was new, but they were soon abandoned. We had other priorities and there are cheaper ways of killing lab rats. So we don't have teleportation. As far as we know they don't have it in the 25th. (The 25th pretend to be pious stay-at-homes but we're sure they're watching us. Or maybe they're too busy teleporting to worry about the past.)

ROBERT DICKINSON

They wouldn't tell us even if they did.

About half an hour later Hayek bips me. "I don't think our girl is going anywhere."

"What makes you think that?"

"I'm watching her now. She's in the arrivals lounge, at a coffee shop. She's sitting in the open, as if she wants to be seen. I think she's waiting to meet someone."

So: no need to go to Essex. "Thanks, Hayek. Keep me informed."

"You'll be told what you need to know."

I'm at least two hours away from the airport. Unless whoever she's there to see has a delayed flight she could have made her rendezvous and left while I'm still on the motorway. Still, now that Hayek has found her he might be able to keep track. Suit and Black Jacket are unlikely to make trouble in a place with so many potential witnesses as well as armed and jumpy police.

I bip Hayek. "The two following our client, what can you find out about them?"

"I wondered when you'd ask." Hayek is deadpan. "The one with the limp is Christopher Gurley. He has old criminal convictions for assault and receiving stolen goods, but nothing recent. His younger associate is Wilson Knight. He has a shorter record and a diagnosis of ASD, whatever that means. Those are the current police records. From another source I learn he dies later this month."

"How?" Briefly I wonder if this is the breach of protocol that gets me sent home. "Who kills him?"

"I don't know, Tunnel Boy. I'm not Geneva. The police records come from a not-quite-official local contact. The other information is pure chance. It's a fragment from one of their newspapers, a summary of gang-related deaths a client brought here two years ago. The client was a retired Safety with an interest in this era's crime. He brought his research with him and thought I might be interested. Of course I added them to our records." He sounds pleased with his own foresight. "I'll send you what I have."

"Thanks." I'd rather he hadn't told me Knight was going to die, or had at least sounded less cheerful about it. I hope *gang-related* means what it says and isn't a euphemism for *murdered by travel rep.* I could almost feel sorry for Knight. He'd drawn a machete on me, true, but he hadn't looked as if he enjoyed the prospect. I'm sure he'd have killed me with the same mournful expression. The information bips to the display screen on the dashboard. It's illegal to read while in control of a vehicle, but this one has been modified and won't let me crash. There's Knight's record, a series of images marking his progress from scowling fourteen-year-old to impassive twenty-seven. The newspaper fragment doesn't say how he died, only that he was one of the casualties in "a vicious struggle for territory" that started after another man, his cousin, was beaten to death. Four other deaths followed. I don't recognise the names or faces. Gurley's history is longer but with fewer pictures and no convictions in the last twelve years. After that the record stops: Hayek's police contact and our amateur criminologist didn't have anything on him. Perhaps he reforms. Or he carries on and his crimes aren't lurid enough to appeal or the records are lost, along with so much else, when the NEE hits the server farm.

The NEE. It's difficult to think about. We've reduced it to three letters, which makes it easier to say. In my time it's history: grim history, but in the past, finished, over. The only people still arguing about it are specialists: historians, techs with a point to make, crank theorists and teenagers discovering crank theories for the first time. (Cantor was an aficionado of crank theories. It was hard to tell if he believed them or simply relished the ingenuity that went into their elaboration.) The NEE attracts cranks because we still don't know how it started. The records start to fragment in the lead-up to it, and the Event itself – or the Events, because it was complicated – are still only beginning to be reconstructed. Before that all we have are the personal testimonies of people who missed the important events. (Their records survive *because* they missed them.) The NEE is like the accident that destroys the surrounding memories, or the kind of fugue state where you wake up in an unfamiliar building with missing teeth and no clothes. It's a hole in our history. Proper, sequential records don't begin again until decades later. That's the NEE: humanity's lost long weekend, the near-death experience that persuaded us to reform. Tragic and terrible, but history.

Except the 21st still has it coming. We haven't told them, of course. They wouldn't do anything. They *don't* do anything. It's just far enough in the future to be somebody else's problem.

These are the kind of thoughts I have as I drive. The lorries and cars, the vans and coaches driving between warehouses and retail points, or office to office; businessmen, sightseers, regional managers, the police, thousands of people on this road alone, all working to maintain a system that in ninety years will cease to exist, all thinking they're at the pinnacle of civilisation.

They are in a way.

It won't help. It *didn't* help.

Hayek sends updates: "Our girl is still alone."

I drive on. The car has safety modifications, and needs them. Too many of the natives drive like they want to die, or believe they can't. Still, I like to exercise some control, even if my destination is predetermined and the only choice I can exercise is what to listen to on the radio, in this case the government classical music station, where Sibelius's Fifth Symphony is followed by a discussion between three natives worrying about the implications for performers of the recordings we released a few years earlier. It was a gesture to show how our interest in the past was benign and that we were willing to share some things as long as they were harmless. I'm curious about what these natives will say. Except for this era's conspiracy theorists and religious hold-outs and all the contributors to DomeWatch, we seem to be taken for granted. Whatever they might mutter in private, most natives don't talk about us in official media, so it's a surprise to hear three of them discussing the impact we've had on musical performance. Or, rather, they talk about the recordings without mentioning who made them, as if they'd simply appeared. It's infuriating. People went to a lot of trouble to make those recordings. Brink and Nakamura, who recorded the 1808 concert, never came back. These natives don't mention Brink and Nakamura. They don't mention us at all, as if they're under some kind of prohibition. Instead they quibble: that there's only one recording of Beethoven conducting his Second Symphony, and how typical is that of his style? And with the Third, we know he was unhappy with the rehearsals ... Oh yes, they agree, the recordings are certainly interesting – the Bach organ improvisations, especially – but they are not definitive. They still leave a lot of room for interpretation ...

I listen, enthralled and outraged. The Bach recordings (a later team, not Brink and Nakamura) are overrated. They're the ones it's fashionable for this era to like. This, I say to the radio, is why your civilisation is doomed. Somebody shows you that you were wrong about something, and, even in a case as apparently trivial as this, you find a way to ignore the evidence. You people *deserve* the NEE. It's an unworthy thought. They're going to get it whether they deserve it or not.

"Our girl is still there. That's nearly an hour now."

"So the person she's meeting might be delayed."

"Perhaps. Or she likes airports."

"I'll be there in another forty minutes. What about Gurley and Knight?"

"Also in arrivals. They're waiting in a bar."

"Have you noticed anything unusual?"

"Are you expecting anything unusual?"

"I don't know. Keep me informed."

The radio discussion is succeeded by a Chopin recital by a native musician who once again ignores the authentic recordings. My car follows the road, along with all the weaving, dangerously unmodified vehicles. The sky, which has grown steadily darker, is now an ominous grey. The rain, when it falls, is just another annoyance. I shouldn't have to deal with missing clients. I work for Happiness. I'm a travel rep, not an honorary Safety. The native musician takes the nocturne too slowly. I ask Hayek, "What's happening with our client?"

"No change. Everybody is still waiting."

The onboard estimates another fifteen minutes before I reach our allotted parking area. Allowing another ten to walk, there's a chance I can reach arrivals before anything happens. If our client is still at the coffee shop I will walk up to her innocently, as if I'm no more than a concerned rep – because I *am* no more than a concerned rep – and offer to drive her back to the resort. If she wants to stay to meet someone, fine – I'll wait, innocently, as if my concern is only for the good name of Tri-Millennium and the well-being of our clients, and then offer to drive her back. The pianist attacks a polonaise at something close to the right speed. By the time he finishes I'm almost at our allotted parking. It's half empty: we rarely travel from public airports although a surprising amount of official business is conducted in their vicinity. I park to routine applause from a hall in Huddersfield. The pianist starts creeping through the berceuse.

"Tunnel Boy," Hayek's voice, less casual than usual. "You need to stop dawdling. Something is happening."

The truth about travel

You don't believe it at first. For as long as you can remember you've been told travel is a Number City lie. It goes against reason; your scientists have *proved* it was impossible. When people you're supposed to trust say *We built our own zone long before you were born* you don't know how to respond.

They begin with the history: how they followed plans taken from the Number Cities; how the work required the sacrifice of resources and labour hours; how it had to be kept secret from their own people. The zone wasn't at Spad. It was further east, at the other place, the fourth one, whose name you can't remember. Mosk, Spad, Sver, a gap. Had you ever known its name? The labourers lived in prefabricated housing near the site and were never told what they were building, the techs and organisers were sworn to silence and all communications with Kat were strictly controlled. Once the zone was complete Kat would be able to face the Number Cities on nearly equal terms. It was, your instructor said, an optimistic time.

It sounds like a fable.

The great effort failed. The zone was never used, or even

tested. They had the theory but there was an engineering problem, an energy problem. It was left intact, sealed, waiting for the day when they could make it work. *Until then, we tell people travel is impossible.*

In Spad they tell you the truth about travel. They also tell you the truth about truth. There are different kinds: that the Number Cities have travel is one kind of truth; that they don't is another. People are given the truth they need. You have shown you can be trusted with special truths.

If the Number Cities can travel, you ask in one class, and they're so terrible, why don't they go back and destroy us when we're weak? It's what you'd do to them.

Because they didn't, the instructor says. They won't. They can't. They have a weakness: they believe the past is fixed, that nothing can be changed. This provokes questions from the other girls. Can it be changed? That's a difficult question. What we have to ask is, Should it be changed? So, another girl asks, could we travel back and hurt *them*? Another good question: how *could* we hurt them? A bomb, you say. Bury it before they can build one of their cities, set it to explode when it will do most damage. No, the instructor said. Who can see why that might not work? Another girl can: The components would either become unstable and explode too soon or become inert and not explode at all. No, you want to say, it has to be the right kind of bomb. Does anybody have a better idea? Fight them there, another girl says. Better. Can anybody suggest how? Find them and kill them. Stop them from starting the Collapse. How? Remember they outnumber us and control the governments. So, if they don't think they can change anything, why *do* the Number Cities travel? They do the same as here, the instructor says. They accumulate resources, steal whatever they can. Why do the people let them? Didn't the pre-collapse have satellites and aeroplanes and millions of people? Didn't they have armies and nuclear weapons? Why don't they resist? Because, the instructor says, they didn't realise what was happening. Could we tell them? They wouldn't believe us. Remember, they have hundreds of people. We have only sent back a handful and they have to be careful.

There are, she says, some Number Cities who rebel against their system. Instead of fighting, they do it by running away. They choose to live in the early 21st. The Number Cities permit it if those people are no longer useful to them. These people give up everything they have in their own time and the Number Cities arrange for them to have credit in the early 21st. The only way we can get our people back for any useful length of time is by having somebody assume the identity of a Number City citizen and becoming one of these so-called extemps. It's a difficult life. They are under continual observation. They mostly work alone. They provide us with everything we know about what the Number Cities are doing. The difficulty is communications. The only way they can send information back is by couriers. If you're sent back, your first mission will be as a courier. The instructor thinks you'll be impressed by this.

The girls have more questions: Can they travel into the future? Couldn't they go there and find out everything we'll do? No, the instructor says. We don't know why, but they don't travel into the future. The Number Cities are powerful but they don't know everything. And there are complications: say they have a record that on a certain date one of their people met people from the 21st to buy a particular mineral. That person has to be sent back whether or not they want to go. What they know creates an obligation; what they don't know gives us an opportunity. That's why we sent a team there.

But but but. What happens if someone destroys the records? What if somebody lies about what you were supposed to have done? The instructor holds up both hands and says she's answered enough questions for one day. If any of you are sent back the important thing is to follow your instructions. You will not have to worry about these deeper questions.

The girls hold long discussions in the dormitory. They don't involve you.

You learn languages, self-defence, use of weapons. When you travel, you're told, it will be from one of their cities. You will have to pretend to be one of them. Hence the languages. Hence the tech. You learn how to use early-21st tech, how to hack a Number City transport.

You see the Assistant Director again. You're summoned to the office she's requisitioned from a senior instructor. You're not told why you've been summoned. You don't think you've made any mistakes but you can never be sure. She greets you coldly and tells you to sit, and then seems to forget you're there while she looks at papers. It's an act, you think: she's making you wait. It's either a test or she enjoys your apprehension. It's the first time you've seen her up close since you were fourteen. She hasn't changed: she's still the person you most want to be. Finally she looks straight at you and tells you the instructors have informed her of your progress. She pauses to see how you react. You keep still and watch her face. *I'm pleased to say they think you're doing well*, she says. Her expression of stern resolve doesn't soften. *A lot of girls lose focus after their first year here. As long as you don't question orders or get distracted by emotions you could be a good fighter. Do you think you're ready to be sent back?*

Yes, Assistant Director.

Do you understand why you have to go back?

To fight the Number Cities.

She nods at your answer. *Not quite. Your purpose is to follow orders.*

Yes, Assistant Director.

Do you have any questions?

You have many, but you know the one she wants to hear: What are my orders?

If you are sent you must understand you may never see your friends again.

She must know you haven't made any friends: that's why you were chosen. Out of all the damaged girls you're the most solitary. Not the most vicious, not the cleverest or the funniest, or the best fighter or the prettiest, but the one who can live surrounded by strangers and not care. You were made for this.

Yes.

Yes, Assistant Director. There is an agent called Picon Delrosso. You don't need to know his real name. He is one of our best people, the first to go back. We haven't received a report for two years. The last courier we sent did not return. We want you to contact him and find out what happened. Do you think you are ready?

Yes, Assistant Director.

The machines are always listening

There's a small crowd gathered just outside the coffee outlet, two of them police in lurid yellow jackets. The other onlookers are dressed in the miscellaneous clothes of native travellers, a few are in civilian uniforms, workers from the shops and exchange bureaux. Our client isn't among them. "Hayek, what can you see?"

"A gathering of people. You walking towards them."

I stop moving. "Our client?"

"Not visible."

"What are they gathering round?"

"The cameras are fixed, Tunnel Boy, I can't make them move. It appears to be somebody on the ground."

"Our client?"

"Somebody would have to get out of the way before I could tell."

There's shouting. Two medics run across the hall. The crowd separates, then closes in on them again. I glimpse enough of the person on the ground to tell it's native and male.

"It's not our client." I look around, but can't see her. "Gurley and Knight. Where are they?"

"Still in the bar. I haven't seen them leave."

That's where I find them, at the back, in a place with no clear view of whatever happened. I suspect they moved there so they wouldn't have to answer questions about what they'd seen. They probably don't like dealing with any kind of officialdom.

Gurley has a nearly empty pint glass. Knight is halfway through an orange juice. He notices me first. He doesn't say anything: just gives me the stare. He probably thinks it's menacing, but it just looks like he's posing for one of his regular police images. Gurley turns to see what's caught his attention. "Oh Jesus fucking Christ," he says. "Not you as well."

I sit at the table. "What just happened?"

"Jesus fucking Christ," Gurley says again. I briefly wonder if this means he's religious. You can never tell with natives. Knight, meanwhile, is looking at his orange juice as if he hates it.

Gurley drinks the rest of his pint. "We don't know," he says. "Was there something to see? We must have missed it. We only came here for a drink."

"I'm not the police," I say. "Tell me what you saw."

"I told you. Nothing."

"I know you've been following our client."

"It's not your business." Gurley glances at Knight, who's still staring at his orange juice. In a few days he's going to die. I hope it's nothing to do with me.

"She's our client. It is my business." I take Gurley's glass. "Let me buy you another."

He glares at me. It is not frightening. "If you insist."

I stand. "Don't run away."

94

"Fucking Christ. As if."

The woman behind the bar remembers what he's drinking. She's from Eastern Europe and seems surprised I can speak This English. "This is his fourth," she says disapprovingly.

"He's not driving."

When I get back to the table Gurley hasn't tried to run away. Knight is still staring at his drink.

I slide Gurley his pint. "Start with why you're following my client."

"Because we were asked to." Gurley sips tentatively, as if he thinks I might have slipped him some futuristic truth drug. "By one of you."

"Who asked you?"

"You expect me to give you a name?"

"And an address. And the reason they asked you."

Gurley drinks about a quarter of his pint in a single gulp. "If you're from the future," he says, eyes narrowing, "how come you don't already know?"

"It doesn't work like that."

"Glad to hear it." He grins, or something close to a grin. "You people," he says, trying another approach. "You think you're so fucking superior with your gold and platinum and your fucking tattoos. We're not idiots. We didn't need your signal."

"Signature."

"Whatever. But we were told to find her and keep an eye on her. And guess what, we might not have your fancy toys but we got here first. And that's all we did. We kept an eye on her." I assume he means watching her until she went somewhere less public. He'd chosen to wait in the bar because he felt comfortable there and hadn't realised she'd be staying this long. He sneers. "What are *you* doing?"

I can't let him sidetrack me, something I suspect he's good at from years of practice with weary investigating officers. "I'm not the police. Just tell me who sent you here."

"Or what?"

"Or I'll signal those police officers and show them film of your friend waving his machete." There is no film, but he won't know that. I'm from the future: he probably thinks I can record with my eyes. (Hayek can, but that's more to do with Hayek's personality type than a job requirement.) "I'm fairly certain that would count as a criminal offence." It's a bluff. My grasp of 21st-century law comes from watching this era's entertainments and they're not always reliable. The criminals, for example, always get caught.

He thinks about this. I can see the effort it takes. Knight doesn't say anything. He's still staring at his orange juice.

Gurley says, "Fuck it, this isn't our mess. If you lot want to talk to somebody try Picon Delrosso. He's one of yours."

"And where do I find him?"

"You can work that out for yourself. Is that it? Are you going to leave us now?"

"Not yet. What happened here?"

He looks sly. "You don't know, do you? Well, your client shot somebody."

I hadn't expected this. "Who?"

"I don't know. Some bloke off a plane. He came out, she walked towards him, pointed something and he fell down."

"She had a gun?"

"She had something. I thought it was a phone and she was taking a picture. Looked like a phone. She points it at the people coming out, she walks away. I was watching her. And then he collapses. And she keeps on walking. Like she expected it to happen. Didn't look back."

"Did the police do anything?"

"Those muppets?" His professional contempt shines through. "Looking the wrong way, as per. They didn't see anything. We were the only ones who noticed." He glances at Knight. Knight doesn't confirm his story. Knight isn't paying attention. He's still focused on his unfinished orange juice. Gurley looks back at me, resigned. "If she can do something like that in a place like this I'm steering clear."

"You're certain she did it?"

"She pointed at him. He fell down. What do you think?"

"What do I think? I think she took his picture and he had a heart attack." Heart attacks are what kill people in this country, in this era. Heart attacks, cancers, pneumonia and strokes. Later on it will be malnutrition, hypothermia and a range of once-treatable diseases. "Are you sure you don't know who he was?"

Gurley glares at me. "Don't know. Don't care. You should talk to Picon Delrosso."

I stand up. "You've been helpful."

Back in the car I bip Hayek. "What do we know?"

"I would have started with the threat about the police. Their account of events is fanciful."

"So what happened?"

"The medical services are treating it as a health problem. Probably, as you suggested, a heart attack. There's no sign their police are involved in anything more important than crowd control."

I'm relieved. It means I'm not following a killer. "And our client?"

"Headed back to the station. She is now on a London train."

"London?" It doesn't mean she plans to stay there. London is still a transport hub. She could be on her way back to the resort. "Hayek, isn't there some archive you can consult? Notable deaths, or deaths at airports?"

"I've told you, Tunnel Boy, I'm not Geneva. If it's just medical it won't be reported."

"Unless he's notable for something."

"I'll do what I can."

"Thanks, Hayek. Do you want me to continue following the client?"

"No. It's too easy for her to lose you in London. I want you to come back. I have an address for this Delrosso. He's a registered extemp." He sends it: it's on the other side of town from my flat, but on the way home. "I'll do what I can with our girl. You should pay Delrosso a visit."

I want to tell him I'm a rep. I shouldn't have to talk to extemps about their involvement with criminals. "Isn't this a job for your people?"

"I've cleared it with your manager." Hayek is having fun. "All you have to do is ask questions."

"Questions. Should I start with a threat?"

"Imply one. He's an extemp. He'll crack."

Two and a half hours later I'm in Picon Delrosso's expensive neighbourhood. Big houses in a wide street with a lot of trees. His neighbours, according to native lore, are businessmen, football players and, mostly, other extemps. At home Picon was a regional resource administrator with a spotless record, unremarkable mid-level Facilitation. Here he lives in a walled-off house large enough to hold an entire kin. According to Hayek he lives alone. It's not uncommon with extemps. Kinship obligation, along with the rest of our *oppressive society*, is one of the things they're trying to escape.

His gate, a wrought-iron thing in an antique style, is slightly ajar. There's a silver vehicle in the drive that looks as if it hasn't moved for a while. It's tarnished and streaked and, around the wheels, weeds have pushed through the paving. There's a stone path through a lush and overgrown lawn ringed with trees dripping from the recent rain.

I push the button next to his door. There's faint music coming from inside the house: rapture, which fits Picon's age. Wandering lines over a rhythm like a slowing heartbeat, a favourite with the early users of tonin.

The door is opened by a native woman. It's always tricky guessing their ages. This one could be fifteen or she could be thirty. Her blank expression might be childish or it might be tonin or some native opiate. She stares up at me without saying anything.

"I'm here to see Picon Delrosso," I say.

She continues staring.

"I'm with the security team at Resort Four."

For a moment I wonder if she doesn't understand This English. I'm about to try my Early-19th German when she steps back, turns and walks away. As she hasn't closed the door I take this as an invitation.

The hallway is big and empty. According to Hayek, Picon registered as an extemp ten years ago, which means he must have been among the first. He's spent the last nine in this house. He hasn't done much with the place. There's no furniture in the hallway, the walls are a plain beige and the wooden floorboards an unpolished dark brown. The early tonin users – we used to call them *raptives* – usually prefer plain decor. It's less distracting.

The woman pads towards the source of the music. I follow with a sinking sense that Picon is going to embody all the worst stereotypes about extemps.

He does.

At the back of the house is a large room with big windows looking out over a garden as lush and untended as the one at the front. There are long sofas around the walls. The woman heads straight for one of these and lies down.

Picon is sitting on the sofa on the right, talking into a phone. He's a thin man with fine features and transplanted black hair. He talks while staring at a screen on the opposite wall. He's using This English. "Fifteen per cent. No, fifteen. That's what we agreed. Fifteen." He sounds fluent, but then he should be after ten years. I can't make out the other side of the conversation but I recognise the tone of somebody who wants more than fifteen per cent. If it's a deal this could be interesting: extemps aren't supposed to engage in business with the natives. Picon doesn't seem concerned at being caught mid-negotiation. He glances at me and shakes his head as if he thinks I'll sympathise with his difficulties. There's another woman, similar to the first, sitting at his right. She's staring at a mobile phone, native fashion. There are six or seven small devices on the cushions on his other side. None of them look like weapons. The screen shows images of natives milling around in the open as a horse is led across a patch of mud. "Thank you," Picon finally says. He lowers the phone and glances up at me again and then sends a message. He picks up one of his devices and points it at the screen, which goes black. He picks up another and the music stops. He smiles at me. The smile is not friendly. "I don't believe I know you."

"I'm from Resort Four. I'm here because of one of our clients." I tell him our client's name. I tell him she left the resort without informing us and we're concerned.

"You're Safety?"

"Happiness. A rep."

He relaxes slightly. "I see a lot of people here. I don't remember that name."

"How about Christopher Gurley and Wilson Knight?"

He pauses. I can almost hear him asking himself how much I'm likely to know. "I know Christopher Gurley, yes. That is," he qualifies, "I've *heard* of him. I wouldn't say I know him well."

"He's following our client. When I asked him why he told me to talk to you."

"That doesn't surprise me." He tries to take control of the conversation. He'd been a regional resource administrator after all: he outranked me. He thinks he still does and – consciously or not – assumes the manner of an overworked manager listening to the tiny problems of a subordinate. "He's trying to deflect attention from himself and I'm a known local figure. I have social contacts with many natives. Gurley knows *them*. He's one of these people who hang around on the fringes, hoping to make money. But I wouldn't use him."

"Why not?"

"I hear he's unreliable."

"Have you any idea why he might be following our client?"

"What makes you think I should?"

"We believe she was carrying tonin."

He shrugs. "I haven't broken any protocol."

It's the guiltiest thing he could have said. I gesture at the devices on the sofa. "Are you sure?"

I was referring to his discussion about percentages. He misunderstands: he thinks I mean his native woman. "They're old enough. Besides, the protocols prohibit the *sale* of technologies," he says in a why-are-you-wasting-my-time voice. "They don't say anything about personal use. If they did every rep at your resort would be in breach."

One of the devices next to him starts playing music. It's another phone. "Sorry," he says. "I should take this." He hunches forward and talks quickly and quietly. It's a brief conversation, this time in Modern. I hear enough to tell he's giving directions. From his weary tone it's information he's had to give more than once. When he's made his point he puts the phone down beside him and shakes his head. "I'm sorry about that. Visitors from the mainland. You were asking about your client. It's true, yes, she was supposed to be bringing me tonin." He sounds like he's about to blame me for whatever went wrong.

"Is that all she was doing?" There are other questions I could ask. How did he know to expect her, for example. How does he communicate with his old home? He must have a contact at the resort. I don't push the point. I don't want to cause trouble for some low-tier Happiness who isn't doing anything illegal. "Do you know why she was at an airport?"

"I don't know what she's doing. Perhaps she wanted to see the planes. When she didn't turn up where she was supposed to I was concerned. A young person, alone, here for the first time. It can be confusing. I wanted to make sure she was safe, so I asked a friend to look out for her. He must have involved Gurley. Or Gurley heard about it and thought it was a chance to make money."

"You should have contacted the resort."

"That would have involved a Safety Team. I came here to avoid that sort of entanglement."

"So you involved people who know people like Gurley. Did you know his friend threatened me with a machete?"

"With what?" He blinks at the word. "Whatever that is, I'm not responsible for it. I didn't ask him to get involved."

"He was asking about signatures. Did you tell your friends about those?"

"Of course not. Besides, what good would it have done them? When I heard she hadn't gone back to the resort I said I'd look out for her in the usual tourist places and asked them to use their own resources. Like I said, one of them must have blabbed to Gurley. He's acting on his own initiative."

"They followed her to the airport. Do you know how they might have found her?"

"They're resourceful, in their own way." He looks thoughtful, as if he's reconsidering his opinion of Gurley. "You have to remember these people aren't stupid," he says in a tone that suggests this is an important lesson I would do well to take to heart. "You can't judge them by the standards of home. How long does a rep spend here? A year? Two years? And you spend most of that time in resorts, talking to tourists who are here for a month. Probably following the same script every time, taking them on excursions to the same few places. You might as well be back in the 24th. It's different for us. We live here. We're not entirely outside your society – how could we be? But we're definitely not part of theirs. We know both sides watch us. Nobody trusts us. Why should they? We've turned our back on one side and we're not allowed to join the other. Even if we wanted to, we'd never be able to belong. Other than prisoners, we're probably the most carefully monitored people in history. Our credit is controlled by Geneva. They can tell us where to live and decide how much we spend. At any moment they can take everything away from us. The locals could do the same. One day enough of them might decide we're the cause of all their problems. Have you seen this so-called March for Humanity? If their government agrees it can happen, things could get uncomfortable for us. But with all that, our life is better here than it was back in the cities. Our position may be insecure, but that's the price of freedom. That insecurity has two consequences: we follow the protocols and we stick together."

It's a fluent speech. I wonder if he's adapted it from the one he gives to new arrivals. When he stops it's a pause rather than a conclusion. When he starts again he's a regional resource manager giving a dim subordinate the hard facts. "One way we keep together is by helping each other. It's a system based on mutual obligation."

"A favour for a favour."

"Exactly. And tonin is the favour I provide."

"And what do you get in return?"

"Contacts. Support. It's hard to quantify. Sometimes there's no immediate return. Sometimes it's there just to make life more tolerable."

"Is it possible somebody else is selling your favours?"

"It's possible. But it's unlikely. Everybody knows the rules."

"How are these favours shared?"

"People come here. As guests. This is a big house. I get many visitors. Some of us like to travel. I'm one of the stops on the way."

"My last question: we know she went to London. Do you have any idea why?"

"No," he says sourly. "It's a famous place. Maybe she grew tired of watching the planes and decided she wanted to see famous monuments instead. Maybe she's found a buyer for my tonin in the community there. If I hear anything—" As if on cue his phone starts playing music again, a different piece this time. "For all I know this is her now." He picks up the device and glances at the screen. "It isn't." He hunches forward and lowers his voice. Modern again. "No, that's the day after tomorrow. It's not here. It's at Adnam's . . . " I back away. The women don't look up from their phones.

Outside Hayek says, "That was a slight improvement, Tunnel Boy, but I'd still recommend formal training."

"What did you make of him?"

"Based on what I could hear he had good taste in music."

"I wouldn't have guessed you were a raptive."

"I was young once," Hayek says in a faraway voice. "And human." I assume it's his idea of a joke. "But he was lying about something."

"How could you tell?"

"Extemps are always lying about something."

An hour and a half later, I'm back at my typical single-person dwelling. I turn on my 21st media devices – laptop, television – and promptly fall asleep.

I'm woken by a bip from Hayek. "We have news."

Three hours have passed. I'm still groggy. One day we will learn to do without sleep and all the inconvenient stages of semi-consciousness. I'm staring at a television screen. It shows a still picture of a flooded street and rolling text about a cricket score.

"Our heart attack victim has died."

"Do we know who he was?"

"I'm still waiting to be told."

"And our client?"

"I will let you know when we find anything. In the meantime you should sleep. Your heart rate is elevated. You run the risk of hypertension."

"Thanks, Hayek." He is monitoring my signature. "You can stop listening now."

"Tunnel Boy," he says, "don't you know the machines are always listening?"

I recognise the question. It's from *Artegal*, one of the earnest entertainments his generation listened to as children, a series about a benign superintelligence from the future. Cantor used to quote lines from it all the time: he thought it was hilarious. "Yes," I recite back, "but do they understand what they hear?"

"No, Yonec." Hayek finishes the quotation. He can't help himself. It's probably burned into one of his augmentations. "But they remember until the understanding comes."

The state of the road

You stop for a break. The back of the vehicle swings open and you see they've reversed into a hangar from which everything belonging to this era seems to have been removed. There are toilets at the far end and some food has been set out on a folding table. Their driver tells you they will stop for half an hour. Then they will drive for another four hours. Then you will be given a new driver. "So we should be there tomorrow?" It's the first time you've spoken to her.

She hesitates before answering. "The day after."

You realise you already knew this: you'd asked the same question that morning. You hope they haven't noticed.

Riemann waits until she leaves before he talks again. "When you travelled," he begins. He considers the bread rolls in one of the containers. Eventually he picks one up and tears it open. "Could you eat the food?" Casually. You're wary. That's how they ask the important questions: quietly, while they pretend to be concerned about food.

Or he really is concerned. This is his future. Maybe this

thing that looks like bread isn't bread. You remember having the same doubts.

"I went back to the 21st." You refused to answer questions at your trial and wouldn't talk to Consideration Panels. You're not sure why you're ready to talk to him. Is it just because of his name? "The food was strange."

"What was it like?"

You want to tell him: One day you'll see for yourself. "How long have you been here?"

"I arrived the day before I collected you." He's still considering his piece of bread. "I had one day for briefing. How long were you in the 21st?"

He's sly. You have to stop yourself from answering. Then you realise you couldn't answer because you don't remember. You thought you did, but it's gone. "Everything in the 21st was made in factories," you say. "I went to one of their markets. There was food from India, America, Africa. All over the world."

"I read about that. Did you try anything?"

"I wasn't there for the food."

He chews thoughtfully. "Why were you there?"

Their hosts have been careful. They've provided only basics he might recognise: fats, protein, plant matter for decoration. It's no better or worse than the food they gave you in prison. You take a mouthful of bread, partly to put off answering his question, partly to show him it's safe. "We had to know what you were doing," you finally say. You don't know what he's been told.

"You should have asked. It was no secret. What we were doing was a salvage operation. We were rebuilding civilisation. Learning from the mistakes." He says it as if he believes it. He's young. "Nationalism, the way they organised society.

The waste. But we also wanted to learn from the things they did right. Technology, culture. Things that were useful." He nibbles at a crust. "Apart from watching us, what did you do?"

"Culture." Once again, you wonder how much he knows. Your trial and what happened next are in his future. "You sound like a Consideration Panel." How much would they tell him about that when they won't even let him travel in a vehicle with a window? "We knew about your culture. The clearances." He doesn't respond. Maybe he's too young to have been told. You try a different approach: "These people you're trying to find: why are they worth all this trouble?"

"They're well connected." He doesn't elaborate. He pretends to be fascinated by his food. You try to imagine his life. He's sent forward to search a ruined city. When he goes back the city will still be alive. He'll live to see it destroyed. And then, if it's the same person, he'll go back to the early 21st and look for you. Why? Because of what he sees? Or because of something you tell him?

You say, "Two weeks."

He's forgotten he asked the question. "What?"

"The 21st. I was there for two weeks." That's all he needs to know.

He chews thoughtfully. "It must have been memorable."

"I had instructions. Like you."

He eats in silence. You feel a growing resentment: you want to tell him about your time in the 21st. You feel like telling him about the earlier meetings. It's still too soon. You can't yet see how it will help. You can't be sure they happened as you remember. The memories are vivid but they might not be true.

Once back in the vehicle you feel drowsy. Only the bumps and the jolts of the road keep you awake. Riemann remains alert the whole time. You've never seen him asleep, or even inattentive. He studies the dents in the side panel while you try to remember the earlier meetings. There was one in a car park outside an airport. And the other?

The gaps and jumps in your memory are worrying. You've spent too long with the same few thoughts, tapping the walls, looking up at the ceiling. When you try to remember the past it's like entering a storeroom and finding rats have been there first: all that's left are scraps, mixed up and unsafe.

You had walked together down a street. Was that the first meeting? The first, that is, in your line: he would remember them in a different order. Or he will, one day. You remember a teacher explaining how travel had given the Number Cities new tenses: one for completed actions in the future, another for actions in the past you hadn't yet done. You grope for the names but the rats have been there first.

You can remember the first meeting with the other Riemann: you stood at the edge of a paved street under a blue sky. You remember the buildings as grey, the road ahead filled with vehicles travelling impossibly fast. The air made your throat burn. There was the sound of hundreds of engines. *One day, a long time from now, you meet me again.* The vehicles that filled the road suddenly stop. *I'm here because of that meeting.*

You jolt awake. Riemann turns away: he'd been watching you. You hope he doesn't notice your panic. You don't want to show signs of weakness. "Was I asleep for long?"

"Not long enough."

The vehicle hits another bump on the road. You can infer a lot from the state of a road. If a road isn't maintained it's because it's not being used. No traffic, or no ground traffic. Therefore no population. The space between cities.

Or the space *beyond* cities. Are they really two days away from home?

Is it home after all this time? You think of a question. "It's the first time you've travelled, isn't it?"

"And the last, I hope."

"You didn't want to come here?"

"I didn't volunteer."

"Do you know why you were chosen?"

"Because I was available."

"You were the only one?" You think you know the reason: because there's no risk of him meeting his older self in this era. That older self is in the 21st, looking for you. You wonder if he's realised this.

"The only one," he says flatly. "It had to be me."

He's making fun of you in a way you don't recognise. You resent it and can't think of an answer. You sit in silence until you fall asleep again. Your latest prison jolts along the old road east. Mosk, Spad, Sver.

DomeWatch

The next day I'm awake at my usual time. I scan the native media. The news programmes are still excited by pictures of flooding in Central Europe and an election in Africa. No mention of any deaths at airports. They must happen all the time.

Hayek bips me: "We have a name for our airport casualty."

It's a start. "Who is he?"

"Alexander Metzger."

Metzger, I remember, is German for butcher. Apart from that the name means nothing. "What is he?"

"Lecturer in philology, recently appointed to a new post in this country," Hayek recites. "Fifty-two years old. Known for his work on" – his voice thins with contempt – "Greek lyric poetry."

I'm at the laptop, tapping on its keyboard.

"For the time being there is no suspicion of illegal activity ... " Hayek trails off. "There is no obvious connection to our girl."

Their internet produces some information about Alexander

Metzger: gifted scholar, specialist in Parthenius, author of numerous papers and two collections of his own poetry and, latterly, president of the German–Hellenic Society. Dutifully, I look up the German–Hellenic Society, expecting to find a worthy survival from the last or last-but-one century, a home of rarefied scholarship and occluded sexuality.

I find Nazis.

Now, Nazis have a special place in the mind of the early 21st, a significance even casual visitors find hard to miss. They're symbols of deliberate, conscious evil in the same way that City Two East is our symbol for primitive fanaticism. If a native wants to imply a rival political movement is bad they will compare them to Nazis and, in entertainments, all a character has to do to represent evil is wear an armband with some kind of cross. Entertainment Nazis are shorthand for monstrousness, simplified versions of a movement that was simple to begin with. So finding an organisation that actually approves of them is like stumbling across a group of other mythical horrors, werewolves or vampires. (Except the 21st has grown to love its imaginary monsters. They've humanised, as they say, their old night terrors, while telling themselves the real killers – Nazis, people designated as terrorists – are inhuman and remote.)

So Alexander Metzger was a Nazi. Or a member of an organisation that included Nazis. Or (I read on) an organisation that was said by other people to include Nazis. The German–Hellenic Society itself did not make any public statements of its values. Other natives insisted this meant Nazi, and quoted examples of various members expressing nostalgia for the Third Reich.

It's interesting, but it doesn't help.

I'd hoped learning why our client had gone to the airport would provide an explanation. A clandestine drug deal made perfect sense. But what was the connection with the president of a fringe political movement? Perhaps Picon was right: she'd gone to see the planes and a man collapsing from a heart attack was a piece of irresistible local colour.

"Hayek, have you found our client?"

"She seems to be avoiding cameras. And masts."

"Or something has happened to her."

"That is also a possibility." Hayek sounds like he's enjoying himself. "I will let you know if we find anything."

I switch off the various devices and step out into the filth and noise of the street.

The car has been vandalised. There are wavering lines scored along both sides and paint tipped across the windscreen. There are no words, though there's something like an X scratched into the boot. I can't tell if this is an accident or if whoever did it was interrupted before they could finish a whole word. Extemp? The cars parked on each side haven't been touched. Mine has been singled out. It looks no different from the surrounding vehicles. The modifications are not visible from the outside. It doesn't have special plates, or a badge identifying it as belonging to Tri-Millennium. Whoever did it must have seen me getting out. Which means they must have been watching. I look up and down the street. I can't tell if anybody is watching me now.

I bip Erquist. His first questions: "How bad is the damage? Does it still work?"

"I'll need to clean the windscreen."

One of the vehicle's modifications is passive recording (we're not allowed to install countermeasures). As I drive to work an hour or so later (windscreen smeared but usable) I send the records to Hayek. He finds the minute when the incident took place and extracts some clear images and accompanying data (height and approximate weight of the vandals; a sound file in which one uses the other's name) and sends it to the police who respond by giving him a number. (The native police don't always prevent crime and can't always catch criminals, but they'll give you a number you take to an insurance company.) Hayek tells me he hasn't heard of any other attacks on our vehicles. "You could be present at the beginning of a trend." There is, he adds, still no sign of our client. The only thing he can tell me about the vandals is that they weren't Gurley and Knight. "These are younger men. One of them is called Justin. That's all I have until I can talk to my police contact."

"You think the police already know them?"

"I would be unsurprised."

I listen to music as I drive: recordings of Schumann songs from the 1950s. They're close enough to the originals. There's a news bulletin. The top story (as they call it) is the African election. Apparently the wrong people have won, always a problem with democracies. The last item is that the government has agreed to allow the March for Humanity but haven't decided on a date. I try to remember what Picon said about the march. Hayek comes back: "Justin Bayer." He sounds pleased with himself. "Twenty-two. Previous incidents of damage to property and starting fights in public. It seems he chose our property to damage."

"Will the police do anything?"

"I'm told that despite the pictures and the name and address they don't have enough information to act. Still, why should you be worried? You can look after yourself, Tunnel Boy."

"I shouldn't have to," I say. "I'm a travel rep." He's already gone.

*

I go straight to Erquist. "Well," he says. "You've had some interesting times." He shows the appropriate degree of concern. "I hope you're bearing up."

"I'm fine," I say. "We must have reported some of this."

"We do report what happened to your vehicle."

"What do we say?"

"That the damage to the vehicle was slight and you were unharmed. Operationally there's no need for concern." Erquist looks sorry about this. "Is there anything else I can help with?"

"There is one thing."

"Please ask."

"In a few weeks I'm supposed to be sent home for breach of protocol."

"Ah." Erquist looks, if anything, sorrier. "You know I can't tell you what it is. Agency."

"Could you at least tell me if I kill anybody?"

"I'm sure it won't come to that."

"How sure? Is it on the records?"

"Spens, I understand your anxiety," Erquist sounds as if he understands anxiety the same way he knows about the local transport. "I wish there was some advice I could give you, but there really isn't. Geneva has to take the long view. Take this morning's events. One damaged vehicle belonging to one resort might seem important when it happens but from their perspective it's not significant. Operational requirements are different from personal ones. And that means, in many respects, we're in the same position as any native of this era. It means we have to deal with events as they arise and try not to exaggerate their importance." Erquist's voice is measured and slightly pained. He's trying to justify the system to himself and failing. "It all comes down to agency. The sense of agency is so important . . . " He's lost for a moment. "All we can do is try to live in accordance with our principles. And remember the Tri-Millennium code of conduct. And, where possible, avoid men with machetes."

It's weak, and he knows it. He looks abashed. It's likely he's always dreamed of one day making a stirring speech to his employees, and now that day has arrived and this is the best he can do. He stares at his blank desk for a few seconds. "Apart possibly from the business with the tonin," he says brightly, "there's no sign that our client is doing anything wrong. And if this Delrosso can be trusted, even the tonin isn't strictly illegal. So there's a good chance this is just a week-long panic over nothing."

It's not reassuring. Erquist is too much part of the Happiness Executive. No matter how high-ranking he is (and he is, we reps know, *very* well connected) when it comes to access to information he's always going to be subordinate to Safety and Facilitation. And in the background – so far back you don't see them – are the Millies. Erquist doesn't just accept the official line, he's the living embodiment of it, bred and conditioned. He's only ever going to give you good news. I go to the reps' room. It's empty: the other reps are greeting the latest arrivals or jollying people along in the Entertainment Areas. I lie down on one of the couches and for a moment consider staying there for the rest of the day. Perhaps giving up is the breach of protocol for which I'll be sent home.

It's still morning and I'm tired as if I'd worked a full day. If I'm having this much trouble in the early 21st, what can I expect in the 19th? It will be a long trip, much longer than my stay here, all to witness a performance of music I've heard a hundred times already. And it won't be a holiday. I'll have to work to earn the right to attend.

The concert is on my handheld, one of the recordings I take

everywhere. I start it now. There are crowd noises, picked up by the eight concealed microphones Anders Brink and Jim Nakamura had planted the week before. (They had been travelling as a Swedish count and his oriental manservant. Earlier they had travelled as a Persian prince and his Christian slave. Their book about their experiences is wonderful.) The microphones were good: they caught snippets of conversation, mostly complaints about the cold. I've often listened and wondered if I'm in the audience. If I am, I'm keeping quiet, probably pretending to be a merchant from Finland or the United States (both neutral countries) and keeping to my seat so my height doesn't spook the locals. There's a long wait before the music actually starts: Brink and Nakamura couldn't be in the hall so had to record everything. On the night of the concert they were negotiating with the Viennese authorities about their right to stay in the city. As well as having recently been a war zone, Vienna was a police state. They missed their only chance to attend the concert. They couldn't even be sure their microphones had worked until they returned to collect them two weeks later.

Brink and Nakamura were my heroes. They gave their lives to recording music. For thirty years they travelled around Europe pretending to be eccentric foreigners. They wheedled, dodged and bribed their way across borders, into concert halls and the homes of the wealthy and, at the end of that time, when they realised there was no hope of coming back, they prepared their archive, wrote their book (in ink, on good paper) and buried it in a prearranged spot where it remained undisturbed through several wars and the NEE. They weren't the only musicologists to travel, but they were the first and the bravest. They're the reason I became interested in music. And their book is hilarious.

I've listened to the recording so often I know the audience noises as well as any of the music. If I am there I do nothing to draw attention to myself. You're not supposed to, in the 19th. You get only one chance and you have to be discreet. When I was studying I heard about a man who loved Wagner so much he attended the premiere of *Tristan und Isolde* twice. That kind of thing is impossible now. Being in two places at once is bad enough; being in the same place twice is strictly forbidden. Even then, when the authorities were less careful, he had to take precautions. When he came back from his first trip he changed his name, moved to a different city and retrained as a field medic so he could be included in another mission to the same era. On the second visit he had to make his way from Egypt to Munich; at the theatre he had to be careful to sit in a part of the hall where he couldn't be seen by his younger self (he had no memory of having noticed his older self, and wouldn't have realised if he had, but overlaps make people behave irrationally). He even made sure his absence from duty wasn't included in the official report. He would have got away with it if he'd been able to stop himself talking about it to everybody he knew. Eventually, some colleague or kin must have heard the story once too often. He was arrested, of course, and then released when the authorities realised what he'd done wasn't yet illegal. Now there are stringent rules for any kind of cultural contact, and your record is checked carefully. Otherwise people would be trying to buy van Goghs straight from the painter or commissioning requiems from Mozart.

The Pastoral has just started when I get a message from Hayek. "Have you heard of the Anachronists?"

I stop the music but don't get off the couch. "What about them?" The Anachronists date back to the early years of travel,

when the only people who dared use it were techs. They had access to a research prototype and a philosophy about testing history. We're more careful now: there are protocols for all interactions with natives, strict rules about what we are allowed to say. We don't intervene in their affairs. We *can't* intervene. Really, all we can do is sightseeing or shopping. Brink and Nakamura were as much sightseers as our clients in a shopping mall; materials acquisition is just shopping on a larger scale. This wasn't enough for the Anachronists: they wanted to intervene at Major Historical Events.

The problem is that Major Historical Events are both dangerous and surprisingly easy to miss, as Balaman Okscay, a specialist in the 17th, discovered. Unless you're fluent in the language and up to the minute in religious and political disputes you're likely to become the target of a mob. Okscay ended up stuck in the lost city of Bristol, pretending to be a merchant. He barely escaped with his life. He said later that for all his research into the period he never knew from week to week what would happen next. And, between religious wars and various plagues, the rest of Europe was worse. Even if you survived the fanatics and mercenaries you could still die from the plague or an impacted molar. The Anachronists, the story goes, didn't allow for any of this. They wrote their manifesto ("Testing the Self-Consistency Principle"), made their translations and are remembered as idiots. There were even entertainments about them (for children, with pictures) which used to be cherished for their sadistic slapstick. Cantor loved the one about the inquisition.

"There's a possibility our girl is an Anachronist," Hayek says.

"An actual Anachronist? Aren't they all dead?" All except one: he turned up in Southern California at the end of the last century under the name Quentinder Ward and formed his own religion – the First Church of Christ Transhumanist – with ecstatic dancing and carefully inaccurate prophecies. He's still alive in the early 21st. Geneva keep a close eye on *him*.

"Not all of them, Tunnel Boy. It turns out our girl has a connection to one of the signatories of the original manifesto, one of the ones who never travelled."

I sit up. This is possibly relevant. "I thought they all travelled."

"Some were caught while they were still setting the controls. They were planning to reach early-21st Europe."

"Do we know why?" It sounds unlikely. The Anachronists were supposed to be keen on Big History: assassinations (William the Silent, Bobby Kennedy), even, supposedly, the crucifixion of Jesus. (So far nobody's travelled back further than the 14th, and that was just to see if it was possible. There's nothing of much use to us before then.) The early 21st is an unlikely choice for an Anachronist. Apart from us declaring our presence, nothing significant happens. That's why it's a popular Tri-Millennium destination. "What were they looking for?"

"If I had access to the records I could tell you. There is only so much information they let us have." Hayek sounds as if, for the first time, he's beginning to resent this arrangement. "However, I'm still in contact with Geneva. They may be able to provide more information."

"Do you think they'll tell us anything?"

"If it was about drugs, no. If it was about a missing tourist, no. If it's about old history like the Anachronists then maybe."

"Good luck."

"If you want to do something before then," Hayek says casually, "I can tell you Justin Bayer's address."

"Why? Do you want me to damage his car?"

"You could ask him why he damaged yours."

"Is that an order?"

"More of a suggestion, Tunnel Boy." He bips me the address. "It's three streets from where you live."

"I've never heard of it."

"It exists even so."

After which I'm in no mood to listen to music. First it was follow our client, then question an extemp. Now I'm being asked to talk to a native. Whatever Hayek says, it's an order, except one I'm supposed to *choose* to follow. Agency.

I will choose to follow it. Justin Bayer damaged my car. It felt personal. I want to know why.

I wonder if he has a machete.

Edda bips me. She's waiting outside a cathedral. Her party of tourists are inside, amazed at how small it is and mixing up their civil wars. According to Li it's how clients usually spend time in cathedrals. We agree to meet in Bar Five. If it's busy – or if Ivan shows up – we can move to that dead place round the corner.

At least I know what I'm doing this evening. It gives me a tiny sense of agency.

Erquist, who's noticed my mood, hasn't assigned me any rep duties for the rest of the day so I spend an hour in the gym in Entertainment Area One. Resort gyms are the traditional place for reps to prey on the younger clients. I'm not in the mood. I spend my hour in the back room pounding an Auto Combat. It's satisfying and unsatisfying at the same time. The machine remembers your last session and tells you how much progress you've made (none, in my case). This detracts from the brute pleasure of hitting a heavily padded machine and trying to avoid it when it hits back. I set it at Level Three, the hardest I can manage. (At Level Four it taunts you; at Level Five it tells you how it will beat you and alerts the medical area in advance. Only the mad – Safeties, ex-Millies – use Level Five.) After an hour of punching and occasionally being punched I'm bruised and exhausted but there's no catharsis. And there's no word from Hayek. I let Erquist know I'm leaving and go to see Justin Bayer.

My apartment's in a house built in the 19th. We lease the older houses because they have larger rooms and, importantly, higher ceilings. Justin Bayer's block dates back to the later 20th, when builders seemed to think people were getting shorter. It has an external staircase, so I don't have to identify myself before I reach his door. The stairwell is as fetid as I've come to expect. The 21st has working sewers but the natives will still piss in any enclosed public space. They've written on the walls as well: the names they wish they'd been given, libels about their neighbours. I wonder if these scrawled testaments were left by the children I saw waiting in the street on my way here. The style is childish enough.

Justin's apartment is one floor up. It's a standardised, modular building, like a child-sized version of the structures at home. All the doors are the same colour. His is the third one along. To reach it I pass three identical windows giving views of three once-identical kitchens.

There's a button by the side of his door. I push it, producing a weak buzz that's surely too faint for anyone inside to hear. I don't expect him to be in. I wait anyway, just in case.

The door opens. It's not Justin, but another native, smaller and thinner than the one in the image Hayek extracted. As soon as he sees me he tries to close the door. I put my shoulder

124

against it and hold my position. The door bounces open, and there's the sound of somebody falling over. I step into the hallway. It's narrow, only slightly wider than the door. I have to dip to avoid a hanging light bulb. "I'm looking for Justin Bayer," I say to the person on the floor. I use This English. I doubt he speaks Modern.

It's a teenager, as far as I can tell. He crawls away, still on the floor. "He's not here."

I give him time to get to his feet.

"Jesus." He retreats into one of the rooms. "Hulk smash. You've broken our door."

"It's not broken." I close it behind me. It shuts perfectly, despite the splintering around the hinges. "I just want to talk to Justin Bayer."

"He's not here." His voice is out of its usual register. He's too scared not to be telling the truth. "I'll call the police."

"Justin damaged my car. I've already told the police."

"That was his idea," he says very quickly. "I didn't want to do it. I like you people. I don't have anything against you. I think you're . . . " He can't find the word he wants. "I mean, I've got nothing against you."

"Why did he do it?"

"Because he *does* hate you." He keeps moving backwards, one small step at a time as if he hopes I won't notice. He'll have to stop when he reaches the television, a big screen in the far corner. It's switched off. That's the first thing I notice about the room. The second is a bookcase. It's small but full of books. This is unexpected. In the early 21st literacy usually depends on income. Poor people are supposed to watch entertainments and self-medicate.

The next thing I notice is the furniture. Everything looks worn out. Even the television is last century.

He stops when his back touches the screen. "Justin, man. He hates everybody."

"Why did he attack my car?"

"I don't know. Because you were the nearest?"

I'm curious about the books. I read the spines, expecting to see swastikas. I don't recognise any of the titles. 20th and early 21st isn't really my period.

He sees my curiosity. "We call them *books*," he says. "I don't suppose you have those."

"We have books." Print survived the NEE better than electronic records and we were printing books long before we rebuilt the networks. The materials – rag paper and hemp – were easier to find. "Our time isn't what you think," I tell him. "Are these Justin's?"

"They were our dad's. Now they're mine. I've read everything here." He sounds hurt. "Nearly everything. Justin – he started one book two years ago and hasn't finished it yet. So what do you read?"

"Just tell me about Justin."

He crouches on the edge of a grey sofa. "So what is this? Is this where you ask me questions, I answer them and you send me back to the Jurassic?"

There's another chair in the room: brown panels on a chrome frame. It looks fragile. I remain standing. "I won't send you anywhere. I'm just a travel rep."

"Jesus," he says. "I'd hate to see the fucking police. What-ever. It's still weird. I've never spoken to one of you before."

"We're not so different from you."

"Yes, you are." He snorts. "Can I take a picture? Just to prove you were here."

"Don't, please. I came to talk to Justin. I want to ask him why he damaged my car."

"I told you. Because he hates you. Not you personally. You people."

"Why does he hate us?"

He snorts again. "How long have you got?" I'm not given a chance to answer. He rattles off a list: "He hates you because he thinks you think you're better than us. Because you're rich. Because he thinks all the gold you carry around is *our* gold. Because he's scared of what's happening in Geneva. Because he can't work out if you're white or Asian or what. I mean, does it even matter where you come from? Because you won't let us into your domes or tell us what's going to happen." As he talks he relaxes, his voice sinking to its natural register. "Because he thinks you're freaks. That squad in Mexico – were they even human? And, really, that's just the start."

There's nothing I haven't heard before. All it tells me is that his brother reads DomeWatch or talks to people who do. "So what made him do it *now*?"

"I don't know. I don't think they're that well organised. He's known about you for weeks. Maybe he couldn't hold back any longer. Maybe it was the first time he saw you had something he could damage. How long have you had the car?"

"Did somebody tell him to do it?"

"You mean, did he receive orders?" He laughs, as if the idea is ridiculous. "No offence, it doesn't work like that. Look, he talks to people. Social media. They encourage each other. He might have read something. He might have thought, you know: *This time they've gone too far.* And, like I said, you were the nearest."

"So he was watching me?"

"I wouldn't say watching. But he knew about you. I mean, you stand out. Look at you."

"The people he talks to, who are they?"

"I thought you'd know. Aren't we history to you? Can't you look it up?"

"It doesn't work like that."

"How does it work? I mean, if you don't mind my asking, why are you here?"

"Because your brother vandalised my car."

"No. Why are you here, in this century, now? Why do you people keep coming back? What's so great about us?"

"People are curious about the past." It's a bland answer, but I don't want to mention Material Acquisitions or the NEE. "Your people visit museums. It's the same with us."

"So we're a museum to you? Thanks. But is that all? I mean, what you do can't be cheap. Those domes. They're too big just for a few tourists. I thought you'd be living on Mars rather than coming here."

Mars! I should know more about 21st aspirations. "People want to see something they feel a connection with." There's nothing on Mars we want. It's emptier than the 14th. "What else can you tell me about these people?"

"Not much. I don't know who Justin talks to. They use code names. You should hear them. Snow White, Happy Diggers, Sleeping Beauty. For a while I thought he was talking about drugs, but he's always been funny about those. I don't know if they're people or things they've got planned or what. His laptop's in his room. Can't you copy his files or something?"

"Not quite." With the right connection I could load them onto my handheld and read them on my own laptop. But I don't have the right connection. The code names don't tell me anything: Snow White and Sleeping Beauty are children's stories and I've never heard of the Happy Diggers. "Can you show me his laptop?"

"No. He keeps everything in the cloud." The cloud. I

remind myself it means something different here. When we hear the words the first thing we think of is a sixty-kilometre-wide toxic weather front. Our parents grew up in its shadow, sometimes literally. When the Cloud arrived you sealed all the doors and stayed inside until it was safe to inspect the damage. If an entertainment set in the past wants to add drama they'll usually have a character run in and shout, "The Cloud! The Cloud!" When I left it was somewhere over the South Atlantic and not expected back. In the 21st the same word means all the information that will be lost. "I don't know his password. He uses at least three. He's paranoid. He doesn't trust anybody."

"He took you with him when he damaged my car."

"That's *because* he doesn't trust me. He wanted me to be involved. So I wouldn't talk." He laughs again. He seems amused by his own thoughts. Or it's terror. "I mean, I'm talking to you. But I wouldn't talk to the police. No, actually I would. If I thought he wouldn't find out. I'd tell them like a shot."

"These people he talk to, who are they?"

"I don't know their names. It's all codes. 'This is Grumpy5', like it's a big conspiracy. They're probably all EPP."

"Who?"

"Do you know, like, anything? You must have heard of them." He spells it out. "English People's Party. He used to be a member."

"Are they connected to the German–Hellenic Society?"

He smiles, but doesn't laugh this time. "I've never heard of that. The EPP were politics, sort of.

"Sort of?"

"They have one idea. They hate you. Sorry to break it to you, but you people are not exactly popular. Especially round here. I've got nothing against you, but you should be careful. It's building up."

"What is?"

"Everything." He's confident now, playing out a scene from an entertainment: the truth teller and the official who doesn't realise what's happening. "It's not just people like my brother. The March for Humanity? You must have heard of that. It's proper politicians. They're starting to get involved."

This sounds unlikely: politicians with actual power are the last ones to make trouble. "Tell your brother we're watching him."

"That's why we don't like you. You think you can control everything. You think you're the only people who matter."

"Tell him."

I let myself out.

Hayek bips me. "That was your worst interrogation so far."

"It wasn't an interrogation." I've held my breath as I descend the stairwell and gasp as I come out to the open air. A group of native children are sitting on the wall. They watch as I walk past. *You people are not exactly popular.* "Aren't you supposed to warn me when you're listening?"

"When you load Safety functions onto personal tech you give me permission." Hayek is nonchalant. "Implicitly. Besides, you were asking questions at my request. It would have been irresponsible of me not to listen."

"He didn't know anything."

"He could have told you more, Tunnel Boy."

"Would it have helped?"

"Are you asking me to evaluate information you didn't obtain?"

A click, and he's gone. I take the handheld from my pocket

and turn it off. It's a gesture. Hayek can turn it on again when he chooses and I don't want to miss any messages from Li or Edda. I turn it back on.

What I've learned is more about mood than information. Justin's brother thought something was coming and Justin probably thought the same thing more fervently. It doesn't mean anything is going to happen. People without power often look forward to a reckoning – a disaster, a revolution, the return of their gods, a levelling event that will show the rest of the world they were right all along. But the vindication doesn't happen, and goes on not happening until the NEE arrives, and nobody wanted that.

In the meantime, while they wait, there's politics, or what passes for politics in the English People's Party. The big parties aren't a problem. The small ones can damage your car. Back at home, while the television news shows people expressing their concerns about the African elections and floods in Central Europe and nobody mentions Metzger, I see if there's anything about the EPP on their internet. I expect to find something. In the early 21st there is no faction so small it doesn't occupy some server space.

The EPP has an official page. It's bland, the politics-as-usual in this era – smiling men in suits, inoffensive slogans about caring passionately and putting England first. The only sign they're cranks is the link to DomeWatch. Another link which says "Latest News" leads to a blank page. I'm not going to learn anything about the EPP from the EPP.

But they've attracted some attention. Another site, put up by people who don't like them, has a brief history: they're a fraction of a fraction of another small party, who broke away because the other group didn't recognise the threat we posed to the English way of life and Western Civilisation. The EPP aren't just a typical hate-all-outsiders group: the outsiders they hate are us.

Still, I'm intrigued. How big is this group? If it's Justin and a few friends it won't matter. If it's popular it's something we should know about. Geneva should be told. They have resources Hayek can only dream of. They'll find Justin's passwords and analyse every message he ever sends or receives.

I remember the name Justin's brother mentioned and type in Grumpy5. I find an online conversation between EPP members on an entertainment site. It's part of a long sequence where natives discuss their favourite native actors; somehow three of the participants have recognised their shared beliefs and carried on exchanging messages long after everybody else has left. It begins with speculation about the possibility of making a film of something they call TWO (or *two*, or just *2*) and then gets sidetracked: *1 come in my shop ystrdy. Wanted to smash his smug face.* Answered by: *They come in my place all the time. Can they spk English? Dont be stupid.* It's hard to follow: their spelling isn't standard and they don't punctuate. One of them comments: *Shame cos wmn r hawt.* Some things stand out: *They are dstrying our country. We shd do something.* Answered by: *Have 2 b careful, frends with Govt. Russians best bet. More independent.*

But Russian films r shit.

Its a Russian story.

Still shit films.

That's when I realise they're not talking about a sequel to an existing entertainment. TWO is *The War Ouroboros*.

EPP members are *that* kind of crank.

The War Ouroboros, like DomeWatch, is one of those things reps find amusing at first. A Russian bestseller from a few years back, it's never been published in the West, although there is a translation, a collective, volunteer effort on their internet. Millions of natives are supposed to have read the idiot thing. As part of my attempt to be the best possible rep – understanding the local culture – I once started it.

It pretends to be the diary of an FSB officer sent to investigate a group of ex-army and intelligence officers who are believed to be stockpiling weapons in a remote industrial town. The hero infiltrates the group and learns they're not terrorists: they're preparing for war – against the future! They have evidence that our so-called resorts are staging posts for a planned invasion. The Whites (as we're called) have been planning the invasion ever since they arrived. This is explained in a lot of detail – pages and pages and pages. The hero breaks into a resort to see this preparation for himself. There's a description – a *long* description – that seems to have been provided by somebody who'd possibly seen the shell of a resort as it was being constructed and imagined the rest. These are the parts reps will tell you are hilarious. Anyway, convinced of the reality of the threat, the hero goes back to Moscow and tries to alert his superiors. They don't believe his detailed and very specific warnings and give orders for his new friends to be arrested. Before this can be done the invasion begins: heavily armoured monsters storm out of resorts all across Europe and the United States. Moscow and other big cities are under attack. The hero's superiors realise the hero was right and beg him to help them. He tries, but the only one he's able to save from the initial assault is Natasha, his Chief's beautiful assistant. They make their way through the war ravaged countryside to the remote industrial town and prepare to fight back.

That's the first three hundred pages. It's usually about as far as most reps get. I was determined to be the best possible rep.

The hero undertakes a series of foolhardy missions, all of which would have failed had anyone tried them in the real world. He survives every time: weapons misfire; guards look in the wrong direction. After another two hundred pages – it's a very long book – he finds out why: the leader of the Whites is his remote descendant, which means he can't be killed as long as he doesn't father any children. Fortunately he's what they call Orthodox and believes sex has to be approved by a church. He tells himself he has to be pure "like the ancient warrior knights", and insists the people fighting with him live the same way. I stopped reading after the chapter where the leaders of the demoralised NATO forces beg him to be their leader. The descriptions of the atrocities committed by the Whites were getting monotonous and there were still about a thousand pages to go.

I've probably read further than Justin Bayer.

Maybe it's better in the original Russian, but the version I read was a dull and obvious daydream of power. The descriptions of the Whites – us! – start by being wrong enough to be amusing, including the obvious mistake that, for a number of reasons, we don't have any resorts in Russia. It gets more disturbing when you realise the author actually hates us and that some of the natives take him seriously. They believe the invasion plans are real. They want the film to be made so that more people will hear the message. Plus the 21st doesn't really believe a book exists until they've turned it into an entertainment in a different medium.

If EPP are impressed by this rubbish they can't be a serious threat.

DomeWatch has a new story. Under the headline "Killed By Fanatic From The Future?" they have a picture of Alexander Metzger ("soft-spoken, scholarly defender of traditional values") and one of arrivals taken on a different day. "Eyewitnesses claim that seconds before Dr Metzger collapsed several 'visitors' were seen in the vicinity, yet the police made no effort to apprehend them. It is not enough that whole areas of our capital city are effectively no-go zones. It appears they are now taking their violence into our public spaces. We demand, etc." It's lurid, laughable stuff, and not a surprise they're sympathetic to the hardships of Nazis. There are no *no-go zones*, just a few streets the natives can no longer afford. As for our violence, apart from the occasional Safety Team intervention (always in other countries and always carried out with the approval of the native authorities) the only trouble I've encountered was when two of them attacked me. With a machete! The next two stories are more typical: one claims that, by not taking sides, we are unfairly influencing climate change debate; in the other, a Reverend wonders if we are not the biblical nephilim ("giants", etc.). He admits we haven't shown much interest in the daughters of men – he clearly hasn't met Picon Delrosso – but claims this is just a sign of our dangerous cunning.

Happy Diggers doesn't find anything useful. *Diggers* by itself brings up an ancient political movement and, unsurprisingly, more Nazis, this time in Australia. It's depressing. I push the laptop away. I've seen enough for an afternoon. I can always ask Li about the March for Humanity.

Twenty minutes later the routine pictures of flooding in Central Europe are interrupted by an excited native in a studio. "We're getting reports of an explosion and a fire at the so-called Resort Number Three just outside Chichester , , , " And there's a jump to shaky film of one of our resorts (they really do all look alike) where there's smoke rising from a spot just to the right of the entrance. It's filmed from about a kilometre away, and whoever's holding the device can't keep their hand still. There's some incoherent talk – variations of, "Wow! Look at that! It's on fire!" – before the programme cuts back to the studio, where the excited native now looks piqued. "Breaking news there. We'll go back as soon as we have more details." He gazes out hopefully. "No? Oh. The Prime Minister was surprised yesterday ... " I stop listening. The Prime Minister's surprise is unimportant. After a few minutes they're back to the fire at Resort Number Three and this time they have information: it's the result of a car being driven directly into one of the glass walls of the dome. Whether it was an accident, or the driver believed he could smash through the walls in a native vehicle isn't clear, but there was an explosion on impact and the remains of the car are still burning harmlessly as the reporter speaks.

I suspect it's the work of somebody like Justin Bayer. More car-related crime ... The driver, they say, is believed to have died in the explosion. He hasn't yet been identified. I expect a message from Hayek but nothing comes.

Li bips me. "Have you seen what happened at Resort Three? What do you think it means?" She's excited, as if events are confirming her theories. "Are you meeting Edda later? I'll see you there."

I have a feeling Bar Five is going to be busy.

Welcome to the anterior

Your chance to travel comes when Adorna Mond from City Three West strays too close to your home territory. She was picked up by scouts, held in an isolation ward and told she had an infectious disease. They gave you an implant to mimic her signature, turned on and off by a device worn on your wrist. Adorna Mond was roughly your height and build. The resemblance is useful. If the signature isn't enough to fool their Safeties you can always claim to have had elective surgery, another Number City extravagance.

You slip into City Two West, close enough to Adorna Mond's home city not to arouse suspicion, far enough away that you don't accidentally meet her kin (she gave her "doctors" a list of people to contact so you know who to avoid).

The inhabitants surprise you at first. You expected slaves and monsters and find cheerful people who want to be friends. You repeat your memorised answers and soon learn the best way to deflect questions is to ask your own. Number City people are grateful for any chance to talk and quickly forget you haven't told them anything. The other surprise is that they rarely mention your own city. You'd expected it to be a common topic of conversation, or at least to be mentioned in official announcements, but they don't seem to care.

The company that arranges travel has three different names. You're surprised it uses names: you'd been told the Number Cities used only numbers, but City Two West has restaurants named after the people who make the food and buildings named after architectural features. It seems the rules are softer for new institutions. You wonder if it will spread and the cities will be given names again.

Adorna Mond, whose credit you use, could afford to travel with Heritage. You choose Tri-Millennium. It's the cheapest and your instructions are to travel with low-status people to attract less attention. You might need Adorna's credit when you return.

The travel is easy to arrange. As long as they think you're Adorna Mond they have no reason to stop you. You answer the questions and days later climb into the transport with other tourists, sit for several hours, then disembark in a resort.

Your first task is to buy a device locally (they're called *phones*) and contact Picon Delrosso using a memorised number. You can't contact him from inside the resort in case communications are monitored. Picon will tell you what to do next. You carry a Dolman box, a Number City invention but useful. You don't know what the box contains. It was closed when it was given to you, and locked using Picon Delrosso's signature as the key. The only people who can open it are your contact, the tech who locked the box or the real Picon Delrosso, whose identity had been taken the way you've taken Adorna Mond's.

You spend the first week in the resort, avoiding the reps and trying to look like you are taking part in the cultural activities, surrounded by people you despise. They are complacent, frivolous; they think of nothing but pleasure. Worse, they keep trying to talk to you and you have to listen to them and try to smile. Finally there's what looks like a chance to buy a phone: an excursion to a shopping mall that includes, as a bonus, a minor accident. You ask for a place.

Everything about that first trip outside the resort is a shock: the crowded streets, the thousands of vehicles jamming the roads, the clamour and dazzle of the mall, the terrifying and pointless abundance – you could clothe and feed a city with what you see on display. Everything is bigger and brighter and louder than you imagined. Even the Number City idiots from your resort are shocked by it, and drawn to dimmer, quieter rooms that offer books or elaborate underwear. Fortunately you remember your training and brave one of the noisier shops to buy a phone using a card in your assumed name. The natives don't question it: to them you're just another traveller. They nod and grin at everything you say but you can recognise their contempt. You charge the phone in their shop and make the call. A man answers. When you tell him you're Adorna Mond and give the code he sounds exasperated. "What's taken you so long?" You tell him this was your first opportunity to leave. "At least tell me you've brought something." "I have it now." "Does the coach go straight back?" You tell him yes, but there's going to be an accident. "What sort of accident?" "It says minor." "How long do you stop?" "About fifteen minutes." He sends you a tiny image of his face. "Get out then. I'll be following the coach." "Why can't you come here?" It seems the obvious thing to do. "I can't go to a mall. They're watched." This seems like excessive caution. The mall is crowded; the box could be passed on easily. You assume he knows what he's doing and spend the next hour being appalled by window displays. This is the world the Number Cities will destroy. You're meant to be outraged, but can't help wondering if it's a world worth saving. It's a relief to get back to the coach and wait for the accident. When it happens you follow some of the other passengers off.

In the next street a vehicle with tinted windows is waiting. The door slides open as you walk by. A man smiles as if he's delighted to see you. "Welcome to the anterior." He's about the right age but he isn't the man in the picture. You're wary. You don't trust the smile but you trust what Picon told you. You climb in.

Mish talk

It's raining as I walk from the station to Bar Five. Even after a year and a half in the 21st I still have an instinctive distrust of rain. It looks pretty enough if you're inside and damps down the usual stink of the city for a while, but I walk a little faster whenever it happens. I'm still uncomfortable when it touches my skin.

There's a crowd in the street outside Bar Five, mostly natives. Beyond them are a police vehicle and one of the red things they call *fire engines*. Two small, vicious-looking native police are keeping a row of people back. Fortunately I can see over their heads.

Bar Five's windows have been broken. There's glass strewn across the pavement as if it's been spat out. The inside, usually pristine white, is black, and not just because the lights are off. The interior is scorched, smoke-damaged.

It's building up.

Li is at my side. "Let's get out of here." She's with Edda and Jorge, a Heritage rep I've met before and didn't like. On the other side of the cordon I notice Ivan gesticulating at a policeman. He keeps pointing at Bar Five, as if explaining why they need to let him in. I can tell he's serious because his sleeves are rolled down.

I follow Li to her native friend's failing bar. There's the same rigmarole of admission, the same bearded man guiding us through the storeroom to the same empty sofas. It's no busier than the last time. The few native customers look like the same ones as before, in the same places. When we walk in they don't react.

"So," Li asks once the bearded man has brought us drinks, "what's going on? Resort Three, Bar Five. Is this connected? Is it the start of something?"

"And don't forget Spens was attacked," Edda says.

"You?" Jorge studied Early-20th History and Culture and thinks cinema is serious art, or was, until they started adding sound, and can explain why at length. He isn't sure whether to believe Edda. "Where?"

"By gangsters, a few nights ago. Leaving this bar." Edda makes it sound like an achievement. "Did that have something to do with your client? Did you ever find her?"

"She's still missing. Our Chief Safety is in touch with Geneva."

I expect Li to be scornful. She doesn't disappoint. "Geneva? They won't help."

"They might in this case."

"You seem to attract trouble," Edda says. "Wasn't your car vandalised?" I wonder how she knows. Possibly Erquist mentioned it to another rep in one of his pep talks ("At least you haven't been as unlucky as Spens . . .") and it spread from there. The world of reps is small.

"A local," I say. "I think he was acting independently."

"Bar Five and Resort Three," Li says. "And now your car. This could be organised."

"You think that's organised?" Jorge says. "Where are you from, City Three North?"

"They might not be accidents," Li insists.

"Resort Three was," Jorge says. "You've seen how the locals drive."

Li ignores him. "The question is, why now? What's changed? Is it to do with your client?"

"That's three questions," Edda says.

"You know what I think?" Li ignores her. "I think Geneva knew this was going to happen. Bar Five is too big. How could they not know?"

"Because it's not important," Jorge says. "It might inconvenience a few reps, but it's not Big History."

Li turns to me. "If they included your accident—"

"Operational reasons." Li's theorising about Geneva is the one thing about her that makes me uncomfortable. It reminds me of Cantor, except he was never entirely serious. For him it was always a joke. He might keep talking long after everybody else had lost interest but he didn't believe he was revealing a great truth. "They didn't include my client going missing."

"But there might be a pattern. Your client, Bar Five – neither of them were in the records."

Jorge is delighted. "Are you're saying they're *connected*? His client and Bar Five? Are you saying she might be *responsible*?"

"Of course not," Li says sharply. Jorge seems to bring out the worst in her: the last time they were out together, I remember, they argued the whole evening. "There are two answers here. Either Geneva knew about Bar Five and didn't tell us, or their own records are wrong. Look, maybe they didn't tell us because their records said something else."

"How can they be wrong?" Jorge, of course, objects. "We've had a few events we weren't told about. So what? They're all minor. The bar burned down, but was anybody hurt? If we were in danger we'd have been warned. So maybe it wasn't an attack on us, but an accident. You can't build an argument about their records based on what we're *not* told. You'd have to find something they have told us is going to happen that doesn't. If Spens is still here next month you'll have a case."

"Or" – Li changes tack – "they suppressed the information because they didn't want us to be prepared. They want us to panic."

Edda stays cool. "Why?"

"So that they can intervene." Li says it as if it's a long-held conviction. She has contradictory ideas and can sound passionate about all of them. Jorge isn't passionate about anything: he just wants to win arguments. It can make for a difficult evening. "Geneva isn't enough for them. They want everything else."

"What do you mean by intervene?" Jorge slumps back to signal her opinion wearies him but he can't let it go unchallenged. "Don't we get everything anyway?"

"We get what's left. And you can bet somebody in Geneva's wondering what we could do in the 21st if it wasn't for the people already here."

"Isn't that the plot of *Ouroboros*?" Jorge seems to think this is a killer strike.

Edda is lost. "The Russian novel? Have you read it?"

"Li finished it," Jorge says. "It changed her life."

"It's an interesting cultural artefact," Li concedes. "The question is, do they know what's happening or not?"

"Is there any point discussing this?" It seems like a good time to change the subject. I can see the argument getting heated on both sides. We don't want to be the ones shouting in a native bar. If the natives are friends of Li they might understand Modern. "We don't know why the bar burned down. I don't know why my client went missing. Until we do, all this is mish talk."

"So what's your solution?" Li turns on me. "Keep quiet and let the grown-ups sort it out?"

"What else can we do?"

Li is fierce. "I don't trust the grown-ups. What happened was an attack on us."

"It might be what it feels like," Jorge says. "But we don't know that. Not yet. And if we speculate without information we're as bad as DomeWatch."

"Who are funded by Geneva," Li says. "Think about it," she adds when Jorge groans. "It's a classic way of discrediting real concerns. Associate them with nonsense."

"I read it this morning," Edda says. "I think there's a simpler explanation."

"Edda's right," Jorge declares, as if he expects her to be grateful for his support. "The people here don't need our help to generate nonsense. Domeheads, DomeWatch – we don't have to tell them what to say. We corrupt them simply by being here."

"Not all of them."

"It doesn't need to be all of them. It only takes a minority. The trouble with you, Li, is that because you know a few reasonable locals you underestimate how much the rest of them hate us. And I don't blame them. Look at it from their perspective. Ten years ago they didn't know we existed. They're not yet used to us. Or they're used to seeing us but only just beginning to realise what that means. Remember the protests in America? All those people who thought the world was going to end in their lifetime and they'd go to heaven? The second coming of Jesus? They *can't* believe that now. Remember why we don't go to the Middle East? We're an awkward fact they can't acknowledge. This March for Humanity?"

"It won't happen," Li says.

"It'll happen. Enough of them hate us, and it needn't be because of anything we do. The fact we exist is enough. The minority that don't like us is going to have their march and make trouble. And your minority, Li, will be happy to sit back and watch."

It's annoying, but Jorge's probably right. For all we tell clients the early 21st is advanced and sophisticated, the people will still turn into a mob if they're given the right enemies. The Justin Bayers may be one in a thousand, but a dozen others will join in readily enough, and the rest won't try to stop them.

"Geneva," Li begins but doesn't finish. She's realised Jorge is just trying to impress Edda and isn't going to be swayed by arguments. "All I'm saying is there's more going on than we think."

"I don't know," Jorge can't let her have the last word. "In your case, Li, there's probably less going on than you think. Spens is right," he adds reluctantly. "All we can do is wait."

"Speculation helps," Edda says. "We can't talk in front of clients."

"Perhaps we should." Li softens her tone. "They're not children. Has anybody else been asked to report on people's opinions? Ban asked me this afternoon." Ban is their version of Erquist. According to Li his management style is based on appeals to pity. "When I refused he started crying."

146

"He asked me." Jorge looks dismayed. He probably thought he'd been singled out. "I thought it was easier to say yes and do nothing. There's no point upsetting him."

"I wasn't asked," Edda says. She turns to me. "So what happened when you were attacked?"

I give a brief account. Jorge is surprised by the machete. "And this was about your client? She's trouble." He laughs. "Maybe she did have something to do with the bar."

"The latest is my head of Safety thinks she might be an Anachronist."

"Please," Jorge says. "I know your lot have older clients, but how old is she? Aren't they extinct?"

Edda makes a point of asking me, "What's an Anachronist?"

"Idealists," Li says before I can answer.

"Idiots." Jorge is emphatic. "They didn't know where they were going or what they would do when they got there. And they all died. Apart from the one in California."

"They knew what they were doing," Li insists. "Did you read their manifesto?"

Nobody answers.

"I didn't think you had." Li is scornful. "They were concerned by the implications of travel. They thought that information brought back from the future would mean the end of freedom. That whoever controlled that information would have the perfect means of social control. They wouldn't even need it; they only had to claim they had it. They could make it up, and people would do what they were told. The Anachronists weren't playing a game. They didn't even call themselves Anachronists."

"You sound like a fan." Jorge is once again delighted. It's clear he thinks this is an easy target. "But they failed, didn't they? You can't just turn up in the 10th century and expect an audience with the Pope. It's a fundamental mistake."

"That's not what they were trying to do. People say it was all about Big History, saving a Kennedy, killing a Hitler. They knew that was impossible."

"So what were they trying to do?" Edda sounds as if she really wants to know.

"They wanted to see if they could be more than a passive observer of the past. They wanted to see if they could actually have influence."

"They didn't," Jorge says. "They couldn't. They died."

"True," Li says. "But we don't know how they died. How could we? They left no traces. It doesn't mean they failed. Most of the population of the world leaves no trace. We'll leave no trace."

Jorge glares. "I still think they're cranks."

Edda turns to Li. "You sound like you'd have joined them."

"I don't think I'd have had the nerve. When they left they knew they had no hope of coming back."

"Like Brink and Nakamura," I say.

"No. They were supposed to come back. If it hadn't been for Brink catching typhus they'd have made it to Siberia in time. Besides, I know you're a fan, Spens, but they were just passive observers. They made their recordings and were careful not to change anything."

"What could they have done?" Jorge says. "Given Beethoven a hearing aid?" He stands up. "Last bus. Li? Edda?"

Li accepts. For all their disagreements they're friends. When they're gone Edda complains about Jorge. "Typical Happiness with the clients. Then he tries to make himself interesting by arguing with everybody. At least you and Li have been other things." She isn't typical Happiness: her kin, she admits, are mostly Safety. Her eye modifications are not entirely cosmetic. She chose to be a rep because it was an easy way to travel. She wants to go to Africa. "It doesn't matter when. It's just easier to get there in the 21st." I ask why she wants to go. She says, "Aren't you curious?" and lists reasons: the history, the wildlife. "Megafauna, Spens. They're still alive, as we speak." She can almost make me feel her enthusiasm. And then she says, "I read about the 28 incident."

I assume this is an African thing and look blank.

She prompts. "That was the accident that killed your parents, wasn't it?"

I don't usually talk about my parents. It seems either presumptuous – other people's parents die – or manipulative. Why would I tell you unless I was trying to win your sympathy or claim some kind of exemption? Besides, showing too much interest in your kin is a Happiness trait and, despite my occupation and the people I work with, I'm not really Happiness. I was in the Tunnels, with everything that entailed – and that's something I don't talk about either, because you don't talk about the Tunnels with civilians. We didn't even discuss it among ourselves. We took tonin and stared at the ceiling or rambled on about what we'd rather be doing instead.

And I've never heard of the 28 incident. "It didn't happen in 28. In any 28."

"It's not the year. It's the number of the site where it happened," Edda says, as if it's common knowledge. "Just before I came out there was a scandal about a recovery team. There were radioactive elements in a cache. They hadn't been warned so they weren't wearing protective suits. The contamination wasn't even noticed until they reached a storage hub and the people there weren't protected either. They said it was the worst incident since the 28 site. I looked it up because I remembered the date. The 28 incident happened the year you were twelve. Wasn't that your age when your parents died?"

It would explain why their bodies were never brought back. Cantor had been intrigued by this. Something was being concealed: of course he was intrigued. "Does it say why we were burying radioactive elements in the first place?"

"No. The story was there only because some of the last team were able to contact their families. The authorities had to acknowledge something had happened, and that's when they mentioned the 28 incident."

I'm relieved Li isn't here for this: the way the authorities manage information is one of the things that makes her angry. They say nothing and then, suddenly, without announcement, the information is there, as if it had been available for years. "How much do they say about it?"

"They don't give details. Just that it happened and that it was bad. You didn't know?"

"I was told it was an accident. They didn't say what kind." I don't know what to make of this information. My parents died because somebody didn't make a proper inventory. It's bad, but people have died for worse reasons. "Where was site 28?" I don't know why I ask. It's not as if I can go there now and put up a warning sign. The materials might not yet be there. Geneva could still be trying to secure the land.

"On the main. They don't say exactly where. I'm sorry, I thought you knew."

"I'd have found out when I returned." By accident, probably. I wouldn't have been looking. There would be a reference in the Arc, with no indication it hadn't been there for years. Or I'd meet Cantor again and he'd tell me. *See? I was right all along.* I wondered how he'd get on with Li, and dismissed the thought. She'd probably think he was frivolous.

An hour passes. I ask how she'll get back to her resort. "I thought I'd walk you home," she says. "I want to see how people live outside. And you might be attacked again and need my help."

You're not Picon

There's the extemp who isn't Picon and, in the front, two locals. One drives while the other continually checks the mirrors. "You have something," the extemp says.

You don't trust him. It's the way he smiles. "You're not Picon Delrosso."

He keeps smiling. "Does that matter?"

You feel a jolt in your chest, a sense of the world sliding away from you. "I'm supposed to give it to Picon."

"He's not here. You give it to me."

"That's not the arrangement."

"There's been a change."

The extemp gives instructions to the locals. You've studied the language but he talks too quickly for you to understand. He shouts at them, then turns to you and smiles. "Picon is not who you think he is. How much is he paying you?"

You don't say anything. He's Number City, you decide, but not Safety. A criminal working with local criminals.

"So how does it work? Are you paid in advance? When you get back? What is his system?"

He keeps talking: "Or are you acting from pure altruism?" He sounds bitter. "Are you kin?"

You don't answer. If you'd been stopped by the authorities – a Safety, a local police – you'd know what to say: you are Adorna Mond, a tourist. You weren't told what to say to criminals. You wish you had a pin gun. Or a knife. They taught you how to use weapons, then told you not to carry one.

It must be part of the test.

The locals seem to be driving in circles. You begin to recognise the names of shops and the posters in windows. The streets are still crowded. You have already seen more people today than in the whole of your previous life and here are hundreds more. You remind yourself this is before the Collapse. There are billions of people alive in this era, millions of them on this island, at least a million in this city. At home the numbers had always sounded impossibly high. The superabundance of the mall begins to make sense, even if you can't think of the people as real. There are too many of them.

The driver stops. At first you think they've taken you back to the street where you climbed in. It's been a test after all, and you've passed: you didn't give up the box. Picon will appear and congratulate you, and then you'll be taken back to the resort. Instead they half push, half drag you towards a shop that, like the car, has tinted black windows. The locals don't look happy until the door is locked behind them. They hold your arms while the extemp pats your sides until he finds your phone and the box. He takes both. "Now, that was easy, wasn't it?" You expect him to ask you to open the box; instead he hands it to one of the locals, who leaves.

You're confused. He's Number City, but he doesn't recognise a Dolman box. Meanwhile, Picon will notice you've missed the rendezvous. All you have to do is wait. Or is this a test of initiative and the box is going to be given to Picon?

The remaining local keeps in the background. It's obvious he doesn't trust the extemp.

The extemp is old, soft. You wouldn't need a weapon against him. The local is younger, possibly dangerous. He leans against a wall by the window, sighs to show he's bored and keeps looking at you. You know the look.

"You haven't met Picon yet, have you?" The extemp keeps talking. He's trying to make you think he's on your side. "Have you seen where he lives? *How* he lives? You should. He lives easy. The longest T-break in history. Do I sound envious? It's because I am. Every few months another of you turns up with another delivery. How does he find you? Does he have a contact in Two West?"

You're not sure what to make of this. You thought the box contained instructions. How can they be valuable to criminals? You were told the last courier was over a year ago. Who are the others?

The extemp keeps talking. "And what was he at home? Some intermediate administrator. Facilitation, or whatever they call it." He complains about their castes: "If you're born into the wrong family . . . " Typical Number City, you think, rebelling by running away.

The local is getting impatient. His sighs are becoming louder. He's like a child who wants to join a game.

"Don't worry," the extemp says. "This will soon be over. As soon as we get the clear sky they'll let you go. They might even take you back to your resort."

There's a burst of noise: a bad recording of a man shouting over a kind of music. The local snatches something – it's a phone – from his pocket and the music stops. He holds it to the side of his head and growls. The extemp stops talking and watches him.

This would be a good time to run. The local is preoccupied; the extemp is weak. But you don't move. You need the box. You need to carry out your instructions.

The local and the extemp shout at each other. You can't understand everything they say but it's clear the extemp wants the box brought back and the local is adamant it can't be done. "I'll talk to him," the extemp says. "Face to face. I'll see him now." The local gestures at you. The extemp points at the back room. "It seems we have to keep you here for a little while longer," he tells you. "Trust me," the extemp tells the local. "Everything will be fine." The local looks disgusted and steps forward. Between them they push you into a back room. You don't resist. You've been locked in smaller rooms before. It's almost a relief.

They don't tie you up. They're fools.

Within seconds of the door closing you find the switch for the light. You're in a storeroom, with cardboard boxes stacked on metal shelves. A wooden door with a single, antique lock, no window. You make an inventory, looking for anything you can use.

The boxes contain small squares of yellow paper, ring-binders and things called staplers. Half of the boxes are empty.

The shelves are held in place by metal uprights. You clear boxes from one shelf and start loosening the nuts. The first bolt comes away easily. After half an hour you've removed the upright, a narrow metal stick. You swing it like a baton. You can imagine whipping it into the face of one of the extemp's locals – or the extemp himself. It's a gratifying image.

You start working on the lock.

It takes longer than you'd think, but it works. The lock

gives; the door opens. The local is leaning against the wall and looking at something on his phone. He opens his mouth when he sees you and pulls the white plugs from his ears. You run at him and slash down with the upright. You are fast, efficient, angry. Because of him you have missed your rendezvous with Picon. Because of him you have failed. On the third blow he drops to the floor; on the seventh he stops trying to get up. The sense of triumph doesn't last. Within seconds you realise you've made a mistake: you should have left him conscious enough to answer questions. Now you have no way of finding the box ... You go through his pockets: a leather wallet, a phone, some keys. No weapons. They left an unarmed man to guard you. They were fools. They deserve this. You take his phone: you can use it to call Picon. The screen has a clock. You watch the seconds flick past while your breathing returns to normal. The man on the floor groans; there's a splash of blood on your sleeve. You can't make the call: you walked into a trap, lost what you were supposed to deliver and now you might have made things worse. You feel numb, frozen, uncertain what to do next. *Think, girl.* The clock turns to 4.00 and the phone chirps. Two words appear on the screen: Karia answer. Picon, you think. You wonder how he knows your real name. The music blares out again and you answer. It's a woman's voice. You recognise the familiar accent of home. "Karia," she says. "Listen carefully."

Geneva is very deep

We're woken by the call to prayer from the temple on the high street. Edda is impressed until I tell her it's a recording. They don't actually have a local man of proven virtue ringing the bells at set times each day, just the same recording that's played in half the other temples in the country. "And the other half?" she asks. The cathedrals have real bells, I tell her, and some of the smaller rural temples, but most use recordings. It's typical of the 21st. People spend their evenings looking at images of other people's lives and their calls to spiritual duty are automated. She finds this amusing.

She turns on the television, another period detail. There's nothing about Bar Five on the morning news. I suspect pressure has been exerted. Or shops and bars burn down so regularly they're not considered worth reporting. Their news, after all, isn't about what happens every day; the stories are chosen because they're untypical. DomeWatch already has a new lead story: "Schoolgirl Brides of Future Perverts". The headline is misleading: apparently a native magazine asked some teenage girls if they would consider marrying one of us and several of them thought they might. "Living there has got to be better than this dump." The DomeWatch writer is agitated by this and blames "propaganda". I'm relieved: the future perverts have displaced the future fanatics if only for a few hours.

I accompany Edda to the station where she catches the mini-bus for Resort Six. I notice a member of their Safety Team waiting with the reps. She's not as blatantly militarised as Hayek: she looks like a maintenance tech with a utility belt. It's likely some of her tools are in breach of protocol. Edda thinks she's there to reassure the clients. We don't see any trouble on the way there.

My resort bus doesn't have an escort, but then Tri-Millennium's clients are expected to stay at the resort. The bus is for the reps. We're not supposed to need reassurance.

There are no more Safeties than usual at the gates. As soon as I pass the last one I'm bipped about a meeting in Small Hall Two. It's reps only; resort staff aren't included. The rumour, which people are quick to share, is that excursions will be suspended, that we'll be obliged to stay in quarters until we know what's happening.

Small Hall Two is for minority interests – meditation, dance classes – and it's just big enough to hold the forty-two reps Tri-Millennium employs. There's a raised platform at one end where a class leader would stand. Erquist and Hayek are already there. It's the first time I've seen either of them out of their offices, and the first time I've seen Hayek out of his chair. He's shorter than I expected: barely two metres, shorter than Erquist, though broader and probably about three times heavier. He nods at me as if I'm a valued colleague. I feel shamefully flattered.

Once Hayek has finished scanning everyone (I assume that's

what he's doing) he nods at Erquist, who steps forward. Erquist has a clear, comforting voice. A lot of Happiness people train as actors.

"Many of you will have heard about the incident at Bar Five last night. I've never been there in person but I know it was a popular destination for reps. The good news is that apart from the proprietor, two of his staff and a few native customers, nobody was hurt. You may also have heard of the incident at Resort Three. Once again, apart from the driver of the vehicle involved, I am pleased to report there were no casualties. As far as we are aware the two events are unrelated. Some of you, I'm sure, will be wondering why we did not have these events on record. The fact is that the only records we have are the ones that our Central Office considers relevant." Beside him, Hayek shakes his head slowly, as if the paucity of records is a cause for personal sadness. "In turn, they only have the records that have been released to them by the authorities. We are in touch with Geneva" – Erquist glances at Hayek, who lowers his head with a ponderous humility – "to determine whether we can expect any future incidents of a similar nature. Until we receive an answer all we can do is deal with events as they arise and try not to exaggerate their importance. Above all, we must remember the Tri-Millennium code of conduct." He pauses, gives a rueful little smile. "In the meantime, after consultation with our Safety Team" – another nod from Hayek – "we propose the following courses of action. All excursions are to continue as planned. However, in addition to the assigned rep, they are now to be accompanied by at least one additional rep with suitable training. That includes any form of service, whether Foraging Units or Tunnel Clearance. It will mean changes to the staff rosters, but there are enough of you with the appropriate background to make this possible."

As far as I know I'm the only rep who worked the Tunnels. I didn't know there were any from the Dangerous Berry Squad, though; as an old Mole, I can see why they might have kept quiet. "In addition," Erquist continues, "because some of you may have concerns for your personal safety we will make quarters available within the resort for anybody currently living outside who feels they might be at risk. Those of you who wish to take advantage of this, please talk to your section chief."

There's a general murmur of approval. Erquist raises his hand. "I understand many of you will still have questions. But the two measures we have proposed should enable us to keep this resort running in accordance with our principles. Remember, this is all about client satisfaction *and* client safety. A safe experience of the 21st. That applies to employees as well, to *all* of us." The murmuring hasn't stopped; his audience's attention is slipping. "One more thing," he says louder, his pitch less secure, "these are interim measures subject to change if there are further developments. We will, of course, keep you informed." He steps back, shrugs at Hayek. The once evenly spaced reps are beginning to coalesce around their section chiefs. I stay where I am. I've been reporting directly to Erquist ever since our client disappeared. Besides, I don't want to move into quarters. I like my flat, even if Justin Bayer lives a few streets away. Erquist steps down from the stage and indicates I should follow him.

There's a space behind Small Hall Two, a dressing room of sorts. Chairs, tables around the walls, mirrors. One of the rooms in the resort I've never seen before.

Hayek lumbers away. Nobody tries to talk to him.

Erquist closes the door. "How do you think that went?" This isn't politeness. He really wants to know. "I've never been very good with crowds."

"I thought it went very well."

"I did wonder if I wasn't coming across as too authoritarian."

"No. Relaxed."

"It's kind of you to say. But how are you? I heard you were at Bar Five last night."

"I saw the aftermath."

"Terrible. But no further incidents?"

"Not so far."

"Good. That's good." He looks, by his standards, sombre. "As you've probably guessed, Geneva haven't been exactly forthcoming. There's also no new information on our client, though Hayek is still analysing exactly what happened at the airport. He's trying to backtrack through the records but it seems there are technical difficulties. However, if it does turn out that our client is in breach of protocol she will face appropriate charges on her return." He gives a rueful half-smile. Actions committed in the past are classic legal problems. "That is, if there *are* any appropriate charges. One thing Geneva has asked" – he's sombre again – "is to report on the mood among the reps and clients. What do people think, what are they saying, that sort of thing. They think it's important we don't indulge in too much speculation. It could harm morale." He looks at me hopefully. Li and Jorge were asked yesterday. It's another sign of Tri-Millennium's low status.

"So far, the people I've spoken to have been confused." I'm not going to name names. "Geneva could end speculation by telling us what they know."

"Well, quite, exactly. But obviously there are issues with the kind of information they feel they can release. Now this needn't have any sinister implications. It might just mean they have no useful information and feel embarrassed about admitting it. It was a native bar after all, and there was no harm to any clients or reps. But they are concerned about rumours circulating and feel they can best counteract these if they know what kind of rumours are circulating." He pauses. "And who is responsible for circulating them."

"Don't they monitor this anyway?"

"Apparently they don't. Or they want us to think they don't. Geneva is very deep."

I don't say anything. Apart from fascinating Li, what Geneva knows or doesn't know is the stuff of all those entertainments about heroic individuals confronting faceless omniscience. I used to be surprised the authorities allowed them: it was as if they relished being shown in a poor light. Cantor thought I was naïve. The authorities are never shown as evil or incompetent, just occasionally overzealous. The conflict usually turns out to be a misunderstanding and any mistakes are corrected. All of them, he used to say, were made with a purpose. His idea of what the purpose might be changed from week to week.

Erquist leaves. I remain in the room, alone. Edda sends a message that she's confined to her resort for the next few days but I can visit her there if I'm able to leave mine. I check the roster. I've been rescheduled to accompany an excursion to a Scene of Natural Beauty. It's supposed to be uneventful. I stop at the staff mess. A few reps are there, engaged in the kind of speculation I'm supposed to report to Erquist. As I eat I get another message from Hayek. "I see you've got an excursion planned. Meet me in my office when you get back. *If* you get back." I'm now an unofficial Safety Team member. Is this how the recruitment works? First they make you feel like an insider, and then the requests for favours begin. Before you know it you're wearing their uniform and reporting to their bosses.

The only advantage is it might give me more freedom

outside the resort. It might get me out of accompanying excursions. Or it leads to the breach of protocol that gets me sent home.

Or I refuse, and that's the breach.

The excursion is a tour of the Pennines. The scenic tours aren't the most popular with our clients, most of whom are older generation and uncomfortable in the open air. However, when I reach the vehicle zone there's twelve of them waiting, a respectable number. I check the list carefully, which annoys Olav, the rep who was supposed to take the tour alone. He'd already checked the list: "You really don't have to do anything on this one. Just stay at the back and be reassuring." I do as he says. We drive out to the Scene of Natural Beauty, our clients walk around for as long as they dare, we drive back. There are no unrelated incidents: nobody goes missing; it doesn't even rain. Our clients return to their quarters to write sonnets expressing their disappointment and I go to Hayek's office. "Tunnel Boy," he says before the door has closed behind me. "I've been reviewing the incident at the airport. The cause of death is officially a heart attack. Apparently this is not inconsistent with Dr Metzger's age and medical history. There is no indication of any external influence." He dismisses the file with a gesture. "But what do they know? There are at least two methods our client could have used to achieve that effect. One would not have worked at that range. The other would have worked but would have also affected bystanders. We can conclude that our client's intentions did not include killing Dr Metzger. I am currently investigating another possibility. There's no need to involve you with that for the moment." He gazes at me with benign menace. I wonder if he's also had dramatic training. "I have had one small piece of information. The client's card reports from your excursion have come through. Our girl bought something at a shop that sells their phones."

"Can we trace the phone?"

"You follow too many entertainments. All I know so far is how much she paid for it. But it does suggest she intended to contact somebody already here. Which means she probably chose to leave."

"She could have been acting under duress."

"She didn't appear to be at the airport. For now, even if she is following her own whims, this doesn't mean I'm happy. She might not be murdering people but she seems to be doing more than carrying tonin for extemps. Which means she could be putting herself at risk. Our duty is to protect our clients, even the reckless ones."

"I was told she wasn't in danger."

"By your mysterious stranger. Did he tell you who he was working for? Did he give you a reason? Have you seen him since? Do you really think I'm going to put my faith in that?"

He has a point. "What about Geneva?" If I'm working for Hayek he might as well keep me up to date. "Have they said anything?"

He's guarded. "They have not said *nothing.*"

"And the Anachronists?"

"A dead end. As dead as Dr Metzger."

"The kin?"

"Not relevant. Everything she's done here seems to be a complete break with her previous behaviour. We need, as I said, to find out what she's doing. If I arrange for you to be exempt from your usual duties, will you help?"

"Do I have a choice?"

"We can always find more excursions for you to accompany.

You complain, Tunnel Boy, but isn't this more fun than work? Start with Delrosso. He lied to you last time and there's something odd about his history as well. He doesn't fit the extemp pattern. His decision to move here was described as *sudden and uncharacteristic.* You might find you have to talk to his local contacts."

"Like Gurley and Knight?"

"I'm sure you can find others."

"They might not talk to me."

"Aren't you a friend of Li Tran? She's known to have nativist sympathies. She might also be more alert to the nuances. They might talk to her. And see if you can ask the right questions this time."

There's another message from Edda. If I want to meet later she'll be in Entertainment Area Three in Resort Six. She's left my name with their Safety Team: I can use their resort bus. I reply that I'll try. There are things I need to do first.

I consult the Arc about the 28 incident. It's exactly as Edda said: a reference in a story about a more recent disaster ("the worst event of its kind since . . . ") and no details beyond the year. But it's the right year.

I still don't know what to make of it. Information can change our understanding of what's happened or confirm what we already knew. This feels like a confirmation. It tells me that a mistake was made and the authorities kept quiet about it for as long as they could. And they're still keeping quiet: the item doesn't list the victims or apportion blame or explain how the contamination occurred. Why did we store radioactive waste in the first place? We don't need it, we can't reprocess it; the only use we'd have for it would be to make what this era calls "dirty bombs" – fantasy weapons effective for spreading fear but useless if you're trying to reclaim land or build anything. I knew my parents died in an accident, and now, thanks to Edda, I have a slightly better idea of what kind. But that's all. I go back to my apartment.

One of their more serious newspaper sites has an obituary for Dr Alexander Metzger, "Scholar, Poet and Dog-Lover". His early work on 5th-century lyric fragments is described as "useful", and his short book on Parthenius "exhaustive". The German–Hellenic Society was (I learn) originally founded by three admirers of Hölderlin and only became political around the 20s of the previous century – their politics was mostly about refusing membership to Jews. Thereafter it stayed in a bubble, an odd survival with about a dozen members until the start of the 21st, when a charismatic new leader started forging ties with more directly political groups in Germany and Greece, cranks with a few dangerous friends. According to the obituary, it's likely Metzger was a naïf who hadn't understood the nature of the politics: there was no public history of any previous involvement. His death came just days before questions were to be asked at his university.

Another dead end.

I bip Li and tell her about Hayek's orders. Does she want to help?

She sounds surprised. "You've agreed to this?"

"I don't have a choice."

"You always have a choice. You could say no. You *should* say no. It might be the thing that gets you sent home. She's not your concern, Spens. If your Safety Chief thinks there's a problem he should send out a team. Haven't you done enough already?"

"He doesn't want to involve a Safety Team."

"He doesn't have to send you. I'll help, but only because it gets me out of dealing with people like the Shins. What's the plan?"

I tell her about Picon Delrosso. "And then we'll see if we can find Ivan."

I watch a news broadcast. It follows its usual pattern: war, crime, disaster, crime, war, disaster; an endless litany of what is wrong in some parts of the world, presented with very little background and abandoned as soon as the next story comes along. There are pictures of flooded streets followed by an interview with a politician who describes the March for Humanity as a dangerous provocation. He doesn't say who would be provoked and the interviewer doesn't ask. It seems designed to induce a feeling of helpless rage, while leaving you with no clear idea what is actually happening.

Picon answers his own front door. "You again." He tries to give the impression I've interrupted important business, and fails because he's wearing a kimono and no trousers. "What do you want?"

"To ask more questions."

He seems to notice Li for the first time. "I suppose you're a rep as well?" His tone makes it clear he doesn't believe either of us is a rep. "You'd better come in."

He leads us to the big room at the back with a view of the garden. There's no music playing this time and the screen on the wall is blank, a dark mirror. A native woman sits on one of the sofas staring at a slate. I can't tell if she's one of the women who was here before. She glances up at us and then looks back at her slate. She seems used to Picon having visitors.

Picon takes his place on the sofa next to his collection of phones and controls. "You had questions."

"Regarding my client," I say.

"You haven't found her yet? I've given up."

"So she hasn't been in touch?"

"Since yesterday? No. She hasn't called. She hasn't turned up at my door to apologise. Like I said, I've given up. She's your client, after all. She was never my responsibility."

Li sits next to the woman and says something I don't catch. The woman is surprised, as if she's not used to Picon's guests talking to her. This makes Picon uncomfortable. "We may need to talk to your friends," I say. "They may know something about our client."

"They wouldn't talk to you."

"Why not?"

Li and the woman have started a whispered conversation. He watches Li carefully. I wonder if he's trying to lip-read. "Because they don't like dealing with the authorities."

"Because they're criminals."

"That's going too far. We may be marginal people here but we're not that marginal. We can't afford to break the law."

"So how does it work? How do you pay your couriers?"

"I don't." He's casual. "About a year ago I had a visitor, a work colleague. She was fed up with her position and wanted to start a new life. She decided that one day she'd like to live here. So we came to an agreement. She finds people who are prepared to carry tonin and pays for their time here. And every time I receive a delivery I put some credit aside for her. It's like any other banking system: two sets of ledgers and trust. When she's able to leave she'll have enough to be comfortable here."

"Like you."

"Exactly."

"Won't Geneva give her credit?"

"Not enough to live on. Not comfortably. Does that answer your question?"

Li and the woman are still talking. Li asks long questions; the woman gives short answers. She laughs at one of Li's remarks. Picon tries to maintain his relaxed/bored posture but the tension is obvious.

"Can I ask why you became an extemp?"

The question surprises him. He opens his mouth but it's several seconds before he can speak. "The usual reason." He tries to sound casual. "Freedom. We might complain about all the prohibitions and the protocols we have here, but they're nothing compared to where I lived before. Every aspect of life was monitored, controlled. You're younger. You can't imagine what that kind of society was like. Everything was a test, and everything was set up so you would fail." He warms to the subject, as if he's only just realised how much he wanted to talk about this. He even forgets the other conversation in the room. "Everything we're told is a half-truth. You've realised that, haven't you? One of the tests is how well you can pretend to believe in it. The pretence all the time, the acting – it was exhausting. I played the part for as long as I could and as soon as I saw a chance to escape I came here. It was like being reborn. I wouldn't want to endanger that."

The woman stares at him, speechless. I wonder if it's because she understands Modern or she's just not used to hearing him speak.

"I see," I say. "Do you know a local called Alexander Metzger?"

He slumps back against the sofa. "No. What is he?"

"An academic. Greek lyric poetry."

"Not my scene."

"An organisation called the EPP?"

"I've heard of them. Politics. They're the sort of people who

171

think DomeWatch is too accommodating. The fringe of the fringe. Do you think your client's involved with them?"

"I just wanted your perspective."

"Glad to be of help. Any other irrelevant questions you'd like to ask?"

"Just one. Do you know an extemp called Ivan Ho?"

"I used to." Picon grimaces. "We had a disagreement."

"What about?"

"He denied he'd stolen money from me." Picon relaxes: Ivan is a safe subject. We're not asking him to blab about a friend. "Cash, some local currency I was holding. I wouldn't waste time talking to him. He's a liar, a fantasist." Meaning: don't believe anything he tells you about *me*.

"Do you know where we might find him?"

"Not around here." He smiles. "Stand in the street and whisper tonin three times. That should make him appear. There's a native pub you can try. He used to go there a lot, I remember. Or he used to talk about it a lot. Is there anything else you want to ask? Because I am expecting guests."

Out on the street Li says, "That wasn't quite what I expected."

"Did the woman tell you anything?"

"She's taken tonin, but didn't know about anything else. She hasn't been there long. She said I should ask the other girls. All she knows is that he lets them sit around in his big house and take tonin. He doesn't talk to them much. She thought he thought they were stupid."

"What did you think?"

"I felt like contacting DomeWatch. Did you notice his accent? When he did his big speech it changed. I've heard the accent before. When I was growing up some refugees were settled in my quarter. Unskilled workers, so of course they sent them to Three North. They learned the language quickly enough but there was always still a trace. You don't forget it. I think he's from City Two East."

"Really?" Depending on who you ask City Two East is either a joke or a threat. It's closed, uncooperative and one of the reasons I had military training. "Two East doesn't have extemps. They don't travel. According to his records he's from One West."

"Did he sound like he was describing One West to you? And he had the accent. It was faint, but it was there."

"Maybe he was one of those refugees."

"Refugees didn't become regional resource manager. Not in his generation. And they don't have names like Delrosso."

"He could have changed his name. Worked his way up." We head for the taxi rank. I wait for Hayek to tell me I've asked all the wrong questions but he's silent. Perhaps I'm doing something right.

Edge of the territory

You're suddenly awake. "How long was I asleep?"

Riemann turns away. He was watching you. "Three hours."

"And you never sleep?"

He shakes his head, looks pleased with himself. He's young, of course. You remember how it felt: it felt like nothing. You wonder how he occupies himself on this journey. Perhaps he listens to music or one of those interminable dramas they seem to like. When you broke out of the room the local had been listening to music; that's why you were able to hurt him. Riemann seems too careful for those distractions.

"We'll be at the perimeter soon," he says.

"Already?"

"Yesterday you complained about how long it was taking." He looks at you with something like concern. "Are you sure you'll still know your way around?"

"I'm sure."

He looks doubtful.

*

175

When you reach the perimeter you're allowed to walk in the open. It's because there's nothing to see except low clouds moving slowly in the direction you came. The land ahead is flat.

Riemann leaves you to wait outside the vehicle while he makes arrangements for the last stretch of the journey. Or has the arrangements explained to him. He looks anxious, as if expecting a reprimand. When he walks away there's an exaggerated swing to his step you recognise as bravado.

You feel sorry for him.

You're at the edge of Number City territory. As a child you'd imagined there would be fortifications, a wall of some kind. When they talked about the Number Cities spreading you pictured a wall moving outwards, crushing everything in its path. Instead there are only the remains of a road and a few concrete blocks with weeds sprouting between them. The rest is scrubland, wild grass, dust and dirt. A few people walk from one building to another. They're wearing uniforms rather than protective suits. They ignore you.

Before he left Riemann said, "This is your chance to run." He knows you won't. You're still half a day's drive from home. No food, no tools, no shelter if it rains. You walked home once but that was a long time ago and you carried a week's provisions and a tent. Lately your only exercise has been to walk twice a day from your cell to Room Two. It isn't enough preparation. Even looking at the flat road to the horizon makes you feel weak.

And you begin to feel apprehensive about what you might find. Every time he asks you assure him you haven't forgotten. How could you? But each time you try to remember, say, the route from the home to the school you have the sense you've missed something – a stretch of road, a building. You tell yourself you'll recognise everything when you see it but what if you don't? Home will have changed when the bombs fell, if they'd used bombs – you were already in captivity when it happened and were never given details. They used euphemisms, like all cowards. *The action has been taken; the area has been cleared.* You knew what they meant by clearance. As a girl you were shown the pictures: charred bodies stacked on open ground, corpses dragged from crude underground shelters. Clearance meant murder, Burn everything and hide the evidence. You were raised on stories of atrocities. Even now, you can feel an echo of the anger you felt as a child. You shouldn't feel sorry for Riemann. He isn't on your side.

He returns alone. "They've found us a vehicle. The medical team arrive tomorrow. They'll wait here until they receive our signal." He looks tired, as if the meeting hadn't gone as he expected. "The sooner we leave," he says. He leads you to what looks like a smaller, dustier version of the vehicle you came in. A solar: it won't be fast, but it's sturdy. You'll search during the day, sleep in the vehicle at night. It will shield you from some of the damage. He opens the back to show you how it's divided into two compartments, one for supplies, and an inner one just large enough for a cot. "That's where you'll sleep." Another cell. He'll sleep in the cabin. You've been given protective suits in case the levels are dangerous but won't have to put them on for another fifty miles, if at all. As long as you stay in the open for less than an hour at a time you'll be safe. "We leave immediately."

"You know the direction?"

"We follow the road. What's left of it."

You climb into the cabin beside him. The landscape doesn't change as the solar rolls east. After twenty minutes you fall asleep. When you wake up the landscape is still flat and unfamiliar. You close your eyes: perhaps when you open them you'll find this is a dream and you'll be back in the prison. You try to think of the cell and the image that comes is the safe house where you were sent after escaping from the shop. It puzzles you why you can picture this so clearly when you were there for only a few days – three or four; the exact number has gone. You remember the disposition of the rooms and the views from the windows. Three or four days, out of how many years? You try counting them up: your life started when you were brought to Kat. The time before that is lost. Ten years in Kat, five in Spad; two weeks in the 21st; everything that's happened since, up to Riemann's arrival at your prison. You add it up and somehow you seem to have missed at least a decade.

You open your eyes. You're driving along a straight, uneven road through a grassy plain. Riemann glances at you. Once again he looks concerned. You grope for a question to show you are in control. "These people you're looking for, are they worth all this trouble?" It's a question that's been nagging you. Riemann doesn't answer.

Traditional native

The pub where Picon thinks we'll find Ivan is in a commercial area built around the middle of the last century, a precursor to their malls. The shops are closed but the street is still busy with natives, most of them young and already drunk, circulating around the dozen or so bars that are dark and raucous, as if, Li says, they can't bear to look at or listen to each other. Ivan's pub is traditional native: cluttered, uncomfortable, not quite as loud and selling drinks for which I may never acquire a taste. Ivan isn't there. Li buys a pint of one of the drinks. "Try it," she says. "You'll have worse in the early 19th." Everybody else in the pub is native. We attract the usual covert attention. "So," she asks, "how do you feel about playing *detective*?"

She uses the old word from this era's entertainments. "It's what Hayek wants." I've told her about Hayek. Her resort has an equivalent. Oberon Petkov. Stays in his inner office, is rumoured to have had his entire alimentary tract replaced and to need no sleep. She's never seen him. "How do you feel about playing *sidekick*?"

"It's better than dealing with the Shins. So you're Safety now? Is this what you want to do?"

"It's an unofficial secondment." I'd had one before, in the Tunnels, when supplies went missing. We were too far out for proper investigators to travel and, as the chief said when he assigned me, *At least you can write a report.* The people who worked the Tunnels were not sophisticated criminals. All I had to do was ask the obvious suspects, "Was it you?" until one of them said, "Yes." It was the easiest promotion I ever earned. "Whatever she's doing, she is my client."

"That's a careful answer. And you think Ivan will tell you anything? What happened to the Anachronist connection?"

"Ruled out."

"Shame. That might have made it interesting. You know, don't you, that Ivan is going to lie."

"He'll let something slip."

"Because you're an experienced interrogator? You're going to read between the lines? You should have brought Edda. I bet she's had training. I bet she was top of her class—" She stops abruptly. "Here comes somebody."

It's a native. He's wearing a jacket that looks like one of our cast-offs from a few years ago, a real one, not a Domehead imitation. The fibres are starting to lose their lustre: the yellows have gone and the tonal range is a shifting blue-grey. It's too big for him, but he's rolled up the sleeves and wears it as a three-quarter-length coat. I'd say he was about fifty, but it's hard to tell with natives. He could be thirty. He could be nineteen. He's dark and has very black hair which he's brushed so it stands straight up. He pulls a chair from the next table and joins us. There's a swagger about the way he does it. "We don't see many of you here." His Modern is passable. "Are you friends of Ivan?"

Li answers in This English. "We thought he might be here."

"He might be along later." Natives look at us and see money. Already I can see this one asking himself: *What can I make out of this?* "Yes, Ivan comes here a lot. He says we're helpful here. Very helpful."

"Really."

"Yes. We don't see many people like you. Mind you, we had one the other day. She was asking about Ivan."

He stops there. I can see his ploy. He establishes he's of value then waits for one of us to make an offer.

Li doesn't have the patience. "Another friend of his?"

"Depends on what you mean by a friend."

"Did you know her?"

"Never seen her before." He addresses Li. He hasn't heard me speak yet. It's possible he thinks I wouldn't understand. "But then I've never seen you before."

Li is cool. "Ivan knows us."

"He likes to be careful."

"I'm sure he'd talk to us. Why don't you ask him? Tell him it's Li Tran."

"I'll see." He walks out of the pub. Either Ivan is waiting outside or the local doesn't want to make the call in our presence.

Li watches the door. "People looking for Ivan? Is that likely?"

"It might happen. He must have some friends."

"Not in this era. People don't look for Ivan. He looks for them."

The man re-enters. "Left him a message." He sits down, and waits with the air of someone expecting payment.

"So," Li says more casually than I could manage, "the one who was looking for Ivan, did she find him?"

"Not that I saw."

"Did you tell her anything?"

"Didn't get a chance. She looked around, asked a few questions and left."

"Could you describe her?"

He stares straight at Li. "She looked like you."

Not helpful. "Is that all you can tell us?"

"She might have been a bit younger." He turns out his palms. "And a bit taller. But that's all. Apart from that, she was like you."

I take out my handheld and show him the client's image. "Was this her?"

The man stares. "It might be."

"You're not sure?"

"No. But it might be."

"You mean," Li says, "we all look the same."

"I didn't say that."

"Thanks," Li says. We're not going to get any more out of him. "Get you a drink?"

The man accepts glumly. Li takes him to the bar where he chooses a triple measure of the most expensive whisky on display. She pays in cash. He mumbles his thanks and drinks it alone, at another table without looking at us. First he sips it, as if he wants to make it last, then he seems to change his mind, gulps it down and leaves. The other customers manage to not quite ignore us. Perhaps they're waiting to see who'll talk to us next.

"A person," Li says, "looking like me. Or your client. You should have shown him a picture of Edda to see if he could tell the difference."

"I don't have one. Besides, whoever was looking for him was an extemp. A civilian. If they were official they'd have tracked Ivan's signature. They wouldn't be asking around in places like this."

Li frowns. "So this extemp is what? Your client's contact?"

"No idea. It might have been the client herself. Ivan might be involved with whatever she's doing. He must do something when he's not bothering reps."

Ivan walks in. He notices us immediately, and looks carefully at the rest of the pub. His expression is serious, as it was on the night of the Bar Five fire. I've seen him intent, when he thinks there's tonin to be had, and I'm familiar with his usual bonhomie, his glad-handing, back-slapping, effortful impression of cheerfulness. I've never seen him like this. In the second or so it takes him to peer round the room he's almost thoughtful. Then, abruptly, the mask is back on, and he rolls towards us with his dancing walk, arms swinging just enough to suggest high spirits. His sleeves, I notice with relief, are rolled down.

"This is rare." He sits in the same chair as the native who called him, who, I now realise, must have been wearing one of Ivan's old jackets from home, probably what he wore for the translation. Ivan's clothes are native now: a dull burgundy jacket over a checked blue shirt. His skin is lightly tanned. Seated, with his arms out of sight, you could almost mistake him for a local. "What brings you to the anterior?"

Li responds. "What brought you here?"

"I just found I was happier here, you know?" He holds out his hands in an expansive gesture. "It's my kind of period." He grins. "Why the interest in me?" The grin broadens. "Are you still trying to find your runaway?"

I answer: "We're interested in the people she's talking to."

"She's quite a personality." Ivan looks around the room again. "I'm a fan."

"You've met her?"

"You don't need to meet someone to recognise their quality."

183

"Do you know anybody who has met her? Do you know Picon Delrosso?"

"Picon?" He looks sly, and suddenly very old. It's the exposure to sunlight. Ivan is ageing at the same rate as the natives. "I know a thing or two about Facilitator Delrosso."

"Such as?"

"It all comes down to tonin."

"It always does," Li says. "With you."

"Not in the way you might think. I going to make a confession to you. I'm not a heavy user."

"Is that why you're always asking for it? Come on, Ivan, you're notorious."

"See? You've misunderstood. I ask for it because it's my only source of income."

"Don't you get credit from Geneva?"

"I left too soon for that arrangement. And there were special circumstances." Typical Ivan: dark hints, not much information, almost certainly bogus. "I used to scrape it from reps and sell it to fellow members of the extemp community."

"Not locals?"

"I still have some principles. I could have made more, true, but my needs are simple. A lot simpler than Facilitator Delrosso's. Have you seen how he lives?"

"We've seen," Li says.

"You've seen only the surface. About a year ago Facilitator Delrosso started receiving a direct supply." He grins at me. "Every month or so, another one of your clients. I don't know how he arranges it. I suspect he has a contact in Two West. You might want to look into that when you go home. But your clients come here and they know how to find him—"

I interrupt him. "We know this part."

"But do you know the full story? He probably told you he gives the stuff away."

"A favour for a favour."

"So he's still making the speech." He nods, looks around the pub again, is content nothing has changed. "If people can get it for nothing from him then they're not going to buy from me. Suddenly I have no money. How am I supposed to live? Meanwhile, Facilitator Delrosso hasn't just destroyed my livelihood, he is selling to locals."

"So he's not just giving it to his women?"

"You didn't know?" Ivan overplays the surprise. "The locals – some of them – have started using it. It's probably not on your Archive because the people selling it are careful. You see, tonin isn't a street drug. It's sold to a very particular social segment. High-status, well-connected. Of course, they call it something else and don't know where it comes from. Well, it comes from Facilitator Delrosso. He sells it to local distributors, and they tell their customers it's a local thing that's still being tested. That way if they blab about it you don't get to hear. It avoids complications."

"How do you know this?"

"What can I say?" He shows his teeth. "I've been here for a while. People trust me. I hear things." For a second or two he smiles happily, as if accepting silent applause.

"And my client was a courier."

"That's what everybody thought. Another tourist after a free holiday, doing something a little bit daring but not illegal. They deliver to Facilitator Delrosso and he sells it for local money to his contacts, and they sell it for even more to theirs. It was good business. Until the money attracted some other people."

Like Gurley and Knight. "How did they find out?"

He shrugs. "Don't know. Probably through one of Picon's contacts. The people he sells to, they manage the distribution. They're breaking the law, but then they're people who break the law for a living. Naturally they know other people who also break the law. Somebody must have talked. And that's where I became involved." Another tease.

"Ivan," Li says in This English. "Stop pissing around and tell us what happened." She sounds like she's ready to get up and walk away.

Ivan grins to show he's not offended. He'd sooner be insulted than ignored. "This group" – he pauses, searching for the right word – "decided to *intercept* your client before she could make her delivery. They knew she would be in a certain place so they made sure they got there first."

"How did they know?"

"Easy. Picon's women. He thinks they're stupid. And, between us, most of them are. But one of them understood Modern. They paid her to listen to his calls. She heard Facilitator Delrosso talking to your client and it sounded like there was a delivery on the way. She sent them a message about it while he was in the room. He never noticed. They worked out the courier was on a Tri-Millennium mall excursion with an accident on the way back. They knew the route and the approximate time. All they had to do was get there first, and wait."

"How did they know about the route?"

"That's why they involved me." Ivan looks – it's hard to say what his expression is: smug but nervous, pleased with himself but ashamed. I'm glad his forearms are covered: those snakes would be a distraction. "I know a lot of reps. It's not hard to get schedules of planned excursions. They knew the courier had been told to get off where the accident would be. They wanted me to tell them the spot. You know what they're like:

they think we know everything. I told them that accidents don't just happen. Somebody has to go out and make them happen, and they should pick the spot that suited them. That's why they used two cars: one to stop your coach; one to take her away. It should have been simple. Have her hand over the tonin, and put her back on the coach thinking she'd made the delivery. The tonin would have been in London before Facilitator Delrosso knew what had happened. And this is where it gets interesting."

"Finally," Li says.

Ivan smirks as if she's kissed him. He leans across the table and, even though he's speaking Modern, lowers his voice. "You ought to know your client isn't just a tourist. She's something else."

"Just tell the story, Ivan."

"She wouldn't cooperate. Kept saying she could only deliver to Picon. Very stubborn. They had to take the delivery off her. And then there was another problem."

"You're spinning this out."

"It was complicated." Ivan shows a flash of irritation. "I'm just trying to make you see. Firstly, they can't let her go in case she contacts a Safety Team. And then there's a problem with a box."

"You mean like a Dolman box?"

"Exactly. Whatever that is. The point is, they locked her in a room—"

"And she escaped." Li is deadpan. "And now she's missing."

Ivan glares at her. "Yes." He rallies. "But before she escaped she beat up the local who was supposed to be guarding her. Badly."

"How badly?" I remember the newspaper fragment. The first casualty in a vicious struggle for territory. "Did he die?"

187

"Does it matter? The point is, she did it as if she knew what she was doing. Like she had training. She escapes from a locked room, beats him up and disappears. And she's still missing, isn't she? You wouldn't be here if she was back at the resort. Does that sound like an ordinary tourist? These locals are after her because they need her to open the box. If they find her, they'll make her open it. But she's gone, vanished. So she either knows where to go or has somebody helping. And that's not like a tourist."

"Maybe Picon helped her," I say. He'd claimed to have contacts. His version of events seemed to fit with Ivan's. "If this story is true."

"It's true. I was there, in the car when they picked her up. They needed a translator."

"You agreed to it?" Li has a low opinion of Ivan but this surprises her. "You needed money so badly?"

"I wasn't given a choice. Yes, they were going to pay me if things worked out, but if I didn't help them – let's say I can't rely on a Safety Team. Besides, this was supposed to be *easy money*, as they say. Nobody was supposed to get hurt. But there's something wrong with your client." He leans back again. "She's not a tourist. She's dangerous. You have to respect that."

Outside there's the blare of an alarm, then another from a different direction. Ivan starts.

Li stays calm. "Have you heard anything about her since?"

"I think I've said enough."

A third alarm starts. It sounds as if it's in the street outside. Ivan is ready to run. "It's been a pleasure," he says, and glances at the door.

I have an obvious question. "Why have you told us this?"

"Why do you think? Because I want you to tell the

authorities what Facilitator Delrosso is doing. I want my business back."

"And my client?"

He's half out of his chair. "She's your problem."

And that's when the trouble starts.

What I see is the door suddenly open and two native men walking quickly towards us, with three others following them. One of them has an arm round Ivan's head before he can stand up. They don't say anything, as if they can't talk and run at the same time. I'm on my feet before the second one gets into range. His range, that is: he's already in mine. I put my hand against his chest and push him into the men behind him. Li jumps to her feet. The first man is struggling to keep Ivan down. I don't intervene. This is Ivan's local, his problem. He can solve it himself. The man I'd pushed recovers his balance and throws himself towards me again. I use a Level Three palm strike and feel his collarbone give way. He stops, staggers backwards a few steps and turns to vomit into one of their gambling machines. Ivan, meanwhile, has finally managed to stand up. He shoulders his man away and shouts something in This English I don't catch. Li is stuck behind the table. She looks terrified, probably having a flashback to that gig in 1976 when somebody punched her in the face. The four remaining men try to box us in. They're warier now. There's a native phrase: *mob-handed*. I wonder what kind of *mob* this is: angry crowd or organised crime? Are Gurley and Knight going to walk through the door? Is this the gang-related activity that ends with Knight dead? For the moment there's a pause, a stand off. Perhaps five against three looked good to them. Now they're down to four they seem less certain. They don't know that Li isn't a fighter. The pub's customers have backed away. Some have left. The ones who stay watch from the other side of the bar: this is an entertainment. Two more natives appear at the door talking animatedly. They see the man leaning against the gambling machine and retreat. The other four hold their position.

It's a moment when I wish I'd brought Edda. I have a feeling she'd be useful in a situation like this.

There's a crash from directly outside, like a crate of iron nails dropped from a third-storey window. The sound encourages them to charge. I say to Li, "Stay behind me." Ivan tries to say something as well but doesn't get a chance. The man who'd held him by the neck throws a punch. From the way Ivan recoils it's clear he's no more of a fighter than Li. I run at the door, swinging my elbows when necessary and clear a path through them and out to the street, Li following, and then Ivan, who's finally realised that affability isn't going to work with this audience.

They stay in the pub.

Outside is confusing. There are too many people, mostly younger men, running in too many directions. They're even running along the parts reserved for vehicles. Alarms sound from all sides. At the north end of the street a plastic bin is on fire. There are sirens in the distance.

"Station," Li says. I know what she means. From the main station we should be able to get a bus to a resort, any resort. We start walking, Li beside me, Ivan trailing as if he'd rather not be with us. We don't talk, in case it attracts attention from anyone who hasn't noticed our appearance. Fortunately the natives are more interested in running away or breaking windows than attacking strangers. From time to time I look back: the men at the pub haven't come out. It takes only a minute or two to reach the edge of the disturbance, a residential street blocked by a police vehicle parked halfway along, lights flashing. There are three native police in their lurid jackets. One of them, male, makes a move to stop us. Another, female, says "Let them go" in a voice that suggests stopping us would give them more trouble than they need. Other natives have gathered behind the police car. They're peering along the street, as if waiting for a parade. We keep walking. The sirens are still coming from every direction. The few people on foot seem to be moving more quickly than usual, but no more than if they were late for a meeting. Ivan pulls out a native communication device and pokes at its screen. "That was fun," he tells us with relish.

Li isn't amused. "Those people who attacked us, who were they?"

"Let's just say it's a misunderstanding." We've reached a junction: broad streets, high, old buildings, empty sandwich shops. It's quieter here: the buildings are offices, with nothing the rioters seem to want. Ivan stops walking. "Well, it's been an interesting evening, but I have to be elsewhere."

Li is surprised. "You're not coming with us?"

"Why would I go to a resort?" He looks around casually, as if the danger is past. "I live out here."

"Because a resort is safer," Li suggests. "Those people looked like they were after you. If it hadn't been for Spens you would have been in trouble."

Ivan holds up his arms in mock surrender. "Your logic. If it hadn't been for Spens I wouldn't have been there."

"They might still be after you."

"Then that's a situation I'd have to do something about it, isn't it? And I can't do that from a resort. You never know who's listening. Who might draw the wrong conclusions." He's already walking away. "I'm freer out here than in the resort. That's why I came here in the first place."

Li doesn't give up. "What about when his client finds you?"
"I'm not worried about that. She's already found me."
"Ivan . . . "
But he only waves and keeps walking.

It's not she

The first meeting with Riemann begins with a parcel arriving at the safe house with a charger for your phone, a change of clothes, another bracelet like the one that controls your signature and a pin gun. The charger works; the clothes fit. When the phone is charged it rings. It's the woman who called you after you escaped from the shop. How did she know you'd taken the local's phone? She didn't say. You wondered if it had been a test after all: the local would have given you his phone if you'd asked; you'd hurt him for no reason ... In her first call she told you not to worry about the box or Picon Delrosso. A taxi would come for you, she said, and it came, the driver also carrying a key for a flat on the outskirts of the city, the safe house. You remember the disposition of the rooms and the view of the street. Later that evening food was delivered. The woman seemed to have thought of everything.

Now she tells you to be at an address at 4.15. A taxi has already been arranged. "Take the gun. If you meet a man called Riemann Aldis do what he tells you."

"Is he with us?"

"It's important you do what he says and listen carefully to what he tells you. When he asks what you mean to do next, you must tell him you're going home. Today."

You wonder why: you're supposed to be here for another two weeks.

The taxi arrives. In your memories all the taxis are driven by the same man: dark-skinned as if from the far south, bald and bad-tempered, with a soft roll of flesh at his neck. The address is for a row of little shops like the one where you were imprisoned: one sells raw food, another cooked food, the next two are empty and the one after that, the one you want, is closed, metal shutters drawn.

A man steps out of the door of the nearest empty shop. He's dressed in a shabby coat, like a transient. Fifty, perhaps, white-haired with weathered skin. At first glance you'd think he was a local. Those are the only details you remember. "Adorna," he says, as if he knows you. "Are you still calling yourself Adorna?" It's the Number City language.

"Riemann Aldis," you say.

He's not surprised you know him. "I didn't expect to see you here after the airport. Have you thought about what I told you?" You look at him blankly. He's disappointed. "You should. Do you know who's in there?" He nods at the drawn blinds. "I thought they were following you. It seems you're following them."

You don't understand the reference to the airport. You start to walk away.

He takes your arm. "I used to wonder what you were like when you were younger." The grip is casual but firm. You could twist free if you chose. You don't. You've been told to listen. "The childhood of the monster, that kind of thing.

Not that I believe in monsters. You weren't what I expected."

You wonder what it means when somebody from the Number Cities calls you a monster.

"I take it you're here for the same thing." He loosens the grip on your arm without letting go. "One minute. Then I follow you in."

"I don't need help."

"I'm not offering it." He lets go and steps back into the doorway. "I'm just curious about what's going to happen. One minute."

The door opens on the first knock. The local who answers is squat and heavy and wears a suit like a member of the business caste. You've never seen him before. He seems to recognise you. "Jesus fucking Christ."

A religious. To put him at his ease you return the greeting and add, "I'm expected."

He steps back awkwardly and waves you in. "About fucking time."

Inside the shop it's bright. The walls are lined with empty glass cases, like a museum without exhibits. The Dolman box is on a glass-topped counter next to some kind of long blade. So *that's* why you're here: you're being given another chance.

The man outside must be another test.

Another local, as tall as you, stands behind the counter. He's dark, in a shiny black coat. He's unfamiliar but, like the man in the suit, looks at you as if he knows you.

The blade is a concern: it isn't the kind of tool you'd use to try to open a Dolman box. It doesn't look like any kind of tool. They're prepared for trouble.

You point at the box. "I've come for that."

The squat one shrugs. "So open it then." He's nervous. He must know about the local you hurt. "Get it over with."

A surprise: they expect you to open it. The woman hadn't said. Even if you could open it, what then? What would they do with Picon's instructions? And if you've been told to forget Picon, what are you supposed to do with them? Perhaps the woman needs them.

The one in the jacket is still staring at you. "It's not she."

The squat one is surprised. "What?"

"It's not she." The tall one's voice is low, pained. He seems to find it an effort to talk.

"Of course it's fucking her."

You take out the pin gun. The squat one limps towards you and peers warily. "What's that?"

"A key."

"She's different," the tall one insists. "The one at the airport is different."

The airport again.

"Don't be stupid. Of course it's her." The suit sounds as if he's fed up with both of you. "Didn't think they needed keys. Thought you just touched it and it opened."

"There are different kinds." You wonder what happened at the airport: both Riemann and the suit think they saw you there. You pick up the box, not sure what to do next. "This one needs a key." You don't know if they'll believe you. You can't decide which one to shoot first.

The tall one simplifies matters. "It's not she." He reaches for the blade. "*Telling* you."

You shoot him in the face. He spins away, making a choking sound.

"Fuck," says the squat one. You pivot to face him. Instead of running at you as a trained person would he retreats to the door. It opens before you can fire a second shot. Riemann steps briskly inside, closing the door behind him. The local stops so suddenly he stumbles and almost falls. "Fuck," he repeats. "Another one."

Riemann has his own weapon, or a device you assume is a weapon. It is levelled at you. "I'll take the box."

"Leave me out of this." The local limps over to where the other one has fallen. "You fucking people."

You remember your instructions and surrender the box. Does this mean you've passed the test?

Riemann doesn't congratulate you. "Do you know what this is?" He balances the box in his hand, testing its weight. "Do you know where it came from?" You weren't told to answer questions so say nothing. He shrugs and slips the box into his coat pocket, lowers his own weapon and walks over to the man you shot. "A tourist," he says.

His back is turned to you. You realise this is a chance to shoot him. You also realise it's one you won't take. Or can't. His coat might be heavy enough to stop a pin; even a shot to the back of the head might not be effective. You keep your hand at your side. Killing him wasn't in your instructions.

There's a door behind the counter. Riemann pushes it with his foot and looks through. "You," he says to the local in their language. "Drag your friend in there." The local, gasping for air, does as he's told. "Now get the weapon." The local limps slowly back to the counter. He picks up the blade, holding the handle by his fingertips. "Put it next to him." The local does as he's told, moving with exaggerated care, as if the blade might explode in his hands. "Now empty your pockets on the counter." The local takes a deep breath. "Easy money," he says, not quite talking to himself. "No trouble. Nobody gets hurt. We all end up laughing." He makes an effort to look calm but his hands shake. "I should have known I couldn't trust somebody like him." He lays out what he has: keys, a leather purse, two phones. No weapons. "You people." He looks exhausted. "Get in the room," Riemann tells him. The local looks at you as if he thinks you might help. "You can't do that to people," he warns. He's trying to cheer himself up. "You tell your friend there's going to be repercussions." He retreats into the room and stands as far as he can from the body.

Riemann locks him in.

You follow him out to the street. It's busy: locals pushing their children, carrying the plastic bags that will outlast them. Old women who stare at you. You're a long way from a tourist area. Here, you're the sights to be seen. People will surely remember seeing you leave the shop.

Good. They'll blame the Number Cities.

You were told to listen to Riemann; you wait to hear what he has to say.

"I know you were at the airport because of Metzger." Riemann strolls along casually, as if he hasn't just seen you shoot somebody. "I know there's a connection between you. I will work it out."

You've never heard of anybody called Metzger. "Who are you?"

"I was impressed with your act," Riemann says. "For a moment I almost believed it. But you can't expect me to believe it now. You've never heard of Alexander Metzger but you turn up at exactly the right time and place to watch him die. And now I've seen you take a Dolman box from criminals and you're carrying a gun which you obviously know how to use. There's no point pretending you're a tourist. You weren't at the airport to watch the planes land. So, the box." He taps his pocket. "What are people like that doing with a Dolman box? Do you know what's in it, or are you

198

just a messenger? It's too light for currency. Is it information? Something nasty to bury in a mine? Which of our sites were you planning to contaminate with this? Or are you going to tell me we've got everything wrong?" He doesn't give you time to answer. It's a technique. They ask questions and try to read expressions. Non-verbal responses. You're from City Two East, trained at Spad. Not responding is natural. You had to learn *how* to respond.

"Not talking? At least you've stopped lying. That's a start. Do you even know what you're doing here? Are you just following instructions? Go there, carry that, shoot this person in the face? I know what that life is like. I can sympathise." He stands in front of you. "I used to wonder what it would be like to meet you before you, well, did what you did. I wondered if I'd want to kill you. I knew I wouldn't, obviously, but I wondered if I'd want to." He pauses for a second or two, as if he's still undecided. "So, what will you do next?"

It's a question you know how to answer. "I'm going home."

"No, you're not." The woman told you the right thing to say. He's surprised. "You can't be. When?"

"Today."

"I don't believe you. Of course I don't believe you. What do you mean by home, anyway?"

"City Two West."

"Now I know you're lying. It's too late for another translation today."

You keep walking until you reach a place where people are allowed to cross the road. He walks beside you. You have to wait for the traffic to be told to stop. "I don't believe in monsters," he says. "I'm going to break protocol again.

Do you know why I didn't kill you at the airport? Why I don't do it now? Because one day, a long time from now, you meet me again." The traffic stops. "I'm here because of that meeting."

It makes no sense. You walk away quickly. He doesn't follow.

Resort Six

The big screen outside the station shows pictures of burning buildings. They alternate with adverts for shops, which is the first sign the rioting is not as bad as it looks. There's a Resort Six bus outside the station with a two-person Safety Team which, they tell us, will leave in twenty minutes, sooner if there's any sign of danger. A message has gone out to reps: everybody to head for the most convenient resort. They want us off the streets as soon as possible.

It explains why I haven't heard from Hayek. He probably has his own problems.

Inside, the station looks the same as usual: natives waiting for a train, a handful of beggars, most of them watching the screen above the concourse. The burning building seems to be in London. According to the text scrolling across the screen buildings have been set on fire in a number of cities, including this one, but the images of the London building are all they show. Back at the bus a few Heritage reps and clients have gathered. Jorge is there. He can't see why he was summoned: there hadn't been any trouble in *his* neighbourhood. A rep I don't know tells him her clients were surrounded by a group of natives demanding currency. She'd scared them off. "I told them I'd called for help," she says, "with my mind." The clients, who were supposed to be attending a Typical Nightclub, are excited, as if a riot is a local festivity. Li shares the story of how we were attacked. They find it hard to believe we didn't know this would happen. Why weren't we warned?

"Events like this evening are nothing unusual," Jorge tells them. "Paradoxically, they're a sign of stability. They have what they call a summer of unrest every ten years and a winter of discontent every fifteen. A crowd will break shop windows and set fire to a few vehicles. A few days later everything goes back to normal. Tonight's events were not on our records because they're trivial."

"But what about the attacks on you?" one of them asks Li.

"The attacks on us are opportunistic." Jorge answers for her. "They're made for the same reason as the attacks on their own shops. Because we have something they want." He takes out a Dor and holds it so the pale metal catches the light. "Currency. This might not be much to us, but it's worth more than most of them will earn in a week. And when those people look at us all they can see is this."

Li looks unhappy about his speech, but doesn't want to contradict another rep in front of the clients. The clients are pleased: they've learned an important lesson about the early 21st. When he finishes Jorge turns away from them and stares out of the window, sunk in thought or possibly just admiring his own reflection. We sit, listening to the sirens: ambulance, fire, police. Li sends messages to her native friends. When the Safety Team decide no one else is coming I bip Edda and tell her I'm on my way to Resort Six.

*

From the outside, Resort Six is the same as all our other resorts – a giant dome set a few kilometres from the nearest town, surrounded by the usual acreage of well-tended trees and discreet safety measures. There are supposed to be subtle differences between them, making each one a unique experience, and so on, though it's rare for our clients to see more than one. A trip to the early 21st is usually once in a lifetime, and the few who make return visits prefer to visit the same resorts. The three I've seen have been functionally identical – Travel at the centre, the Entertainment Areas and Living Quarters disposed in the same optimised patterns, an experience of home even here, in a time before homes like ours became necessary. Resort Six had the same vehicle bays, the same gates to the interior. There's a more obvious Safety presence than I'm used to, but that's probably the same across all the resorts tonight.

There's a room marked Private at the back of Entertainment Area Three. The techs have set up a connection to the native broadcasts. There's a dozen reps there, some off-duty and toning, some still in uniform, all watching one of the native channels. One of the more experienced ones (I don't know her name) is translating the scrolling text. It shows the same clip of a burning building. We watch for a while, but it's soon clear the native reports either don't have much information or they aren't sharing it with their own people.

Edda bips me. She's in the Entertainment Area outside, by the Theatrical Hall. I can't see any reason to stay in a room full of Heritage reps. I leave Li talking to her friends.

The area between the different halls is the same as in the other resorts: a broad avenue, with a central line of trees hung with lamps. The only difference is in the arrangement of the halls. The Theatrical Hall in Resort Six is by the entrance where Resort Four has a Sports Hall, Tri-Millennium clients being supposedly more interested in games than classic drama. It was late now, and most of the events are finishing. The clients have spilled out into the Entertainment Area and seem unwilling to settle. They move from bar to restaurant without staying at any of them, the same infected with mild form of the fervour outside. And then, among the crowd, I notice a familiar face: our client.

She's just stepped out of the Science Hall and joined the stream of people moving towards the Area gate. It's her, unmistakably her.

I bip Hayek. "She's here, in Resort Six."

The response is almost immediate. "Are you sure?"

"I'm sure."

"I'll advise their Safety Team."

"I want to talk to her first."

"If you must. Just don't get in anybody's way."

"I won't." Our meeting will look like an accident. The riots will give us something to talk about. So you've been brought here as well? I will pretend to be no more than a rep concerned for the welfare of a client. So what have you been doing? Seen any sights? No mention of tonin or airports or beating up local criminals. No hint that I know about her suppressed signature. Her replies will be equally fake, but I want to hear her say them. Tougher questions will follow when the Safety Team become involved.

She walks slowly, unobtrusively, blending perfectly with the other clients. I follow, keeping to the other side of the line of trees. I let Edda know I'll be another few minutes: something has come up. She's waiting, as she said she would be, outside the Theatrical Hall, under a sign announcing a Günther Eich double bill. I wave at her and point to the exit; she points at Bar 3.2 next to the Hall.

I think we understand each other.

By the time I reach the exit gate our client is only a few paces ahead. We're on the concourse on the Western half of the resort. There are people moving in all directions, between the Entertainment Zones and the Living Quarters. It's a good place to disappear.

She doesn't disappear. She hasn't seen me or hasn't recognised me or doesn't think I'm important. She stops for a moment and studies the messages on the big screens above the entrance to the approach: tomorrow's entertainments, restaurant menus. I'm only a few paces away when someone seizes my right wrist.

It's Riemann. He has a firm grip. "Not yet." He's no longer dressed like a native. Here, he looks like another client, a retiree come to see the 21st before he (and it) dies. Our client walks away, more quickly this time, as if she hadn't been looking at the screens for information but steadying her nerves. She walks like somebody with a purpose.

She is heading towards the travel zone.

I ask Riemann, "What's she doing?"

"We'll soon find out."

"Do you mean you don't know?"

He doesn't answer. Our client pauses at the Zone Gate long enough to be waved through by the Safety.

This should not have happened. She's not scheduled to travel for another few weeks, and from a different resort. The Safety Team is supposed to know she's here. Even if the one at the gate hadn't been told he should have noticed she didn't have a signature.

"See," Riemann says.

"What have we seen?"

Riemann releases his grip. "What we're meant to see."

"And what's that?" I don't expect him to answer. "So where is she going? She can't expect to travel."

"She doesn't. This is a trick."

We watch as the Safety at the gate seems to get a message. He puts his hand to his ear and stares at the gate. He looks around the hall as if he's hoping to see someone there. Then, his mouth moving – either arguing with his superior or swearing to himself – he runs through the gate.

Riemann says, "Ha!" delightedly. He strolls towards the now unattended gate. I follow him. He doesn't try to stop me.

"What kind of trick?"

"That's what we'll find out."

We walk through the gate. The actual transport is about half a kilometre ahead, but, because of the shielding the approach isn't a direct route. The corridor spirals round for about five times that distance. The approach to the zone is our clients' least favourite part of travel. No matter how many subtle lighting variations we build in we can't hide the fact that it's a walk along a very long corridor. We've tried food kiosks at the halfway stage and calming music. We found that after half an hour in the approach the clients were often confused about what they wanted to eat and the calming music hadn't always had the expected effect. The kiosks had to be automated when staff refused to work on them. The problem wasn't just the stress of dealing with bad-tempered and confused clients: there's something about the approach itself that quickly becomes seriously disturbing, even, it seems, for the machines. They break down regularly; food spoils at unpredictable rates. Maintenance won't make repairs on-site. They go in, disconnect the machines and carry them out as fast as they can. Nobody goes into the approach unless they have to. That's why it needs only one

Safety at the gate. And once inside there are no short cuts or back doors. You either walk all the way to the transport or go back the way you came.

But there are barriers: fire breaks, precautions against the tech nightmare of uncontrolled energy. There hasn't been an accident since the very early days but precautions are still taken. Every few hundred metres there's a point where a barrier can drop and the corridor be sealed. In theory our client could be boxed in until the Safety Team arrive to escort her out again. At the least, they can stop her reaching the zone. Each time we turn a corner I expect to see her and the Safety standing by one of these barriers. This wouldn't present a problem for me. I have a reason to be there: she's my client, after all. Riemann might have a harder time of it. Any good Safety would be wary of a second civilian without a detectable signature.

But they don't seem to have lowered any barriers yet. Possibly because they don't know where she is (no signature) and can't tell which doors to close; possibly because this is the approach and the barriers have developed a fault. They're relying on the old-fashioned method of having a Safety run after her.

Riemann doesn't run. He keeps to a steady, almost casual pace. His expression remains one of alert amusement. He doesn't seem inclined to talk and I don't expect him to tell me anything.

I ask anyway. It's going to be a long walk. "Why has she come here?"

"You know I can't tell you." He sounds almost regretful. "But I'm interested in what she does next."

He might have a reassuring calm and an air of competent authority but I preferred him when he was ten. He'd been serious and quiet, the sort of boy who always thought carefully before he spoke. Back then his reserve came across as respectful. "Can you give me a hint?"

"Have you seen Cantor lately?"

He's trying to change the subject. "Not for years. Not since I went to the Tunnels." I change it back. "We thought she was carrying tonin."

This stops him. "It was more than that." He keeps his eyes fixed on the corridor ahead. He still thinks carefully before he speaks. Then he starts walking again. "Cantor used to talk about you."

"We were friends for a long time." I don't want to be distracted by reminiscences. "What else was she doing?"

"I liked you, Spens. I could never see why you were Cantor's friend. You never had much in common. You were more mature than him. He was always getting obsessed with stupid theories."

"He didn't believe in them. He thought they were funny."

"That didn't matter. He couldn't tell when people were bored. You were always patient with him even when you didn't have to be. I always thought you had more in common with me. I used to think we'd be friends when I was older. And even now there's a part of me that still thinks the same way. You're always that friend I might have had. But you have to understand I can't tell you anything."

I understand. It's still infuriating. You're always at a disadvantage. You can't tell if someone is exploiting what they know or trying hard not to. Either makes them look smug.

It's not hard to see why some natives hate us.

"But you don't care that I'm following you."

"I can't stop you."

Interpret that. He could mean he doesn't care if I follow

him; he could mean he can't stop me because in whatever report he once read (in his past, my future) I was among the people recorded as being present. If that's the case he wouldn't be able to stop me: his weapon would jam (we're in the approach, after all, where tech fails all the time) or he'd walk onto one of my Level Three punches. I know he can't hurt me: it's not in my line. I'm about to be sent home for breach of protocol. A few years after that I join a kin, and, forty after that, die. It's not his job to hurt me.

At least, not for another forty-odd years. Perhaps that's how it ends, with me looking up one morning to see him walk into wherever I am, just the same as he is now, or slightly older or younger. Perhaps that explains his little speech: somewhere back on his line he's already killed me, when I was an old man and he was a bright young recruit for whatever department selected him. The talk about a friendship that might have been is his way of saying there are no hard feelings.

It's the delirium of the approach. When a translation is scheduled you reach a point about halfway in when your skin begins to tingle and then crawl. Even behind several metres of shielding, you feel nauseous. The walls seem to move, the ground ripples and lights seem brighter. In the transport itself it's not so bad: you're strapped into a comfortable seat and soothed by gentle lighting and ambient noise. The translation itself is easy. It's the effects on the periphery – the hallucinations and mood swings – that are unsettling.

Riemann stays calm, as if he's used to this.

"Were you at the airport?" I ask. I have to say something.

"Why would I be?"

"We tracked her there. I talked to Gurley and Knight."

He frowns. "Who?"

"Locals. They were following her."

"Oh. Them." He assesses this new piece of information. "Did they tell you anything interesting?" His tone is amused, smug.

"Nothing useful. Do you know why she was at the airport?"

"Spens, you have to stop asking questions. I can't tell you anything."

He knows I know why he can't. Protocol, as well as common courtesy. If you know something about a person's future you don't tell them. *The next time you see me I will be younger and you will be about to die.* You don't say it. It's an abridgement of agency.

It doesn't stop me asking. "Does that mean you don't know? What does she have to do with Alexander Metzger?"

"What do you know about him?"

"Not much. Fringe politics. Greek lyric poetry. She wasn't here long enough to have known him."

He nods. I've told him nothing he didn't already know. "Why did you think she was carrying tonin?"

"We were told by an extemp. Picon Delrosso."

There's the faintest flicker of surprise. "You traced it to him?"

"Gurley gave me his name. When I asked Picon he admitted it."

"I can see why he'd admit to that. What did you make of him?"

"We thought he might be from City Two East."

Another faint flicker. "What made you think that?"

"His accent."

"City Two East. Did you draw any conclusions?"

"Not yet. Should I?"

"It's not worth it. He isn't the problem."

"But she is?"

Ahead of us I can hear what sounds like a faulty air pump. We turn a bend and find the Safety leaning against a wall, noisily sucking in mouthfuls of air. His face is pale pink. At first I think he's hurt, but he's just winded. He watches us approach as if he's been expecting us. "She's a runner."

"She would be," Riemann says mildly. "Have you closed the final gate?"

The Safety nods miserably. He's gasping at a slower rate now and the colour is leaving his face. I guess he's in his sixties, too old to be running along a corridor even in a lightweight Safety suit. "It was the first thing I did when I lost her." He speaks to Riemann. He's spotted the authority and is trying to impress him with competence. "I was going to retrieve her. Once I got my breath back."

"Good work," Riemann reassures him. "You stay here. We'll retrieve her."

The Safety looks grateful. "Do you know who she is?" He'd do whatever Riemann asks.

"His client." Riemann indicates me. "We think she spent too long in the open."

"I thought so," he says, as if it's something he sees every day. "Why else would anybody come in here? Should I alert medical?"

"Good idea." Riemann has started to walk away. "Don't call them here yet, but you can let them know they might be needed."

"Yes, sir." The Safety does his best to stand to attention. "I'll let them know."

We leave him. Once we're out of his sight Riemann lets himself smile. "A runner. I bet she didn't have to run very fast."

We keep walking. I let Edda know I may be longer than I thought. I don't know if she'll get the message through the shielding. I wonder if we'll meet our client coming in the opposite direction. She could stand and wait to be retrieved or try to slip past an exhausted Safety. I doubt she's the kind to stand and wait. We keep walking.

"What has she done, Riem? What is she going to do?"

"Spens, stop."

"Why is she so important to you? You can tell me here. Nobody's listening."

He sighs. "I've broken enough protocols already."

We keep walking.

Riemann says, "I'm trying to correct a mistake."

I don't say anything. If he's going to talk I don't want to interrupt.

"I've tried to understand this for years," he says. "Ever since I first met her. I can't tell you the circumstances. I shouldn't tell you the circumstances." His voice has changed. He talks rapidly, almost nervously. It's disconcerting. "So I came here. I volunteered sixteen years of my life for the chance to come here. You'll learn how they work. They let you travel, but you have to do something for them in return. So I worked for them and now I'm here. But the events aren't any clearer. You should turn back. It'll be easier for you."

"What are you going to do?"

"I tried talking to her. I told her what would happen. It didn't work." He grins like somebody finally understanding a joke. "Of course it didn't work. How could it?" He takes a thin tube from a side pocket. "So now I'm going to try something else. I'm going to try to change history. Like an Anachronist. What do you think will happen when I push the button?"

It's a mad question. Some people, when the delirium hits, crack completely. "You told me she returned safely."

"I wanted to protect you." He walks more quickly now, brisk, neat steps as if he's eager to finish this. "Do you think we'll find ourselves somewhere else with no memory of this? Or does the paradox apply? The first time I met her – the first time I met her *here* – I began to think I might be wrong. I warned her about the consequences of her actions. I thought I'd made an impression. The second time it was obvious she didn't care. I should have ended it then, this afternoon. I had the means, the right location. Instead I tried to talk. That's what stops us. Fear. No matter how badly things turned out, at least the past is known. What if you can change things, and they're worse? The devil we know. There isn't much further she can run, Spens. You should leave."

We reach the marker for the last hundred metres. The gate is ahead of us. It's still open.

"What now?" I ask him.

Riemann keeps walking. "You should leave."

"So? She's trapped, isn't she? What can she do now?" Ivan had said she was dangerous: he may have been exaggerating. She beat up one local in extreme circumstances. That doesn't make her a threat. "Can't we just wait for a Safety Team?"

"There's a protocol. If she knows that . . . " Riemann shakes his head. For a moment he looks helpless. He reaches into his coat as he's about to call for help. "I have to do this." But he sounds uncertain; he doesn't move.

"Riem." The nausea hits me before I can say anything else. *This* is the verb. I stagger backwards and fall to my knees. The walls seem to pulse around me. Even Riemann looks queasy. His own knees buckle and he drops whatever he's taken from his coat.

213

There shouldn't be a translation. There is. And the gate is open.

"Either we're wrong about everything . . . " Riemann somehow manages to stay on his feet. He steps into the cordon. "Spens, you have to get out of here. The next time you see my brother—"

I don't hear the rest. I start crawling away. It's instinctive. After a few metres I'm able to get off of my knees and start stumbling. The floor still seems to ripple and shift and the soft approach lights have turned into sharp-edged stars. I move faster. Or try to move faster: it's hard to tell if there's any difference. I feel heavy, the way I did for the first month after I had the Tunnel augs. But that was because I *was* heavier, and hadn't yet adapted. This is just a side effect of travel when there isn't a barrier between you and the cordon. I could be sprinting or I could be lying on the floor, hallucinating that I'm sprinting.

I run into a wall and fall over. Behind me, very close behind me, is the click of a lock releasing.

The gate is closing with Riemann on the other side.

I get up again and run. I hit another wall. The approach lights go out, which doesn't help. I manage a dozen or so steps without a collision. If one gate closes the others should close. It's the protocol. I can't tell if I've run into a wall or a gate. I might be running in the wrong direction.

I keep moving. If I am moving.

For a second the corridor is flooded with light. I see everything with ridiculous clarity: the whorls of fingerprints on the walls, the impressions of hundreds of different shoes on the smooth floor, the glow of the power lines behind the walls, the corridor itself, spiralling all the way out to the concourse where a Safety Team is reassuring onlookers that the sudden dip in lighting is nothing of concern, that nothing's happening, and beyond them, the resort and the surrounding trees, and, further out still, more cities and fields, the images superimposed but every single one distinct and perfectly clear: our client, standing in a dark room and Li and Edda walking across a yellow field while the sky overhead is a terrifying unbroken blue.

Long walk home

Back at the safe house your phone rings. It's the woman again. "What did Riemann tell you?"

"He took the box."

"That isn't important. What did he tell you?"

You repeat everything you can remember: how he mentioned an airport; that he claimed to have been following the locals and that he allowed you to face them alone for the first minute; that the locals seemed to recognise you; that both of them had also mentioned an airport; that Riemann hadn't been surprised when you shot one of them. That you let him take the box. You didn't think he'd followed you. "What is he?"

"It doesn't matter. Did he mention any other names?"

"Alexander Metzger. He said he was also at the airport. And that he died. Who is he?"

"Did Riemann say what he thought was in the box?"

"He thought it was information. Or something to bury in a mine. He asked if we were contaminating their sites. He said

217

he would meet me again. He said he was here because of that meeting. He took the box."

"The box isn't important. Did you tell him you were going back?"

"Yes."

"Good. Because that is what you're going to do. You've done well, and now it's time to go home ... "

She explains how. You're to go to a particular tourist bar and meet a woman, Arne Vasilis. She's travelling with Heritage and has a room at Resort Six. She's due to return in a few days and wants to stay for longer. She thinks she can swap signatures with you and the authorities will treat it as a minor breach of protocol. Once you have her signature you're to go straight to the Resort and stay in the public areas and then ...

The instructions are detailed. The woman makes you repeat them back to her. "Good. You've done very well."

"How do I recognise this woman?"

"She will recognise you."

"How?"

"That is not your concern. When you get back you need to report to the Defence Committee. This is what you need to tell them ... "

It's a long report. You had a good memory then.

You find the bar, take a table and wait to be recognised. Travellers come in, some accompanied by reps. None of them pay attention to you. They seem more intent on a screen that shows images of a building on fire.

A woman joins you. Mid-thirties, bright clothes, their strange cheerfulness. "Adorna! I didn't think you'd come." She seems to know you.

"Here I am."

"I nearly didn't come myself." The woman leans in, excited, conspiratorial. "I've never done anything like this," she whispers. "I didn't think it was possible."

You do your best to smile back. "It's possible." You take out the new bracelet and find the tiny panel. You ask her to put it on and count to fourteen and then remove it.

She does what you say without asking questions. She trusts you more completely than you've ever trusted anyone. "I did have second thoughts about this when I heard what was happening." She glances at the screen, which, instead of the burning building is now showing film of a man driving alone on a mountain road. The woman seems mesmerised. "There's a rumour they're thinking of calling us all back to the resorts. But then I thought: I'm never going to be here again, I might as well make the most of this. If they ask I'll just say I missed the message. Besides, I read all about this time before I left. I don't remember anything about any serious trouble. I'll be safe."

You take the bracelet. "I keep this one," you tell her. "This is yours." You pass your old one across in its pouch. "You must remember not to put it on until you're ready to go back. As soon as you put it on it tells them you're me, understand?" It's not true but she believes you. You slide the new bracelet onto your wrist. "And now, as far as they're concerned, I'm you."

"Where did you learn how to do this?" The woman is delighted. She puts the pouch with her bracelet into her bag. "No, don't tell me. It's probably better I don't know! Thank you so much for this. I'm so grateful for all this extra time. And I'm just sorry it didn't work out for you."

You try to look sad. "Thank you for helping me." For a

moment you wonder if you've gone too far. But the woman looks pleased. The Number Cities like excessive courtesy.

"I'm sorry you didn't enjoy your time here. I've loved it. There are still so many things I want to see. And I'm sorry to leave you so suddenly but I really have to go." She jumps to her feet. "I'm catching a train. To London!" She expects you to be impressed. "A train!" you say with appropriate awe. "I want to see the march," she says as if she expects you to know what she's talking about. "I would have missed it otherwise. I can't thank you enough." She backs away, and waves one last time when she reaches the door. You wait for the prescribed time, then leave.

After that everything happens exactly as the woman said. You take a bus back to Resort Six. The other travellers crowd on, still talking about the trouble they've heard about or seen for themselves: broken windows, fires in the streets, police riding actual horses. They wonder about the cause: a new tax, politics. Do you think it could be us? Once in the resort you walk around the Entertainment Area until it's time to enter the corridor that leads to their travel zone. You tell the Safety at the gate you think you dropped your mother's kin ring when you arrived. Has anything been found? Do you mind if I look? Allowing you in is probably against their rules but the Number Cities are sentimental about kin. He waves you through with a smile and jokes about not spending too long. Number City people are usually reluctant to enter the corridor. You can't understand why: you find it soothing. You break into a run as soon as you're out of sight and keep running until you reach the zone. The barriers don't fall, just as you'd been told. You cross the zone, throwing away the bracelet that identifies you as Arne Vasilis, and climb into the transport. It astonishes you that it's left unattended, the door unlocked, as if a winding corridor is enough to protect it.

You find the panel and carry out the memorised procedure. Twelve switches, a precise sequence. You strap yourself into a seat and promptly fall asleep. That's the end of your first visit to the 21st.

Millies

Edda says, "He's awake."

It's true. I am.

I'm looking at the ceiling of a medical room. I can move my head. Edda is on my left side, in her rep's uniform. I wonder what I could have done to inspire such loyalty.

There is nobody else in the room.

Which means she's here as a proxy, reporting back.

She says, "What can you remember?" Her gaze is level, as if she's been told to keep her head still.

I say, "What happened to Riemann?"

There's a pause. "Who?"

"The person who was in the corridor with me."

Another pause. "There was nobody with you."

"The Safety saw him. Spoke to him."

"You were the only person we found."

"And my client!"

"It wasn't your client."

"I saw her."

"You need to rest."

223

I break eye contact. You never get used to talking via proxies. I'm not even sure whether I'm talking to Hayek or Erquist in official mode or Resort Six's equivalents, self-pitying Ban and the unsleeping Oberon Petkov. Now I'm no longer gazing into Edda's eyes I look at the rest of the room. A standard medical bay of the kind I've seen twice before, both times to check up on clients who'd eaten the native food. I'm not, I'm relieved to notice, attached to any machines. Nothing seems to hurt. My arms are fine, I can't feel any bandages on my face. There seems to be nothing wrong.

I look down. My left foot is missing.

I throw back the sheet to make sure. My left leg stops just above where the ankle should be. The wound has been dressed so the leg ends in a soft white stump. I look back at Edda. I can feel my foot. I can feel the toes flex. Except it isn't there.

"We're very sorry." Edda repeats an official condolence. "But you're lucky to be alive."

"How long have I been unconscious?" Long enough for the wound to be treated. Long enough for Edda to have been recruited to her new role.

"Three days." Edda uses a different intonation. It means a different person is now speaking through her. "We tried waking you yesterday but you were incoherent."

"Three days," I repeat numbly. Knight, it occurs to me, may already be dead from his gang-related activity. I feel sorry for him, though also relieved that I don't kill him after all.

"There was a translation." Edda switches back to her first voice. "It's being investigated. We don't know if anybody was present."

"There must have been somebody."

"That's being investigated."

"It was our client."

"The person who entered the tunnel was a guest of the resort. She returned yesterday via Resort Two. I'm sorry, Spens, but there's no record of anybody else entering the approach."

"But the translation—"

"Is being investigated."

It's no use arguing. "So what now?"

"Now? We apologise to two hundred and thirty-six Heritage clients for a delay in their homeward journey. And we report a technical failure leading to an unfortunate injury."

"My foot."

"We're very sorry."

"And what happens to me?" Is this – finally – my breach of protocol?

"You'll stay in Resort Six until you've stabilised." The second tone again. Edda distinguishes between the two voices well. She's probably had dramatic training. She'll go far in the Happiness Executive. "We've sourced a prosthetic design from one of our South American centres. We don't, as a rule, see many amputees in resort medical bays. It will serve you until you get home. It won't be ready until tomorrow afternoon. You should be free to leave the day after that."

"And then?"

"We'll let you rest now. No, I don't think more questions are appropriate." Edda smiles. "Sorry, I wasn't supposed to say that last part. They're arguing among themselves. I'm going to disconnect." There's a pause. She seems to be listening for something. "They've gone." She relaxes.

"They're probably still listening."

"Not through me." She sits on the bed. "They're probably

monitoring this room anyway. But at least they're out of my head." She lowers her face close to mine and whispers, "I don't know everything that's happening, but all excursions have been cancelled. All the reps living outside have been ordered back to the resorts. There are rumours that extemps will be called back as well. The clients are being sent home early to make room."

"For what?"

"There's nothing official." She kisses my cheek, a gentle smudge with her lips. "I'll let Li know you're conscious. She was concerned."

"Thanks." She leaves. I try to think about what she said and immediately fall asleep.

I wake up alone. The lights are dimmed. I lie on the bed, not moving, staring up at the blank ceiling screen, a black rectangle surrounded by dark grey. If I move my arm the lights should come on. I think about my foot. There was nothing in my record about losing a foot: I should have been told. It's important information, more important than losing a job. I flex the toes under the sheet, rotate the ankle. I can feel every movement, and half expect it to be enough to turn on the lights. Except there's no movement and nothing to move. I'm surprised at how detached I feel: I'd have expected to be more upset. One of my team in the Tunnels lost a hand after being bitten. He was never the same afterwards. I'm relieved the accident happened in a resort and that I didn't wake up in one of the native hospitals. Instead I have modern treatment and medication that promotes a mood of calm acceptance. I wonder – abstractly – why I wasn't sent home. Instead they're bringing a prosthesis from halfway around the world.

The thought of South America reminds me of Riemann.

There was an entertainment when I was young about a team of adventurers who kept finding themselves in different periods of history: one week they'd be in 13th-century Spain, the next in 5th-century Byzantium. At the beginning of each episode they would arrive somewhere and get separated from their transport. Their only way of getting back to it was to find out as much they could about wherever it was they'd crashed. Because they didn't speak the language they usually spent a lot of time hiding. Each episode ended with them back in the transport and hoping that this time it would get them home. Schools liked the show because it was educational – you really did learn a lot about the different periods and there were usually actual images from the times in question. Older children liked it because it was fun to spot the same actors and extras turning up week after week – last week's Martin Luther was this week's unnamed boyar and the week before's Mayan priest. There were, after all, only a limited number of performers short enough to play people from earlier periods. (Li claims her mother appeared in several episodes.) I remember the series fondly because of the episode in which the characters meet Brink and Nakamura – or actors pretending to be Brink and Nakamura. The series presented them as amusing eccentrics, but I thought there was something heroic about them. I was so impressed I mentioned it to a teacher who told me that Brink and Nakamura were real people whose archive – the account of their experiences and their recordings – had been recovered only a few years earlier. That entertainment, in a way, changed my life.

The people who reliably didn't like it were techs, for tech reasons: the depiction of travel was nonsense, their transport should have disintegrated after the crash, and even if you conceded it was a special experimental model that could generate its own energy the passengers would still have been torn to pieces. Some of those pieces might have been large enough to survive a second trip, but the attrition would have been deadly. Without proper medical intervention not one of the team would have survived the loss of their first limb.

Riemann had stepped into the cordon. He was unlikely to have survived. He wasn't stuck in the Cretaceous with only my foot for company.

A shame. I'd liked him when he was ten. The loss seems remote, a theoretical sadness. It must be the medication.

He'd mentioned Cantor in the approach. *The next time you see my brother . . .* If I see ever Cantor again it'll be back in the 24th, when Riemann is still young and alive. It's probably a good thing I've lost touch. I wouldn't know what to say to either of them.

My foot. I'll have to get used to a prosthesis. Neith, who lost his hand in the Tunnels, never got used to his. Even after he was given the customised replacement he used to say it didn't feel the same. He would find himself staring at it, waiting for it to move. On bad days, he said, he didn't feel like himself any more. Even when performing ordinary actions – holding a cup, turning a key – he could never be entirely sure if it was what he wanted to do or what the hand had tricked him into doing. He'd lost his sense of agency.

A foot shouldn't be such a problem. What do you do with a foot? You walk on it, or stand on it. Occasionally you might run or kick with it, or dance. A prosthesis can manage all that. A foot is not a hand. It's not in front of you the whole time. We don't say: I know it like the sole of my foot. It's possible to work with somebody for years without ever seeing their feet.

But still. It's gone. The part of you that was your contact with the ground has gone. Even when the prosthesis has been replaced, the nerve endings spliced into a cultivated mirror image of your remaining foot, a connection will have been lost. You'll be walking on a simulacrum, indistinguishable from the real foot, but not the same. It will be a foot without history. (Neith kept his new hand gloved for the first week. When he removed the glove the skin was as pale and soft as a baby's. He was told it would take years before it was properly conditioned.)

Poor Neith. I hadn't thought about him since reaching the 21st. I lost touch with him after I left the Tunnels and he signed on for another five years. It's said if you don't leave after your first term you never leave. I'd had enough. When I left I lost touch with all of them: Neith, Ansah, Joneson, Hindemith, Oyego ... For me, the Tunnels had been a means to an end. For them, the Tunnels *were* the end. I feel a wave of nostalgia that probably owes more to painkillers than any fond memories. Fond memories are what we make later, when we're at a safe distance.

I sit up, which turns on the lights. I point at the screen. It remains blank. This is a medical bay: possibly it's been set to ignore what might be involuntary movements. There must be a manual control somewhere. I look around for a box or a sensor. Nothing. Everything here is managed remotely. The patient is no more than a subject to be studied, a baby who can't be trusted around elaborate machines. I swing out of the bed, intent for a moment on marching out to seek help, and stop when my foot – my remaining foot – touches the floor. I stop for what seems a long time. If I'm in a medical area then I'll be between an Entertainment Area and the Safety Office. I calculate how far I could comfortably hop and swing back onto the bed. This time my stump starts to tingle. For the first time it feels like an end point. There is no ghostly presence beyond it, no illusion of normality. I lie back on the bed wondering if my movement has attracted any attention.

It's only a foot. We can replace feet. Brink had typhus. He never got home. He died, years later, in Moscow. Nakamura buried him, wrote the postscript to their joint memoir, concealed the archive and then disappears from the record. A foot is nothing.

When I open my eyes the lights are still on. Edda is standing by the bed next to an older woman wearing the traditional whites. "One," she says. She's been counting down. "Welcome back. How do you feel?"

I look down the bed. My foot has returned, or something that has the shape of a foot. My stump tingles. "How long was I asleep?" I twist my leg. The foot-thing moves.

"Two days," Edda says, smiling. This time she's not connected.

"Two days?" Asleep isn't quite the word. "Why?"

"It seemed the safest course." The doctor doesn't elaborate. "How does your foot feel?"

"Which one?"

"Is there any pain?"

I move my leg again. "There's no pain." But there's something, a shimmer of nerves, which might, without the drugs, eventually become pain.

"Are you ready to try walking?"

"Should I be?"

As if in answer she throws back the sheet. The thing at the end of my leg is what a foot would look like if it was encased in a flesh-coloured plastic sock. It's slightly darker than my leg, and narrower than my other foot. There's a white strap at the join. When I move my leg it doesn't fall off.

"We had some trouble finding one that would take your weight," the doctor says. "That should be adequate until you can get a proper replacement. If it had been my decision I would have sent you back. It would have been less trouble for everybody."

I sit up in the bed, turn to face them, and swing my feet onto the floor. Edda and the doctor move so they're on each side of me, Edda on my right. She puts a hand gently on my shoulder. I wonder if she's here because she wants to be here or because she's following orders. It's an unworthy thought. The room is already full of monitoring devices. She's chosen this.

I stand up, putting as much weight as possible on my right leg. It doesn't hurt. There's a sensation of pressure that doesn't quite rise to pain. Slowly I shift more weight onto my other leg. The doctor watches me coldly. She's seen this before. They don't have many amputations in resorts: I wonder if she's been brought in from outside, possibly from South America. I wonder if she ever met Riemann. The sensation of pressure changes, still without becoming pain. It's pain at a distance.

I ask Edda, "So what's been happening while I was asleep?" I can't quite believe another two days have passed. Unconsciousness is its own form of travel.

"Worry about that later." The doctor keeps glancing from my foot to my face. "Shift all of that weight. You're doing very well." Her tone suggests she's used to working with children.

"They don't tell us what's happening," Edda says. "But they've started sending back clients. Two transports a day."

"Is your weight evenly distributed?" The doctor steps back

and waves at Edda to do the same. "Good. You can stand unassisted. Now try to take a step forward."

I move my right leg. For a split second all my weight is pressing down on my stump. It's uncomfortable, but no more than wearing the wrong-sized shoes. I say, "What are they telling them?"

"That it's precautionary," Edda says. "They'll be compensated. There's been a few complaints but most of the clients are pleased. They've seen as much as they want to see and they'll get some of their money back."

The doctor ignores this. "Now try another step."

"Have there been any more incidents?" I step forward. Another five paces will take me to the door.

Edda squeezes my shoulder. "Officially, nothing."

"Now try two steps. How does that feel?"

It feels the same: not exactly painful. "Unofficially?"

"We don't go out. We can't talk to the other resorts, and they've cut off the native feeds."

"Now turn and walk back to the bed." The doctor doesn't even look at Edda. "How is that?"

"It feels odd."

"Of course it feels odd. You're walking on a prosthetic foot. What matters is if you are in pain."

"There's no pain."

"Good. Do you want to try walking along the corridor?"

The corridor isn't very long. It leads to a T-junction I take eight paces to reach. We are the only people about. With each step the sensation in my leg gains in intensity. It reminds me of an animated sequence about the birth of a star: particles slowly coalescing until they form a core. The doctor watches my face carefully. "Let me know when it hurts. There's no point being brave."

I turn left at the junction. It's familiar. I've walked down its counterpart in my own resort. It hadn't looked so long then. I push on. It seems to get easier. The pain, if that's what it is, levels out. Unless there's a sudden spike I should be able to make it to the Entertainment Area; though, as I'm still in a hospital gown, I probably shouldn't. It might upset the clients, if there are any left. Every few steps the doctor asks how I feel. "Remember you'll have to walk back."

But the door opens before we reach it. A Safety stands there, helmeted and armoured, though his visor is still up. "We need to clear this area," he says. "Take him back to his room." He sounds almost apologetic.

"Why?" the doctor asks. "What's happening?"

The Safety hesitates. There's a question of rank here. He wouldn't need to say anything to a rep; a Medical might merit an explanation. I have the impression he's been told not to explain anything. "There isn't time now. We need to keep this corridor clear." He looks unhappy saying this. "I can help you, if you like." He gestures towards me. He's noticed the foot. "It's fine," I say, and, to his evident relief, turn back. The doctor and Edda follow me. The Safety says, "One more thing. All reps are to gather in Entertainment Area One."

Edda takes my arm. "I'm off duty."

"It doesn't matter. You need to be there."

"Why?"

"It will be explained there."

"What about me?" the doctor says. "Am I supposed to go anywhere?"

"The main medical centre."

"I presume it will be explained when I get there," the doctor says to nobody in particular. "I don't see why they can't just bip me."

"I'm sorry," the Safety says. He's young, possibly younger than Edda. This might be the first time he's had to give orders. "But this corridor has to be kept clear."

Edda releases my arm. "I'll let you know." She walks past the Safety. The doctor takes my arm and guides me back to my room, as if I might have forgotten the route. At the door of the room we hear the Safety shouting "Clear!" and then we hear the thunder of boots. Two abreast, a column of armoured personnel move along the corridor at a steady pace. For close to a minute we watch them jog past. They're not Safety. No resort needs a Safety Team this size. These are Millies.

"I'm not sure we were meant to see that," the doctor says once they've gone. "They must have jammed them into the transport. A good thing they have a high tolerance for boredom."

I sit on my bed, suddenly aware once again of the sensation in my leg. It's definitely pain, but manageable. "Everything seems to be normal," the doctor says. "Now I'll go and see what they want us to believe. Will you be all right here? I'll see to it that you're not forgotten."

"I'd like the screens to work." I indicate the ceiling. "And something to eat."

"I'll see what I can do." She smiles. The encounter with the Safety has made her friendlier. We're united against a common enemy. "But for now you need rest."

"I've had too much already," I start to say. But she's gone.

It's two hours before I see anybody else. It's not the doctor, but a low-grade med-tech, the kind who keeps the simpler machines working. He hands me a control for the screen. "I was told you wanted this."

"What's happening outside?"

"I don't know." He retreats to the door as soon as the plastic is in my hand. "I wasn't at the meeting."

"What about the Millies?"

"I had inventory." He's already through the door. "They didn't tell me."

Typical med-tech. Not good enough with people to be a Happiness, not sharp enough to be a proper tech. I point the control at the ceiling. The screen comes on at the Heritage resort menu. I call up information. There are no recent announcements. I check the summaries of world news: election results and wars in countries where we don't have resorts. There's nothing about riots or demonstrations in this one. The summary is bland, designed to reassure, if not lull. I try connecting to the native channels, but I'm not good enough to cheat the machine. Finally I scan the available entertainment and settle on an old recording of Mahler conducting *Tristan* which I've heard about but never listened to. The prelude has barely finished when the med-tech returns, this time with a tray of food. He winces at the music, so I switch it off. "Find what you wanted?" he asks.

"Not quite. Are you the only person here?"

"I seem to be."

"Where is everybody else?"

"Still at the meeting, I presume."

"Must be important." The food is bland, made up of the safest choices for a patient with unknown health problems.

"Not necessarily." He seems slightly friendlier. "You know what meetings are like."

"Who's looking after the clients?"

"Safety. They had their meetings earlier. Whatever it is, they'll probably tell us last. They need somebody to keep the place working."

"Have you heard anything about the Millies?"

"Not a whisper. Do you need anything else?"

"There's one thing. I had a handheld."

He perks up. "It'll be with your clothes."

"Do you think I can have it? I need to talk to my own Safety Team."

He seems pleased to have a job. "I'll see what I can do."

I eat the bland food and restart the music. *Entartet Geschlecht!* Isolde sings. *Unwerth der Ahnen!* Degenerate race, unworthy of your ancestors! For some reason this makes me think of Dome-Watch, our degenerate forebears. What are they saying these days? For a few minutes it seems important to know, but the screen won't give me access to their internet. I listen to the attenuated yearning of the music. I am in a bubble, unable to find out anything. It feels like I'm being kept here *so* I won't find out. *If it had been my decision I would have sent you back.* I wasn't sent back. The benign interpretation is that they don't have the space: the clients go first.

Act Two is drawing to a close when the med-tech returns. He has a bundle of clothes, clean and folded, and my handheld. "We found only one of your shoes," he says apologetically. "I've found another pair. I don't know if they'll fit."

"Thanks. It doesn't matter."

"And I don't know if your handheld will still work. It might have been fried."

"I'll soon find out."

"And then there was this." He hands me a Dolman box. "It was in the tunnel. They assumed you'd dropped it."

It's a small one, about two centimetres deep, the kind used for carrying information or small pieces of tech. I turn it in my hands. There are no identifying tags. It doesn't open at my touch. It doesn't, as in old entertainments, turn out to be a box I closed, or will close.

"You're lucky you didn't lose it." He backs away. "If you need anything else . . . "

"Thanks. You've been very helpful."

He nods and retreats. As soon as he's gone I put on my real clothes. The shoes fit. Pushing my temporary foot into the left shoe adds to the feeling of strangeness. My left trouser leg is frayed at the ankle.

Ivan had claimed our client was carrying a box. Could this be it? Is this the reason she went missing? It seems unlikely. She wouldn't have gone to all that trouble only to throw it away in the approach. The last time I saw Riemann he had been trying to take something from his pocket. Could it have been this? Had he meant me to have it? I'll decide what to do with it later.

The handheld springs to life at my touch. I bip Erquist: nothing. I bip Hayek: nothing. I try Edda: busy. Li answers, "Spens, are you all right?"

"I'm fine. I'm still in the bay. What's going on?"

"Nobody knows. Honestly, nobody knows. I'll come and see you."

"I'll come to you."

"Are you sure? Are you well enough to move?"

"I've spent long enough here."

The walk along the corridor to the Entertainment Area takes me longer than I'd thought. The medical bay is empty. I don't even see the med-tech. The doors open; a relief. I'd half expected them to be locked. The hall outside is empty, and dark. The sky above the dome looks black. There's a 1.00 a.m. feel, except without clients returning from dance rooms and meditation tanks. The local time, according to one of the screens, is 23.06.

The hall should be busier. It's the place where clients come to avoid the Entertainment Areas. But there's nobody about, not even a lone Safety. The emptiness makes the hall appear larger. The sensation in my leg gets closer to pain as I walk. Before I'm halfway across it's become actual pain, an axe blow to my ankle at every step.

I stop at a bench with the gate to the area in sight. It's barely a hundred metres but I can't walk any further. It feels as if the foot is about to fall off. I almost wish it would. How long would it take to crawl the remaining distance? I bip Li. "Wait there," she says. "We'll come for you." Minutes later she appears at the gate with Edda. They run over to me, hoist me from the bench and, between them, drag me to the area. "We don't want to stay out too long," Li says. "We've been told to stay in Area One or quarters."

"What's happening?" My usual question.

"Let's get out of here first."

It doesn't take them long to reach the gate. Edda is stronger than she looks. A *lot* stronger. The Entertainment Area is nearly as empty as the interzone. Most of the restaurants and bars are closed. The remaining clients are subdued but it's hard to miss their repressed excitement. An evacuation wasn't part of their itinerary but it's either an exciting bonus or something they can complain about for the rest of their lives.

Li and Edda guide me to 3.2, which is still open.

Li goes to the bar. No table service tonight. There's one man working instead of the usual nine.

Edda says, "You should be more careful. Your leg could be infected."

"I couldn't stay there any longer."

"Does it still hurt?"

"Less now, thanks." I look around the room. Bar 3.2 is built to hold two hundred people. Tonight, the only other customers are reps, six of them, sitting gloomily at a table in the opposite corner. "Where is everyone?"

"Getting ready to leave." Edda speaks softly. "Half of the clients have gone already. The resorts are being brought under military control."

I'm pretty sure there's a protocol which forbids this. "Why? Are we being attacked?"

"We've been told it's a precaution."

Li returns with drinks. "The service staff will be gone by tomorrow. Mack says they're leaving just enough to keep two of the bars in Area Three open. The Millies need to drink."

I wonder if the beer will react with whatever drugs are still in my system. I sip anyway. "Is it happening everywhere, or just this resort?"

"We don't know." Li is excited. "The first thing they took over was communication."

"What about your friends outside? What are they saying?"

"Their signals are blocked. We're cut off."

I feel dizzy. It's not just the beer. "Look, we studied the history before we came here. I don't remember there being anything that needed this."

"We'll be home soon enough." Edda says. "We can look it up then."

"I don't want to go home," Li says. "I like it here. I've got another five months on my contract. I *need* those five months."

"They'll reassign you," Edda says. "They'll send you to another resort."

"If there's one to be sent to."

"It needn't be a resort. They could send you earlier."

"They won't. I was here in the 70s. You know what they're like about overlaps and backtracking. 'A rep'," Li quotes,

"'may not work in more than two periods and those periods are required to be sequential.' Besides, I've seen enough
resorts."

"Where would you like to go?"

"I'd like to see the 1930s."

"You're mad," Edda says fondly. "You know, you could
go to another continent. Africa is supposed to be amazing."

"Maybe."

"And if you're sent back now, they have to compensate
you." I try to remember the rules. "I was supposed to be sent
back for breach of protocol."

"Your record is wrong." Li turns to Edda. "Did you read
yours?"

"There was nothing. So, do we think the authorities know
what's happening?"

"They know." Li is emphatic, happy almost. Her conspiracy
talk is being proved true, or less wrong than I'd like. "Every
step of the way."

Edda laughs. "I'm not so sure. I think they're as surprised
by this as we are."

"Does it matter?" I'm uncomfortable, and not just because
of my foot. One day you think you're living an ordinary life,
and suddenly you're caught up in a Major Historical Event.
You walk home from the factory or the orchard and see the
first conscription notices being posted. "It's like you said:
we're about to be sent home. We can find out what happened
when we get back."

"The Millies are here for a reason." Li doesn't give up.

"But is it a good one?" Edda asks. "It's not like we're about
to declare war on the 21st."

"*The War Ouroboros*," I say.

"Why not?" Li says. "Competition for resources. It's what

nations have always done. And the past is just another country. Why wouldn't we use force?"

"Because they outnumber us," Edda says. "Heavily. And I'm not sure the 25th would let us. And if we're beaten we don't have a clear line of retreat." She looks at me. "How's your foot?"

I swig the beer. "Which one?"

Edda laughs. Then says, "I shouldn't laugh." She sits up straight. "Tunnel Boy," she says. "I'll keep this short. This link won't last."

"Hayek."

"Obviously. I want you to get here as soon as you can."

"Hayek, I can barely stand."

"I don't expect you to walk. Take a vehicle. Bring your friends if you need them."

"What's happening?"

"This link won't last. Go to the vehicle bay now. If they stop you tell them—" Edda frowns. "He went dead."

"Your Safety Chief," Li says. "Do you trust him?"

"I don't know." I've had half a glass of beer and an unknown quantity of painkillers. Somebody else will have to drive. "But I don't want to stay here."

By the time we reach the vehicle bay I'm limping again. Hayek has approved a vehicle, a heavy black box only a Safety would find beautiful. Edda offers to drive. I wonder if this is where I find she's had military training.

She takes the wheel. Protocols are engaged, so even if this is her first time we should be safe. She drives us smoothly to the exit. When we stop at the barrier she tells the Safety, "We're collecting a client from Resort Four. Kinship issue." He looks at us, checks a screen, looks at us again, seems about to say something, then nods and steps back. Hayek must have called in a favour, trading on the old resentment between Safeties and Millies. The barrier is raised. Two minutes later we're on a public road. There's not much traffic: an occasional lorry, a coach full of sleeping men. I tell Li, "You didn't need to come."

"I did. You can barely walk. What else was I going to do? Wait to be sent home?"

"That might be all that happens at Four."

"Maybe." She stares out at the road. "But at least I get a last look at the 21st."

It's an unimpressive last look. A straight dark road with steep concrete verges. Still, we're under an open sky, and every now and then there are lights in the distance, houses, small towns.

There's a concentration of traffic ahead. It's not the kind of queue that usually forms behind an accident. This one is slow, but still moving steadily. As we draw closer we can see it's made up of a line of canvas-sided vehicles. The drivers are wearing camouflage jackets.

"He's back," Edda says. Her voice becomes flat. "Do you see those? We have seen similar movements all over the country. That's why you had to come now. By tomorrow there could be roadblocks. I don't want you blabbing what you know if they stop you."

"What am I supposed to know?"

Edda gives it the right tone of weary disdain: "Just get here." Then, in her voice: "He's gone."

"Really gone, or just listening in?"

"Gone. I'd know if he was listening."

"The machines are always listening."

Edda doesn't recognise the quote. "They might listen, but they don't always know what's happening."

The convoy is behind us now. The road ahead is clear.

Li says, "Geneva knows."

Edda keeps her eyes on the road.

Half an hour later we pass another convoy heading in the opposite direction.

The gate to Resort Four opens automatically. There are, we're pleased to see, no angry mobs outside. I'd turned on the radio after seeing the second convoy, and caught one of their news programmes, one that was broadcast for a fixed number of minutes at set times no matter how much or how little there was to report. There seemed to be not much. There was no mention of troop movements. The main stories were overseas: refugees from the flooding in Southern Europe, tensions on the Turkish border.

The natives were being told as little as we were.

As soon as the bulletin finished Edda told me to turn the radio off. Something about it was giving her a headache.

There are two Safeties at the dome entrance. They wave us through. I manage to walk from the vehicle bay to the main concourse before my stump starts hurting again. It's as quiet as the place we left. No Millies yet: they're either being kept out of sight or, Resort Four being Tri-Millennium and low status, they'll be deployed here last.

Hayek is in the outer office with Erquist and two of his team. They're examining native camera feeds: empty streets and stretches of motorway. It's only the second time I've seen them out of their offices.

"Tunnel Boy," Hayek says when I hobble through the door, "how's the de-augmentation?"

I drop into an empty chair. "I don't think I'll keep it."

Hayek grins. "Edda," he purrs. "My eyes and ears." He

ignores Li. "Sorry to have dragged you here at this late hour, but events are proceeding." He turns back to the array of screens on the wall. They seem to display nine different locations. I don't recognise any of them.

The pain subsides from hot skewer to severe bruising. "Have you heard from Geneva?"

"The weather is lovely. They're expecting a mild winter." Hayek's attention is on a row of small, terraced houses on the top left screen. A native male moves unsteadily along it. "You saw the soldiers?"

"Ours and theirs." The native male disappears from the screen. I expect him to reappear on another one. He doesn't. "Why did you want me back?"

"A pattern." Hayek's eyes follow a white van along a stretch of otherwise empty road. "Your friends can stay in the quarters here until you have to go. We have room." He turns to one of his team. "Try the west side." The images on three of the screens change. "Tunnel Boy, while you were in the medical bay you mentioned a name. Riemann."

"That's the man who was in the approach with me."

His eyes narrow. "So your mysterious stranger had a name. Who is this Riemann?"

"The man I saw before. The one without a signature."

Hayek doesn't take his eyes off the screen. "You never mentioned you knew him."

"He told me not to tell anyone."

He turns slowly in my direction. "But you did tell us. You disobeyed him and withheld information from us. Apart from his name, and the fact you recognised him, is there any other information you've withheld?" This isn't mock anger. Hayek is actually angry. If it wasn't for the pain in my leg I'd probably be more scared. "How did you know him? Was he kin?"

"He was the brother of an old school friend."

"And what does he do?"

"I don't know."

"What did he do the last time you saw him?"

"He was a boy. When I met him here he was older."

"How much older?"

"About forty years."

His eye is caught by something on one of the screens. "And you're certain the person you met was this school friend's brother?"

I can't be, of course. I met someone who told me he was the adult version of a boy I knew. "He was plausible."

"Plausible." Hayek's usual tone of superior amusement vanishes. "After forty years. What was the connection between your friend's brother and our girl?"

"He said he was there to stop her doing something."

"Which you didn't mention earlier."

"It's what he told me in the approach."

Hayek pivots away. "Did that sound plausible as well?" He nods at a screen. "That one." It's a street of rectangular buildings, offices rather than dwellings. The pavement is empty. I wonder what he's seen, if his attention hasn't been caught by a fox or cat. It takes months for us to not be surprised by animals in the wild. Clients often cry out when they see their first squirrel or cow. "See?" Hayek says.

It's faint: there's a patch in front of the garage door as if a flaw has suddenly appeared in the image. The patch becomes easier to see when it moves in front of darker, more consistently patterned walls, like tiny, transparent creature sliding across the lens. "We looked again at the information from the airport. We noticed anomalies. At first we thought there were flaws in their tech, but then we looked closer. This data has been manipulated. It has been altered by a protocol embedded in our systems. Certain images are systematically removed."

"Do we know who embedded these protocols?"

"Geneva," Li says. "There are things they don't want us to see."

Hayek ignores her. He cycles through different images of the airport. "The local surveillance is incomplete. We can't track continuous movement. There are blank spots; their cameras don't always work or they're connected to networks we can't overlook. But once we recognise a pattern we can look for it elsewhere." The images change: office buildings, a street of small apartment blocks. The blur appears briefly in all of them. "I can trace distortions, interruptions in the signal, erasures. There are patterns. I found this one reviewing the records from the airport. We tracked this one from the airport to one of those buildings. It hasn't reappeared since. Could this be your school friend's brother?"

"He was with me in the approach. I saw him walk into the cordon."

"No." Hayek continues staring at the screen. "You did not see him. There was nobody with you. You were alone."

"The Safety saw him. He talked to him."

"That man was sent home before he could be questioned. Besides, I wouldn't trust human testimony concerning anything that happens in the approach. According to the information I do trust you were alone. It was a hallucination. Or you have a false memory now. A recollection generated by your numerous anxieties. These are not uncommon after a" – he pauses as if the phrase sickens him – "traumatic event."

I take out the Dolman box. "He left this." I pass it to Erquist, who passes it to Hayek.

"It means nothing." Hayek peers at the narrow edge. "Why would he be carrying this?"

"It might have been our client's. Ivan said she was carrying one."

"And is Ivan a person whose information you trust? Any one of our clients could have dropped this."

"It might explain why she's here."

"It might. If it was hers. If I could open it. People use them for a reason." He tosses it back to me. "Take it back with you. Somebody might thank you for returning it. Or you can keep it as a souvenir. This school friend's brother, whoever he is, whatever he is, could still be at large. Normally I wouldn't care about him. But there's this." He indicates one of the screens. The sky above the apartment block changes. "From yesterday." A figure walks into view, one of us in a hooded jacket. They stop outside the building, look up and down the street and walk up to the door. They keep their head down, seemingly aware of the camera. When the door doesn't open they step back and look around again. This time they're less careful. The film stops the second they turn to the camera. "See?" Hayek says.

It's our client.

The film resumes. Our client walks away. "Do you see now? This is why I overruled your return and why I called you back here. I want you to go to the medical bay. They will give you something to control the pain you so obviously feel. Then you will sleep. Tomorrow, you will go where I send you and you will identify this acquaintance. You shouldn't need to talk to him. You can sit in the vehicle and look at a screen. Edda will be your eyes."

"Can't I do that from here?"

"The protocols are embedded in our systems. You will need

to be outside the resort. A short-range transmission from her to a screen with no other connections. Otherwise all I could show you is a blur. Or you could confront him, face to face. Whichever you choose, you have to be outside."

"If Geneva are going to all this trouble, should we even be looking?"

"This concerns our client. She is our responsibility. And looking for her is within our jurisdiction." He's still angry, but it's not directed at me. He's been the invisible king of this resort for a long time now. He can feel his authority slipping away and is making one last assertion of autonomy before the Millies take over. "You have a personal contact with this man. Make use of that. And if you're concerned about any trouble you might find outside, Edda is quite resourceful." He smiles at her again, the same benign appraisal. Of course: they're kin. That's why she's so at ease with him. He could be an uncle. "Besides, it will be safer than the Tunnels."

I glance at Erquist. He nods, but doesn't look happy.

"I'll go with them," Li says.

"You won't be needed."

Li doesn't give up. "I might help."

"How?" Hayek is amused. "Have you seen his school friend's brother as well?"

"No. But I know the people." Li, as usual, refuses to say *natives*. "That might be useful."

Hayek considers this. "It can't hurt. Now go to the medical bay."

It's four in the morning. The bay has been told to expect me. The doctor is military. I wonder if the bay is being converted to cope with combat injuries. I ask the doctor if she's expecting trouble. She doesn't answer. The Millies don't like dealing

248

with civilians. She gives me some field meds and warns me to use them carefully. "On standard dosage that foot could fall off and you'll be able to run for twenty minutes on the stump. Not that I'm saying you should." I take half the standard dosage. The effect is immediate. I walk to the assigned quarters with the faintest of limps. Without the stimulus of pain I fall asleep in minutes.

Overlap

When you come back it's as En Varney, a Two North woman assigned to Material Acquisitions. She was picked up at a recovery site just inside Number City territory, a daring raid by the heroic border scouts. Like Adorna Mond before her, she was kept in an isolation ward, where she demanded to be released. She was, she said, about to be sent to Geneva as part of a trade delegation. Her work was important; she'd be missed.

She was perfect: the right age, the right profession, travelling to the right period, a close enough resemblance to you and about to work with people who had never seen her before ...

It had taken years to reach that point. Not just waiting for the right person: you had to win the argument with the Defence Committee, which meant making an enemy of the Assistant Director. She'd recruited Picon and took any criticism of him personally. The missed rendezvous, she insisted, must have been your fault. The stories about selling drugs to locals were either lies or part of a plan you had misunderstood. The supposed corruption of the other courier was hearsay. What were your sources? A Number City extemp with his own criminal involvement and a voice on a telephone? Could either of them be trusted? She questioned your proposed course of action. Even if you could do it without being detected, what would it achieve? She accused you of being an agent provocateur for the Number Cities and tried to kill you by assigning you to an insect factory.

You survived the insect factory. You endured the long hours and bad food, the heat and the bosses. You didn't faint once, sustained by the conviction it would end. After three months the Committee called you back. They had received reports of a second contaminated stockpile, just as you'd predicted. The Number Cities had blamed their own workers. The logic was inescapable. Your plan had been carried out, therefore it would be approved. The Assistant Director protested. She was overruled. You moved to barracks in the suburbs to recover from the factory work and resumed training. Then they put you in the same ward as En Varney, where you pretended to be Adorna Mond, a patient from Two West with the same infectious but asymptomatic disease. En Varney was grateful for company. By the time you reached Geneva you knew her life story and could tell it as if it was your own.

You arrive earlier than on your last visit. You start in Geneva, working as En Varney, performing her official functions punctiliously for three months, cataloguing and classifying mineral purchases around the world, identifying suitable recovery sites. The work takes you to other cities and, thanks to Riemann, you know who to contact.

Alexander Metzger has an apartment in Berlin and walks his dog in a nearby park regularly morning and evening. You approach him one morning and tell him you need his help. At first he's terrified, then suspicious, then fascinated.

By the second meeting he would do whatever you ask. He has contacts, a network of locals who have already formed their mad little conclaves. Metzger vouches for you at their meetings. They listen while you confirm their worst fears: Geneva is working to take over their governments, their lives. A disaster is coming. Enough of them believe you. You're from the future, after all: how could you not know? They accept you as a renegade from the class they believe is oppressing them.

You explain your plan and why you need their help. Your own city is too weak to take action in your own time and their groups are too weak to attack them here. Geneva and the resorts are too well defended; their own governments have been bought. The only way to harm them is indirectly. They are only here for what they can take; make that dangerous for them and they'll leave. You don't use the argument that convinced the Defence Committee. You want these men to think they have a choice.

It takes cajoling, veiled threats, promises of rewards and the constant assurance they're on the right side, but you teach them how to enter and leave secure facilities without arousing suspicion, and – the hardest part – how to work together. You give them skills and a sense of purpose, reconcile them to their previously miserable lives. The damaged girl has come a long way. Metzger shows you how to organise them without leaving a digital trace. He is, he likes to boast, something of an expert when it comes to lost information. After giving you his contacts across Germany and France he promises to introduce you to groups in England — HumanTruth, Not Our Future, EPP. You make plans to meet in London, knowing he will die at the airport. You do all of this without arousing the suspicion of En Varney's fellow workers. They're soft: they complain about the difficulties and stress of their jobs and work fewer hours than anybody at Kat. Nobody seems to care how you spend your evenings.

You arrange a week's holiday in England. It's more hectic than your work: you have to follow a strict schedule.

While crossing France you contact Picon and tell him to arrange two apartments: one for you in London, another for the woman he knows as Adorna Mond. He protests: "I don't know where she is. She missed the rendezvous."

"No. She was in the right place. *You* missed the rendezvous."

"By one minute." He's offended. "Two at most. Traffic was bad. She should have been more careful."

"You should have gone to the mall."

"Don't be ridiculous." He talks as if he's still in charge. "Where is she now? Has she contacted you?"

"I know where she is." You tell him to arrange the apartments and call you back with the details. "This is what the Defence Committee wants." When the time is right you call the woman on the phone you know she'll have just taken from a local. She doesn't sound as surprised as you remember feeling. You tell her how to get to the safe house.

On the next day you go to the airport to see Metzger die and meet Riemann for the second time.

The case for war

At noon I'm back in the vehicle bay. Edda is already there, dressed in a black coat which contrasts with her pale skin and probably conceals at least one weapon. She's also carrying a metal case that might as well be stencilled "This technology breaches protocol". Li has chosen native garb that's more a political declaration than a disguise. "Do we know where to go?"

"Hayek thinks he's in north London." Edda has been briefed. "A district called Enfield. We're going there first."

We've been assigned the vehicle we came in. Once again Edda drives. Li sits in the back. The roads are as quiet as they were on our journey here: a few trucks and coaches, not many smaller cars. We don't pass any military convoys. The radio news (Edda allows me to listen to it once) makes no mention of them. The Prime Minister and the leader of the opposition are reported as calling for calm. There's been a slight improvement in export figures: the trade deficit is at its lowest for five years. There's no mention of any disturbances which makes the calls for calm sound hysterical.

Edda turns off the radio as soon as it finishes.

Li is still intrigued by Riemann. Last night was the first time she'd heard of him. "Why didn't you tell me you'd met someone like that?"

"He told me not to tell anybody."

"You told your boss and your Safety Chief."

"I had to tell them something. It might have been relevant to our client."

Li stares out of the window. We pass another lorry and then a coach filled with short-haired men in identical black tops. "So who is he?"

"What I told Hayek. Somebody I knew as a boy."

"What do you think he's doing here?" She wants to speculate. Mish talk.

I'm not in the mood, and Edda is too intent on the road and whatever instructions she's receiving to take part. Li, who probably feels isolated in the back, fidgets for a while, then tries again. "I don't know why they're mobilising. There isn't supposed to be any real trouble now. This is meant to be the managed democracy stage. The first signs of real trouble are years away."

"Fascinating," Edda says flatly. We pass another canvas-sided truck, a relic pulled from a military museum. We're driving through suburbs, miles of cramped houses, each with a car parked outside. Occasionally we pass a pedestrian, but no more than one or two at a time. "What do you think?" Edda asks. "Did we miss an announcement for a curfew?" We pass a commercial zone, the great boxes of supermarkets and furniture stores. They look like they're closed but there are four, no, five couples pushing trolleys across the open field of the car park. They're behind us before I can see what they've bought. Canned goods, water, survival provisions? "Maybe one of their royal family is getting married," Edda says. "Or it's a football match. Don't they love sport?"

"Not all of them." Li takes out a phone. "Not this much."

Edda turns off, heading towards the heart of the city. Military vehicles pass in the opposite direction, and, once in a while, a smaller one that might be civilian. We slow down when we reach a street of office buildings. Outside one of them, a native stands next to a cleaner's cart. He wears the shabby green overalls of the local poor, and pushes repeatedly at a button set in a wall. We're gone before anybody opens the door. Another turn, another row of office buildings and deserted sandwich shops, and then we're in a residential area: blocks of flats, rows of identical houses.

London, the natives like to say, isn't one city: it's a collection of villages. Most of them are badly organised jumbles of styles and shabbier than you'd expect for such a famous city. You grow up with the descriptions and the old images: the original world city, the heart of an empire, etc. Apart from a few older buildings the place itself is a disappointment. Extemps love it, which tells you everything you need to know about *them*. After the NEE the parts that survive become villages again.

Edda stops outside a block of flats. "Double yellow lines," Li says. The city has millions of vehicles and strict rules about where they can be left. There's no sign of our client.

"We'll pay the fine." Edda turns off the engine, but makes no move to get out. "Li, pass me the case." Li complies wordlessly. Edda rests it on her lap and opens it, revealing a small, flat screen, another piece of local tech we've adapted. "Let's see," she says, not to us. She pauses, waiting for instructions. "I'm ready." She lowers her window and looks at the block of flats. "Take the case," she tells me. I lift it off her lap. There's an image on the screen: the block of flats seen from Edda's perspective. The colours are distorted. The walls are various shades of green. There are red blobs in some of the rooms. People. They blur if she moves her head. "Is this what you see?"

"No. My vision is normal. But the layers are sensitive to other frequencies. It's just a matter of applying the right filters. Are the images getting sharper?"

"Yes." From simple blobs they're resolving into recognisable human shapes: torso, head, rudimentary limbs. The big one on the second floor left turns out to be two people in close proximity. "How much detail can you get?"

"A little more." The arms slowly become articulated. "You won't be able to tell which way people are facing until they move, but you should be able to distinguish one of us from a native. Top flat left. What do you think?"

A male figure, tall enough, is sitting on a chair with his back to the window. He could be eating a meal or cleaning a weapon. I check my handheld. "No signature." The blinds are drawn. Whoever's there is sensitive to natural light. Or depressed.

"Right then." Edda releases the seat belt. "Shall I go and see?"

"What?"

"I'll go up to the flat and knock on the door. When he opens I'll ask him if he's somebody else, then apologise for my mistake. You'll see his face on the screen and confirm if it's him. Simple."

"You'll need to get into the building first."

She's already out of the car. "I'll image the lock." And strides confidently off.

"Image the lock," Li says. "She's like a spy in an entertainment. You're impressed, aren't you? What is Hayek trying to prove?"

Whatever imaging the lock means, it seems to work. Edda disappears inside. The picture on the screen changes to the normal human frequencies. Edda is looking around the hallway. It's clean, as if it's been recently renovated, and it's empty. There's a staircase leading upwards. Li switches cards in her phone and starts making calls. She uses This English and talks quickly and softly: "Ricky, yeah, it's Li, what's happening, man? Call me, if you can." The second floor is a copy of the first and equally empty. Edda skips up the next flight of stairs while Li leaves another message, or the same message with somebody else. Edda reaches the top floor, goes through a door to a hallway with a window at the other end and two doors facing each other at midpoint. She pushes a button by the side of the door. The door opens.

It's a man, one of us. Riemann and not-Riemann. This version is in his thirties. The features are not quite right: he might be an older version of the boy I knew but I can't see how he becomes the man I saw in the approach. He smiles guardedly at Edda, who looks straight at him and recites her story. He shakes his head, closes the door. Edda retraces her steps. The hallway is still empty. I see myself on the screen as she runs back to the car. Then the screen goes black. She jumps into the seat and closes the door. "They don't tell you how strange channelling feels. It's like the back of my head has been removed." She takes the case from me, closes it and hands it back to Li. "Was that him?"

"No." I realise why I was perplexed, why I thought it was Riemann and not. "It's his brother, Cantor."

Edda drives to the next street and parks in a space outside a terraced house. We're close enough to walk back, far enough away to be out of sight if Cantor looks out of his window. "At least," Li says, "he's not overlapping."

Edda is more serious. "What were your friend's interests?"

"When I last saw him he was eighteen. I was about to go to the Tunnels; his kin were moving to City Five South."

"What sort of things interested him? It might tell us why he's here."

"He was a tech. His whole kin were techs."

"Travel?"

"Bio-chem. His parents were med research."

"But what were *his* interests?"

"All sorts of things. He'd have a different subject every month. The last time I saw him he was interested in reconstruction politics." *Interested* is putting it mildly. He was cranky without actually being a crank, obsessed with theories about distortion in the historical record. There were people who thought the whole history of the period immediately before the NEE was a fabrication. Cantor was fascinated by the different claims – that it was the consequence of a failed attempt to halt climate change, an accident caused by the Richardson expedition, or an earlier, secret incursion, and so on. He had tech friends who could talk for hours. I'd stay and listen out of loyalty, but thought they were all wrong. The NEE was too big to be the result of a single cause. It was a relief when I left for the Tunnels. "He was young then. It could be nearly twenty years ago on his line. He must have grown out of it by now."

Edda is silent, listening for instructions. Li says, "Not all of those ideas were stupid."

"They've made a decision," Edda says. "Hayek wants you to talk to him."

We leave Li to mind the vehicle and walk back to Cantor's block. There's still nobody about. It's beginning to feel ominous. Yet people are around: we can hear voices and snatches of music as we pass the houses.

A solitary police vehicle drives slowly by. Two people in the front seat, one in the back. The passengers look at us as they pass, but they don't stop.

Edda opens the door. I follow her up the stairs, along the hallway I'd previously seen through her eyes.

Cantor opens his door as if he's expecting someone. It isn't us. "You?" he says to me. "Spens?" And to Edda: "I knew you couldn't be a rep."

"Can we come in?"

"Are you Safety?"

"We're just reps," I say.

"*You* might be." He stands aside to let us pass.

It's strange seeing him in the flesh. The last time I saw him we were the same age. Now his face has lost its adolescent edges. You could see how he'd look at fifty: softer than his brother, less self-possessed.

I duck through the door and into his hallway. It's a standard native unit, about the same size as Justin Bayer's. One wall of the main room is stacked with equipment, some native, some probably in breach of protocols. There's more equipment on a table, along with a pizza box. It's a telling detail: Cantor has been here long enough to acquire the taste. Apart from a chair there is no other furniture.

"I heard you were becoming a rep. Long time ago."

"I'm still a rep."

There are printed images on the wall above the table. Cantor stands in front of them, blocking our view. "I remember when you went into the Tunnels. Riem was so impressed he decided he'd do the same. I tried to talk him out of it, but he was stubborn." The words come in a rush. I'm reminded of his brother. The difference was that Riemann needed the delirium of the approach; Cantor was always like this. "Of course, it was different by the time he started. Mostly, they just patrolled. I thought it was a strange choice for you, but you always seemed to make strange choices. There must have been an easier way to qualify for the education. And then I heard you became a rep. Riem went into Awareness. They recruited him the day he finished. I'm surprised they didn't do the same for you. It would have suited you better. I know you did it for the travel but they make you travel as well. They set him forward."

I've never heard of Awareness. I'm not sure I like the sound of it. "Where did they send him?"

"Never had the chance to ask." Cantor grimaces. "I tried to, when he came back. They wouldn't let me talk to him and then, well, we both had work. That's the trouble with forward. People get so precious about what might have been seen. All I know is it was a charter, and asymmetric. He was gone for about two years. I don't know how long he spent wherever they sent him. It might have been five years; it might have been days. But it's obvious he saw something they didn't want him to talk about. That's Awareness for you. They don't even like admitting they exist. Did you ever do that Beethoven thing?"

"Not yet." I wonder if he knows his brother was also here. I try to do the calculations. How old was Riemann when he left for the 21st? Will Cantor have returned by then? Does Cantor tell him about this meeting? The adult Riemann hadn't been surprised to see me . . .

"Sorry. Of course you haven't: you're still a rep." Cantor looks down and mutters something under his breath, an old habit. I realise he's also making calculations. "How long since you last saw me? On your line?"

"About five years."

"On mine it's fourteen. Fifteen. It must be the same event." He grins. It's probably meant as a grin. "Travel is confusing. What are you doing here?"

"We said. We're reps."

"I mean, what are you doing *here*, in my flat? I'm not a client." He turns to Edda. "Which brand are you with – Heritage?"

"We wanted to talk to you." Edda looks at him with the same attention she gave to his tech. "We think you might be in danger."

Cantor shakes his head. "No. I'll talk to you but I can't go to a resort. I have work here." His attention is caught by her eyes. "I assume you're relaying this? Are you using third-gen layers?"

"Second."

"Had them long?"

"A few months."

"Have them stripped out as soon as you get back. Second gen is unstable. They start to break down after a year. You can repair the damage to your eyes but you won't be able to use augs again."

"Thanks." Edda is amused. "I'll probably do that. But we are concerned."

Cantor turns away. "Do you find listening to their radio gives you headaches?"

"Cantor," I say.

"Just trying to help." He steps away from the display. "I'd thought of getting third gen. They're less obtrusive. Then Awareness turned up and made it clear I shouldn't."

I step around him and look at pictures on the wall. Most of them are maps, a few of cities, most of open country. There are also images of buildings and faces. Two of them I recognise immediately: our client and Alexander Metzger. The Metzger picture is the one that's been used to illustrate every story about him. The picture of our client shows her leaving an office building. She's not the focus: it's a picture meant to illustrate something else, financial success or the pressures of urban living. She's one of us among a crowd of natives. "This is the reason I'm here." He watches Edda's gaze sweep across the walls. "Got everything?"

She indicates the picture of my client. "Do you know who she is?"

Cantor gazes at it as if she's the love of his life. Perhaps it's as simple as that: a romantic entanglement across decades, centuries. "We're not sure. There's a hypothesis she's from City Two East."

Two East again. He doesn't know she has stood outside this building. "Why do they think that?"

He gestures at the image of Alexander Metzger. "He was my main concern." We expect an explanation, but he falls silent.

"Why?" I ask. "What did he do?" Metzger should be a safe subject: he's already dead.

"I saw him die."

I'm too surprised to say anything. Edda asks, "Who is he?"

Cantor looks at her as if seeing her for the first time. "I was told to. Awareness, City Five South." He's fascinated by her eyes. "I'm sorry. I haven't seen anybody with those for years. I was thinking of having third gen. There are some applications for my work ... " He shrugs, or twitches. "Awareness. They approached me after Riemann returned from whatever he did. They told me they wanted me to come here. I was a climate historian, part of a project trying to reconstruct the NEE. You know I was always interested ... They told me I could do important work here." He gestures at the array of equipment.

"And that's what I do. What happens in the early 21st is part of the picture. It helps us reconstruct what actually happened. We're beginning to get a clearer idea of the sequence of events. And in return for them helping me . . . " He stops and wanders over to the window.

"In return," Edda prompts.

"I've spent five years here, gathering data. It's not what I would have chosen to do, but it's still important work. Did you know we had no detailed records for the first half of the 21st? It was almost all maintained on computers, hundreds of them spread all over the world. All lost." He peers through the blind.

"What's out there?" I stand next to him. "Are you expecting somebody?"

He moves away from the window, stopping exactly half-way between me and the table. "Five years. In all that time I'd never left this flat. Almost never." I can't be sure if he's ignoring my question or didn't notice it. "Six, seven times. They contact me. There's a joke they have in Awareness. If they ask you to do something you don't understand you shrug and say it and nobody laughs. One of those jokes. *Go there, carry that, shoot this person in the face.* They send me equipment, instructions. I don't see anybody. No contacts, except with a few locals, and you can't really make friends with them. So I collect and analyse data. That's most of what I do. About the weather, about these people." He indicates the pictures of the other natives. They're the kind taken from official records: men of different ages, most with shaved heads, which gives them a family resemblance. "And then I was told to fly to Berlin. There was a conference. Climate scientists from this era. I couldn't participate obviously, but as an observer . . . It was all so I would come back on the same plane as him. That's how they work. They make your work possible, but there's a

265

price. You'll find out when you go to your concert. They'll want something in return. They arranged the tickets. I sat next to him on the plane. Do you know how uncomfortable they are, those seats? My back still aches." He catches my look and stops himself. "He was terrified the whole flight. Something scared him. He wouldn't look at me. So I sat in this uncomfortable seat and tried to read the conference papers. All the time I'm watching him, thinking, why him, why him. And I follow him off the plane and through all the security checks. And then, as soon as he reached the hall, he fell over, like he'd been tripped. And then he was surrounded by people and I left."

Our client had been there. Gurley and Knight had been there, watching our client. "Did you see anybody else?"

"No. I just wanted to get away as quickly as possible. They told me to pay attention to him. I did that."

"Did they say why?" I ask.

"Why doesn't matter. They said I had to be on the flight. I wasn't given a reason." He's puzzled, resentful. "It was an obligation. Five years of collecting data, then they tell me to do this. I'm supposed to be here another two years, collecting data. Then I go back. After that, I have agency again."

I indicate our client. "And what about her?"

"I don't yet know. It's the others I'm interested in." He jerks his arm at the pictures of the natives. "You remember the polonium traps?" We look at him blankly. "Ah," he says. "When did you leave?"

"47," Edda tells him.

"Ten years before me," Cantor says. "Then you know about the contamination of sites 28 and 49? 52 and 71? Spens, you must remember site 28."

Edda looks at me. "You mean the 28 incident?"

"We don't call it that any more. Not with what we know now. They weren't accidents or mistakes."

"Should you be telling us this?" Edda asks.

"Your parents, Spens. Even at the time I thought ..." Cantor shakes his head like a small child refusing food. It was a gesture he still had at eighteen, one of those character traits it was safe for his friends to mock. "Those resources were bought in the 21st, buried and marked for recovery. Hundreds of sites. Rare metals, material archives. Some of them were contaminated. Mill tailings, spent fuel rods from local reactors. Whatever they could find. The name 'polonium trap' stuck. People liked the sound of it."

"And you think he had something to do with that?" Edda has slipped into the past tense.

"After the disaster at 71 we started taking precautions. There'd been protests; teams were refusing to work. It slowed us down and it meant some of the materials couldn't be recovered. And then we found human remains at 83. They were well preserved. It was him." He points at one of the images on the wall. "Miko Halaz. He had identity papers from the 21st. They were still legible. They think he'd been accidentally contaminated and his accomplices sealed him in. Or maybe they just didn't like him. But it gave us a place to start." Cantor gazes at the man's face. It looks to me the same as all the others. "Awareness think they weren't acting on their own initiative. Somebody was organising them."

"Metzger?" It seems unlikely. His face doesn't fit with the others. It's the only one not taken following an arrest.

Cantor shakes his head vigorously, as if trying to loosen something. "They told me they had evidence City Two East was involved. It was based on personal testimony, inconclusive. That's why I'm here. To see if it's true."

"City Two East don't travel," Edda says.

"That picture, it's from a newspaper, a physical copy. A few years ago South Four were interested in the activities of extemps. They went through the archives, all these scraps of paper they had. They saw that picture and sent it round. Somebody from Awareness saw it and recognised the company. It's a report about an energy company winning a government contract. The picture just shows the company's main office. The contract was for securing radioactive waste materials. I'm supposed to find out if there's a connection."

"Without leaving the room," Edda says.

"I don't need to. The body we found in site 83, Miko Halaz, he's alive now. I track his contacts. They communicate through their internet. They use code but it's trivial. They're wide open. I monitor their network the same way I monitor the weather. I'm waiting to see if she contacts them. I'm waiting to see if his death" – he nods at the picture of Metzger – "is going to make a difference ... "

I wonder if Justin Bayer is one of these contacts. Justin's brother had mentioned code names: Happy Diggers, Snow White, Sleeping Beauty. I wonder why Cantor has been given this job, why he's working alone in a London suburb. Then I realise: what he's doing is a breach of protocol. If it's ever reported, Awareness – whoever they are – will claim he was acting alone. "Have they mentioned her?"

"So far, no. They talk among themselves. If she contacts any one of them personally we'll have our evidence."

"And then what?" Edda asks.

It's Cantor's turn to look blank. "Then I report back and go home. I have agency again."

Edda won't let it go. "If she's responsible and she's working for City Two East that's an act of aggression."

Cantor is glum. "That's a possible interpretation."

"You're here to make the case for war."

"That isn't my decision. I'm just here to find out what happened."

"*If* it's her," I say. I remember Riemann's last words: *The next time you see my brother.* Did he know Cantor was here? Was he here *because* of Cantor? Gurley thought our client had killed Metzger. He might have misinterpreted what he saw: our client was taking a picture, but not of a man having a heart attack. "Do you have any evidence?"

"It's inconclusive." He shakes his head. "That is, I don't have any. Yet. Apart from a picture, and it might be an accident she's in that. It hasn't been taken yet. See that newspaper stand in the corner? There's a headline, the death. That hasn't happened. You know, I've looked into *him*." He gazes at the image of Metzger. "Afterwards, when I learned his name. I read his book on Parthenius. I can't see his connection to this. I can't see why his death was important." He begins pacing up and down. "Have you ever heard of Parthenius?"

"The woman—" I say.

"It's relevant," he says. "Or not relevant, but important. Parthenius was a Greek poet. That was his subject, Metzger's, old poetry. Parthenius was brought to Rome as a slave. Ancient Rome, Julius Caesar, Nero, that time. You know me, Spens, history isn't my subject. But Parthenius – he wrote poems, but they're nearly all lost. It was like the NEE, except without the extinctions. All Metzger had – all that's left – is one little book about unhappy love affairs. Everything else is fragments, allusions. A reference in a poem here, a line quoted there to demonstrate a point of grammar. He *may* have taught one Roman poet, he *might* have known another. Fragments, allusions. Metzger tried to make sense of them. There's one thing he wrote, Metzger: even if the written record was complete we'd still have only a part of the story. The most important events in people's lives are unrecorded. The only trace they leave is in their consequences. I can read the messages they send each other but I can't hear what they say when they talk. I don't know if the woman is already involved. I don't know her name."

"It's Adorna Mond," I say. "She's my client."

He stares, open-mouthed.

"She's here already," Edda says. "She's been here for weeks. We think she's looking for you. You should come back with us."

"No." He scowls, his lips moving, miming a harangue. Something else he did as a boy. "I don't go back. I stay here. Two more years. The record says I stay." He jabs a finger at the floor.

"She's been seen outside this building."

"Then I won't let her in."

"It might not be safe." I look through the blind. Outside is still quiet. It looks completely safe. "Do you know what's going on out there?"

"I track communications," he says distractedly. "I monitor the weather. That's important. What's out there – it's a mostly peaceful decade."

"The military has taken over the resorts. Their army is being mobilised."

He's unmoved. "That's theatre."

"Are you sure?"

"That's what they told me. They tell me what I need to know." Cantor suddenly appears to remember he's in a room full of equipment, some of which might be listening. "What they *think* I need to know. If I was in any danger here they would tell me. The work I'm doing here is too important to them. They want me to find this evidence. Last week, after the riots, I asked if I was safe. They explained. People are upset, so their government pretends to be upset. Then they pretend to take a stand and we pretend to take them seriously. There's a conference, and we agree to some trivial changes and carry on with whatever we were doing. This march? It's just theatre. Their government didn't want to allow it. We told them to let it happen, give people a chance to let off steam, show they're still independent. I'm in no danger." He stares at the faces on the wall. They seem to calm him down. "I need to stay here. I'm not supposed to leave."

"She knows where you are."

"It makes no difference. Perhaps she's supposed to know." He gestures at the equipment. "Perhaps they told her. I don't leave this."

Edda doesn't argue. She turns to me "We should go. Unless you have any questions."

Of course I have questions. They're ones I can't ask. "Let's get back."

She heads for the door with no more than a nod to Cantor, who's still staring at the image of our client. I touch his shoulder as I pass. "Be careful." He grimaces and makes no attempt to stop us.

The man who collapsed

Metzger had been soft, asthmatic, overweight. You could tell he was marked for an early death simply by listening to him breathe.

You're not sorry: Metzger was useful, but there was something unnerving about the way he would gaze at you in meetings. Even as other people talked his eyes would be fixed on you. His attention reminded you why you'd once carried a knife: this teacher, that guard. He wasn't a physical threat but after the second meeting in the park you were careful never to be alone in his company. You didn't want to be in a situation where you might have to hurt him.

His death simplifies things. And it's useful: a story to inspire the others. When he collapses you photograph the crowd that gathers around him, meaning to examine the pictures later, even though you're not sure what you expect to find. Any face belonging to a Number City traveller will be enough. *This person was present. There must be a connection.* Show it to the diggers, let it circulate through their networks. Given them a reason, an enemy, and a moral.

You don't see Riemann until you're almost back at the station for the London train. Even though you've been expecting him he still manages to surprise you. He steps out of nowhere and catches your arm in a grip as casual as it is firm.

You allow yourself to be led out of the building and across a road where taxis and coaches disgorge their passengers. He never once loosens his grip on your arm. You reach a fenced-in plot with spaces for twenty vehicles, half of them taken. The low metal gate swings open as he approaches. "I almost didn't recognise you."

He expects this to unsettle you: he thinks it's the first time you've met him. You wait until he talks.

He talks. "I shouldn't tell you this, but on my line this isn't our first meeting."

He stops at one of the vehicles. Four doors, a dull silver-grey, the usual tinted windows. Empty. He lets go of your arms and produces a key fob and pushes a button, holds open a door. "Please. It'll be easier to talk inside." You climb in and sit next to the driving seat with your arms folded lightly across your chest, a defensive posture. You want him to think you're frightened.

He climbs in the other side. "I can take you wherever you want to go." He looks at you carefully, as if he still can't believe it's you. "Or we can sit here and talk. It's up to you."

You face him. "Who are you?" You need him to tell you his name. "Are you a Safety?"

"No." His expression is mild, almost regretful. "My name is Riemann Aldis. Ever heard of the Anachronists?"

"What are you?"

He rests his hands on the steering wheel. "How about the self-consistency principle?"

An interrogation technique: change the subject, keep the prisoner off balance. You don't answer.

"You should look it up," he says. "It's what's keeping you alive." He doesn't wait for a response. "I'm in a strange position. I know what happens. I know what you're going to do and what you might be doing already. I can't help thinking I could stop it all now."

"Stop what? I am a tourist."

"What are you doing here?" He looks straight ahead. "Meeting a local contact?"

I came to see somebody die. You wish you could tell him this. *I came to see who was implicated in the death.* It would be a pleasure to see his self-assurance punctured. Instead you play the frightened tourist. "I wanted to see an airport." You hold his gaze, wide-eyed. "I wanted to see what it was like when ordinary people travelled from one country to another."

He seems amused. "Did you notice what happened back there? The man who collapsed? Do you know anything about that?"

"No."

"Did you know you're being followed?"

You're wide-eyed again. "Why would anybody follow me?"

"Two locals. I was watching them. So you don't know why they would be following you?"

You'd spotted them moving to the back of the bar when the crowd started to form. The squat, red-faced one and the taller, dark one you're going to shoot. "No."

"Have you ever heard of Karia Stadt?"

Even with your arms loosely folded across your chest you can feel your heart beating. He knows more than you expected. "Who is she?"

"A woman I met, a long time ago. At least, on my line it's a long time. Travel is confusing, as they say. I was younger then. I hadn't heard of her, didn't appreciate who she was. I wasn't

275

even sure what she'd done. I could have asked, but it wasn't in my instructions. I had to be careful I didn't learn anything I wasn't supposed to know. Forward is like that."

Your throat is suddenly dry.

"I did some research." Riemann doesn't look at you. "Later, when I came back. There was the trial, the whole show. It turns out Karia Stadt wasn't even her real name. It was the name given to her by the people who killed her parents. Her real name – and you might find this interesting – was Ester Liens. Her parents had been part of one of those communities that rejected all the cities. Religious, left over from some old cult from before the NEE. Does any of this sound familiar? According to the survivors they were attacked by soldiers from City Two East. The soldiers killed every adult they could find and took the children. There are a lot of similar stories from the time. Two East had a low birth rate and high infant mortality. They had to get children from somewhere. If I met Karia Stadt, I'd want her to know this."

"Why?" It has to be a lie, a provocation. You change the subject. "Who were the Anachronists?"

"You haven't heard?" He brightens. "You don't remember *Kai and Victor Meet the Inquisition*? I thought everybody knew that one. I always felt sorry for poor old Victor. You really haven't heard of them?" He's mocking you. He knows you haven't. It's the technique again. At any moment he's going to ask a question. "The Anachronists wanted to see if they could change what had already happened. It's understanda-ble – you see somebody about to make a mistake and you try to stop them." He stares out at the car park. "When I was a lot younger, I was sent forward. That's rare. I suppose it was a privilege, though I didn't appreciate it at the time. I saw City Two East. What was left of it."

Another provocation. You don't respond.

"What I saw there . . . " He stares at the windscreen as if overwhelmed by the memory.

You recognise this trick. He pretends to be lost in thought, leaving a silence you're supposed to fill with a confession. You count to twelve and ask, "Why did you go?" A tourist question.

He ignores you. "They poisoned us. They were ingenious. They came back here and found where we were stockpiling materials and added radioactive elements. A long-range weapon. They're doing it now, or maybe it's next week or next year. They think they can get away with it. But, like I said, we find out eventually." He falls silent again. This time you don't have to prompt him. "We responded. Collective punishment. It was controversial. I didn't know this when I was sent. When they send you forward you travel in a bubble. This woman, Karia, Ester, whatever, was also in the bubble."

"Why are you telling me this?" They travel, and then they invent elaborate protocols to avoid the consequences. If his story was true he wouldn't tell you. "I'm just a tourist."

He smiles. It's an interrogator's smile, the smile of someone who wants you to think they have information. Smug. "But there I was, in a bubble with *this woman*. She's older, more *scattered* than you, but you still have a lot in common. I didn't blame her at first. I thought she was a soldier, brought up in a closed city and taught to follow orders. But I discovered she was responsible for a lot of deaths. They were her idea. Should I try to stop her? It might be she thinks she's doing the right thing. What if I told her that what she's doing leads to the destruction of her city? And that it's destroyed using the same materials she used against us? What if I told her she not only gave Five South the reason they'd been looking for, she provided them with the tools? If you knew this, what would you do?"

You stare, as if you haven't understood. "I would tell the authorities."

"I wish I could." He smiles again. It's hollow. He'd thought he could – what, persuade you? "I used to wonder, would she still do it if she knew what was going to happen? Or was the destruction an end in itself? What was she trying to do?"

You don't answer.

Panic response

On the stairs Edda says, "Do you think he was telling the truth?"

"He was telling us what he believed."

"Yes," she says, not to me. "We're on our way now. Nothing? There was a lot of equipment in there. It must have created interference. I'll report when we get back." The street outside is empty. "They didn't get a thing. There's no signal." I take out my handheld: she's right. I bip Hayek and Erquist: nothing. "Come on," Edda says. She breaks into a jog, and quickens her pace as we reach the next street. I don't feel comfortable running, and stride along behind her. Edda comes to a dead stop at the corner, allowing me to catch up. Our vehicle has been boxed in by two police cars. Two native police, a man and a woman, stand on the pavement, talking into the wound-down passenger window. The man looks up as we approach. His hand moves to his belt. He's armed, but not with a gun. It's a crude electro-shock device. His partner takes a step back, giving him room. "What's going on?" I say in This English. I stop at what should be an unthreatening distance.

He keeps his hand at his belt. He's jumpy, nervous out of all proportion to any threat we might pose. If this is theatre, not everybody has been told. He looks if he's been expecting trouble all day and thinks we might be it. Or he's the sort who believes what he reads on DomeWatch.

He says, "Is this your car?"

"It belongs to our resort."

Li puts her head out of the window. "That's what I've been telling him."

"I need to see your identification."

I take out my card and hold it up. It's rare to be asked. Normally they can see at a glance we're not local. He doesn't move. The woman steps round him and takes my card, squints at it, then back at me, returns the card and nods at the man. He doesn't relax. "What are you doing here?" His voice sounds constricted. A third policeman, another man, appears behind him. Two more, both men, stand behind us at a safe distance.

"We had a report a client was in the area." I try to sound calm, pretending this is a routine conversation. I don't want him to use his device. I've heard electrocution is unpleasant. I don't know how it would affect Edda's augs. "We offered to take them back to the resort."

The policeman stares at me. "So where is this client?"

"He declined our offer."

"Where is he now?"

I don't immediately answer. Edda says, "Why do you need to know?"

The policeman stares. His hand twitches. "You people."

"We would like to leave now," I say without moving. I don't want to give him an excuse.

He doesn't move either. None of them move.

"Is there a problem?" Edda steps forward. "I am relaying this to our Safety Team." She looks into his eyes.

The policeman's face goes blank. The woman puts a hand on his shoulder. "Sir."

"You people," he repeats. He turns on his heel and walks away. The man behind him takes his arm and guides him to the forward car. The two behind us drift away, like a tiny crowd realising there's nothing to see.

"Thanks," Li tells the policewoman, the last to move away. She nods in acknowledgement. Edda gets into the driver's side. I wait until the police are in their cars before stepping into the road. I don't say anything until the door is closed. "What happened there?"

"They said they had reports." Li watches the two cars pull away ahead of us. At the end of the street they drive off in different directions. "They wouldn't say what they were about."

Edda starts the engine.

"I don't think we were in danger." Li is still excited by the encounter with the police. "The one asking questions seemed to have problems. The others weren't there in case *we* caused trouble; they were to stop him. Did you see the way they kept their eyes on him?"

Edda watches the road. "If he'd attacked us they'd have sided with him."

"I don't think so. They'd have stopped him. Or dragged him away."

"If he'd attacked us they would have arrested us." Edda is emphatic. "That's what security services do. They don't like admitting mistakes. Let's see if we can get back without any more trouble."

"I think I know why he was anxious," Li says. "It's the March for Humanity. It's happening today. The government's telling people who aren't going to the march to stay at home. They're saying there might be repercussions. That's why the streets are empty."

"They have demonstrations all the time," I say. "They didn't empty the streets like this."

"This is different," Li says. "This is big. They're saying a million people. And the government is encouraging it. The media has been telling stories about extemps. That's unusual. The Prime Minister has said enough is enough and lines have to be drawn. They're saying they don't care if it provokes us, they have to make a stand. They're stirring up a lot of fear."

"It's theatre," I say. Cantor's description.

"It's a mess," Edda says. "Everything's a mess. They pretend to make a stand; we pretend to back down. Your friend thinks he's investigating your client. I wouldn't be surprised if she's investigating him."

"Cantor always liked elaborate conspiracies."

"Well, he's part of one now. I hope he's happy. But he's an idiot. I'm surprised they thought they could trust him. He shouldn't have told us anything."

"He's a climate scientist. He doesn't have the training. And I'm an old friend. He probably thought it was safe to tell me."

"He was an idiot. He should have known better. You don't tell people what's going to happen. You don't tell people you work for Awareness. He shouldn't have mentioned them." She frowns at the road. "They shouldn't use people like him."

"Perhaps they didn't have a choice. He was at the airport. He had to be there. He was distraught. He had to watch somebody die."

"I think he did more than watch. But we can't report this, any of it. When Hayek asks what he said, tell him it was all climate science and you didn't understand."

"What did he say?" Li asks.

"We could save lives," I say. "At least we could warn them about 52 and 71. We don't have to say how we know. We could tell them it was a rumour."

Li repeats, "So what did he say? Is something happening?"

"We can't tell you," Edda tells her. To me she says: "It would make trouble for everybody. If we say we heard a rumour do you think they'll pay any attention? But when it happens, then they'll remember what we said. And then they'll want to know exactly where we heard this rumour."

"We tell them. Awareness, Five South."

"You can't mention them. They'll disown your friend. Look, they probably know about us already. You saw the equipment. How do you think they'll react when they hear what he told us? The only way to avoid trouble is to say nothing and pretend you didn't understand."

"Understand what?" Li asks.

"That Five South and Two East are playing at espionage," Edda says coldly. "And Five South is looking for an excuse to start a war."

"Is that all?" Li is disappointed. "Don't we assume they're doing that anyway? What else did he say? Did he know about his brother?"

"He didn't know. I'm sure if he knew anything he would have told us."

"Did he say anything about what's happening now?"

"He was the one who said it was theatre."

We sit without talking until we're back on the motorway. There are more vehicles on the road now. It's closer to, but not quite, an ordinary day. My thoughts are going in all directions, none of them cheerful. Meanwhile there's a noise that's been disturbing me for a while, a chugging sound that has slowly been getting louder. It isn't made by our vehicle. Then I look up. "Is that thing following us?"

Li looks up as well. "It's called a helicopter."

"If it's just watching us I don't mind," Edda says. "We're not doing anything wrong."

"Right," Li says. "Do you think that will make a difference?"

It is following us. It follows us all the way to the approach road for the resort. There are native vehicles – trucks, armoured vehicles – lined up on both sides of the road, but the road itself is clear. The men standing around them are obviously military. Whatever they're waiting for, we're not it. They glance at us as we pass but nobody tries to stop us. "Look, more theatre," Li says. "Are they here to protect us? Or are they planning to storm the place?" She looks at them intently. "How many of them do you think have read that stupid novel?"

"What novel?" Edda keeps her eyes on the road. The flying contraption hovers overhead.

"How many do you think have finished it?" I say. "How does it end?"

"What do you expect? They win."

The soldiers aren't simply lined up by the road: they're also spread across the surrounding fields. Many of them are facing the resort.

Not here to protect us, then.

But they don't try to stop us. Possibly they prefer to keep us all in the same place. The outer gate opens as we approach. Once through the inner gate, in the dome itself, the usual Safety Team has been replaced by twenty-odd Millies, who sit or stand, as obviously bored as their counterparts outside.

In the vehicle bay engineers are working on the coaches and cars. Ours is requisitioned as soon as we're out of it. Naturally we go straight to Safety. Entertainment Area Two is now full of Millies, drilling in the open spaces or preparing their weapons. "This is ridiculous," Li says. "This is the kind of thing that starts wars."

Edda walks briskly, careful not to make eye contact. Individually, Millies are still human. Collectively they can be unpredictable. A sudden loud noise can trigger a response cascade like the one in City Four South, Sector Three. There's a reason Millies have been kept away from civilians ever since. Nobody wants another Sector Three.

We leave Entertainment Area Two. There are Millies at every doorway. Li lowers her head. "Twenty years from now they'll have more to blame us for. That's when they could get more aggressive. Do you ever ask yourself if the NEE wasn't something we wanted? Think about it. Who benefited from it the most?"

"The cockroaches," Edda says. "Some viruses."

"I'm just saying—" Li stops: we've reached the Safety Office. Hayek is in the outer room. His team have gone. There's a man in his thirties sitting at the back, an obvious Millie despite a civilian jacket. Hayek looks grim. It isn't hard to guess it's because of the interloper in his domain. "Glad you could make it back," he says, his voice flat. "Unfortunately, as you may be aware, communications were shut down for security reasons. We were unable to share your discoveries. Geneva has decided you will not be able to report at present. You will be on the next available translation. Until then you are to stay in your designated room." He gives the Millie a carefully neutral stare.

*

Our designated room is in the client quarters, a family suite with four beds. A meal is delivered by a military caterer. Subsistence food. Edda decides to sleep. "I don't know if we'll have a chance for a while . . . " Translation, including the long walk at each end, usually takes about six hours and people who can sleep in a transport are rare. Reps' advice to clients is always to get as much sleep as possible before leaving. When we say it we try to sound like experts, even if we've never yet made a return journey.

I stretch out on one of the beds, close my eyes and remain awake. Li, who's made a return once before, paces up and down the room until Edda tells her to stop. Li sits on one of the beds between us. "So, Spens, you're being sent back. And nobody has said anything about breach of protocol."

I'd been thinking about our client and my parents and war with City Two East. If Cantor is in his thirties and has another two years before he returns (if he returns) and City Five South consults the other cities before taking action . . . By the time the war starts (if you can call it a war: against a state as isolated as City Two East it will be more like an execution) I'll be in my forties, part of a kin, probably a career Happiness. Tri-Millennium and Resort Four will be a memory. And Riemann goes back a few years after that. He tries to change history and disappears in the approach.

My breach of protocol seems trivial. "We're not home yet."

"It's an administrative excuse." Edda can't sleep either. "It'll go on all our records as the reason we came back early. It sounds better than militarised panic response."

"I don't know," Li says. "They'll find a reason. You've had a bad few weeks. There's all those locals you've attacked."

"Self-defence."

Edda joins in: "Withholding information from a Safety Chief."

"Following orders."

"Allowing a resort vehicle to be vandalised."

"Not my fault."

Edda has the winner: "Losing a client. Seriously, Spens, you're lucky your record doesn't say anything worse."

None of us manage to sleep. Eventually there is a knock on the door. A Millie, bare-headed, unarmed, walks into the room, nods at each one of us to make sure we're all present. "Time to go. Translation is in one hour." Her tone has a don't-blame-me edge without being apologetic. We're civilians, after all. She doesn't have to be polite.

We don't argue. We follow her out of quarters, all the way to the approach, exactly like we're clients who need to be shown the way. At this point we'd be making small talk, anything to reassure people and take their minds off what's about to happen. Our guide does none of that. She's not here to add the final grace note to our stay in the 21st. She's here to make sure we get out of her resort. She leaves us at the entrance to the approach. "Don't dawdle," she says, as if we've been dragging our feet. "Translation is in fifty. You know the way." She marches off, and is soon lost among all the other uniforms moving back and forth across the interzone. We enter the approach with the usual combination of boredom and foreboding. "I've made translation three times," Li says. "I've never seen one as empty as this. We can't be the only ones leaving. They wouldn't go to this trouble for three people."

"Militarised panic response," Edda says. "It outranks budgetary considerations. But there'll be other people. We're probably just the last ones they've told."

"It's ridiculous." Li walks quickly, in the way people do when they're spooked. I wonder if she's going to talk the whole way. Edda strolls at an exaggeratedly casual pace, another nervous response. My stump begins to tingle, which makes me check my pockets. I still have the tube of military-grade painkillers.

Despite the tingling, I feel a sense of lightness. We're going home. Within a few hours, all of this – the militarised panic response, the questions about the records – will be history, a closed file, at best one of the minor disturbances in the slow run-up to the NEE. Soon the early 21st will be two hundred years in the past and I won't have to worry about it again, at least until I reach my forties and the war against City Two East begins.

If there is a war. Perhaps Cantor doesn't find the evidence. Perhaps . . .

The vending machines at the halfway point are empty.

Li talks the whole way. Nervous chatter. What did Cantor tell us? We can tell her now: nobody's listening. What do we think the Millies will do? Have we made any plans for when we get back? From time to time Edda says yes or no, but refuses to tell her what we heard. She's also distracted. We reach the cordon, where some people get headaches and some behave as if they're drunk and others lose sensation in their fingers or find they can't remember their names. Nobody likes crossing the cordon, even when the power is off. It's a relief to reach the transport.

Edda was right. We're not the only people travelling. There are two Safeties on seats at the back, older men, probably judged unfit for anything more dangerous than monitoring reports, allowed to stay this long because Hayek needed them and the Millies didn't object. Erquist is sitting by himself nearer the door. He signals for me to join him. Edda and Li take seats in different rows in the opposite aisle.

The other two hundred and forty-four places are empty.

As soon as we're strapped in place the doors close and the sequence begins. From here on there's nothing any of us can do except wait, or listen to an entertainment.

Or talk. Erquist says, "I've never heard of anything like this." He makes it sound as if being sent home early from his own resort is no more than a mildly interesting experience. "I was sorry to hear about your accident."

"So was I."

"The company will, of course, cover the full cost of any additional medical expenses."

"Will I still be working for you?"

"We can discuss that once we're back."

There's a low hum and a faint vibration. If it wasn't for the transport's shielding we'd be torn atom from atom. But the shielding holds, and energy that could destroy a medium-sized city causes no more than a vibration and a low hum. It will be like this for the next few hours.

"I was not impressed by the military," Erquist says confidentially. "They seemed to be *hoping* for a confrontation. I overheard two of their senior officers talking about how long it would take to clear away those poor natives outside. One of them thought it would take thirty seconds; the other insisted it would be fifteen. They were gleeful, quite bloodthirsty."

"Is anything likely to happen?"

"What concerns me is the possibility of an accident. Another Sector Three could cause a lot of damage."

Typical Erquist: worried about damage to the resort. "I'm surprised you agreed to leave."

"I didn't at first. But you can't argue with the military. Unless, of course, you're Hayek. He's connected to too many systems for him to leave. Did you know he's a key component for a lot of the external surveillance? The military can't replace him. He won't go unless there's a general evacuation." He stops, possibly wondering if he's told me more than he should. "But I've decided to treat this as a holiday, a chance to spend a few weeks in my old city, catch up with friends and family. I'll be back as soon as it's over. I expect the authorities will want to pretend this never happened. You?"

"New foot."

"Of course, but afterwards? Would you come back?"

"Isn't there my breach of protocol?"

Erquist is amused. "That always puzzled me. Of all our reps, you were the one I thought most likely to accept the blame for somebody else's mistake. That said, you haven't had a good record lately. And you missed a mandatory briefing with your section chief."

"I was reporting to you."

"That doesn't mean you can just ignore the rules." Erquist sounds regretful. "Unfortunately, that will have to be taken into consideration."

He closes his eyes. Erquist is, it seems, one of the rare people who *can* sleep. I stare at the ceiling for a few minutes before looking at the transport's library. I finally decide to listen to *Iphigenie auf Tauris*, if only to see if my German is still functional. It's a modern performance. The only drama Brink and Nakamura captured was the spoken passages in *Der Freischütz*. *Iphigenie* isn't a favourite, but the transport's selection under Theatre/Classic German is limited. They don't even have *Wozzeck*.

Iphigenia has barely begun her opening monologue when the vibration becomes a shake and the hum becomes something closer to a rattle. It dies down after a few seconds and we stare at each other in bemusement and relief. Erquist goes back to sleep. Edda goes back to whatever she was listening to. Li remains unplugged: she doesn't want to miss anything. She grins at me, the regular traveller amused by the beginner's fears. I try to concentrate on what Iphigenia is saying. *Doch immer bin ich, wie im ersten, fremd.* From time to time there's a judder, as if we're in an earthbound vehicle that's hit a bump in the road. In the old children's entertainment the transport would always shake just before it stopped in some new era. I remember a teacher explaining to us that if a transport actually shook that much it would disintegrate, end up as dust scattered across some immense distance. "Remember, travel is always dangerous, even if it's a fixed link." Unbound travel, she said, was especially dangerous. You couldn't be sure when or where you'd arrive and you'd need to build some sophisticated infrastructure before you could come back. The Siberian site Brink and Nakamura never reached needed fifty years and two transports of nothing but equipment and was never powerful enough to establish a fixed link. It was dismantled in 1832 and the parts buried. They weren't retrieved until the 2020s.

We're travelling between fixed points, which should be easier. "You could think of it as a lift," I remember our tech teacher saying. "If you could imagine a lift travelling fast enough to enter a low orbit, make several circuits of the Earth, then land in the shaft of a building in another city while decelerating exactly enough to stop at the correct floor." I remember liking the image. The teacher had then spoilt the mood by asking us to consider some equations. They were simple ones, baby steps towards full travel. Cantor once tried to explain them to me and nearly succeeded. He couldn't understand why I found them so difficult. But as he couldn't tell one piece of music from another and kept confusing

Napoleon with Hitler it was clear we were starting to have less in common. He went straight into High Education. I had to prove I was useful in different ways.

And we both ended up in the early 21st. Seeing him again had awoken a kind of nostalgia. Perhaps when I get back, I'll visit him, or his younger, 24th-century self. I could hand Riemann the Dolman box and see if it opens. Surprise!

No. I'd forgotten. I can't see Cantor again. If I did, he would have remembered the meeting. Besides, it would be awkward if he asked what I'd done recently. And I don't think I could face Riemann, who'd be fifteen. *Hi, Riem, I saw you die.*

The play can't hold my attention. I can't concentrate enough to follow the language. I listen as if it were music. On my first translation I'd passed the time reading the political and social history, the background information that was supposed to make me a better rep. It hadn't turned out to be useful. Now I keep thinking about Riemann. Perhaps he didn't die. Perhaps he caught up with our client and changed history.

Except Hayek says he wasn't there and that the woman we followed – that *I* followed, alone – was somebody else, a known tourist. If another rep had told my story and been contradicted by the data I'd have attributed it to the delirium of the approach or post-trauma confabulation or a dream. Because only in a dream would a man like Riemann talk about changing history.

I'd followed a woman I'd mistaken for our client into the approach. There had been a problem with the barriers and an unscheduled translation that was now unlikely to be investigated. Resulting in passenger inconvenience and a non-fatal injury.

I should look it up when I got home. Unscheduled translations from Resort Six. It was a fixed link: there was only one place it could go. Whoever was on the transport would have been stopped by Safety. The report might even name them . . .

There's another jolt. Iphigenia falls silent mid-speech and doesn't resume. The jolt is enough to wake Erquist. He looks around, startled, seems to remember where he is, smiles ruefully and closes his eyes. Edda is jabbing at her control panel. "Is that normal?" She leans as far across the aisle as the straps allow. "I've lost sound."

Li says, "I've heard of it before. Sergei says it happened on his translation. They lost the whole entertainment system for an hour. There were some angry clients."

"At least we don't have those." Edda stares glumly at her panel. "I should have brought a book."

Which is when the lights go out.

"Li." Edda's voice, sardonic. "Did this happen on Sergei's translation?"

"He never said." Li sounds cheerful. We sit in the dark, listening to the hum, which sounds louder now there are no other distractions. There's another jolt, the most violent so far. Beside me, Erquist yelps, then apologises. "What happened to the lights?"

"We don't know."

"Announcements?"

"We've lost the system."

Erquist swears. That's when I realise this is possibly serious. One of the Safeties by the door calls, "Everyone stay calm. This is nothing to worry about," which doesn't help. Erquist swears again, more quietly his time. "Do you know what this means? A loss of power like this could be a sign we're no longer fixed point. Something's happened either at the resort or at home."

"You think the military might have accidentally shut it down?"

"They're unlikely to be that stupid. They would have left travel to the techs."

"Unless they had a response cascade." I can imagine the scene: somebody drops a cup and for the next fifteen seconds the Millies are blasting at everything that isn't another Millie. "Is there anything we can do?"

"In here? Nothing. We just have to wait until the techs resolve the problem."

"Isn't it possible to take control from inside a transport?"

"You can *start* one. *If* there's a fixed link. Once we're under-way there's nothing we can do. Do you remember *Living in the Past*? Well, it's not like that." His sigh merges with the hum, which rises in pitch. We sit in absolute darkness.

"What are you doing?" Edda's voice. I can see her eyes: faint green dots. Or think I see them. It might be a hallucination.

"Everybody stay calm," repeats the Safety. He sounds terri-fied. "There is no need to panic. Everything is under control." Another jolt. This time it feels as if the transport has been hit from the side. The shock reminds me of the accident in the coach, with the difference being we knew what was happen-ing then. We knew nobody would get hurt. This feels like it could soon get worse.

The surprise is that it's exhilarating. If I wasn't strapped down I'd be running – or limping – in the aisle, and not from panic. This is the spirit of Joy itself, the daughter of Elysium, the glee for which tonin is a weak substitute. I'm strapped to a chair in the dark with no idea what will happen next and I've never felt so alive. Even if it turns out that *Living* was good science and we step out into the 9th century I feel I'll be prepared. Within a year I could be running my own fiefdom.

We'd never be able to generate the energy to go home, even if we could reconstruct the tech, and, if what Cantor said about second-generation augs is true, Edda would start going blind after the second year. We'd leave behind a legend about wounded giants and some buried pleas for rescue to baffle future generations.

Another jolt: the whole transport seems to lift and then drop. I have a sudden sense that we are upside down. The sensation soon vanishes. "This isn't normal," Li says. "Are they letting this happen because there are no clients?" Nobody answers her. I can't see Edda's eyes. The hum grows louder than ever, somewhere between a whistle and a shriek. "Spens," Erquist says gently, "it was a pleasure to work with you." And then the noise stops. The lights come on, dimly, just enough for us to make out our silhouettes. There's still no sound from the system, no automated message explaining what just happened. "We must have a fixed point again," Erquist says confidently. He's part of the Happiness Executive: his job is to reassure. "It should be easier from now on." Which is, of course, when we crash.

Loose ends

You travel north to the city where you had your first glimpse of the 21st. You call Picon to tell him you'll see him soon. There are loose ends to tidy up first. Also he needs to send supplies to Adorna Mond. You tell him what to include.

You think about what Riemann said: *She thinks she's fighting for something but she destroys it.* You tell yourself it's an obvious lie.

Even if it's true it's too late to stop now. The plans are laid. Your Diggers are ready to start.

One loose end is the extemp who stole the Dolman box. You have a clue: the word *anterior.* Pretending to be a tourist, you approach a Living History rep, tell him you'd met a man who'd pestered you for tonin and used language you'd never heard before. The rep laughs. He said *anterior?* Everybody knows *him.* He's a nuisance. He's at Bar Five most nights so he's easy to avoid.

Or find.

You don't want to face him in a bar full of tourists. You try asking in a few local pubs; none of the locals you question admit to knowing anything. You have an idea: if Bar Five is closed he'll either go home or somewhere less public. Metzger had given you a handwritten list of contacts. It doesn't take much to persuade a HumanTruth local to heel a bag under a seat in Bar Five, early evening, before the tourists arrive. Nothing spectacular, just enough to start a fire and make sure the place is closed. And then you stand and wait with the other travellers until the extemp appears. He doesn't recognise you: you're part of a small crowd and wearing the headgear and eyeshades of a nervous first-time tourist. Your helper follows him, calls twenty minutes later with an address. Two floors above some kind of shop. Not typical extemp luxury, but he isn't a typical extemp. You take a taxi. You turn up at his door without the headgear. On his line it's only a few days since he took the box and pushed you into a room so when he sees you he's puzzled, pleased and then scared in roughly that order. The snakes on his forearm are frantic. You push your way in, close the door, show him the pin gun. He starts with bravado. *You don't shoot me. I've seen my line. Is that even a weapon?* He'd never seen a Dolman box, doesn't recognise a pin gun. You explain how they work. The projectile breaks down in the target causing immediate systemic damage. A shot to the head or chest is fatal; a hit to a limb causes the loss of that limb. You ask for the box. You know you won't get it, but you have to make sure his people take it to the shop so that you can meet Riemann for the first time. As you were once told, the knowledge of what happened creates an obligation: the meeting with Riemann doesn't happen by chance. The extemp insists he doesn't have the box, hasn't had it since he took it from you. His friends kept it. They're bringing in an engineer, a specialist, to open it. "Call them," you say. "Tell them I'll save them the trouble." You don't need the box, its contents are now irrelevant, but Riemann is following it and you need your younger self to meet Riemann. That needs to be arranged. The extemp hesitates, gabbles, tries to be friends, becomes stern, warns you don't know who you're dealing with and shuts up only when you point the pin gun at his thigh. Finally he makes a call. On the phone he's cheerful, as if passing on good news. Whoever he speaks to seems unconvinced but eventually tells him what he wants to know. He gives you an address. "Tomorrow, four-fifteen." He tries to be a concerned older friend: *I think you're making a mistake.* Offers the benefit of his wisdom: *After what you did to them I'd be careful.* Becomes bitter again: *And you're doing this for that selfish fraud.* You ask him to tell you everything he knows about Picon Delrosso and he does, gleefully. He's a fool and a coward but without him you wouldn't have learned the truth about Picon, you wouldn't have met Riemann and learned what you were meant to do. By locking you in a room he put you on the path that led you here.

You let him live.

Your helper has been waiting in the street outside. You tell him to go home, you don't need him for the next part. "What about him?" he asks, nodding up at the extemp's flat. He's angry, like all of your helpers. (His handle is, in fact, Grumpy7.) You tell him he's done enough for one night.

You make the call, give the address and the time. "Take the gun. If you meet a man called Riemann Aldis do what he tells you ... "

Picon doesn't recognise you. He blinks. You tell him your new name and give the identification codes. He recognises these. "You," he says glumly. And then, as if it's a pleasure to pass on bad news, he says, "We have a problem."

You follow him through his door. It's a big house. You ask, "How many work here?"

"It's just me." He walks briskly. There's a large room at the back of the house with sofas along the walls. A native girl sits on one of them, gazing at a slate. She doesn't look up. "I wasn't expecting you this soon," he says. "It could be serious, the problem."

"What problem?"

He sits on a sofa, next to a small collection of phones and other devices. "Adorna Mond. The courier, travelling as."

You glance at the girl. She's not listening, intent on her slate. You doubt she speaks your language. She's safe. Her slate, however, will be connected to the local networks which might have been compromised. Your helpers have warned you about the extent of the local snooping. Picon takes the hint and picks up one of the devices next to him on the sofa. Music starts.

Now you can talk. "Why do you think she's a problem?"

"She didn't make the rendezvous." Picon tries to sound serious but you can tell he's enjoying this. "That was only the beginning. I've had a rep here, asking about her. He said he was a rep. Looked more like a Safety."

You look around his room. "You're too comfortable."

"That's because I'm supposed to be one of them." He twists in his seat and checks another phone. He's trying to make you think you've interrupted serious business. "This is how they live. Anything else would look suspicious."

"You were sent here for a purpose."

"And I've been carrying it out. I've made a full report."

"Things are going to change."

Now he looks concerned. "Are you sending me back?" The fight goes out of him. Useless.

*

You take a taxi to the tourist area and find Arne Vasilis, the traveller who wants to stay. It's easy: you already know her name and what she looks like. She's soon persuaded. It's an odd conversation: you've met her before, but it's the first time she's seen you. Afterwards you call your younger self again, which is less strange each time. Arne Vasilis is exactly the person you remember – a day younger, no more. Your younger self is less familiar: terse, asking few questions, a good subordinate. You feel something like pride. This must be how the Assistant Director felt about Picon. You tell her she needs to stay in public places at the resort, what time to go to the approach, what to tell the Safety at the gate. You explain what needs to be done at home, what story to tell, which officials to approach, what arguments to make. It only becomes strange when you end the call. You have told yourself exactly what you remember being told, but it hadn't felt like a repetition: it felt like the only way it could have been said. You know you will carry out your instructions because you remember carrying them out.

It's one of the circumstances you were warned not to think about too deeply.

The riots get you into Resort Six. It's busier than its Safety Team is used to: people are coming in from everywhere. Even extemps and reps and clients from other resorts have been allowed to take shelter. As long as you're not a local they won't even look twice. You are able to slip away from the newest arrivals, through an unmarked door and down some stairs to a room where information relays are kept. You would need approval to input instructions at the appropriate desk and even more to enter the rooms where instructions are processed and routed to different systems, but in this resort there are four rooms where information is held temporarily, where instructions wait until it is time for them to be processed. Here, if you know what to do, is a weak point.

There are limits. You can't do anything that would cause serious damage. You can't change translation parameters or start a translation, but you can set a delay on the security gates for the approach so they won't close until the translation sequence begins. Another memorised procedure, a kind of magic: you perform the actions, certain consequences follow.

You don't get caught. Adorna Mond makes her public exit. Riemann, you're sure, would have taken note and will turn his attention elsewhere. And now she's gone you're no longer bound by her schedule.

Resort Six provides a room for temporary guest En Varney. You contact Acquisitions in Geneva and tell them you will be delayed for a few days: local trouble. You'll be back at work as soon as you can. That night you stay in your room and examine the images you captured at the airport, looking for a person you can blame for Metzger's death.

The Richardson expedition

At first it feels like another jolt, no harder than the last one. Then there's the whooshing sound that means the outer door is opening. One way or another, the translation is over. I'm out of my seat before the inner door has unlocked. If I'm going to die I might as well do it on my remaining foot. Erquist stays strapped in. "Don't you think the Safety Team should go first?" They're taking no chances, as if staying in their seats could save them. The inner door opens with a very human sigh.

The good news is that we're not in a field, or two kilometres above a field and falling. We're on the ground, inside a structure. There are dark walls with sparse, dim lighting and solid black material on the floor. There's a ceiling of dark material maybe fifteen metres overhead. It's a zone, but not one I expected. This is starker. There is no marked path to the approach, no message of greeting.

Edda joins me at the door. "What do you think?"

"We've arrived somewhere."

"Military?"

"This is old." Erquist has joined us, carrying two bags of bottled water and energy bars from the transport supply. He hands the heavier bag to me, and looks out. "This is what they looked like sixty years ago."

None of us have yet stepped off the transport. The Safeties have disentangled themselves from their seats and are hanging back. Li pushes past me and walks down the ramp which means the rest of us have to follow. I join her on the floor of the cordon. There's still a sense of residual energy, but fainter than you'd expect. We look around. "Do you recognise anything?"

"It's new to me."

Off to our right a metallic gate opens with a ponderous scraping noise. "We've landed in a museum," Li says. She walks towards the gate. "Come on. There's nowhere else to go."

We follow her. Edda walks beside me, then Erquist. Finally, and reluctantly, the Safeties, who give the impression they're only following us because they don't want to be left alone.

This approach is different architecture. Instead of a spiral corridor like the ones at the resorts this is made of straight lines and right angles. "An early design," Erquist says. "Abandoned around the turn of the century. People found the sharp turns disturbing." I can see what he means. Rather than having a sense of slow progression it feels like we're lost in a maze and about to double back to where we started. There's lighting at each turn, simultaneously harsh and ineffective and the ceilings seem to slope at odd angles. "Of course," Erquist says, "this wouldn't have been for commercial use. This was for research." He's talking from nerves. "I'm surprised something like this is still working. I would have expected it to have been decommissioned years ago." He dutifully emphasises the positive: "At least we landed somewhere. When we lost the fixed point I thought we were going to die."

"Perhaps it was reinstated," Edda says. "The military had requisitioned the commercial ones. They had to divert us somewhere."

"We lost a fixed point?" Li is excited. "Can that happen?"

"It's possible," Erquist says mildly. "Losing a fixed point was not uncommon in the early years. There were miscalculations. It's safer now, but there's always a possibility of error. Mind you, fixed was always safer than unbound travel. *That* was dangerous. Small teams, and most of the transport was taken up with the equipment they'd need to return. The Richardson expedition." He sounds wistful. "I heard an entertainment about it as a boy. It obsessed me. I tried to learn everything I could. Of course, the technical side was beyond me, but the adventure of it – going somewhere and having to construct your own means of getting back – all that was very appealing. Of course, I didn't really understand the dangers. To be sent back only ten years before the NEE when the political situation was so poorly documented – that was a risk. But it had to be somewhere with energy supplies and no strong central authority. So they were sent to a potentially dangerous era with no certainty they'd be able to return. The calculations were crude by modern standards . . . " He chatters on, his voice gentle and even. "Everybody involved wrote about their part in it. Except of course Richardson herself." Richardson stayed behind. If she left an archive it's never been found, which is why she turns up in crank theories where she either causes the NEE or witnesses the real cause and has to be silenced. "I read everything I could about them as a boy. Travel looked like the most exciting thing in the world . . . "

We've been walking for about fifteen minutes. I'm starting to feel tired, the post-translation fatigue all travellers are warned about. My leg doesn't hurt, possibly because of the gentle pace and relief at still being alive. Erquist, who was asleep for part of the translation, is the only one unaffected. He talks about his old enthusiasm for the Richardson expedition ("Look where that led me") until we turn another corner and there's a gate ahead of us. It's open, and leads somewhere just as dimly lit. And silent: no announcements or recorded greetings, no music or any other sound. And no one waiting for us, friendly or otherwise. We step out into a hall only slightly smaller than a resort interzone. It's dark: only a quarter of the lights are working. There are no signs anywhere, no active screens – no inactive ones either: just bare walls in the same dark, metallic grey. The place looks abandoned. The theory that we're in an old, hastily recommissioned zone looks plausible. "They must have been able to activate it remotely," Erquist says. "Still, I'd have expected somebody to be waiting."

I remember I'm carrying a sophisticated communications device and take out my handheld. When I try scanning for signatures the only ones I can find are ours. There is nobody – nobody with a signature, anyway – within a half-kilometre, although with all the shielding I could easily miss somebody. Erquist checks his own device, with the same result. Li takes out her mobile from the 21st. "If this finds anything, we're in trouble." It doesn't.

Edda points at the far wall. "There's a door." I can't see anything but I trust her. It's only as we cross the hall, past the empty booths that appear to be geometrically arranged, that the cold starts to sink in. The floor is covered with a fine grit that crunches underfoot. The door, two sheets of lighter-coloured metal, has no lighting around it, no sign indicating what might be on the other side. Edda pushes against it and it folds back with a squeak.

On the other side it's darker still. The hall behind us is the only source of light, and that seems to be getting dimmer. Ahead of us is what might be a broad avenue in a medium-sized town. There are structures on each side but no sign of light or activity. Overhead is pitch-black. "Definitely an abandoned neighbourhood," Erquist says. He turns to the Safeties, who hang back as if they were hoping not to be noticed. "Do either of you have night vision?" They both raise their hands. "We're going to walk along this pathway," Erquist tells him. *Pathway* seems an odd word. The route seems wide enough for three lanes of traffic. "Could you please lead the way?" he says to the younger one, his Happiness training reasserting itself. "You," he says to the other one. "It would be helpful if you could keep up the rear. We're can't be very far from an inhabited area. The rest of you, keep together."

We start walking, following the luminescent piping of the younger Safety's uniform. Now that we've started building on the surface again most of our cities have uninhabited districts. The authorities either let them slowly collapse or be taken over by former Happiness in the hope they'll generate culture. This one seems to have been left to collapse. "Research facilities," Erquist says. "Probably military. It makes sense. They wouldn't have put a zone near a population centre in those days."

There's still nothing visible ahead of us. No lights, no movement. After the incessant noise of the 21st this place is eerily quiet. It isn't just the absence of traffic and alarms or sirens or people or the continual noise of machines – heating units, air-conditioning units, electrical substations, the ubiquitous grind of their music, all the hums and clicks of hundreds of devices. There's no weather down here: no rain drumming against the ground, no wind, no trees for the wind to move through. We seem to be in a completely dead place. "And I thought City Three North had nothing going on," Li says.

"I always wanted to see Africa," Edda says.

"When?"

"20th, 21st." She's being typical Happiness, trying to distract us. "Any time you could still see the megafauna."

It works. We reminisce about what made us travel: to see the society that existed before the NEE for Li; I mention Brink and Nakamura; the older Safety remembers *Artegal*: "I used to listen to it every night . . . ". It's hard to tell how far we've come. You walk more slowly in the pitch dark; you don't have any points of reference. The lead Safety tells us some of the structures now start to resemble barracks or blocks of flats.

Finally Erquist says, "Let's see what's in this one." He doesn't say why he's chosen this building rather than another. The door is metal, and, beneath the usual layer of grit, glass. The older of the Safeties cuts out the lock and we're inside, the other Safety leading the way. There's a hallway with a concrete staircase, and doors at each side which lead to smaller hallways with more doors. It reminds me of Cantor's block of flats back in the 21st: the same floor plan, almost the same scale. The Safety opens one of the internal doors. It leads to what is recognisably an apartment. Surprisingly, there is still furniture: a table and sofa in one room, a bed in another, a narrower room lined with cupboards that was once a kitchen. Li fumbles at the walls. If there are switches or scanners they don't respond. She finds bedding in a wardrobe, but no clothes. The grit that is everywhere outside hasn't found a way in. The air is stale, but breathable. Something from the surface is still reaching here. There must be concealed vents. The other doors lead to similar rooms.

We gather in the hallway. Erquist hands out energy bars. We chew slowly, sipping carefully from bottles of water, blankets wrapped around our shoulders. "The question is," Erquist says, "do we keep going in the hope of finding help, or do we stay here, closer to the zone?"

"Keep going." Li's answer is immediate.

"We'll stay," the older Safety says. "We'll stay here."

"Here?" Edda says. "Really?"

The Safeties exchange a glance. "It's what we've decided."

Erquist doesn't try to talk them out of this. He goes straight to negotiation: they can have a third of the food and water; we will take a sidearm and a night-vision set. After five minutes the Safeties' resistance is worn down and the equipment is surrendered and we're ready to leave on what look like friendly terms.

Edda takes the NV. "I've used this before." One day I'll have to ask about her training. "Everybody ready?" Erquist takes her left hand. I take her right. Li takes my right. "Like children," Li says, "lost in the forest." She laughs, remembering something. "Follow the yellow brick road." Early 20th-century culture. A children's entertainment. We resume walking, a steady pace, but slow. Edda squeezes my hand.

"What can you see?" I ask.

"A straight path surrounded by boxes." Her visor emits a faint glow, like the after-image of light. "I can't see anything alive. I thought there'd be weeds, moss."

"There's no sunlight," I say.

"I expected rats."

"Tunnel Boy," she says. "Do you think Hayek knows where we are?"

"There'll be enough information," Erquist says. "Hayek will do everything he can." The present tense is jarring: the 21st is long over by now. The resort will have gone, the valuable parts taken home, the rest left to fall into ruins. Erquist talks as if it still exists. It's the logic of travel: the past is just another country, and, if you can afford the translation, you can always go back. Nothing is lost, nobody really dies. *You* die, of course: but, if they have the right resources, other people can always come back and see you. You remain alive for them. "He won't give up easily," Erquist says.

"So maybe we should have gone back to the zone," Li says.

"No. There's no energy left there. Our translation must have used whatever reserves they had. It might even have been the source. Those lights at the zone were fading when we left. They'll be dead by now. Plus if we're traced they won't be able to send a transport to the zone with one already there, but they'll send it as close as they can. And a translation outside a properly shielded zone can be, well, disruptive. We'll want to be at least two kilometres away when it arrives. Especially in an enclosed space."

"Why didn't you tell the Safeties that?"

"They'll be aware of the risks." Erquist is all mild reason. "Besides, couldn't you see how uncomfortable they were around us? All Safeties of that generation get like that eventually. They can only stand each other's company."

"So that's our plan?" Li tries for the same nonchalance. "We just keep walking?"

"Until we find other people. Or at the very least light and food. Then we wait to be found." He makes it sound easy.

"We shouldn't have to wait," Li says. "If they were going to send help they'd have sent it already. Forget rescue, they could have arranged a welcome party."

"Days," Erquist says. "We shouldn't have to wait more than a few days."

For what seems a long time the only sounds are our footsteps, our breathing and the rustle of our clothes. Li's device can produce a tiny beam of light, but it's not strong enough to illuminate anything at further than arm's length. Occasionally we stop to look at one of the structures we pass. There are windows in some of them, as if this stretch was once well lit and busy and people would have looked out to see what was happening. Without landmarks we might as well be walking on a treadmill. I try closing my eyes, thinking that when I open them again there might be a slight difference. There isn't. Occasionally I think I'm starting to adjust and can make out the shapes of the structures around us. It's an illusion. The shapes change when I look again.

"We may have to find something soon," Li says. "I think it's getting colder."

She's right. The temperature has dropped still further, as if night has fallen somewhere overhead. We walk more briskly. "We'll find a suitable building," Erquist says. I can see the glow of his handheld. "Still nothing. Spens, can you read any signatures?"

"Not yet."

"Perhaps they don't have them here," Li says. "Spens," she says, "does this remind you of the Tunnels?"

"No." The painkiller is just beginning to wear off. "They were noisier."

This place is beginning to spook me. I find myself wondering if there aren't people all around us, silent and adjusted to the dark, listening to us pass.

Li breaks the silence. "I could have crossed City Three

North by now," Li says. "Even at this speed. Is anything changing?"

"The roof is getting lower." Edda sounds bored. "None of the buildings are more than four storeys."

"Do any of them look as though they reach the surface?" Erquist says. "There must have been a point of entry."

Edda stops walking. "This one goes all the way to the top."

"Do we really want to go to the surface?" Li says. "We don't know what's up there."

"If there's a chance of a signal, yes," Erquist says.

"We don't know if it will lead to the surface," Li says. "It might just lead to another level."

"We're not so deep," Erquist says. "There's air down here. We can still breathe."

"Small mercies." Li sounds amused. "Well, it has to be better than this. Or different, at least."

We start walking where Edda leads us. When I stub my foot against a step it registers as an ache in my shin. "Here we are." Li's mobile casts its feeble light: there's a flight of steps, perhaps a dozen, leading up to a vast double door with glass panels. Edda finds the locks – three of them – and starts cutting.

While we wait, Erquist talks. There are cities, he says, that are essentially one building extended in all available directions and there are cities made up of prefabricated units thrown up in caverns and mineshafts. This is the second kind. "Definitely some kind of research establishment. That accommodation was basic. Students, military."

Li keeps her torch on Edda. "I can't imagine it ever being cheerful." She notices something by the door. "Can anybody read this?" Erquist goes to look, and then, because there is nothing else to do, I look as well. There are marks in the metal architrave, like the impression of writing left on the page underneath. It's faint, but when the light is shown at the right angle it's possible to make out what look like letters. It doesn't seem to spell anything: random strokes with the occasional H or T. "It's meaningless," I say. "Or initials."

"No." Erquist traces the letters with his index finger. "It's Cyrillic."

Li shines the light around the door, looking for more signs. "So what does this mean? That we're somewhere east? Like City Two East?"

"Perhaps not that far," Erquist backtracks. "It's only one sign. And the alphabet was used from the Baltic to the Black Sea."

"Great," Li shivers. The heat from Edda's cutting tool is making us aware of the cold. "If we meet anybody we can ask if they know Picon."

"Who's Picon?" Edda switches off her cutter and pushes against the door. It doesn't move. "Spens, help me here."

With my shoulder against it, the door begins to move. I try to be careful about putting too much weight on my stump. Eventually it's open just wide enough for us to slip inside. "Some sort of reception area," Edda announces. "Staircases on each side. They're meant to be impressive."

"Or they didn't trust the power supply for lifts." Li releases my hand. I hear her walking ahead of us. "Look!" she says. I stumble forward, not seeing anything. "Look up," Li says. Overhead, about the size of a winter moon, is a disk of light.

The wrong place

It's late afternoon when you reach the Western suburbs. You don't recognise anything. There are nomads living in the ruins. They've put roofs of waterproof sheeting over the bare walls of what were once garages. You watch from the solar as Riemann tries talking to them. The nomads – thin, dark men in faded synthetic robes – are afraid of Riemann. They seem to think he's part of an advance guard. They listen nervously, shake their heads at everything he says and flee at the first opportunity. They'll probably move out that evening, convinced their latest refuge is about to be overrun.

The old city would have welcomed them, you think. The old city was beautiful.

It's gone.

Riemann drives towards what should be the centre, along what had once been the main road to the factory belt. "Recognise anything yet?"

You don't. Apart from a few low walls there isn't much to recognise. The superstructure has been levelled. From above it would look like a plan of a city, as if it was all still to be built.

Weeds have long since broken through the old pavements; there are places where the ground has subsided.

Riemann becomes more sombre as you approach the centre. From time to time you point at a trace of a building: "That was a school" or "That was a district office" or "That was a theatre". They're lies each time: you don't know what the buildings had been. You can't tell if you were ever in this part of the city. You make the claims to see how he'll react. He seems to believe you, and looks gloomier with every passing minute. He hasn't found a trace of whoever he's looking for. He has one of their machines for detecting signatures and looks at it frequently, frowning each time. His information is wrong, you think. His techs have miscalculated. His missing people are in a different place or the time is wrong. They come here, but not until next week, just after he stops looking. Or they came here months ago and are already dead.

Or this is the wrong place.

You wonder why they're so important.

You reach a crater where the lower levels must have collapsed. Riemann stops as close to the edge as he dares, climbs out and peers down. You follow him, keeping a safe distance. You get dizzy sometimes; you don't want to fall. You guess the crater is nearly two kilometres across, wide enough to have contained most of the old city. Cathedral Square, the Parliament Building, the courthouse over the boys' home, your old hidden room with its view of the street, the assembly room with the pipes where you stood with the other girls – everything is rubble and weeds. Riemann doesn't say anything.

It starts raining. You retreat to the shelter of the cabin.

"The nomads." You don't know why you keep thinking of them. It must be the rain. "Where will they go?"

"They came from the south-east." You can't tell how he knows this. Perhaps he recognised their clothes. He watches the rain streaming down the window. "You'll head west. What a shithole."

There was something you meant to tell him. A piece of information you had been holding back until the right moment. When you try to remember it the rats have been there first. There were four special sites: Mosk, Sver, Spad and the other one. The one your instructors talked about wistfully. It was an optimistic time.

You listen to the rain beating on the roof. You remember the day-long downpours when you'd sit by the dormitory window and watch the yard outside slowly flood. In Spad you lived five levels down and could tell when it rained from the gurgling in the pipes. If the rain was heavy enough the pipes would shake. Too heavy and they burst. The crater is what happens when there is nobody to make repairs.

Mosk, Sver, Spad and the other one.

Abruptly the rain stops. Riemann climbs out of the vehicle and waits, impatient, for you to join him. "Are you able to walk?"

"I think so." But you stumble a little. Either the ground beneath your feet is unstable or your ankle is. "Where do you want to go?"

"The crater. There's a path I want to try."

"They won't be there."

He grunts and marches to the edge of the crater, glancing up at the sky. When you catch up with him all he says is "Do you think you can walk down that?" He points at a track zigzagging down the slope about half a kilometre away. It looks as if it's been fashioned deliberately. Nomads looking for shelter in the lower levels. Or salvage. There may still be intact structures underneath the rubble, perhaps even one you'd recognise.

"They won't be there." It looks steep. "If they were here wouldn't we have found a transport?" That was what you'd been about to say. You came back in a transport both times, from one zone to another. A chamber large enough to hold over two hundred people. Twelve switches, a precise sequence.

You remember the walk home. A week's provisions and a tent. It took you ten days, or ten days is the number you now remember. You know you were alone but your memory includes other girls who can't have been there, walking beside you. They don't talk. They're superimposed from some other memory.

You follow him down the path. It's steeper than it looked. You descend slowly, leaning back, one hand on the ground for support. Ahead of you, Riemann has found an opening. He waits for you to catch up. "Recognise this?" He pulls aside some waterproof sheeting, revealing a corridor which becomes pitch-black after a few paces. He turns on a torch. "Well?"

It's a bare concrete tunnel wide enough for two people to walk side by side. The light of the torch doesn't reach to the end. "There were lots of tunnels." You're out of breath. "They were all the same."

He walks quickly. You try to keep to his side. There's smell of stale water that gets stronger. "I used to work in Tunnel Clearance," he says. He shines the torch at the walls, looking for signs, messages. "We spent most of the time on the surface."

"Clearance?" You remember the pictures you were shown as a girl: the stacked bodies; uniformed, faceless men. "Clearance means murder." You stop walking.

He wasn't listening. "Are you good?"

"Clearance. We were shown the pictures."

He's puzzled, then he laughs. "I know the ones you mean. They're old. They were taken before Two East broke away. Those people were already dead. Do you know what killed them? Cholera. The bodies had to be removed and destroyed. That's how clearance started. We'd come to tunnels like this and ... You wouldn't believe me anyway." He pulls you forward, his grip on your arm gentle but firm. "I knew good people who worked the Tunnels. I had friends. Do you know why we had military training? In case we met your people." He pulls you until you reach an opening in the wall, a doorway. The door has gone, probably long since used for firewood or as part of a makeshift roof. Beyond it the corridor widens to a room about twenty metres long. Halfway across it is a waist-high concrete slab. "What is this?"

"A checkpoint." The air is thick. You lean against the slab until the dizziness passes. "You would have had to show papers. They won't be here."

"You needed papers?" Riemann is amused.

"You have your signatures. Aren't they the same?"

"They're not the same." He steps round the slab. There's another opening in the wall just after it, another doorway without a door. The room where the guards would have sat or slept. "They worked in teams of six," you say. "Two on duty, the rest in reserve." Two to watch the checkpoint, two to sleep, two to watch the guards ... There would have been bunks against the wall, lockers for the guards' weapons. Now the room is empty. Anything usable has been taken. "Bodies." It's just occurred to you. "There are no bodies."

"It was twenty years ago." Riemann shines his torch into corners. "What did you expect?"

"Bones. Rags."

"They must have known what would happen. They'd have tried to run or taken shelter." There's a metal door still in place at the end of the room. "Behind something like this." Riemann hands you the torch and pushes against it.

You think of striking the back of his head with the torch and walking away. You decide not to. You will need his help getting out of the crater.

It's the second time you've decided not to hurt him. That time in the empty shop with the pin gun: what would have happened if you'd fired? The memory comes back vividly: the locals, the box on the glass counter with the blade resting next to it. Nothing would be different, you realise. You would still be here. But if you hit him now, if you manage to hurt him ... Then what? He doesn't live to go back to the 21st. You don't meet him because you're not there to arrange the meeting. He doesn't take the box and ask if you're contaminating their stockpiles. He doesn't tell you about Alexander Metzger. And then what? You don't think about what he tells you. You return home a failure. Perhaps you don't even get home, but remain in the 21st, running errands for Picon. You die there, pretending to be an extemp, and the only sign you lived is a name on the Memorial Wall. And then what? You don't find Metzger. You don't recruit the network. The Number City stockpiles are untouched. The Number Cities continue to grow. If you strike the back of his head with the torch, what happens? Would you blink and find yourself back in the safe house in the early 21st or in a barracks in the Eastern suburb? Or would you be dead from work in the insect factory? Do the Number Cities find another excuse, or does your city give up and rejoin them? At the airport he'd invoked a principle. What was it called? You'd looked it up afterwards. A principle, and another word. An. Anterior. No. *Anachronist.* Ever heard of the Anachronists?

"Nobody's been through this for a long time." Riemann gives up on the door. "But that's where the bodies will be, on the other side." He rubs at the dirt on the wall as if still hoping to find a message. "It's probably better we can't open it."

"The self-consistency principle."

He wipes the dust from his gloves. "What?"

"It's all that's keeping you alive."

He shakes his head. "They shut themselves in and thought they'd survive." He's grim. "They'd have been trapped when everything collapsed. How long do you think they lasted?"

You can't kill him. He has to live. His mission has to succeed. If he fails they won't trust him to travel again. If he doesn't travel . . . "They won't be here." You remember what you meant to tell him. Mosk, Spad, Sver. "I know where they'll be."

An der Wien

At the top of the building we find a circular room with a dirty glass ceiling. It looks like a mess hall: there are wooden tables and chairs folded and stacked against one wall, and, facing them, what looks like a service counter, beyond which is another room that might have been a kitchen. The exterior walls are of the same dark material as all the other structures we've seen.

And above the ceiling is the sky. It's overcast: there are pale grey clouds moving overhead. We can hear the wind. We stare for a while at the sky, then at each other, grinning with relief.

Edda climbs over the counter to investigate. I take out my handheld. Nothing. "Atmospheric conditions," Erquist says. The clouds are still scudding overhead. I take two chairs from a stack and sit on one of them, resting my leg on the other.

Edda returns from the kitchen carrying a cardboard box. "There are some rings at the back that seem to use gas. There were bottles in a back room. If the seals haven't perished they may be usable. There's damp in one of the storerooms, so there must be water pooling somewhere. And these." She opens the

323

box. It contains slabs wrapped in silver foil with black lettering. She hands one to Erquist, who stares at it for a few seconds. "Cyrillic. The only word I can make out is protein," he finally admits. He tears open one corner, sniffs at what it reveals and breaks off a crumb. He places it on his tongue as if it's tonin and swallows. "It doesn't taste rotten." He stands up. "Show me these rooms. If there's a water tank and gas we might be able to boil water. We can eat this if we have to." He follows Edda. As soon as they're out of sight, Li leans in. "What did your friend tell you? You can tell me now. Nobody's listening."

"Li . . . "

"Do you think we're here by accident? We could die here," she whispers. "Wherever here is. *When*ever here is. They won't come for us. We're not pioneers. We're not the Richardson expedition. We're travel reps." She seems exhilarated. "How's your leg?" She rests her hand on the foot. For a moment I think I can feel something.

"It's nothing. Brink had typhus."

"And he had the cure for typhus. I'm not trying to depress you, Spens, but we have to face facts."

She's wrong about Brink having the cure for typhus. There was no Archive for Historical Medicines back then. The only treatment was to keep clean, drink boiled water and wait to sweat it out.

Now isn't the time for a history lesson. "They might not come for us." We can hear Edda and Erquist talking, probably having a similar conversation. "But they'll come for them."

Erquist finds a water tank. He's not happy about the colour of the water. "It might be rust. Or there's algae of some kind. Still, as long as we sterilise it thoroughly . . . " Edda finds pots and pans, cutlery, dishes and bowls. "At least," Li says, "we don't have to make implements out of rocks." Because she doesn't have night vision or bone-and-muscle augs she volunteers to cook. Edda searches the rooms below us. Tables and chairs, she reports, empty cupboards. "There are other rooms but the doors were locked. I'll check tomorrow."

"It's getting too dark to do anything," Erquist says. "We should try to sleep."

We think we've had about four hours of daylight, which could mean it was late afternoon when we arrived. It's cold, but not as cold as the sunless lower levels. We sleep on the floor under the blankets we brought from the apartment block. Tomorrow, Erquist says, we will see if we can find a way of providing heat and if it's possible to get outside. It could be a few days before they come for us. "The calculation may not be precise. We did lose the link. They'll have to estimate ... But Hayek won't give up easily."

I'm woken by my foot. It presses against my stump as if fixed at the wrong angle. Overhead it's beginning to get light. Edda, beside me, is still asleep. Li and Erquist have settled in different corners of the room.

When I walk my stump burns. This is only temporary, I tell myself. Brink had typhus. I must remember to remove the foot before I sleep. I limp to the counter. Li is already in the kitchen, watching a deep pan over a small blue flame. "I'm making breakfast," she says. "I don't know if it'll be edible. The problem is measurements. I don't know if one of these bricks is supposed to feed ten people, a hundred, or if it's meant for cleaning ovens. It's definitely add to taste."

Edda says, "Did you boil the water?"

"Boiled, filtered and boiled again."

"It's like eating mud."

"You've eaten mud?"

"It tastes the way mud looks."

"It doesn't have to be delicious," Erquist says. "We should be grateful to Li for trying. And it should only be for a few days." He spends the rest of the morning walking slowly around the room while looking up at the glass ceiling, occasionally standing on a chair to get a closer look. He raps on the walls, searching for concealed panels, and becomes increasingly dismayed. "It's just glass," he says. "Toughened glass. I thought it might be photovoltaic, but it's not connected to anything. It just sits there." He sounds astonished at how the builders could have missed such an opportunity. "They had travel. They must have had the technology for that. I would expect them to have made some use . . . "

Erquist's mood is so disturbing even Li feels compelled to cheer him up. "At least they used something transparent," she says from the kitchen. "And it isn't broken."

"I know." Erquist is not consoled. "We should be thankful for that. But it was still a missed opportunity. Poor management of resources." He realises this is the wrong tone for a representative of the Happiness Executive and spends another half-hour half-heartedly poking at the wall.

On the next level down Edda finds a locked service door. Behind it is a flight of stairs leading to a heavy steel plate welded to where a door should be. I push against it and it doesn't move.

"I don't think this was to stop people." Erquist runs his hand down the wall beside the door. He doesn't find a hidden panel. "I suspect this was here to keep out animals."

Edda is sceptical. "A locked door would have done that."

We leave her in the dark, working with a cutter. Back in the mess hall Erquist admits he finds the sound of the wind disturbing. He will sleep in one of the lower rooms. When he leaves us to look for somewhere suitable Li says, "The hierarchy is reasserting itself."

Edda calls that she has removed the barrier to the surface. Because I limp Erquist and Li get there first. The wind is not as strong as it sounded from inside. We're on a dull mid-brown plain blotched with clumps of coarse vegetation. There are mountains in the distance in one direction. "Do you think we could walk to those?" Li asks.

"You could." I take a few careful paces. In the other direction is a level plain that stretches to the horizon. There are no other visible structures, no indication apart from this that there's a small town below the surface. Erquist returns from a slower walk around. He still can't find a signal or fix a location. Later, Li stews some of the weeds. "I was wrong," Edda says. "*This* is what mud tastes like."

In the afternoons I listen to the recording of the concert. 22 December 1808, Theater an der Wien. I stop the recording before the music starts and replay the sounds of the audience. Am I among them? I'd have a box to myself, and get there early so I don't stand out. The recording includes footsteps, the creaking of furniture, a murmur of talk with the occasional distinct phrase or single word and, towards the end, the sound of an orchestra tuning up, preparing to play an evening of new music.

I should have gone to more concerts in the 21st. But after a while you get used to the idea that the pianist will be able to play the whole étude without making a mistake, that you have a choice of string quartets, that their amateurs, for all the inauthentic style, are better than the nearest we have to professionals. I remember one concert in a church, a young native, my age or younger, playing piano sonatas by a composer I'd never heard of: Ustvolskaya. I don't have any recordings of Ustvolskaya's music. I don't know if any survived. I may have to go back to the 21st to hear it again . . .

Edda looms over me. Her hair is wet, her face scrubbed. "How's your leg?"

"Fine." I'd taken half a painkiller earlier. I need to make them last.

"Let me see."

She removes my boot and unfastens the straps that hold the prosthesis in place. "That doesn't look good."

We eat the powdery protein in the mornings. With the hot water it is somewhere between a soup and a paste. We eat the stewed weeds in the evenings. At midday we allow ourselves half an energy bar each. That way the supply should last us another two weeks. The bars are the high point of our day. Li makes a ceremony of dividing them up; we'll be sorry to eat the last one. Edda suggests we should have half a bar every other day in case the rescue takes longer than expected. Erquist is sure they'll have come before we use them all. Li says it's already taken longer than he expected. "Not much longer," Erquist says, and goes back to his room. We have adopted pre-industrial rhythms: we wake when it is light and sleep when it is dark. I have vivid dreams in which I can run.

Li keeps coming back to Cantor and Riemann. Edda eventually told her what Cantor had said. She was cautious: she made sure Erquist was in his room, and even then took Li outside and warned her never to tell anybody else. "Did Riemann know Cantor was there?"

"Not this again." On some days Edda joins in. On others

she gets impatient. "We don't have enough information. We can look it up when we get back."

"If we get back. We might not be meant to get back. Perhaps they broke the link deliberately. They *wanted* us lost. Think of it." Li speculates. "They didn't want you to tell anybody what your old school friend said. That's why there was a Millie with Hayek. They were making sure he didn't ask. That's why they kept us in a room until it was time for us to go ..."

"But we're not lost. We landed at a place with a zone."

"As good as lost. This could be City Two East territory. Maybe they won't come for us."

"City Two East doesn't have a zone. We'd know about it if they did." Edda is impatient. "Besides, even if we are, they'll come for Erquist. His kin won't let him stay missing."

"They will come for us," Erquist says. He's growing a ragged beard. It's almost the same colour as his skin. From a distance it looks as if his face is starting to fray. "For some of us. But the rest of you will be saved as well. It wouldn't be fair to leave anybody behind." He sits next to me for a few minutes as if he's about to tell me something important. All he says is, "The only question is when. It depends on what information they have. If there's any ambiguity they could easily go to the wrong place, or the wrong time. But I'm sure any ambiguity will be resolved quickly enough." It's a variant of what he says most days, a Happiness inspirational talk delivered in a flat monotone. When he finishes he goes back to his room. We won't see him again until it's time to eat. Li wonders if he's having a breakdown. I tell her he was just the same at the resort. "He rarely left his room then." "And did you think that was normal?" Li says. "Do you think he'd have had that job without his connections?"

*

The Theater an der Wien is about the same size as the Second Theatre in City One West where, as a child, I was once taken to see a City Day festival, a series of speeches about how we children would have to learn important lessons from those who came before us. My parents were still alive then, though as usual they were working away from home. I remember them telling me how lucky I was to have seen City One West: my mother had seen it twice and wanted to move there. I couldn't see why. For them it probably meant better work and accommodation. For me it meant being forced to listen to speeches. I replay the audience noises and stop the recording before the music starts. I need to save energy.

"Or it was an accident," Li says. "We lost the link because the Millies panicked. Or the war actually broke out. Think about it. We lost the link because of the start of the NEE ... "

"Not this again."

"Is it dead? I think it's dead." Edda holds up a worm. It's about seven centimetres long, limp as a piece of string. "It must be dead."

Li peers into a pan. "It might be stunned."

"It'll die soon." Edda holds it up higher, drops it into her upturned mouth, swallows with a gulp and sits very still. "What does it taste like?" Li asks. Edda jumps to her feet and runs out of my line of sight. I hear the sound of her retching. Li laughs, then coughs. "If only we could fry them." Salt, oil: she lists the things we don't have. Pepper, spices, onions, aubergines, cultured pork and mycoproteins, night apples, breads ...

Edda throws the worms out of the door. She claims the

small heap is still there two days later: nothing else had tried to eat them.

The United States is a neutral country, so American should be a safe cover. Their Embargo Act doesn't harm Austrian trade, and there's even some relief President Jefferson didn't use the Chesapeake incident to declare war on the English, who are still in Spain, fighting the French. American should not attract attention.

"What happened to your leg?" A man I don't recognise is standing over me, chewing on an energy bar. We are the only people in the room. I try to sit up. They've come, I think, finally, we're safe. Then I recognise the uniform. Thinner now, with a tangled grey beard, the younger of the two Safeties stands over me, eating one bar after another. His uniform is filmed with grit. His NVU covers his eyes. "Going south," he says, as if talking to somebody else in the room. "Found a tunnel, one k south. Must lead somewhere." He throws another wrapper at my feet. "Don't know how you stand this," he says. "Rain, rain. The noise would drive me mad. And it stinks in here. Who died, Joe? Are we sad they had to go? Found a tunnel. Six metres wide. A place to live, a place to hide. One k south. A track but no train, but a track means what, sir? A connection. Don't know where it leads, don't care. Anywhere's better than." He shuffles as he stands. "I'd take you but you're not fit for transport. Too sick to stand, too heavy to drag. Not a good source of protein. Dead weight. Better off alone, anyway, without. Backstabbing so called. Trying to. In your sleep I walk alone beside the track, remember that one? I walk alone beside the track. Other people hold you back." He walks away, singing softly.

*

"Couldn't you have tried to stop him?" Li is the angriest. "You're the one with the augs."

"He can barely stand," Edda says. "And the man was probably armed. Besides, Erquist was here as well." Erquist is still in his room. We haven't seen him all day.

"He took all the energy bars!" Li moves around the kitchen, coughing and picking things up, pans and broken plates. We all have coughs now. Li's is the worst. "Half of our protein."

"He's welcome to that." Edda squeezes my hand. "It'll probably choke him."

"And five litres of water."

"We can spare it." Edda looks up at the sky. It's still raining. It's dry on this level but the smell of damp rises from the one below. "What did he say about a tunnel?"

The first musicians file onto the stage. There's a conversation in the box to the right: a woman's voice asking if it's true, another woman saying it isn't. They complain about how Old Fritz has gone completely to pieces. *He's always had it easy*, one of them says. *At the first knock* . . . The first woman says something about poor Hans. He's feverish, half the time he doesn't know where he is. Could it be typhus? My leg starts to ache at exactly the place where the scar used to be.

"It wouldn't be giving up," Edda says. "I'll stay here with Spens while you and Erquist find this tunnel."

"And what if we meet the Safety?"

"Stay behind him. It shouldn't be hard. He'll be a long way ahead of you by now."

"I'm not going anywhere near that madman. Why don't you go? You're used to the NV. You know how to use the cutter."

"So does Erquist. And you could learn in half an hour. Erquist, what do you think?"

Erquist doesn't say anything. He hasn't said anything for days. He doesn't even cough in our presence, though we can hear him at night.

Li does cough. Then she laughs. "I can look after Spens as well as you."

"It's not just that. It's that we don't know who'll be at the other end of that tunnel. We don't know how they'll respond to people like us."

"Meaning?"

"People with augs. We don't know where we are. We don't know *when* we are. We don't know what level they're at. At least you and Erquist might look normal to them."

"Thanks." Li coughs again, violently. It's as if she's coughing with her entire torso, every internal organ making its contribution. "Listen to that. He'll hear that coming. And how long is this tunnel anyway?"

"We don't know."

"There's the point. I've looked south. I can't see anything on the surface. We don't know where the tunnel is. We don't know how long it is or what condition it's in. The only thing we know about it is that there'll be a madman in it. Hey, we only know about the tunnel because a madman told us it exists. He might have imagined the whole thing. We're better off here. If they're coming for us, this is where they'll come."

"You're always saying they won't."

"It's better than a tunnel to nowhere. I'm staying here. And so should you. If they're coming for you, this is where they'll come."

*

Li takes a bowl down to Erquist's room. On the way to his room she has a fit of coughing and spills half of it. He doesn't open his door when she knocks. She leaves the bowl on the floor outside. "He said he liked it better cold." The next morning the bowl is still there, untouched, and Erquist is not in his room. After a search Edda discovers the NV unit and cutting tool are missing. We're stuck on the surface now, and she can't open any more doors. I crawl into one of the rooms behind the kitchen. It's noisy: at night the wind whistles through the pipes, and, when the wind drops, I can hear Li coughing. I go through the pockets of my clothes. I'm sure there's a painkiller I've missed. I go through my pockets over and over again.

The strings start to tune up. The woman in the next box raises her voice. "What I can't understand is why there aren't insects. All we've seen are the worms. There aren't even spiders." Her voice is distinct. She could be talking directly to me. "There was an empty section near my second mother's rooms, an empty tunnel and some old offices. We used to play in them, you know, Three-Minute Warning, Rats and Moles. There were spiders everywhere."

Edda tips the warm mush into my mouth. "We've found another box of protein. Water's getting low again, but we have enough for another few days. Once you're better we'll see what supplies we can carry and start walking. We'll head west. There should be something out there. Once we know where we are ... It's a shame you can't go out yet. There are sunflowers not that far away. They look beautiful. Li thinks we can use them." Li goes out every morning, before it gets too hot. She avoids the heat as she used to avoid the rain. The weeds she gathers are yellow or pale brown and seem to be drying up. It doesn't improve their flavour.

"They're further away than we thought, and they might not be sunflowers." The woman in the next box keeps talking. "Liesl walked for half an hour yesterday and didn't seem to get any nearer." The orchestra is onstage. The audience has starting to settle into their seats. "It won't be long now," a different woman says. "Two days, three at most. Then we can go." The first woman says something I don't catch. "It's a choice between dying slowly and dying quickly," the other woman tells her. "This place is killing us. It's actually killing us." The first one replies, "I thought you wanted to stay." They argue in low voices. The hall is already cold and will get colder still when the heating fails. I've brought a good coat, but it might not be enough. There's laughter from the stalls. We wait for the composer.

A bottle of water has been left within reach. It's half full, warm to the touch. The temperature reminds me of the cups in Coffee Monarch. I drag myself deeper into the shadows of the room. My leg has stopped burning. Now I can't feel it at all.

"I heard something." A woman's voice, dry, as if from disuse. "I think there's someone here." She's speaking Modern. It isn't Li or Edda or the Viennese woman who asked about Old Fritz or poor Hans.

I turn my head. From the light coming through the half-open door of the storeroom it's early afternoon. The door opens wider. A woman is silhouetted there. She pauses, steps back. "It stinks in here." She takes a deep breath and crouches at my side. I recognise her almost immediately. It's our client and not. She's older, in her sixties at least. There are lines around her eyes, her cheeks have hollowed and her hair is grey and cut in a style that looks like a punishment. This is new: so far the people I've imagined look the same as they did before we came here: Li's skin isn't blotched; Edda isn't bone-thin; Erquist is clean-shaven and scrupulously neat. The woman puts a hand on my brow. It feels like ice. She pulls it back quickly. "I think this one's alive," she calls. I can hear footsteps in the next room drawing nearer.

"What is it?" A man's voice. It's not the Safety. It's definitely not Erquist. This is also new. In the past, when I've dreamed of rescue, people have come alone.

"He's still alive."

There's the shape of a man at the door. "If he can talk, ask him where the others are."

Our client looks at me carefully. She seems reluctant to touch me again. "I don't think he can talk."

"Are you sure he's alive?" The man moves nearer. "It stinks in here." He's in a uniform I don't recognise. He stands behind our client, looking down at a device in his hand and then at my leg. "He could be a nomad."

"You rely too much on those machines. Look what he's wearing. He's one of yours."

"He's not Ko Erquist. He's definitely not Edda Lang. Those are my primary concern." He's turning to leave when something on the device troubles him. He stoops for a closer look and shines a torch in my face.

"He's one of yours." Her voice is thick with contempt. "Your *civilisation*."

I recognise him almost immediately. It's Riemann. He's about thirty, younger than I've seen him as an adult. He frowns and leans in still closer. "Can you hear me?" His tone softens slightly. "How long have you been here?"

"You're wasting your time." She stands up stiffly and backs away. "I don't think he can talk."

"He might know something." He holds a water bottle to my lips.

"Your important people were here," she says from the doorway. "They must have left him behind."

"Don't go too far."

"It's one accounted for." She steps out of sight. "Your important people can't be far away."

"Spens?" It's as if Riemann was waiting for her to leave before he used my name. "I know you're weak, but I need your help . . . "

You head for the door to the surface. After the stink of the hot, windowless room you need to be outside. As you cross the main room you notice a bundle of cloth under a chair. You can't say what makes you stop to pick it up. You tell yourself it might contain some clue to where his missing people have gone, although you don't need a clue. If they haven't died here they'll be heading west, like the boys who escaped from home under the old courthouse. Always west, towards the setting sun.

Why were they here? You've asked the question before. An accident, he answered each time. You didn't trust him.

The cloth turns out to be a jacket. You hold it up by the shoulders and let it unfurl. It's heavy. From its size it belonged to the man in the back room. The weight isn't evenly distributed: one side is heavier than the other.

He'd changed as soon as he saw the footprints in the dried mud around the doorway. You expected him to contact the medical transport. They'd need to know his people were not in City Two East. He'd dismissed the idea. *Let's account for them first.*

I thought you were here to take them back.

I have to account for them first.

In the right-hand pocket you find a flat, grey box. You turn it over in your hands. There is no obvious opening. It's a second or two before you recognise it: exactly the same as the one you carried to the 21st. The surprise or the heat makes you feel faint. The ceiling overhead is glass, dirty in places but still transparent. There's no doubt that what's overhead is the sky. The heat reminds you of the punishment work at the insect factory. People fainted all the time. They'd be dragged out, have water thrown in their face and, if they revived, they'd be pushed back in to work until they fainted again. You were always proud that you'd never fainted. You'd seen the signs in others; when you recognised them in yourself you slowed down as much as you dared or found some excuse to go to the storerooms, which were cooler.

It's a protocol issue. It involves information. I don't know what kind, I don't need to know.

You go along the short corridor where a tide-mark is a sign of recent flooding, up the stairs towards the surface. By the side of the door is a small heap of dead worms. They're just beginning to rot.

Officially, it was an accident.

For a moment you're surprised you're not in the city. You expected to see a crater: instead there's only open ground with dun-coloured grass. You remember you're in the other place, the one whose name you can't remember, and not in it, but on it. A day's drive away. The secret place. The place with the zone.

It was, it turned out, on Riemann's chart. He knew there'd been something here, but didn't know what it was. A secondary target.

You lean against the wall, taking deep breaths.

They're well connected. Their kin wanted them recovered. Safety agreed. And Awareness seconded me to Safety.

You look at the thing in your hands. The name comes back: a Dolman box. Signature lock. You'd carried one exactly like it. First an extemp had taken it away, then Riemann, the old Riemann. You can still remember the sense of failure in that shop as you stared at the local's phone, not daring to make the call. And for what?

There are official orders and the things they tell you at the last minute.

Riemann's important people must have left the box behind. If he's here because of information it might be in this box. Maybe they'd told the man in the back room to guard it. They'd waited to be rescued and, when the rescue didn't come, they'd abandoned him. Had they meant to come back? Had he known they wouldn't? He'd obeyed orders, remained at his post. A good subordinate. You've known people like that. They look at you adoringly, with angry, fevered eyes until you tell them what to do. You've been a person like that. What do you want me to do? Is that all? It isn't enough.

I was told to account for them.

Once it was simple: there was your city and the Number Cities.

You turn the box in your hands, half expecting it to open. It feels the same as the one you were supposed to deliver to Picon. You wonder what happened to it. It was never mentioned at your trial. Perhaps it couldn't be: the Riemann you'd met in the 21st had taken it back with him. Perhaps it's in a storeroom somewhere, labelled and forgotten, or about to be labelled. Perhaps somewhere in Five South the old Riemann will find a way to open the box without destroying the contents. You can imagine his disappointment at finding nothing but orders to a man who would have ignored them anyway.

What happened to Picon? Did he die in the 21st? He wasn't mentioned at your trial. You assumed he betrayed you. Somebody had. As soon as En Varney returned from her trade mission she was taken into custody. You were put in a cell and left there. No questions, no contacts. You lost count of the days: more than you spent in the 21st, or the insect factory. Then longer, until you thought you'd been forgotten. The trial came as a relief. You showed no regret and admitted no guilt and expected it to end in your death but at least it gave you something to watch. No mention of Picon, your principal contact. No mention of Riemann. It lasted for months: you remember it as a single event, one long afternoon of listening to summaries of circumstantial evidence and refusing to answer questions. Karia Stadt, guilty of sabotage, murder and whatever else they could add to the list. Dozens of Number City workers, Alexander Metzger, Miko Halaz, murdered by persons unknown on your instructions. A representative of the Assistant Director testified that you had disobeyed explicit orders and affirmed his government would not protest a death sentence.

Cowards. They thought it would save them. Instead the Number Cities refused to believe you had acted alone and without authorisation. They put you back in the cell and destroyed your city, just as Riemann told you they would.

You note the position of the sun and walk around the

building until you're in the shade. If anybody walked from here they'll have headed west. You travelled south-east to reach this place: your paths won't have crossed. Next he has to follow the setting sun. Find his people, and account for them.

You wonder how far you can throw the box. Your arm is weaker than it was: you can imagine trying as hard as you can, only to have the box fall at your feet. But your throw is a good one, and it falls far enough away to be hidden by the grass. Riemann won't find it unless you tell him what you've done. It might lie there undisturbed. Rain will fall, the box will sink into the mud. Given enough time it will start to disintegrate and whatever was once considered important will become as worthless as Picon's instructions. Riemann can still carry out his official orders. He won't have this, whatever it is.

It's a small victory. You walk back to the entrance and look out at the yellow band on the horizon. The others will be there, if they aren't already dead. The nausea you felt in the back room has subsided. You take more deep breaths and step down to the corridor. You can hear Riemann vainly trying to interrogate a dying man. Where are the others? When did they leave? Which direction?

I don't answer. I've been rescued too many times before: Li, Edda, Erquist, even Hayek. I've seen them all leaning over me and telling me I was now safe, how it was a chance in a thousand, a chance in ten thousand, a chance in a million. Riemann is surely no different. I blink and he disappears

The hall is full. The conversation dies to a whisper, a faint hiss. I flex the toes of my left foot. The woollen stockings offer little protection against the chill of the hall (it is already getting colder) and, despite everything I've read, I hadn't realised how uncomfortable the seats would be. These are small prices to pay. The orchestra waits for the signal from the composer. He turns his back to us and raises his arms. The music can finally begin.

Acknowledgements

Thanks are due to numerous people: to Tim Holman, Anne Clarke, Joanna Kramer and the rest of the team at Orbit for making this book possible; to Oli Munson at A. M. Heath for knowing where to send the manuscript; and to Candida Lacy, Holly Ainley and Vicky Blunden at Myriad for early support and encouragement.

extras

www.orbitbooks.net

about the author

Robert Dickinson is the author of *Micrographia* (Waterloo Press, 2010), and two novels: *The Noise of Strangers* and *The Schism* (both Myriad Editions). He lives in Brighton.

Find out more about Robert Dickinson and other Orbit authors by registering for the free monthly newsletter at www.orbitbooks.net.

if you enjoyed
THE TOURIST

look out for

AURORA

by

Kim Stanley Robinson

Our voyage from Earth began generations ago.

Now, we approach our destination.

A new home.

Aurora.

Freya and her father go sailing. Their new home is in an apartment building that overlooks a dock on the bay at the west end of Long Pond. The dock has a bunch of little sailboats people can take out, and an onshore wind blows hard almost every afternoon. "That must be why they call this town the Fetch," Badim says as they walk down to take out one of these boats. "We always catch the brunt of the afternoon wind over the lake."

So after they've checked out a boat, they have to push it straight off the side of the dock into the wind, Badim jumping in at the last minute, hauling the sail tight until the boat tilts, then aiming it toward the little corniche around the curve of the lakeshore. Freya holds the tiller most firmly, as instructed. The boat leans over and they go right at the tall lake wall until they almost hit it, then Badim exclaims, "Coming about," just as he said he would, and Freya swings the tiller hard and ducks to get under the boom as it swings over them, and then they're tacking in the other direction, in a reach across the end of the bay. The little sailboat can't point up into the wind very far, Badim says, and he calls it a tub, but affectionately. It's just big enough for the two of them, and has a single big sail, sleeved over a mast that to Freya looks taller than the boat is long.

It takes quite a few tacks to get out of the little bay and into the wider expanse of Long Pond. Out there, all of Nova Scotia is visible to them: forested hills around a lake. They can see all the way to the far end of Long Pond, where afternoon haze obscures the wall. The deciduous trees on the hills are wearing their autumn colors, yellow and orange and scarlet all mixed with the green of the conifers. The prettiest time of year, Badim says.

Their sail catches the bigger wind that rushes across the middle of the lake, which is silvery blue under the gusts. They shift to the windward side of the cockpit, lean out until they balance the boat against the wind. Badim knows how to sail. Quick shifts in the wind, to which they lean in or out; now they're dancing with the wind, as Badim puts it. "I'm very good ballast," he says, rocking the boat a little as he moves. "See, we don't want the mast straight up, but tilted downwind a bit. Same with the sail, not pulled as tight as you can, but off enough for the wind to curve across it the best. You can feel when it's right."

"Look at the water there, Badim. Is that a cat's paw?"

"Good eye, that is a cat's paw. Let's get ready for that, we're going to get wet!"

The surface of the lake winkles in a mirrorflake curl, approaching them fast, and when the gust causing the cat's paw hits them, the boat heels hard. They lean back into it and the boat gurgles forward, slaps into and across the oncoming waves, knocks up dashes of spray that blow back at them. Long Pond's water tastes like pasta, Badim says.

At the end of forty tacks (Badim claims to keep count but with a smile that says he doesn't), they're just a kilometer or so up Long Pond. It's time to turn and make the straight run downwind to their dock. They turn and suddenly it's as if there's hardly any wind: the boat goes quiet, the sail bellies out ahead and to the side as Badim lets out the sheet, the little tub rocks forward in jerks and seems to be going slower. They watch the backs of waves pass them. The water is bluer now, and they can see farther down into it; sometimes they catch glimpses of the lake's bottom. The water bubbles and gurgles, the boat rocks awkwardly, all in all it feels like they're laboring, yet in no time at all they're coming back into their bay, and it's obvious by the way they pass the other docks and the corniche that they're really bombing along. There's time to watch their own dock come at them, and now in the bay they can again feel the wind rushing past, and hear the waves passing the boat, falling over in little gurgling whitecaps.

"Uh-oh," Badim says as he leans out to see past their bellying sail. "I should have come at the dock with the sail on the other side! I wonder if I can swing back out and get on the other beam, and come back in right."

But the dock is almost on them. "Do we have time?" Freya asks.

"No! Okay hold on, take the tiller and hold it just like it is now. I'm going to go forward and jump off onto the dock and grab the boat before you go by me! Keep your head down, don't let the boom hit you!"

And then they're heading right at the corner of the dock. Freya ducks into the seat and holds the tiller hard, the bow of the boat crashes into the corner of the dock while Badim is in the middle of his leap, he sprawls far onto the dock, there is a loud cracking sound where boom meets mast, the boat cants and swings around the dock, sail flapping hard out in front of the mast, the boom loose and flopping out there too. Badim scrambles to his feet and from the dock's side leans out to grasp the boat's bow, just within his reach, and then he has to lie flat on the dock and hang on. The boat swings around on the wind and points up into it, the sail swings around wildly and Freya ducks to get under it, but with the boom disconnected from the mast she has to jump down into the cockpit to get below it.

"Are you okay?" Badim exclaims. Their faces are only a

meter or two apart, and his look of dismay is enough to make her laugh.

"I'm okay," she assures him. "What should I do?"

"Come up into the bow and jump up onto the dock. I'll hold on."

Which he has to, because the boat is still trying to go downwind, but backward now, and into the shallows. People on the corniche are watching them.

She jumps up beside him. Her push almost drags him off the dock; his knee is braced against a cleat in a way that looks painful to Freya, and indeed his teeth are clenched. She reaches out to help him pull the boat closer and he says, "Don't catch your fingers between the boat and the dock!"

"I won't," she says.

"Can you reach down in there, and get the rope in the bow?"

"I think so."

He pulls hard, draws the boat in closer, she leans way out and snatches the rope where it goes through a metal ring in the very bow of the boat. She pulls the rope out of the boat and takes a turn around the cleat on the back corner of the dock, and Badim quickly snatches it and helps her take more turns.

They lie there on the dock, staring face-to-face, eyes round.

"We broke the boat!" Freya says.

"I know. You're okay?" he asks.

"Yes. What about you?"

"I'm fine. A bit embarrassed. And I'll have to help fix this boom. That's a very weak link though, I must say."

"Can we go sailing again?"

"Yes!" He gives her a hug and they laugh. "We'll do it better next time. The thing to do is to come in with the sail on the other side of the boat, so we can curve in toward the side of the dock, just ease across the wind and come in from the side, then turn up into the wind at the last second, and grab the side of the dock just as we're slowing down into the wind. Should have thought of that before."

"Will Devi be angry?"

"No. She'll be happy we're both safe. She'll laugh at me. And she'll know how to make that joint between the boom and mast stronger. Actually, I'd better look that thing up and find out what it's called. I'm pretty sure it has a name."

"Everything has a name!"

"Yes, I guess that's right."

"And since that thing is broken, I think she's going to be a little angry."

Badim says nothing to this.

. . . . .

The truth is, her mother is always angry. She hides it pretty well from most people, but Freya can always see it. It's there in the set of her mouth; also she often makes little impatient exclamations to herself, as if people can't hear her. "What?" she'll ask the floor, or a wall, and then go on as if she hasn't said anything. And she can get obviously mad really fast, like instantly. And the way she slumps in her chair in the evenings, staring grimly at the feed from Earth.

Why do you watch it? Freya asked her one night.

I don't know, her mother said. Someone has to.

Why?

The corners of her mother's mouth tightened, she put an arm around Freya's shoulders, heaved through her nose a big breath in, sigh out.

I don't know.

Then she trembled, and even started to cry, then stopped herself. Freya stared at the screen with its busy little figures, perplexed. Devi and Freya, staring at a screen showing life on Earth, from ten years before.

· · · · ·

On this evening Freya and Badim come home and burst into their new apartment. "We crashed the boat! We broke the thing!"

"The gooseneck," Badim adds, with a quick smile at Freya. "It connects the boom to the mast, but it isn't very robust."

Devi listens distracted, shakes her head at their wild story. She's chewing her salad in front of the screen. When she is done eating, the muscles at the back of her jaw stay bunched. "I'm glad you're okay," she says. "I've got to go back to work. There's some kind of thing going on at the lab."

"I'm sure it has a name," Freya says primly.

Devi eyes her, unamused, and Freya quails. Then Devi is off, back to the lab, and Badim and Freya slap hands and rattle around the kitchen getting out cereal and milk.

"I shouldn't have said that about the name," Freya says.

"Your mom has been known to have some edges," her father says, with an expressive lift of the eyebrows.

He himself has no edges, as Freya knows very well. A short round balding man, with doggie eyes and a sweet low voice, mellow and interested. Badim is always there, always benign. One of the ship's best doctors. Freya loves her father, clings to him as to a rock in high seas. Clings to him now.

He tousles her wild hair, so like Devi's, and says to her, as he has before, "She has a lot of responsibilities, and it's hard for her to think about other things, to relax."

"We're doing okay though, right, Badim? We're almost there."

"Yes, we're almost there."

"And we're doing okay."

"Yes, of course. We will make it."

"So why is Devi so worried?"

Badim looks her in the eye with a little smile. "Well," he says, "there are two parts to that, as I see it. First, there are things to worry about. And second, she is a worrier. It helps her to bring things up and talk through them, talk them out. She can't hold things inside very well."

Freya isn't so sure about this, because not many people seem to notice how mad Devi is. She's good at holding that inside, anyway.

Freya says as much, and Badim nods.

"Good, that's right. She is good at holding in things, or ignoring things, up to a certain point, and then she needs to let it out, one way or another. We're all like that. So, we're her family, she trusts us, she loves us, so she lets us see how she really feels. So, we just have to let her do that, talk things out, say what she really feels, be how she really is. Then she can go forward. Which is good, because we need her. Not just you and me, though of course we need her too. But everybody needs her."

"Everybody?"

"Yes. We need her because the ship needs her." He pauses, sighs. "That's why she's so mad."

. . . . .

Thursday, and so Freya goes into work with Devi rather than spending the day in the crèche with the little kids. She helps Devi on Thursdays. Freya feeds the ducks and turns the compost, and replaces batteries and lightbulbs sometimes, if they're scheduled for replacement. Devi does all kinds of things, indeed

Devi does everything. Often this means talking to people who work in the biomes or on the machines in the spine, then looking at screens with them, then talking some more. When she's done she grabs Freya by the hand and pulls her along to the next meeting.

"What's wrong, Devi?"

Big sigh. "I told you already. We started to slow down a few years ago, and it's changing things inside the ship. Our gravity comes from the ship rotating around the spine, and that creates a Coriolis effect, a little spiral push from the side. But now we're slowing down, and that's another force, about the same as the Coriolis effect in some ways, and cutting across it so it's reduced. You wouldn't think that would matter so much, but we're seeing aspects of it they didn't foresee. There was so much they didn't think about, that they left for us to find out."

"That's good, right?"

Short laugh. Devi always makes the same sounds: Freya can call them up if she wants to, sometimes. "Maybe so. It's good unless it's bad. We don't know how to do this part, we have to learn as we go. Maybe it's always that way. But we're in this ship and it's all we've got, so it has to work. But it's twelve magnitudes smaller than Earth, and that makes for some differences they never thought through. Tell me again about magnitudes?"

"Ten times bigger. Or smaller!" She remembers in time to keep Devi from saying it.

"That's right. So even one magnitude is a lot, right? And twelve, that's twelve zeros tacked on. A trillion. That's not a number we can imagine very well, it's too big. So, here we are in this thing."

"And it has to work."

"Yes. I'm sorry. I shouldn't burden you with this stuff. I don't want you to be scared."

"I'm not scared."

"Good. But you should be. So there's my problem."

"But tell me why."

"I don't want to."

"Just a little bit."

"Oh, I've told you before. It's always the same. Everything in here has to cycle in a balance. It's like the teeter-totters at the playground. There has to be an equilibrium in the back-and-forth between the plants and the carbon dioxide in the air. You don't have to keep it perfectly level, but when one side hits the ground you have to have some legs to push it back up again. And there are so many teeter-totters, all going at different speeds up and down. So you can't have any accidental moments when they all go down at once. So you have to look to see if that is about to start happening, and if so, you have to shift things around so that it doesn't. And our ability to figure out how to do that depends on our models, and really, it's too complex to model." This thought makes her grimace. "So we try to do everything by little bits and watch what happens. Because we don't really understand."

On this day it's the algae. They grow a lot of algae in big glass trays. Freya has looked at it through a microscope. Lots of little green blobs. Devi says some of it is mixed in with their food. They grow meat like the algae, in big flat tanks, and get almost as much of their food out of these tanks as they do out of the fields in the farming biomes. Which is lucky, because the fields can suffer animal disease, or crop failure. But the tanks can go wrong too. And they need their feedstocks to have something to turn into food. But the tanks are good. They have a lot of tanks going, in both rings, all kept isolated from the others. So they're all right.

The algae tanks are green or brown or some mix of the two.

The colors of things depend on which biome you're in, because the lights from the sunlines are different in different biomes. Freya likes to see the colors shift as they move from biome to biome, greenhouse to greenhouse, lab to lab. Wheat is blond in the Steppe, yellow in the Prairie. Algae in the labs is many different brownish greens.

It's warm in the algae labs and smells like bread. Five steps to make bread. Someone says they're eating more these days, but growing less. This means an hour at least to talk it over, and Freya sits down to paint with the paints in the corner of the lab, left there for her and any other kids who might visit.

Then off again. "Where to now?"

"Off to the salt mines," Devi declares, knowing Freya will be pleased; they'll stop at the dairy near the waste treatment plant, get ice cream.

"What is it this time?" Freya said. "More salt in the salty caramel?"

"Yes, more salt in the salty caramel."

This is a stop where Devi can get visibly irate. The salt sump, the poison factory, the appendix, the toilet, the dead end, the graveyard, the black pit. Devi has worse names for it she says under her breath, thinking again that no one can hear her. Even the fucking shithole!

The people there don't like her either. There is too much salt in the ship. Nothing wants salt except people, and people want more than they should have, but they're the only ones who can take it without getting sick. So they all have to eat as much salt as they can without overdoing it, but that doesn't really help, because it's a really short loop and they excrete it back into the larger system. Devi always wants long loops. Everything needs to loop in long loops, and never stop looping. Never pile up along the way in an appendix, in a poisonous sick disgusting stupid cesspool, in a slough of despond, in a fucking shithole. Devi sometimes fears she herself will sink into a slough of despond. Freya promises to pull her out if she does.

So they don't like chlorine, or creatinine, or hippuric acid. The bugs can eat some of these things and turn them into something else. But the bugs are dying now, and no one knows why. And Devi thinks the ship is short on bromine, which she can't understand.

And they can't fix nitrogen. Why does nitrogen break so often? Because it's hard to fix! Ha-ha. Phosphorus and sulfur are just as bad. They really need their bugs for these. So the bugs have to stay healthy too. Even though they're not enough. For anyone to be healthy, everyone has to be healthy. Even bugs. No one is happy unless everyone is safe. But nothing is safe. This strikes Freya as a problem. *Anabaena variabilis* is our friend!

You need machines and you need bugs. Burn things to ash and feed the ash to the bugs. They're too small to see until there are zillions of them together. Then they look like mold on bread. Which makes sense because mold is one kind of bug. Not one of the good ones; well, bad but good. Bad to eat anyway. Devi doesn't want her eating moldy bread, yuck! Who would do that?

You can get two hundred liters of oxygen a week from one liter of suspended algae, if it is lit properly. Just two liters of algae will make enough oxygen for a person. But they have 2,122 people on board. So they have other ways to make oxygen too. There's even some of it stored in tanks in the walls of the ship. It's freezing cold but stays as liquid as water.

The algae bottles are shaped like their biomes. So they're like algae in a bottle! This makes Devi laugh her short laugh. All they need is a better recyclostat. The algae always have bugs living with them, eating them as they grow. With people it's the same, but different. Growing just a gram of *Chlorella* takes in a liter of carbon dioxide and gives out 1.2 liters of oxygen. Good for the *Chlorella*, but the photosynthesis of algae and the respiration of humans are not in balance. They have to feed the algae just right to get it between eight and ten, where people are. Back and forth the gases go, into people, out of people, into plants, out of plants. Eat the plants, poop the plants, fertilize the soil, grow the plants, eat the plants. All of them breathing back and forth into each other's mouths. Loops looping. Teeter-totters teetering and tottering all in a big row, but they can't all bottom out on the same side at the same time. Even though they're invisible!

The cows in the dairy are the size of dogs, which Devi says is not the way it used to be. They're engineered cows. They give as much milk as big cows, which were as big as caribou back on Earth. Devi is an engineer, but she never engineered a cow. She engineers the ship more than any animals in the ship.

They grow cabbages and lettuce and beets, yuck! And carrots and potatoes and sweet potatoes, and beans that are so good at fixing nitrogen, and wheat and rice and onions and yams and taro and cassava and peanuts and Jerusalem artichokes, which are neither artichokes nor from Jerusalem. Because names are just silly. You can call anything anything, but that doesn't make it so.

· · · · ·

Devi is called away from one of her regular meetings to deal with an emergency again, and as it's one of Freya's days with her, she brings Freya along.

First they go to her office and look at screens. What kind of emergency is that? But then Devi snaps her fingers and types like crazy and then points at one screen, and they hurry around to one of the passageways between biomes, the one between the Steppes and Mongolia that is called Russian Roulette, and is painted blue and red and yellow. The next one along is called the Great Gate of Kiev. The tall, short tunnel between the doors to the lock is crowded this morning with people, and a number of ladders and scaffolding towers and cherry-pickers.

Devi joins the crowd under the scaffolding, and Badim shows up a bit later to keep Freya company. They watch as a group of people ascend one of the scaffold ladders, following Devi up to the ceiling of the tunnel, right next to the lock-door frame. There several panels have been pulled aside, and now Devi climbs up into the hole where the panels have been moved, disappearing from sight. Four people follow her into the hole. Freya had no idea that the ceiling did not represent the outer skin of the lock, and stares curiously. "What are they doing?"

Badim says, "Now that we're decelerating, that new little push is counteracting the Coriolis force that our spin creates, and that's a new kind of pressure, or release from pressure. It's made some kind of impediment in the lock door here, and Devi thinks they may have found what it is. So now they're up there seeing if she's right."

"Will Devi fix the ship?"

"Well, actually I think the whole engineering team will be involved, if the problem turns out to be up there. But Devi's the one who spotted this possibility."

"So she fixes things by thinking about them!"

This was one of their family's favorite lines, a quote from some scientist's admiring older relatives, when he was a boy repairing radios.

"Yes, that's right!" Badim says, smiling.

Six hours later, after Badim and Freya have gone into the Balkans for a lunch at its east end dining hall, the repair crew comes down out of the hole in the lock ceiling, handing down some equipment, then putting a few small mobile robots into baskets to be lowered by the scaffold. Devi comes down the ladder last and shakes hands all around. The problem has been located, and fixed with torches, saws, and welders. The long years of Coriolis push shifted something slightly out of position, and recently the counterforce of deceleration shifted it back, but meanwhile the rest of the door had gotten used to the shift. It all made sense, although it didn't speak volumes about the quality of construction and assembly of the ship. They were going to check all the other slides like the broken one, to make sure the lock doors of Ring B weren't impeded in other places. Then they won't stress motors trying to close doors against resistance.

Devi hugs Freya and Badim. She looks worried, as always.

"Hungry?" Badim asks.

"Yes," she says. "And I could use a drink."

"It's good that's fixed," Badim remarks on the walk home.

"That's for sure!" She shakes her head gloomily. "If the lock doors were to get stuck, I don't know what we'd do. I must say, I'm not impressed by the people who built this thing."

"Really? It's quite a machine, when you think about it."

"But what a design. And it's just one thing after another. It's pillar to post. I just hope we can hang on till we get there."

"Deceleration mode, my dear. It won't be much longer."

· · · · ·

The Coriolis force is the push sideways that you can't feel. Whether you can feel it or not, however, it still pushes the water. So now that the water has the deceleration pushing it sideways, they have to pump water across to the other sides of biomes to get it to where it used to go. They have to replace the force in ways that don't actually work very well in comparison to it. They planned for this with their pumping of water, but they haven't been able to make up for the altered pushes inside plant cells, which some plants are turning out not to like. There was a little push inside every cell that is altered now. Which is maybe why things are getting sick. It doesn't make sense, but then neither does anything else.

On Devi goes, talking and talking as they make their rounds. "It's not the Coriolis force that matters, it's the Coriolis effects. Those were never accounted for except in people, as if people are the only ones who feel things!"

"How could they have been so stupid?" Freya says.

"Exactly! Maybe all the cell walls will hold, so maybe it isn't obvious, but the water! The water!"

"Because water always moves."

"Exactly! Water always flows downhill, water always takes the path of least resistance. And now we've got a new downhill."

"How could they be so stupid?"

Devi seizes her around the shoulders as they walk, hugs her. "I'm sorry, I'm just worried is all."

"Because there are things to worry about."

"That's right, there are. But I don't have to afflict you with them."

"Will you have some salty caramel ice cream?"

"Of course. You couldn't stop me. You couldn't stop me with twenty years of fusion bombs going off twice a second!"

This is how they are slowing the ship down. As always, they laugh at how crazy this is. Luckily the bombs are very teeny. They meet Badim at the dairy, and learn that there's a new flavor of ice cream there, Neapolitan, which has three flavors combined.

Freya is confused trying to think this through. "Badim, will I like that?"

He smiles at her. "I think you will."

. . . . .

After the Neapolitan ice cream, on to the next stop on Devi's rounds. Algae labs, the salt mine, the power plant, the print shop. If everything is going well, they'll choose some item that has come up on the parts swap-out list, and go through Amazonia to Costa Rica, where the print shop is, and arrange for one of the printers to print out the part to be swapped out, and then they'll go to wherever the part belongs, and switch on the backup system, if there is one, or simply turn off whatever it is and hurry to take out the old part and put in the new part. Gears, filters, tubes, bladders, gaskets, springs, hinges. When they're done and the system is turned back on, they'll study the old part to see how well it has endured, and where it has worn; they'll take photos of it, and talk its diagnosis into the ship's record, and then take the part to the recycling rooms, which are right next to the print shop, and provide the printers with many of their feedstocks.

That's when things are going well. But usually, not everything is going well. Then it's a matter of troubleshooting, grasping the bull by the horns, seizing the nettle, coping and hoping, damning torpedoes, and trying any old thing, including the engineer's solution, which is to hit things with a hammer. On really bad days, they even have to hope the whole shithouse doesn't come down on their heads! Have to hope they don't end up living like savage beasts, eating trash or their own dead babies! Devi's face and voice can get very ugly as she spits out these bad fates.

· · · · ·

At home in the kitchen, even after bad days, Devi can get a little cheery. Drink some of Delwin's white wine, fool around with Freya like a big sister. Freya doesn't have any brothers or sisters, so she can't be sure, but as she is already bigger than Devi, it feels to her like what she imagines having a sister would feel like. A sister who is littler, but older.

Now Devi sits on the kitchen floor under the sink, calls for Badim to come join them and play spoons. Badim appears in the doorway looking pleased, holding the fat stack of big tarot cards. He sits, and they split up the cards among them, and begin each to build card houses at the three corners of the floor that they always take. They build the card houses low and thick, for defense against the others' nefarious attacks, adding cards at angles so there are no faces presented square to each other. Devi always makes hers like a boat turned upside down, and as she usually wins, Badim and Freya have begun to imitate her style.

When they are done building their card houses, they take turns flicking a plastic spoon across the kitchen at each other's constructions. The rule is you have to launch the spoon by bending it between your hands, then letting it loose to spring through the air end over end. The spoons are light, and their little bowls catch the air so that their flights are erratic, and only seldom do they hit their targets. So they flick, and the spoon arcs across the floor veering this way and that—flick and miss, flick and miss—and then there will be a hit, thwack! But if the afflicted card house has been built well, and gets lucky, it will withstand the blow, or only partly fall, losing an outer rampart or bartizan. Badim has found names for all these features, which makes Devi laugh.

Every once in a while a single hit will simply crumple a card house completely, which always makes them cry out with surprise, and then laugh. Although sometimes a kill shot causes a bad look to cross Devi's face. But mostly she laughs with her husband and child, and flicks the spoon when it's her turn, her lips pursed in concentration. She leans back against the cabinets, wearily content. This Badim and Freya can do for her. Okay, she is often angry, but she can shut that in a box inside her at times like this, and besides, her anger is directed mostly at things outside Freya's ken. She isn't angry at Freya. And Freya does her best to keep it that way.

. . . . .

Then one day one of the printers breaks, and this puts Devi into an immediate fury of worry. No one sees it but Freya, as everyone is upset, scared, looking to Devi to make things right. So Devi hurries down to the print shop, dragging Freya along, talking on her headset and sometimes stopping mid-conversation to put her hand over the little mike in front of her mouth and curse sharply, or say "Wait just a second," so she can talk to people coming up to her on the corniche. Often she puts her hand on these people's arms to calm them down, and they do calm down, even though it's clear to Freya that Devi herself is very mad. But the others do not see or feel it. It's strange to think that Devi is such a good liar.

At the print shop a big group of people are packed into the little meeting room, looking at screens and talking things over. Devi shoos Freya to her corner with the cushions and paints and lots of building parts in boxes, then goes over to the biggest group and starts asking questions.

The printers are wonderful. They can make anything you want. Well, you can't print elements; this is one of Devi's sayings, mysterious to Freya in its import. But you can print DNA and make bacteria. You can print another printer. You could print out all the parts for a little spaceship and fly away if you wanted. All you need is the right feedstocks and designs, and they have feedstocks stored in the floors and walls of the ship, and a big library of designs, which they can alter however they want. They have the whole periodic table on board, almost, and they recycle everything they use, so they'll never run out of anything they need. Even the stuff that turns to dust and falls to the ground will get eaten by bugs that like it, and thus get concentrated until people can harvest it back again out of the dead bugs. You can take dirt from anywhere in the ship and sift it for what you want. So the printers always have what they need to make stuff.

But now a printer is broken. Or maybe it's all the printers at once. They aren't working; people keep saying *they*. They aren't obeying instructions or answering questions. The diagnostics say everything is fine, or say nothing. And nothing happens. It's more than one printer.

Freya listens to the discussion for the way it sounds, trying to grasp the tenor of the situation. She concludes it is serious but not urgent. They aren't going to die in the next hour. But they need the printers working. It's maybe just the command and control systems that are at fault. Part of the ship's mind, the AI that Devi talks to all the time. Although that's bad. Or maybe the problem is mechanical. Maybe it's just the diagnostics that have broken, failing to spot something obvious, something easy. Push the reset button. Hit it with a hammer.

Anyway it's a big problem, so big that people are happy to put it on Devi. And she does not shirk to take it. She's asking all the questions now. This is why some people call her the chief engineer, although never when she can hear them. She says it's a group. Now, from the tone of her voice, Freya can tell it's going to take a long time. Freya settles in to paint a picture. A sailing ship on a lake.

Later, much later, it's Badim who wakes Freya, stretched out on her line of cushions, and takes her to the tram station, where they tram home to Nova Scotia, three biomes away. Devi is not going to be coming home that night. Nor is she home the next night. The morning after that, she is there asleep on the couch, and Freya lets her sleep, and then when she wakes, gives her a big hug.

"Hey, girl," Devi says dully. "Let me go to the bathroom."

"Are you hungry?"

"Famished."

"I'll cook scrambled eggs."

"Good." Devi staggers off to the bathroom. Back at the kitchen table she eats with her face right over the plate, shoveling it in. Freya would get told to sit up straight if she ate that way, but now she says nothing.

When Devi eases off and sits back, Freya serves her hot coffee and she slurps it down noisily.

"Are the printers working?" Freya asks, feeling that now it's safe to ask.

"Yes," Devi says grumpily. It turns out the problems with the diagnostics and the printers have all been one problem, which only made sense. It seems a gamma ray shot through the ship and made an unlucky hit, collapsing the wave function in a quantum part of the computer that runs the ship. It's such bad luck that Devi wonders darkly if it might have been sabotage.

Badim doesn't believe this, but he too is troubled. Particles shoot through the ship all the time. Thousands of neutrinos are passing through them right this second, and dark matter and

God knows what, all passing right through them. Interstellar space is not at all empty. Mostly empty, but not.

Of course they too are mostly empty, Devi points out, still grumpy. No matter how solid things seem, they are mostly empty. So things can pass through each other without any problems. Except for once in a while. Then a fleck hits something as small as it, and both go flying off, or twist in position. Then things could break and get hurt. Mostly these little hurts mean nothing, they can't be felt and don't matter. Every body and ship is a community of things getting along, and a few little things knocked this way or that don't matter, the others take up the slack. But every once in a while something bangs into something and breaks it, in a way that matters to the larger organism. Can range in effect from a twinge to death outright. Can be like one of their spoons knocking flat a house of cards.

"No one wants to hurt the ship," Badim said. "We don't have anybody that deranged."

"Maybe," Devi says.

Badim eyeballs Freya for Devi to see, as if Freya can't see this, though of course she does. Devi rolls her eyes to remind Badim of this. How often Freya has seen this eye dance of theirs.

"Well anyway, the printers are back up again," Badim reminds her.

"I know. It's just that whenever quantum mechanics is involved, I get scared. There's no one in this ship who really understands it. We can follow the diagnostics, and things get fixed, but we don't know why. And that I don't like."

"I know," Badim says, looking at her fondly. "My Sherlock. My Galileo. Mrs. Fixit. Mrs. Knows How Everything Works."

She grimaces. "Mrs. Ask the Next Question, you mean. I can always ask questions. But I'd rather have the answers."

"The ship has the answers."

"Maybe. She's pretty good, I'll give her that. She's the one who caught it this time, and that was not an easy catch. Although it was in part of her. But still, I'm beginning to think that the recursive induction we've been introducing is having an effect."

Badim nods. "You can see it's stronger. And it'll keep doing it. You'll keep doing it."

"We have to hope so."

Enter the monthly Orbit sweepstakes at

www.orbitloot.com

With a different prize every month,
from advance copies of books by
your favourite authors to exclusive
merchandise packs,
**we think you'll find something
you love.**

Newport Community
Learning & Libraries

ROGERSTONE

23.6.17

Sk – 30/9/21